A Tale of the Broken Heart

ROSE PLIESEIS

Text Copyright © 2023 by Dark Rose Publications
Russell Plieseis and Hayley Rose

Publisher Contact:
Dark Rose Publications
P.O. Box 1738
Tempe, AZ 85280
ataleofthebrokenheart.com

Cover illustration and design by Despina Panoutsou copyright © 2023 by Dark Rose Publications Russell Plieseis and Hayley Rose

Interior illustrations by Mark Sean Wilson copyright © 2023 by Dark Rose Publications Russell Plieseis and Hayley Rose

Editing by Floyd Largent

Typesetting by Marcy McGuire

Library of Congress Cataloging-in-Publication Data

Name: Plieseis, Rose, Author

Title: A Tale of the Broken Heart

Description: Arizona: Dark Rose Publications, (2023) | Series: Rellion's Rogue; vol. 1 |

ISBN: 978-1-950842-36-0 (hardcover)
ISBN: 978-1-950842-37-7 (softcover)
ISBN: 978-1-950842-38-4 (eBook)

Library of Congress Control Number: 2023913094

First Edition, February 2024

1 3 5 7 9 10 8 6 4 2

Printed in China

DEDICATION

This book is dedicated to you, the reader, the dreamer, the one who, if only for a few moments, truly finds themselves within their favorite characters and the worlds in which they live.

CONTENTS

Better Than the Streets 1

Bless the Fortunate Souls 7

Shadow Amongst the Crowd 13

Da, Da, DaDa, Dum, Dum 19

The Traveling Medicine Show 25

If It Falls Apart Scatter 31

I Think I Have Seen Enough 39

A Trick of the Light 47

No Honor Among Thieves 53

Rotten Luck Remy 57

Shouldn't You Sterilize That? 63

Prya's Got a Boyfriend 69

Off for a Bit of Fishing 75

Whiskeys of the Manor Hall 81

Hardly a Guest of Consequence 85

Fat Cherry Popped Fizz 91

Count Bobo Mahoney 95

Guest of the State Room 99

Legend It Has Become 105

A Tale of Heroics, Brave and True 109

Not Welcome Anymore 113

The Reluctant Martyr 119

The Eye Behind the Waterfall 125

Your Privileges Have Been Revoked 133

The Cat That's Not a Cat 139

Pretty Girl, Pretty Necklace 145

A Meeting with the Esteemed 151

Sing All Day and Play All Night 155

Pull Hard, You Incompetent Dogs 161

A Tale of the Broken Heart 169

Buffoons and Idiots 173

Hear, See, Speak No Evil 179

Friends of a Sort 183

Weirdly, Creepily, Awesome 191

Their First Dance 199

We Got What We Came For 203

Flushed Down the Toilet 209

A Boy and His Horse 217

I Am Nobody, If You Must Know 223

Other Friends of a Sort 227

A Happy Troupe of Thespians 233

Clan of the Dead Fairies 239

Nevertheless the Deed is Done 245

Remove Your Hats, Bow Your Heads 251

Before You Wasn't Dead Anymore 259

Unlikely Party at the Ward 265

None but the King Could Ride the Stallion 271

Fortuitous Calamity 279

No Matter How Royal the Whelp 283

Damnable Horse Never Did Listen 287

A Good Game of Pattycake 291

Damn, Now I've Committed His Name 295

Pocket Full of Worms 299

Boredom Was Their Lot 307

I Was Hoping Not To Get Stabbed 311

The Whiskey Tea Party 317

King Frobly Wobbly 323

Absolutely Not as Planned 339

Parade of Sycophants 345

Like a Toilet! Whoosh! 353

I Tolerate the Foolish 359

Begone Foul Beast 367

DOING HER BEST NOT THROW UP 375

THE HOPE OF A SINGLE WORD 381

YOU WERE NEVER MINE TO PROTECT. 387

ANYONE WHO DOESN'T LIKE IT WILL BE THROWN OVERBOARD...

BUT THAT'S ANOTHER STORY 395

BETTER THAN THE STREETS

"Ten crawns, three mad stewards, six paupers, and an assortment of fine handkerchiefs. Rellion is *not* going to be happy," Kristane muttered to herself as she tucked a strand of her long, wavy blonde hair back under her hood. Even the copper paupers were worth more than the so-called silver stewards. Everyone knew the Council of Stewards minted those coins themselves, and there was anything but silver in them, just something that looked shiny and bright. Kristane had always thought they were called "mad stewards" because of the scowling face of some long-dead noble that adorned them, but Rellion wouldn't even touch them, saying that if you left them in your pocket long enough you'd go as mad as a Steward. S*eriously, even most of the crawns have shaved edges!*

Today's take wasn't a good one, and there was a shadow of anxiety in the young girl's dark brown eyes at the thought of Rellion's sarcastic reaction: *Oh, my Princess, I do my best to take care of all your needs… and this is how you repay me?* It wasn't as if she hadn't tried. She'd scouted all the usual spots: the Celestial Orrery at noon, the Trade Market, and the gambling halls along the wharf. She'd even tempted fate and caught a lost traveler at the edge of the Tunnels, which housed the Bizzarre. *Stay clear of the Tunnels unless you want to be found floating face-down in one of the bays!* Rellion had told them all repeatedly. He had some sort of agreement with the proprietor there.

At least it had been worth it; the traveler had carried the gold crawns, though he'd also had the stewards. Judging by his black brocade coat and gear-buttoned boots, she'd expected better. Probably he was coming from the Bizzarre, as opposed to going. Obviously he was from out of town for the festival. No self-respecting local would accept mad stewards as payment or change.

There was also that pocket watch the stranger had carried, but Kristane could tell by the look of the antiquated chain that it was probably a keepsake. She knew only too well what a keepsake could mean, and had left it. Her hand moved involuntarily to the neckline of her cloak, brushing against the memento concealed underneath. *Sentiment? Lord knows we have expenses!* Rellion's voice echoed in her head again. He often told her and the others the same dumb tale of a merry band of men who were wrongly persecuted, ending it with, *Redistribution, my rogue!"* What he meant was *thieves*, but *rogue* sounded so much more elegant. Besides, Kristane didn't really like thinking of herself as a thief.

God, why is Rellion haunting my thoughts tonight? Kristane pounded lightly at the side of her head with her palm, as if the action might dislodge the man's persuasive teachings.

The city of Kairos was expansive: to the north and east there were buildings as far as she could see, and as the city stepped down to the west and south into the bays, the streets and avenues became even denser. Here at the center, though, there was room to breathe, except of course on those days when the ocean breeze carried the stench of the fish markets along the docks uphill to offend.

She peeked nervously behind her. Kristane knew she had already lost the Briggers who had been tailing her. All she really had to do was lead them past a tavern, and the thirsty lawkeepers would soon find the bottom of a tankard or mug more interesting than her. Keeping to the shadows cast by the setting sun, Kristane traipsed through back alleyways behind the fancy boutiques of the upper class. Hidden in these dark corridors, away from view and mostly forgotten, she passed the usual crowd of those in greater need than herself. Many of the faces were familiar to her, but there was always someone new, their hands stretched out for a scrap of kindness, or rummaging through the discarded refuse of someone more fortunate than themselves.

Cutting down a side alley at the corner, she passed a small family where they had made their bed for the night. Kristane fingered the ill-gotten crawns in her pocket, and flipped a few of the coins — the whole ones, not the shaved ones — back over her shoulder towards them. A little boy of no more than six scrambled for the coins and held them tight to his chest in his grubby hands, careful not to let anyone else see. Even the unfortunate young knew not to advertise their rare good fortune, fearful that someone else might make it their own.

Kristane stole a look back over her shoulder at the now-smiling boy as he showed his mother and pointed in Kristane's direction. "There, Ma, there," the boy whispered as the mother nervously looked around to make sure no one else had seen. Kristane smiled to herself as she took another quick turn, disappearing from their view. Not what Rellion had meant by redistribution, exactly, but she felt better about the day as she headed toward the Attic.

The Attic was home, of a sort. It was better than the streets, anyway. She could easily be like so many others, dirty and begging; but with the Attic, she had a place to sleep, food, a pet, and a twin brother, Xander. There was Rellion too, of course, but no one would ever mistake him for a father figure — more like the mad uncle that most families pretended not to have. Yet Kristane and the other members of the Rogue had a certain fondness for him. That, or maybe it was fear and loathing; it really was a fine line when attempting to understand Rellion.

The Rogue was made up of a variety of members — mostly boys and a few girls aged around sixteen, like herself and Xander. There were also a few younger ones, eleven or twelve, but the way they smoked, drank, and swore, you wouldn't have known it.

The sun had almost set by now, and the nightly fog had begun to roll in from the twin bays, creeping like eerie tendrils across the cobblestones. Time had gotten away from her. "Only a little late, but probably the last, as usual," she mumbled as she exited the back alleys onto King's Way. With the vendors and laborers already beginning to set up a myriad of stages and temporary structures for the festival, and the Saint's Parade coming up tomorrow, a more direct route was safe enough; she could make up some time.

Somewhere behind her, Kristane could hear the distinctive clomping of a stilted lamplighter as his wooden appendages struck the pavers. The lamplighters were completely unnecessary. The street lamps didn't use gas or anything as antiquated as candles, and automatic switches were hardly a new invention. But after a period of prolonged vandalism, which the union of lamplighters swore they had no part of, their services were once again needed. Rellion claimed that they were one of the few groups to have successfully extorted the Council of Stewards and survived, but insisted that they should change their title from "Official Lamplighters of Kairos" to "Official Switch-Flippers of Kairos."

Every building showed the fading of a long-ago renaissance, but still the city was beautiful. From the spired, pitched rooftops of Arroll's Aeronautical, with all things flight-inspired, to Pendulum Timepieces, with its richly frescoed walls in hues of every color, each building was adorned with an array of silent fairies, dragons, and gargoyle sculptures.

Kristane glanced up at the stained glass doors of the Kairos Emporium. A large sign in elegant scroll advertised the finest of everything, from clothes, boots and hats to imported silver and tapestries. Inside, the shopkeeper was sweeping up and turning down the lights. Occasionally a door rattled loudly at her passing, with the nightly ritual of checking them one last time. *Couldn't have planned that better if I'd tried. I feel like a wraith sneaking through the shadows, only not an evil one like in the old stories.* Kristane smiled to herself at her own musings as the light of the merchant boutiques turned off in front of her and the streetlamps came on behind her.

Down King's Way to the East stood the Abbey. Early cart vendors, vying for the best spots, crisscrossed in front of it. Deep, echoing chimes from the three-faced clock of the Abbey began to break the early evening air, and it felt as if it resounded from below and everywhere at once. Six separate bongs; she was really late, and would probably miss dinner. Great golden and brass gears and silvery moon shapes moved about each of the clock's faces. Intricately carved symbols of silver lay about the outer circles of each of the crystalline globes that housed the clocks and their inner workings. As they spun, they reflected the light coming from within the Abbey. Flanking the old Gothic doors, which were so heavy it took several large men to open them, were thick vines of white roses. Their tendrils grew as high as the darkened gray domes and spires of the Abbey, forming into a natural trellis.

It was laughably ironic that here, of all places, was the Attic and home. Kristane had asked Rellion once or twice why the monks had allowed their accommodations within the Abbey. All she got in return was a condescending reply of, *Let's just say, my Princess, a favor is owed that cannot be repaid.* Kristane thought it more likely that it was because the monks distilled the finest whiskey in all the realms, and were none too particular about to who they sold to. Rellion's contacts with the less-than-savory denizens of Kairos was a necessary evil; the monks, after all, enjoyed their façade of piety. Kristane didn't know why he called her Princess, or for that matter the reason for any of the other titles he used for people. Rellion used titles like others used curse words. No respect or sincerity was truly meant. She often wondered if she should feel offended, but she liked to think that maybe he was being a *little* sincere with her, at least.

Though Rellion marched in through the front doors of the Abbey like any other parishioner, she and the others had to use the backdoor. Well, a backdoor of sorts, anyway. Taking a running start, Kristane leapt to small handholds of slightly mislaid masonry far above her, and swung her body to a decorative ledge. She balanced herself on the tips of her toes and pressed her face to the Abbey wall as the startled inhabitants of the ledge fluttered away. The butterflies glowed with the blue halo caused by the immense power coils located at strategic points all along the borders of the city. Kristane paused to let one rest, admiring how the glow highlighted the purple pattern of its wings, which spanned her entire hand. Flitting its wings, it danced about her for a moment until it was carried away by the evening breeze with its companions, their combined luminescence lighting her way. Shuffling to her right, she grasped for the thorny rose vines and clambered up the trellis they created to the lowest part of the roof. Getting to her feet, Kristane sucked at her forefinger, where she'd carelessly pricked it against one of the thorns. *Why am I so distracted this evening?* After taking a moment to chasten herself, she ran along the back of the building's perilous ledge like a well-practiced acrobat, carefully hopping over any vines that had grown to catch the sun.

Kristane positioned herself between two curved towers that sprang from the roof. With her arms and legs outstretched, she shimmied the weight of her body back and forth to work her way up. Reaching the top, she fumbled for a crawn to feed the Pious Monk that blocked the entrance to the Attic. The Monk wasn't real, just a kind of oversized vending machine that wouldn't move unless a donation was made. Instead of candy or some silly fortune, this one granted access to the Attic. How many times had she slept on the roof as reward for a bad day? Shivering at the memory of one cold night in particular, she again heard one of Rellion's many rants: *Lord knows we have expenses!*

She dropped the coin into the outstretched hand of the clockwork guardian. It closed its fingers about the coin and dutifully bowed low, and with a whir of gears, slid to the side, exposing a spiral staircase that led down. Kristane could hear the raucous din of the end-of-day antics of the Rogue, occasionally punctuated by Rellion's deep baritone. With a heavy sigh, anticipating what was about to come, she entered.

BLESS THE FORTUNATE SOULS

The Attic was a large, oval room with a domed glass ceiling and dark wooden walls. Lining the many shelves were bottled liquids of varying sizes that bubbled of their own volition, some containing just liquid and others with pickled animals. Occasionally, one would explode without warning. Old books and fanciful gadgets sat with an stratum of dust upon them as a stone-framed fireplace warmed the room, its mantel playing home to various clocks and globes, all moving to their own internal rhythms.

Kristane reached the end of the stairs and found Purdy perched on her brother Xander's shoulder. Like so many other things she had only a vague memory of, Purdy had always just been there. Rellion had said he was with her when Kristane was dumped on his doorstep. She thought about his reaction when she'd broached the subject with him once before. *Woe's the day that you and your flea-infested flying rat fell into my care. I grabbed you and your brother from the very clutches of death. Little did I know the burden I had taken upon myself when I exited my door that early morning and tripped over a misplaced basket.* Everything was a little grander in the telling with Rellion.

Purdy flapped over to nuzzle against her neck. "Oh, how I missed you today," she whispered into his long, tapering ear as she scratched him in his favorite spot. Purdy was, well, *pretty*, hence his name. Like all children first grasping at words, Kristane hadn't quite worked out all the consonants and vowels; but the name stuck, and now he wouldn't answer to anything else. The short, fluffy fur that covered his sleek body was so soft; it phased from white to pink as she stroked his face, which was a cross between those of a rabbit and a fox. Kristane had never seen another one; a Faerrier, that's what Rellion called him. He was like those lizards that changed color. She had never seen one of those, either, but she'd seen a picture. Purdy mostly changed color according to what he was feeling. Pink meant happy, or so that's what Rellion had told her. Fumbling in her pocket for bit of leftover bread she'd liberated from a cart for her lunch earlier, Kristane was beginning to believe that it actually meant he was hungry.

Holding the bread hidden in her hand, she teased, "It's not a rat, sorry," which was actually Purdy's meal of choice; the complete absence of them in the Attic proved that. Rellion didn't seem to mind him so much in that regard. "Maybe we should cut back a little? Someone seems to be getting a little chubby." She gave him a poke in the belly, and he swatted back at her. "Okay, just kidding, here you go." She gave Purdy the crusty bread, and he greedily grabbed it in his taloned paws.

Launching himself from her shoulder and expanding large, feathered wings, Purdy flapped to the rafters above instead of returning to his perch on Xander's shoulder. Hanging upside down from his long, tufted tail, he nibbled at the treat Kristane had given him.

Rellion was already deep into his end-of-day pep talk, or in Kristane's case, usually a dressing down. As he sauntered about the room with a pot in one hand and a large-forked skewer in the other, his footsteps fell precisely within the triangles that made up the practice ring at the center of the Attic floor. The roughly-hewn circle of stacked triangle scrapings looked like they had been carved into the wood with a blunt knife. There were the good places to place your feet, and the bad. Rellion liked to call it *tripping the triangles* or *turning the circle*. Whatever it was called, it was the reason the Rogue stood out above the common thieves of the city.

Kristane unconsciously rubbed her backside with the memory of the switch that had struck there every time she'd missed a step in her youth. It had probably been worth it, all the practice; it kept her and the others relatively safe when tripping across the roof tops.

"Tell me, my Rogue, who do we thank for this bountiful feast set before us this evening? Besides myself, of course!" Rellion deposited braised bits of sausages, beef, and potatoes on each of her companion's plates. Like a conductor of an orchestra, he pointed the skewer about the room, occasionally swatting or poking the hand of one of the kids as they attempted to eat before he'd finished serving everyone.

"The fortunate souls!" they all chorused at the top of their lungs.

"Truly blessings upon the fortunate souls for their giving! Whether they be aware of their generosity or not, we thank them nonetheless! A moment of thanks!" Dutifully, each of them lowered their gaze in a mockingly solemn pose, some smirking to themselves, others giggling.

"Enough!" bellowed Rellion, "As I always say?"

"Never too much of a good thing!" chorused the inhabitants of the Attic.

"Ha ha! Too much of a good thing, indeed. We don't need them thinking better of themselves!" Rellion quipped.

Laughter broke out in the room, most of it a rehearsed act of repetition, but they all were smiling.

Kristane took a seat next to Groggle, a portly twelve-year-old boy with greasy brown hair and an affinity for books, maps, and crazy inventions. She emptied the pockets of her cloak, placing the day's haul on the table in front of her. Her Friend Prya leaned forward, catching her attention, and gave her a conspiratorial wink.

"And now for the declarations of the day!" Rellion stopped in the middle of the room and took an absurd pose, his skewer hovering above the steaming pot of food as he held it aloft. He scanned the room with an expectantly comical look. "Cayson, Xander, Prya?" Rellion called out.

Dutifully, each pushed forward their loot. Cayson squared his shoulders with confidence and, smiling broadly, gave an extra shove to his pile. Rellion, noticing his demeanor, playfully skipped over and poked the pile with his skewer. With the tip of the fork, he lassoed a golden necklace with a large jeweled pendent. Swinging it high in circles so the room could see it, Rellion returned Cayson's broad smile and declared, "Ah, Master

Cayson, you do me proud!" If Cayson could have smiled any bigger, his face might have cracked, thought Kristane.

With a fluid sweep, Rellion tossed the necklace high in the air. The jewel spun and glittered as the light caught its prisms. Without missing a beat, Rellion opened the side pocket of his jacket just as the necklace fell within. Rellion gave the pocket a little pat of satisfaction, then, skewering an extra piece of meat, tossed it onto Cayson's plate.

"Cheers all around!" yelled Rellion.

The Rogue responded with a deafening, "Hurrah!"

As the cheer died out, Rellion turned his attention back to the others, and added the prize of extra dinner each to Xander and Prya, though with less fanfare.

Kristane knew Rellion would single her out next. He approached her pile and gave a side-long glance of disapproval. Slowly and deliberately, he arched his arm upwards and brought down his skewer onto Kristane's plate, removing one of her sausages.

"Ooh!" There were a few groans around the room, but Kristane just smirked and thought, *Oh well, I wasn't that hungry anyway.*

"Silence! Shut up and drink your whiskey!" Rellion yelled while brandishing his skewer at them as a pretend threat.

Spinning in place, Rellion gave her a slight wink that only she could see, and tossed the sausage on his skewer high into the wooden rafters that held the dome in place. Purdy swung from his tail, but instead of grabbing it with his paws, his mouth opened wide like a frog's, wide and full of sharp teeth. It definitely gave the cute little foxlike face a different look. It could be quite alarming if you weren't use to it. Snatching the meat midair, he gobbled it down.

Rellion returned to his comical pose at the center of the room and, smiling broadly, said, "And as I always say?"

"Never too much of a good thing…" Only this time the chorus of the Rogue was noticeably weaker in its delivery.

"Quite right." Rellion's demeanor changed to a playful scowl. "Now off to bed, work starts early! Tomorrow is the Hallow's End festival, and a most profitable day indeed!"

Most had already scarfed down dinner, and others were licking their plates clean. Slowly, each of the kids moved towards the hammocks that lined the room. Kristane called up to Purdy, and he swooped down to take a perch on her shoulder. She surveyed the room; everyone was settling in. There would be no end-of day-chatting tonight. Groggle was the only one still moving about, humming to himself in a rhyming sing song that Rellion had taught him. "Ten crawns, twenty crawns, four, five, six. Watch out close for Rellion's stick…." *Funny how Rellion's incorporated a warning into even this*, Kristane thought.

Groggle spent most of his days in the Attic or on some errand for Rellion, but his evening duties included collecting and tallying the day's take. Rellion had always said that Groggle's talents lay in other avenues than thievery. Having watched Groggle practice *tripping the triangles* once or twice, Kristane had to agree.

Rellion had taken up his usual stance before the large, circular observation window that made up half of the top face of the three-faced Abbey clock. The hands and inner mechanisms rotated around and disappeared somewhere below the level of the Attic floor. The view from here overlooked the city's center, and the circular amphitheater of its other clock of note, the Celestial Orrery. Rellion gazed intently at the quickly rising second moon. The Older Brother, as it was called, had just peaked over the ruins of Kaer Kairos and its decaying towers, far to the West beyond the bays. A sense of apprehension filled Rellion for a moment, and he felt rather than saw Kristane approach his side.

"It's called the Devil's Embrace, and it has not appeared for a very, very long time. The time is almost upon us…" he said to no one in particular, but looked sidelong at Kristane.

"Does it mean something, then? The red crescent moon?"

"'When splintered the Brothers on darkest night, beware the Devil's Embrace and the dying of the light.' Soon the Older Brother will embrace the other and try to outshine him. He has always tried to outdo his lunar sibling, or so the fable goes... an epic tale; a nursery rhyme, if you will. Meant to scare the young, nothing more." Kristane looked intently at Rellion. His outward demeanor was the same, but she thought she could see something stirring behind those icy blue eyes. *Fear? No, more like a determined, almost dangerous look.* It was just a quick glint, and remembering that he had company, it faded as he turned his attention to her. "Think no more of it tonight. Off to sleep with you."

Shadow Amongst the Crowd

Kristane peered lazily through half-closed eyes. Rellion seemed to not have slept. He stood silhouetted against the first light of the day where he'd stood the night before. *How early is it?* she wondered; it seemed a little darker than it should be. She didn't hear the familiar sounds and smells of the morning. Lazy yawns, mutterings of complaint, and the waft of over-cooked rashers were not present, just the ticking of the clocks. She cleared her head and opened her eyes fully to check the time. *That late already, and Rellion's not having a fit?*

Dragging herself from her bed, she quietly approached Rellion. He pretended not to notice her and kept his gaze fixed on the embracing crescent of the blood red moon from the night before. Kristane could have sworn that they hadn't moved at all.

The other inhabitants of the Attic were beginning to stir, and Rellion snapped from his reverie.

"Wakey, wakey, you lazy ungrateful layabouts! There will be no breakfast for any of you — the day is wasting and there is work to be done!" His voice boomed like the large bells of the Abbey clock that no one could ignore. "Lord knows this is not a charitable institution!" Quickly and deliberately, everyone moved at once. "Let us mix it up a little this morning, shall we? Cayson, you take *him* with you! What's his name? Yes, you with the ears!"

Kristane was slightly taken back; Lathan had always been on *her* crew. Cayson cared little for those outside his group of boneheads. To him, this was just an extra burden for the day, and his face said as much. Lathan, who did indeed have odd ears, looked imploringly at Kristane.

"There will be none of that! What's his name?"

"Lathan," Kristane volunteered.

"What? Ears? What kind of absurd name is that?" Cayson and his cronies, Creff and the Kressley brothers, Markyn and Munse, smirked at Rellion's seeming incomprehension.

"His name is *Lathan*. He's been here as long as we have," Kristane said a little more irritably this time. Everyone knew that Rellion was aware of Lathan's name; Lathan just hadn't had a very good take in a while. Embarrassed by being singled out, Lathan quickly mussed his hair in an attempt to cover what had now caught everyone's attention.

"What? He's been here since when? Whatever, you, you're with Cayson today. Enough of the babying around here! Lord knows we have expenses! And you, Groggle, you take his place with Kristane, Xander, and Prya! It's time to expand your horizons, my boy!" Groggle gave a whimper, but everyone knew there was no further use arguing the point. Lathan was going with Cayson's crew today, and Groggle was probably going to get arrested.

Rellion's Rogue set off for the day, jumping one by one onto ledges and then climbing down the vine trellis to the street. They wouldn't have to travel far and wide today; with the annual festival of Hallow's End just at their doorstep, it was going to be "a most profitable day indeed!"

Overnight, the city's center had transformed into a splash of colors. Broad-trunked cherry trees had blossomed, and shed flower-shaped confetti down both avenues of King's Way as each led outward from the city's center to the east and west. Vendors ready to sell their wares were tucked in beneath the canopies and in between the white-barked trunks of the trees, shouting out to passersby the deals of the day. At the very center where the two avenues met, an amphitheater carved from the same red rock that supported the city of Kairos housed the Celestial Orrery. Several circular broad-terraced landings, each marked by a thick channel of metal, stepped down to the base of the orrery below the street level. As the orrery hummed and spun on its axis, a single large glass orb pulsed with an ethereal mix of light and gasses held within it as various-sized orbs swung about upon gilded metal arms. Most days, it resounded with a pleasant hum of notes and chimes that no one stopped to listen to anymore; but on the eve of Hallow's End, the orrery's performance always enthralled the crowd.

No one could remember how long it had been there. There were no engravings or commemorative plaques that marked its day of christening, just several round, heavily patinaed plates, almost like extremely oversized medallions, interspersed equally about the circular form that the clock's perimeter created. The plates were embedded flush with the red-rock flooring of the final terrace of the amphitheater, just as the cobbled stone walkways of King's Way met it. Inscribed upon the plates were characters of various shapes, no two the same, in a lost language.

Kristane and the others traipsed across the city's center using the profile of the orrery and the long shadows it cast to observe, somewhat unseen, the many festival attendees as they began to congregate.
Unable to use the back entrance, Groggle ran up to them from the Abbey, sneaking out with the parishioners. "I'm hungry," he said, reaching for his rumbling stomach as the smell of freshly baked sweet and savory pasties filled the morning air from the wheeled carts.

"Shut it, Groggle, none of us ate this morning," Prya hissed in a low tone. Groggle lowered his head and kicked at one of the plates with the strange markings. "Listen, sorry, Groggle, it's just that we're one down today…" Prya stopped herself short, hearing the poorly masked insult she was about to make. Groggle was definitely not on par with the others, and he was a bit awkward, but he had his attributes. "Well, I mean, I'm pretty hungry too," she stammered out as she attempted to recover.

As Prya looked at Groggle, his head still bowed dejectedly, a fruit cart passed directly in back of him. Without skipping a beat, she sidestepped him and the large wheels that rumbled across the cobble, and spun back with a bright purple fruit, the merchant none the wiser of his lighter load. "Here, there's no reason to go hungry today." She held the fruit just under his nose.

Groggle lifted his head and grinned, the sun catching the lenses of his goggled cap, which he always donned when outside the Abbey, making him look like some weird, oversized bug. He fancied himself an aviator; but the farthest he had ever gotten off the ground was climbing the stairs of the Abbey. Groggle took a big bite of the fruit, and the juices ran down the corners of his still-grinning mouth. Prya smiled back at him.

Kristane, sensing that the conflict had passed, came to a decision. She glanced towards Xander, who was still scanning the opposite side of the festival, pretending not to be aware of what was happening; he gave her a nod. "All right, we have time, so let's split up and visit a food cart or two. But be careful — the Briggers are out in full force today, and if you haven't noticed, they're carrying their sticks." She looked at the pair meaningfully, and they nodded their assent. "Meet back in front of the Black Kettle just before the one o'clock show. It's always the biggest."

Prya tapped Groggle on the shoulder and shrugged back towards the pasty cart. "Come on, let's go broaden your horizons." Groggle didn't need to be further coaxed. Pulling at his too- big pants, which were in constant danger of falling down despite his portly frame, he ran off beside her, with not even a backward glance at Kristane.

Xander gave Kristane another nod, a brotherly smile, and pointed to his eyes and then back to her. The message was clear: be careful. Xander never said much when they were out, and didn't need to. Abandoned together while very young, they'd really only had each other, despite all the others in the Rogue. It had connected them as more than just siblings, though their rare arguments, epic in nature, were an easy reminder that they were as normal as any other brother and sister. As her twin moved off, melting in with a large group of people dressed to the nines, Kristane absentmindedly fondled the necklace beneath her clothing. A clockwork heart, made from a combination of shiny metals and a pretty, hard wood, was the only tangible item of a supposed past in her possession. She had once asked Rellion why he allowed her to keep it. His offhanded reply was typical. *What, that cheap, atrocious trinket? It's hardly worth the time to pawn, with what little profit would be garnered from it.* She really didn't care if he thought it was worthless; it had a certain beauty to it that went beyond some forgotten past. '*What past was that?*' she wondered. Her single memory of her origins was of a beautiful, long-haired blonde woman with a loving smile who she supposed was her mother. The woman left her with brown eyes that mirrored her own, a careful whispering of love, and a delicate kiss to her cheek.

"Hey, movin' it, you!" The shout came from a craftsman waving his fist at her as he stood up from his cart seat, his accent thick with the cant of the eastern realms.

Snapping back from her reverie at the sound of the man's gruff voice, Kristane pulled her hand away from her cheek, where the memory of the kiss had been, and looked at her palm intently. With a whip of the reins from the hand that wasn't still clenched in anger, the muzzle of the craftsman's large mechanical draft animal began to nudge at her back, along her shoulder. The animal was surprisingly gentle, despite its enormous size and outward appearance. Hammered bits of bronze and thin sheets of riveted brass were draped across a patchwork skeleton of metal spines. Long, ox-like horns spanned the breadth of the sizable animal, and stretched out much farther to each side of the cart it pulled. Through the well-worn and dented metal skin, the whirring and grinding of the oversized cogs and wheels that gave the beast movement could be seen. Being a perpetual beast of burden and self-winding, the energy that kept it moving was a result of its own toils as its internal pendulum wound a spring attached to a gear train. For it to stop for too long meant its own kind of death, leaving it at the mercy of its master until it was slowly wound-up again.

Kristane reached up and gave the beast a pat on its snout, her arm brushing against the frayed straps of leather that made up its mane and descended down into an ox-beard. A low grunt rumbled from within its shell-like voice box, its chambers resonating the flow of air in an attempt to approximate that of a live animal. Carefully, it bowed a little lower, and its eyes blinked appreciatively at her.

"Consarn ya! If you don't min' what yer about, I'll give it to ya!" The craftsman was turning a fair shade of red by this point, his anger obviously reaching a peak, the reins in his hand snapping repeatedly against the back of his charge.

Others had begun to notice the commotion.

Great! If Rellion could see me now! Kristane reprimanded herself silently. *So much for being a shadow amongst the crowd.* Nervously, she dropped her head, averting her eyes from others, and headed for the nearest alleyway.

DA, DA, DADA, DUM, DUM

Rellion paraded down the curved and spiral staircases of the monastery. A scent of burning cinnamon struck his senses, like when a baker opens the oven door to check on some delightful confectionary creation. The monks were deep into their prayer. Rellion made it a point of stomping the heels of his boots just a little louder down the stairs as he exited the building.

Reaching the large wooden doors, he spun around and, with a condescending tip of his hat, shouted, "Blessings be onto you, Lord Monks, this day!"

Rellion made sure to give a patronizing look to the young monk leading the blessing of the Saint's funerary casket. Cristobal Zekel was intelligent, ambitious, and indifferent to the plight of those outside the Abbey, traits that didn't always meld well with those responsible for the enlightenment of others. The weak-shouldered man didn't look in Rellion's direction; he merely dabbed at his nose with a handkerchief. *'By the King's grace, does that man's nose run insistently,'* Rellion thought. Cristobal did his best to ignore the interruption, holding his arms grandly above the casket as other monks swung thuribles by their trailing chains. The fragrant incense smoked in wafts of violet vapor, obscuring the final resting place of the Saint interned within, explaining the burning cinnamon smell. Cristobal began to chant again, and Rellion loudly tapped the ferrule of his cane upon the stone floor. Each of the monks turned to look over their shoulders, some gaping in astonishment, others cringing with annoyance. Smiling, having given the young priest an extra dose of contempt for the day, Rellion spun in place and exited the large doors of the monastery, which had already been thrown wide to greet Hallows End and the Saint's Parade.

The brightness of the Older Brother, in contrast to the subdued light of what should have been noon, caused Rellion to pause and focus on the slivered red moon of the Younger Brother, which had still not set. He murmured to himself, "The Devil's Embrace. Could so much time really have passed?"

With a few quick hops down the stairs, Rellion headed down a back alley next to Wyndom's that led towards Serpentine Lane, his path taking him to the one place that the news and gossip of the day wasn't filtered by the city's regime. The Drunken Chymist had held the corner of High Street and Serpentine Lane for centuries, and though Old Man Pope was long dead, his offspring had done an excellent job of continuing the tradition of "just one more is never enough." In fact, the pub had had continuous service 'round the clock since its opening day. Rellion could only remember once, when a fire had broken out, when the drinks had stopped flowing. Even then, with the help of some regular and thirsty patrons who would not be denied drunkenness due to a blazing inferno, kegs were moved to the opposite side of the street to watch the blaze and cheer on those tasked with putting it out.

The pub stood three stories tall, due to the many years of building on to it to provide more space for the many who called it their second home. The additions seemed very comical at first glance: slanted walls hung out into the street and then unexpectedly jutted back into other curved outcroppings. Brocaded arches, bay windows, and double doors — some that opened to small patios — were adorned with fanciful wrought iron fairies and dragons.

The craftsmanship that made up much of the exterior, though slightly askew, was the finest in the city, probably due to the fact that some of the finest craftsman and artisans of the ages had contributed to the spectacle before Rellion, their handiwork mostly traded out for some past-due bar tab or other nefarious dealings. The slightly off-kilter nature of their work was due to the attempt to run up their debt at the bar a little farther before beginning a renovation.

The interior was best described as a theater in the round. The performers of the day held the audience captive by mixing up a wide array of concoctions. The center of the bar bubbled with large glass jars of whiskey, scotch, vodka, gin, and beer, with all the traditional flavorings in every color, and the ones that were popular today but not so much tomorrow. Piping and cone- shaped collectors made of copper caught the vapors from the jars and collected and cooled them as they were trans-ferred to the spigots for the bartender's use. Each spigot was made of hand-polished brass and decorated as a fallen angel, a private joke of Old Man Pope's that wasn't lost on anyone.

About the exterior walls, the seating for patrons was in grandstand fashion, marked by several staircases and landings consisting of small tables and large banquet-sized ones that could seat many, occasionally punctuated by the odd staircase that led to a single table perched high above the ornate bar for secret conversations or private interludes. Each came equipped with large burgundy drapes that could be pulled into place to hide the patrons and dealings within, but nowhere was there a bad view of what was happening below, if one so chose.

At the Chymist, race and social order meant little. The privileged and the haggard stood elbow to elbow, cheering one another on for the duration of their stay. Rellion scanned the bar, looking for those who spoke more than they should and those whose drunken gossip sometimes held some truth. Plenty of both, usually.

"Red? I haven't seen that, and I've been here all night. I mean, on duty all night." A Brigger, Kairos' esteemed law enforcement, slurred and swayed where he stood. The Brigger smiled goofily at his guffaw, and overly happy bar patrons and his other on-duty buddies slapped him merrily on the back, splashing more liquor on his already-stained uniform.

Briggers were so nicknamed due to the fact that before the Manor Hall was converted to a prison and the Bastille built, the guilty were interned upon an old brigand ship docked in the Bay of Merrow. The makeshift prison was abandoned for a couple of reasons. Firstly, the corruption of the

Briggers meant an easy escape for the price of a few crawns, and secondly the ship, barely seaworthy, had sunk some years back in a storm, drowning all those held in the brigs.

A grizzled old dwarf spoke breathlessly into his drink, his head just peeking above the bar top to the left of Rellion. "By the Blessed Tree, I tell you, something is lurking in the dark of the Tunnels near the Bizzarre. I am not the only one to have seen it. Quick it is, like a shadow."

"A visit from you is long overdue!" Smirking innocently, a pretty young bartender had leaned over the bar, capturing Rellion's attention.

"Ah, Lady Kate, as lovely as ever you are! Just a touch of the usual, will you?" Rellion held his forefinger and thumb apart slightly, but then extended them dramatically with a wink. Kate smiled and turned to a small cabinet of intricately carved rosewood. Brushing aside her long auburn hair, she unfastened a necklace she was wearing, with a small key that hung from it. She pulled from the cabinet a crystal decanter shaped like a dragon, its wings tucked back into a handle. Pouring a generous amount into a short glass, she placed it in front of him.

"Thank you, Lady Kate." With a flourish of his hand, he said, "If you would just add that to my tab."

"I often wonder, what tab that is that you talk about, Rellion? It never seems to come due."

Rellion leaned sideways onto the bar top, gave a slight wink, and whispered with an air of mock confidentiality, "It is for services rendered, my dear."

Kate Pope tossed her hair playfully and smiled, turning her attention to a boisterous group that cheered to an unknown celebration nearby. Rellion considered her for a moment as she spun away, and thought, *Smart as her grandfather, that one.*

Absentmindedly, Rellion spun his glass in slow circles. The music in the room had taken on a decidedly upbeat tempo. In turn, the general din of conversation had responded with a cacophony of more frequent cheers and salutations.

The band sat on an elevated and divided circular stage just off of the bar, the musicians an assembled combination of clockwork and steam-driven parts, long ago built to replace their living and sentient counterparts in an attempt to save old Pope some money and hassle. Over the many years, staff and patrons alike had come to call them by nicknames. Count Bobo Mahoney and the Steam Powered Swing had entertained the nobles, the thieves, and the unique alike for going on two centuries. The horn section, known as Hot Lips, Dizzy, and The Professor, swung in unison, sometimes playing more than a single instrument at once. Sliding trombone arms and bell cones reached for the ceiling at each up-beat as they exhaled steam from the breath of the players. Big Benny, the bassist, had the appearance of almost playing himself, the instrument so much a part of his body it was hard to tell where one started and the other began. Rabbit was a blur on the drums, and of course Count Bobo himself held court and played the upright grand piano stage left. The Count and his entourage, though being slaved to the stage that housed the workings that powered them below, were eerily human in their mannerisms.

"You haven't touched that." Kate had returned, breaking Rellion from his thoughts.

"Sometimes it is as much having as wanting that matters, Lady Kate."

"What is it that you will be wanting this day, Rellion?"

"Just the news of the day, my dear. What whisperings have come in from the long-traveled?"

Kate's usual bright attitude faded as she looked intently at him. "You've heard of the shadow in the Tunnels?" Rellion nodded, to further press her on. "Sightings began about three months ago. There are stories of missing items, but it's the stealth of the shadow and the odd tinkling of a bell as the shadow retreats deeper into the dark that has given everyone a sense of fear."

"Merely the antics of the Wee Folk or a capable thief, Lady Kate," Rellion said with a dismissive gesture of his hand. Kate smirked and raised an eyebrow at the mention of "Wee Folk" and waited for Rellion to smile at his own joke. He obliged. "No more, then?"

"Rumors of attacks along the borders of the Fairy Chimneys near Desolation, their inhabitants all found dead. With the Younger Brother shining red, people are beginning to speak aloud the old rhyme. There are whisperings of the Forgotten Ones returning, as silly as that sounds."

Before Rellion could respond with another pithy retort, which he of course already had in mind, there was a resounding *bong* that brought the bar to complete silence.

So strange the sound, and so unlike what anyone was used to, it brought most of the patrons to a brief moment of clarity. Almost like the clanging of the Abbey bell, it was, yet the pitch was wrong; there were too many underlying tones, and this sound had come from within the walls of the Chymist. Slowly, the realization was coming to Rellion as to the source of the disruption. As he turned, others had also begun to bring their attention towards the stage. The Count sat slightly hunched above his piano, his geared and brass-plated arms held high above the black and ivory keys. The other members of the band stood prone, their soulless gaze fixed upon the Count, awaiting his next orchestral cue. Once again the Count performed a piano slam, every hammer to corresponding key striking a chord, playing every note at once. As a hazy mist of steam blew out of the Count's mouth, the whirring gears of his elbows brought his fingers back to within reach of the keys. *Da, da, dada, dum, dum.* He stroked the keys twice in the same pattern. Rabbit and Big Benny began to follow in turn, the low bass and ringing cymbal beginning to unnerve everyone in the room, yet everyone stood silently transfixed. The band members began to hum a low, reverberating chorus. Steam puffed about them …and then the Count began to sing. "When splintered the brothers on darkest night, beware the Devil's Embrace and the dying of the light. So shall strike the hour on the clockmaker's hand, and silence will fall across the land. For there comes one to claim a throne, by faith, by curse, by bone…." Holding the last note, the Count turned to the stricken crowd and froze in place like a puppeteer had cut his strings, with the other members of the Steam Powered Swing following suit.

The silence that followed was only now beginning to be broken by panicked murmurings. Rellion turned to leave, but stopped himself and turned back, giving Kate a quick wink. "I do believe I will be wanting this today!" In a single gulp he emptied the contents of his glass, spun upon his heel, and made for the door.

THE TRAVELING
MEDICINE SHOW

Kristane had made a fairly unnoticeable retreat, except for the ragman — or Raggabrash, as everyone called him — who was standing at the mouth of the alley, occasionally looking back at her. She wasn't actually sure that was his name; she just figured it was because of the unusually colorful monk's habit he wore that was torn into strips above his waistline. She often wondered if he had stolen it from the trash and dyed it with the splash of colors, or if he was just some monk that had been driven crazy by his oath of silence. She hadn't ever spoken to him. Raggabrash didn't really talk to people; he yelled at them, mostly obscenities and dire predictions of the future, but usually a combination of both; and just in case they missed his intent, he had them spelled out on a large pieces of parchment that he wore on both his front and back. Kristane remembered one time, as a little girl, she had asked Rellion why the funny man was talking to his feet. Her mentor's reply was that he wasn't talking to his feet, but to the Wee Folk. Kristane remembered giggling at that as a young girl.

"I thought we were being careful today?"

Kristane gave a startled gasp as Xander dropped down from a low rooftop next to her. It was just like her brother; probably he'd been keeping an eye on her this entire time.

Staring down at her feet, hands on her knees with her back against the wall, she looked up at him defiantly at first, but eased her mood when she saw him smiling at her questioningly. Nodding in the direction of the Black Kettle, Xander gave her a lift off the wall, coaxing her forward. "Let's go; it's almost time. Groggle should be good and fed by now."

Kristane returned his smirk and trotted off down the alleyway with him.

With the festival of Hallow's End, the population of Kairos swelled to three times its already sizable normal, as vendors, tradesmen, and tourists traveled from afar to witness the festival and engage in commerce. The Black Kettle was housed in an elaborate building that fronted the city center, just where one of the sloping hills that made up the topography of Kairos climbed steeply upward. Most of Kairos was made up of these long stretches of steep, climbing roads punctuated by an occasional patch of flat space. The architecture of Kairos matched the meandering of the land, creating commanding views from almost everywhere, but mostly for the wealthy.

Fastened to the roof of the Kettle, beautiful paper kites of dragons, fish, and other odd creatures flitted in the cool breeze. Distinctive round chimneys spiraled upward in a herringbone pattern, spewing out bright, colorful smoke, the color dependent on what tonics and cures were being brewed within. Pink was always unicorn horn, for whatever plagued the skin. A deep blue generally meant a cure for maladies of the head, and green meant a mixture of slobber and fat from some beast, a salve for things unmentionable. Today the air above the Kettle was infused with a bright amethyst, which meant something very unusual was bubbling within.

The Black Kettle, which did a good trade most days of the week, pulled out all the stops for the festival. A grandiose stage of varying tiers was set up to entice would-be buyers towards the front doors. To either side of the stage sat big-mouthed spring-loaded cannons with half-drunk dwarves perched atop them. They toasted each other with large mugs, splashing the booze over themselves and the stage as they worked up the gathering crowd. Amongst the hanging colorful flags and balloons near the back of the stage hung a canvas backdrop stamped with an elaborate font: *Doc Fatterpacker and Peg-Leg Noodle's Traveling Medicine Show.*

"There they are." Kristane motioned toward the front of the stage. At the front of the stage stood Groggle, a pasty in one hand, a tankard in the other, and a combination of smears across his face from food he hadn't quite gotten stuffed in his mouth. Prya stood a few paces back, occasionally glancing about, but it was obvious she was caught up in the fanfare.

"Take up a position and wait for clean-up. I'll get them." Xander looked skeptically at Kristane. She repeated through gritted teeth, "I'll get them." He nodded and melted into the crowd, dodging a tray of mugs that a drink maiden was serving to a pair of already-swaying well-dressed men.

Kristane approached Prya, bumping deliberately into her shoulder. Prya looked coyly at her. "Guilty, I know, but it's hard not to…. You know he's supposed to be here today?"

Just as Kristane was about to reply, Peg-Leg Noodle took the stage, and the crowd surged forward. Groggle was nowhere to be seen, lost in the assemblage as the circle about the stage closed in. Noodle's peg-leg was a prosthesis made of alloy gears that creaked and squeaked as it hit the stage flooring with great, solid thumps. A tale had been woven of great heroics regarding his missing limb, but was most probably an act of great stupidity that had deprived him of it. Lanky, with sizable eyes — one slightly larger than the other — and a lopsided hairpiece of bright red standing on end, Noodle didn't give the appearance of one endowed with great intelligence. In his left hand, Noodle carried a heralding trumpet. If it weren't for his long arms, it was doubtful that he could have even held it aloft. At a blaring blast, the spectators began to cheer even louder.

"Prya, we need to get to it." Kristane scanned behind herself but had lost her bearings on her brother, and of course Groggle was nowhere to be seen, though she knew where he probably was.

"You heard me, right? He's supposed to be here!" Prya was nodding in a hypnotic way, doing her best to pull her friend in.

Rare were the moments when Kristane was able to act her age instead of what life had dealt her. She knew this wasn't the time for it, but…. "Oh, all right, just until he comes on," Kristane relented with an exasperated sigh, but smiled slyly. *What's wrong with me today? First a few memories I don't know whether are real or not, and now I'm just another girl enjoying the festival with her best friend.*

Peg-Leg continued his heralding, as the dwarves waved animatedly from atop the cannons, taunting the crowd. "What's that you're saying?... Can't hear you!" It was hard to understand the guttural accent of the dwarves, not to mention that they were slurring every other word through mouthfuls of ale, but they finally relented to the prodding crowd.

Along the first reinforcement, and just before the breech, were oversized keys that wound up the cannons like very big child's toys. Miraculously amongst the cheering, the tooting of the trumpet, and the swaying of the dwarves, the cannons were armed. Retreating to the butt end cascabels, the dwarves grabbed hold of braided ropes that acted as firing pins and, with a last high note from Peg-Leg Noodle, pulled them.

BANG! BANG!

Sparkling confetti of lavender, green, and gold blasted out from the cannons, floating and dancing in the breeze. Thick blue and green smoke erupted along the back of the stage, occluding the colorful backdrop banner, and cheers filled the square. As the smoke began to dissipate, Doc Fatterpacker appeared through a slit in the canvas, catching his shoe on the threshold and causing him to trip into view. While not overly mystical or graceful in presentation, by this point the inebriated crowd hardly cared. He gave one of the dwarves an irritable look, pointing to the offending bit of fabric, but as he turned back to the crowd, a brilliant smile greeted them. With his black-gloved hands and black-sleeved arms outstretched, he bowed graciously, so low that the abnormally large purple stovetop hat nestled on his head, adorned with peacock feathers and flashy trinkets, brushed the floor.

Off to the side of the stage, the cannon riders had dropped down to crowd level and were manically cranking a handled wheel. Up from trapdoors emerged various contraptions bedecked with horns, stringed instruments, drums, and piano keys self-playing a lively tune. Well, not exactly *self*-playing; another pair of dwarves was cranking a series of wheels just as frantically as the others.

"Welcome! Welcome all! To the greatest show in all of the realms! Let us entertain you!" As he swept his burgundy velvet cape backwards with a flourish of his arms, a matching brocaded fitted suit underneath a number of price tags popped into view. The implication was clear: everything had its price and was for sale when it came to Doc Fatterpacker.

"And now, without further ado, I give you Eidolon!" The Doc bowed off the stage as one more trapdoor opened and a sole figure rose onto center stage. There was a decidedly more female burst of applause with accompanying hoots and whistles; but one could tell that Eidolon definitely had a following among all.

Standing prone with his head bowed until the applause dimmed and the mechanical band dropped the tempo, Eidolon's thick, black, wavy hair cascaded about his shoulders and curtained his eyes. A haunting, soulful voice raised in cadence as Eidolon's head raised and his hazel eyes met the crowd's. Singing into a silver-plated receiver with large gratings, Eidolon longingly gripped the pedestal that it rested upon. His voice in turn emanated from a pair of flanking high-reaching pavilion horns, their long elbows disappearing into the stage.

> *The long, long road upon which I have travelled*
> *Has kept me far from you*
> *Nights of quiet and a heart's longing*
> *Within your eyes the sun does rise*
> *Within your eyes I have no disguise*
> *I find my love within your eyes*

"Did you see that? Did you see that? He looked right at me!" Prya squealed as the troubadour ended the chorus and continued to sing more of a lost love.

"No, not you! It was me!" Kristane replied with the same delight. Both girls were now clutching each other's hands and jumping up and down on the balls of their feet, swaying to the final chorus.

> *Can it be that there is nothing more*
> *Than just my long search for you*

I find my love within your eyes

"Wow, he is *a*-mazing!" "He knows exactly how I'm feeling!" the girls said in unison as they laughed together giddily.

"Blending in?" Both girls jumped at the sound of Xander's voice, immediately coming back from the moment that they'd shared.

"Well, it's my fault, Xander... I made Kristane stay... Well, you know?" Prya said, suppressing a smile.

Xander just nodded toward the stage. "At least someone is profiting today."

IF IT FALLS APART SCATTER

Doc Fatterpacker had once again ascended the stage, and Eidolon, with his head bowed, was slowly disappearing beneath it. The audience had responded with thunderous applause at the conclusion of the performance, and coins and certain articles of clothing were strewn about the stage. As Fatterpacker broke into a long-winded monologue, the dwarves dove for the haul around his feet, occasionally punching one another in the face as they wrestled for a particular coin, though none of them touched the mad stewards. Even more interesting, though, was Groggle, who had abandoned the remainder of his minor feast and, with his elbows spread wide atop the stage, was busily shoveling unnoticed loose coins from the edge of the stage into his pockets.

"Remember, ladies and gentlemen, unmentionable finery and inscribed handkerchiefs for sale following the final performance. I will now need a volunteer from the audience…"

In response, a lanky woman with a long skirt and golden hair climbed to the stage. Catcalls and whistles followed from several groups of tall-hatted young men, but their appreciation quickly ended in guffaws of laughter as realization dawned. The obviously Peg-Leg Noodle dressed in drag had turned to wink and fuss with the golden tresses of his wig. "With Doc Fatterpacker's Miracle Elixir in chocolate brown…."

"We still have the distraction, but everyone's purses are lighter now. Let's get moving before the day is a waste." Xander was still smiling, but what he said was true.

"Sorry, Xander… right you are. I'll get him." Prya trotted off, the bob cut of her hair bouncing as she moved to retrieve Groggle.

Kristane knew that her brother didn't care, but nonetheless she found herself feeling guilty due to her own recent giddiness. It also made her angry. It was so unfair that others worried for nothing, yet she had to worry about just surviving, every single day. *I wouldn't mind wearing a dress and attending a ball like some young noble lady. Well… I* guess *I wouldn't mind. I've never actually worn a dress before.*

Groggle marched up grinning, hands in his pockets, purposefully jinglingly the purloined coins. "Good job, Groggle, but please wipe your face." Kristane discarded her anger and gave Groggle an approving smile as he wiped his chin clean with the back of his sleeve. "Everyone knows their part. We work the crowd in sections, no repeats. If it falls apart, scatter and head for the top of Gallows Alley." Kristane kept her voice low while talking to the others, so as to not be overheard. Also doing her best to keep up the façade, she kept her eyes bright, and sported a congenial smile. Just one of the crowd.

Turning her attention to Xander, he nodded in response to the group of catcalling younger men from earlier. It was a good mark. They were certainly of means, based on the number of layers in which they were attired. All wore paisley-patterned vests of richly dyed colors, embellished with brass and silver buttons; and their coats showed no wear, with more the appearance of being just recently tailored at the Emporium. Each man carried a walking stick adorned with a gilded topper, signifying their status and availability within society. Still more importantly, each was now to the point of drunkenly leaning against one another. They were laughing and raising their canes in the air in boisterous response to the on-stage antics of Peg-Leg, who was now standing next to the Doc, his sparsely haired pate showing sans wig. Fatterpacker was lowering an oddly shaped cone to his head that was attached to a hose and made a dramatic sucking sound.

Nodding to one another, Kristane and Prya separated, each moving to their respective positions. To work a mark was a simple enough concept in thought, but the reality of what could go wrong was without measure.

There was no need for a bump with this group; with the ongoing slapping of each other's shoulders, they provided enough of their own distraction. Prya and Kristane approached from opposite sides, winding through the crowd. Out of the corner of her eye, she suddenly saw Groggle giving a wave-off sign, a little too frantically not to be noticed, but the fearful look in his eyes was enough for Kristane to stop short. Prya, on the other hand, had not seen the warning. Quickly scanning the surrounding area, she caught sight of Lathan also signaling.

"Oh, no! Those idiots are working the same mark! Those moronic gingers stand out as it is. They'll get us all caught!" Kristane said a little too loudly. Sure enough, Cayson's cronies, the Kressley brothers, were coming in just behind Prya. Markyn and Munse, while not stupid, weren't too quick on the uptake, either. Whether or not they saw Lathan's signal or Prya, it was obvious that they weren't veering off. Kristane knew she should just head for the rendezvous, but Prya, probably intent on making up for earlier, was already lining up. Moving quickly towards the unfolding spectacle, Kristane waved off Groggle. She couldn't worry as to him; he knew where to go. Xander, in his position as drop, would be too far out to help.

"What's this, my fair little pixie?" Too late, Prya had made a clean take; but as she turned, the two moron brothers had bumped into her, knocking her into the mark and onto the cobblestones. Seeing things had gone badly, the two brothers backed into the crowd. No honor among Cayson's crew; it was every man for himself. The man who had spoken looked down at Prya, smiling; but as he noticed a shiny chain clutched between her fingers, his own hand moved to his vest pocket.

"Why, you little thief! Mates, look to your pockets — we have a spider in our midst!" Closing in, he stood nearly on top of Prya, holding the end of his cane very close to her face.

"Ah, let her have it!" joked one of his friends as he slapped him on the back.

"It was a favor from a lady!" the young man replied indignantly in turn.

"A lady? Ha! Probably from your grandmother, if the truth be told!" The rest of the small group of gentlemen began to laugh hysterically at the young man's blush.

Prya just sat scared on the cobblestone, her eyes fixed on the end of the man's cane. This section of the audience had now shifted its attention from Doc Fatterpacker to the scene playing out just in front of them. The Doc, who had moved on from the Sucking Barber, was displaying yet another one of his wares as Noodle juggled an outrageous number of balls of various colors at angles that defied gravity.

Kristane was just wondering how the situation could get any worse when Lathan came to her side, motioning to where the sounds of whistles and crackling could be heard. A phalanx of a half-dozen Briggers were pushing through with their sticks, dark wooden cudgels capped at either end with a brightly polished pieces of copper, held high above the heads of the crowd. "Move to the side, move to the side!" could be heard in between the occasional burst from a whistle.

A gruff but fit-looking sergeant of the Briggers, who was very thick through the arms and chest, addressed the well-dressed men with a bit more respect than he would have normally. "Gentlemen, what's this disturbance about, or are we just on a tear this afternoon?"

Looking to the scene, he came to his own conclusion quick enough. He pointed to Prya, indicating to two of his fellow Briggers to detain her. As the two men moved forward to take hold of her, they shook their cudgels up, down, and then upended them with a twist of their wrists. The distinct rattle like a child's plaything emanated from within the hollowed-out wooden sticks. A mixture of magnetic and voltaic metal pebbles skipped through the internal chambers, created by the decay of the softer fibrous material within the cut-away branch of the quidel tree. Blue bolts skipped about the copper-capped pommels of both ends of the "burning torches," as the giants of Brobdin called them.

As the victim began his tale of a lady's favor, Groggle snuck in behind the two men who had Prya clasped between them. Fidgeting through his many pockets of the oversized jacket he wore, he drew out something that looked like a long strip of metal, pliable as a piece of thread. He first attached one end to one of the cudgels, his chubby fingers shaking a little as he attempted to tie the noose-like knot; then, as he moved to the other, he looked intently at Kristane and Lathan.

"Be ready," Kristane mumbled to Lathan.

"What are we going to do? Is there a plan?"

"Yeah, be inventive. You get Prya." Kristane nodded back to Groggle as he attached the other end of the metal strip to the second cudgel, then dropped to his hands and knees, moving behind another pair of lawkeepers. Instantly, the two Briggers holding Prya shuddered from the connection that had been made, blue bolts tracing up their arms to their comically distorted faces. Prya had taken a small shock, but the Briggers no longer had a hold of her.

Lathan and Kristane, seeing the chance that Groggle had created, sprang into action. Lathan ran at the thick-chested sergeant, stopping just short of him, and bowed while grabbing his hands. "May I have this dance, sir?" He did not wait for a reply. Swinging the lead Brigger about, he let go of the man, who tumbled headlong into the electrified pair. All three fell, twitching convulsively.

At the same time, Kristane stepped up to the two in front of Groggle, smiling. "Nice day for a festival!" Taken aback by her attitude and the scene playing out over her shoulder, the men kind of half-smiled back. Bouncing into a backwards handspring, she kicked at their chests with her feet. As the pair tumbled over a kneeling Groggle, she sprang back from her hands to her feet and, picking up a grinning Groggle, turned to flee.

"I think that will be enough playing for the day, missy!" growled the one Brigger who was left standing, his crackling stick hovering over both Kristane and Groggle.

"Crawns! Crawns for everyone!" Groggle emptied his pockets and threw the glittering coins high into the air. The ensuing push of the crowd, eager to get a share of the windfall, pushed the yelling Brigger backwards, his cudgel held high over his head.

Lathan and Prya, seeing the coins tumble through the air, knew their friends were in the clear. "Come on, Lathan, better stick with us. The usual place." Prya said, while prodding him forward.

"I believe you have something of mine!" Their mark had once again caught them, but in place of the cane he had unsheathed a rapier that was hidden within its wooden shaft. Pointing it at the pair of thieves, his cohorts followed suit, each brandishing their own weapon — though most were still leaning up against each other and laughing. In fact, it had become apparent to Prya that the young man's tone was far from menacing, and the entire experience for the gentlemen was probably something they would just boast about later over several more drinks. Giving the chained pocket watch a little kiss and donning an endearing smile, Prya tossed it to the owner. His gang of friends nearly fell over with laughter.

Chuckling to himself and holding the watch aloft, the young man said, "Aha, mates! Look, truly a favor from a lady! Off with you then, pixie!" Sheathing his thin-bladed sword back into his cane, he turned to his friends. The congratulatory slapping and laughter could still be heard as Prya and Lathan made their escape.

In the distance, more whistles could be heard from a couple of different directions. Time was up; this was all the luck they were getting today. "You know where to go!" Kristane pushed Groggle into the crowd. "We need to split up; it's safer in the crowd that way." He nodded his understanding. She felt guilty, but then again, Groggle had more than proved his worth today. "We wouldn't have made it without you, you know…"

He smiled and turned in the direction of Gallows Alley before she could finish.

Kristane quickly moved down the side alley next to the Emporium, the same one she had taken the night before. The rooftops were the safest route. Using the acrobatic skills she had learned over a lifetime, she leapt upon a large trash bin to her right and kicked at the opposite wall, the momentum carrying her back across the alley to a height where she could grasp the parapet wall of Arroll's, the entire time making sure that her feet were "tripping" the right "triangles." Gaining the roof, Kristane could see all the way west towards Gallows Alley. It was easy now; she could almost see the old cemetery, and the gathering crowd forming there for the Saint's Parade.

Meanwhile, Groggle stood clutching at his chest against a wall, behind a pile of crates. He had backed himself into a dead-end alley. He could still hear the whistles of the Briggers, meaning they had not yet given up their search. *That's so unlike them.* Groggle could have sworn he had passed at least two taverns already. Worse yet, their search was coming closer and closer to where he was hidden. "That's what you get for reading books all the time, and not going out seeing the sights… maps sure are different when looking down on them," he panted out loud to himself. "Little chance of getting up there; that's what you get for being short and slightly afraid of heights." Eyeing the rooftop ridge, Groggle already knew that he would never reach it. Even standing on the crates that littered the alley and on the tips of his toes, it was a feat beyond his stature, but he had to try. After a winded climb, his knees wobbly from fear, Groggle stood precariously with his arms stretched high above his head.

"Yep, too short."

The whistles had stopped, but heavy footfalls where coming closer. His hands still reaching fruitlessly above him, Groggle glanced towards the entrance of the alley. A quick shadow like that of a bird, but much bigger, passed along the alley floor just below him.

"Feeling your horizons broadened?" Xander grabbed Groggle's hand and began to pull him upward.

"A little too much for one day," Groggle said with a toothy grin. "Thanks!"

"We're Rogue. No one left behind, right?"

"Right!" Groggle exclaimed proudly at the inclusion. "Oh, but please, Xander, don't tell the others, or…. um, especially Rellion about the crawns."

Xander smiled back his understanding.

I Think I Have Seen Enough

Gallows Alley, to the west of High Street, led to the necropolis of Saint's Hollow. Gallows Alley wasn't so much an alley as it was a corridor of trees leading to the ancient cemetery. The massive rainbow eucalyptus that canopied the walkway rose to more than fifty feet high. The bright and uniquely colored strips of purple, blue, red, and green bark were caused by the shedding of the tree's outer skin during differing seasons. The effect was wondrous and foreboding at the same time.

Kristane walked casually along the path amongst those who wished to pray, and the monks of the Abbey who had transported the Saint's Casket here. Twice a year, on Hallow's End and King's Eve, the monks paraded the nondescript wooden coffin upon a palanquin from here back to its home at the Abbey along King's Way, in honor of something about a path traveled and a dragon, and some other nonsense about a burning tree and a sword. She couldn't remember, and then wondered if she'd ever heard the story clearly. *Groggle would probably know; he's always reading those dusty old books in the Attic.* Kristane promised herself she would ask him sometime.

"I can't be the first one here — Prya, at least?" Fear that her friend or one of the others might have been caught gripped her. "Just being silly, of course they're all fine, I'm not even to the tombstone yet," she grumbled as she scanned the throng of people for a familiar face.

Above her, the branches that had once, long ago, been looped with hangman nooses were now adorned with a regalia of banners and pennants, marking the festival and where the parade began. *Wait, I remember — something about the Saint's Path, but it was the ruins of Kaer Kairos where his path began, not the cemetery… but no one ever goes there.*

"Hey, Kristane, over here. God, we're glad to see you. You won't believe what happened to us." Prya had called to her from just inside the ornate wrought iron gates that stood ajar, each hanging from a stone archway that continued around into a wall encircling the entire necropolis.

Lathan stood attentively at her side, scanning those who were lining up. The ruling class, the Council of Stewards and their families, took up most of the procession. Their dress was so ludicrously more garish than anyone else's that one couldn't help but notice them, which was their intent, after all. As with many things within Kairos, those nobler ideals that had first formed the Council of Stewards had been lost to corruption. Leaders were no longer elected; control was now passed down within in the hands of families, each Council seat usually represented by the very worst of their lineage, each of them fearing their grip on the masses while still plundering the city of its resources.

"Have you seen Xander or Groggle?" Kristane asked.

"No, I thought Groggle was with you…?" Prya eyed Kristane with a look of worry. She had obviously grown more attached to Groggle in the span of a single day, given their shared experiences.

"We have company, and you're not going to like who it is." Lathan nodded back to the bottom of Gallows Alley. Cayson was marching determinedly towards them with Creff and the moron brothers in tow.

"Come on, this can't go down here." Kristane weaved her way through the parade-goers with the others trailing. As the entrance dropped down into the hollow, a light fog gave off a musty stench that permeated the air and the ground on which they walked. So low was the hollow, and so protected by the nearby hills, that the gathering fog that came from the bay never quite burned off each day. Everything was covered with a glistening dew that puddled and caused a greenish moss to grow unchecked.

The grounds were interspersed with hillocks, each crested with grand headstones, and the same colorful trees that lined the entry, though their colors were muted here and made one see images in the layers of bark that weren't really there. "God! That still freaks me out!" Prya exclaimed at an imagined and seemingly disembodied spectral face that appeared within one tree in particular.

The others nodded silently their understanding. Everyone was a little unnerved after the events of this afternoon.

"What are they still doing here?" Lathan nodded his head to the right.

A small group of shabbily dressed mourners were gathered around a particularly large, old mausoleum, with a carved marble lion covered in the same green moss as everything else. "Just Wailers," Kristane offered in explanation.

The gravesite group was thrown into relief by candles that dotted the plot. Wailers were paid to mourn by wealthy families who cared little for the entombed, but wished to keep up pretenses. "Oh my beloved! Gone too soon! Why, oh why?" A particularly large woman was bellowing and feigning tears into a ratty handkerchief over a plaque that read some death date of two hundred years previous. Eyeing the three friends over her pretended sobs, she stopped abruptly. "Oh, never mind, it's just some waifs!" And sure enough, seeing that Kristane and the others were no one of particular importance, they dropped the pretense and set about making a picnic of the items left for the dead and downing the expensive spirits.

"Oi! Look at this pretty glass, it'll fetch a coin or two!" gurgled one as he sloshed down its contents. To them, this was a much better party than the festival or parade.

DING! DING! DING! A muffled bell clanged somewhere above them.

"That's got to be the three o'clock cable car coming around. The parade should have started by now." Lathan peered upward into the gloom. The fog was so dense that one could easily lose their bearings or, as they were doing, walk unseen. Ancient were the headstones and mausoleums in this area of the necropolis. Those that weren't crumbling under their own weight still showed a majesty and respect for the people interred there.

"We're going to wait for Xander and Groggle. Then we head for the Attic. Hopefully, the tail end of the parade will cover us," Kristane said to the other two, hoping that it would be just that easy, and that Xander would appear out of the fog at any moment. The two nodded their assent. Prya laid back upon the stairs of a nondescript crypt that served as their rendezvous point, rolling a coin across the knuckles of one hand. The cracked door of the plot was embellished with engraved angles, and whoever was buried here was lost to the green moss that had overgrown the name.

"Oi! You lot! We wouldn't have to be hiding to get back if you hadn't —"

"Shut it, Cayson, you know you waved them on even after my signal!" Lathan pointed at the Kressley brothers.

"Waesucks U' sarder! U' dalcop arse!" Kristane had always just thought the Kressleys were idiots, until Rellion had informed her that they were swearing at her. In fact, she really didn't even know which one of them had just insulted Lathan. Both always had either a pipe or cigar hanging out of their mouths, and they always mumbled out their litany of abuse.

"Jeez o' Cripes! Eat it … RAW!" Both chuckled and turned to each other, nodding in appreciation of the other's chosen slander. *That one must have been Markyn,* Kristane thought. He was the one who wore the bowler. The brothers were close in age, eight and nine, and with their shocks of red hair it was no wonder you couldn't tell one from the other.

"That's *it*, you two little ginger morons!" Lathan didn't even know what he had been called, but he was intent on not letting it slide. He lunged at the boys threateningly. Markyn, the older, raised his fists, set his jaw, and took a long draw from his pipe. Munse, capped with a black newsboy hat, spat out his cigar and gave Lathan a double one-fingered salute. Lathan understood that last one. Enraged by the further insult, he marched forward with a clenched fist above his shoulder, intending on bringing it down upon the boy's head.

"Whoa, whoa!" Creff was the first to step in, just as Kristane was advancing to do the same. Kristane was always a little surprised by Creff. He chose the oddest times to give a damn. She suspected it was just the luck of the draw that he was crewed with Cayson. Creff was a little younger than them, and under the domineering ego of Cayson, he hadn't grown into his own yet.

"That's right, Creff, we don't want to have to explain to Rellion why these two messed up 'what's his name' here." Cayson wasn't boasting as to the prowess of the brothers. They did have a certain brutality hidden under their freckled faces that made Kristane think that Lathan might not fare as well as he thought he would. "Anyway, you should have let the... what did they call you? Pixie? Get caught instead of exposing yourselves."

"Cripes, 'ayson! Frickin' 'ixie! Ha ha ha!" The Kressleys were beside themselves with mirth. Cayson gave a wry smile; his attempt at provoking them was working. Prya had stood and was walking into the fray. This situation was getting worse, and it was obvious that Creff wasn't going to step in again. He'd fallen back into Cayson's shadow, not participating but not making eye contact either.

Just as Kristane was of the mind that this could only end one way, and as she took a step forward to intervene, Xander appeared out of the gloom with Groggle, mouse-like quiet, a couple of paces behind him. "Is there a problem?" Kristane relaxed a little inside and nodded appreciatively at her twin. She felt that she was up for the confrontation, but knew that Cayson and the others would back down far quicker with her brother present. "I said, is there a problem?" he repeated.

Munse bent over and picked up his cigar, and began chewing on it as smoke puffed out. His brother and he stood respectfully silent. Cayson looked as if he was going to say something more, but sensing defeat, stayed quiet as well.

"Something is happening. We all need to go." He glared at Cayson. Cayson responded by nodding back toward the gate, and his pack fell in behind him.

Xander gave his sister a brief hug as she approached, and then pulled her around. "We need to go, Kris."

Kristane could see the foreboding look within his eyes. Her anxiety returned. '*What could possibly unnerve him?*' she wondered as she nodded at him, and the fog above them began to swirl ominously.

As they exited the canopy of Gallows Alley, what should have been a festive scene was all but. Most, if not all, of the parade participants had abandoned the procession, dropping their long sticks bearing their family heralds to the side and darting for cover. Gale-force winds were buffeting the city center, and by the look of it, all of Kairos. A collection of parasols, tall hats, and pink flowery blossoms were being whipped about like so much other debris. Craftsmen, in a fruitless battle, attempted to secure their temporary stands and carts that skidded across the length of King's Way. Descending from the higher elevations of the city, a rolling bank, a wall, of darkened clouds encircled the area from all directions. Regardless of the gathering storm, the subdued and crimson lighting of the lunar Younger Brother's umbra was weighing heavily upon everyone's senses. What should have otherwise been the pleasant beginning of a sunset was chaos.

"The Younger Brother is nearly covered in shadow!" Lathan's fearful exclamation drew their attention upward. Within the eye of the clouds, the darkened moon suddenly blazed with a halo of red as the last bit of blood colored crescent fell into shadow behind its full Older Brother.

BONG!

The Celestial Orrery began to chime. Abruptly, the wind ceased, and everything seemed to slow in place. The eye of the storm was directly over the mechanism, yet the wind continued its frenzy along the edges of the city center. The orrery was eerily humming, its tone reverberating to the point where it felt as though it was shaking Kristane's bones. She instinctively clutched at the necklace about her neck, hoping that it would provide some comfort, as it always had. The normally colorful orbs of the orrery continued to swing about the center, but instead of bright and happy colors, they mimicked the storm above it. In the distance, the hastily retreating monks of the Abbey were attempting to stay on their feet as the wind buffeted them and the violently swaying cherry trees. Many of the monks attending the palanquin poles and the casket that rested above it had abandoned their charge, leaving those who refused to, infused with some undying devotion to the holy relic, to drag it up the Abbey stairs, its head-end more often than not bouncing against the ascending steps.

It started in the upper clouds: a series of lenticular forms spiraling downward, their cones angled towards the center orb as if drawn there. Ball lighting bounced about the interior of the cloud wall, and then white ribbon-strikes vented from the cones, striking the center orb of the great Celestial Orrery. The orbs in turn became charged by the energy of the storm, and they began to shoot strikes in reverse, lightning colliding repeatedly mid-air. Soon, a dome of electrified space formed completely around the workings of the mechanism, extending to the cobbled edge of King's Way, where the encircling metal bands separated the terraced red rock from the Orrery.

"We've got to move!" Xander pulled at his sister, and grabbed Groggle by the back of his coat, dragging him.

Lightning strike after lightning strike buckled the cobbles as they ran, tossing blackened stones into the air. With their arms raised above their heads for protection, the cascading debris kept them from moving in a straight line. Lathan and Prya, who had run to the forefront, waved them to the abandoned staging of the Medicine Show in front of the Black Kettle. Diving under the wood stage, they found that they were not alone; a wide eyed Peg-Leg Noodle and several dwarves looked at the new arrivals with panicked terror. Huddled farther back was Doc Fatterpacker, exclaiming to another, grumpy-looking dwarf, "I ask you, is the weather something we now control? Adjust our contract next appearance to include meteorological and astronomical events… Amendment to clause twenty three, acts of God shall be compensated regardless…"

BONG!

Kristane watched in fascination as the embedded rings of the Celestial Orrery rose up from the surface and began to rotate. Four rings, one for each descending tier, spun around and disappeared back into the surface of rock until their momentum was so quick it was hard to determine if they were still there. *How many times have I walked across those brass bands, thinking they were just decoration?* Kristane wondered. Only the displacement of the detritus-filled air gave any indication that something moved. Kristane was reminded of an armillary device within the Attic, and how the rings spun about the spheres with the tap of her finger.

BONG!

The third chime reverberated as though it was trying to break through something, like time had stopped and she was just hearing the echoes of an event that had already happened.

Some of the large, round plaques with their mysterious engravings moved aside, and black-cloaked figures rose up through the darkened holes revealed. Kristane looked about to make sure the others were seeing the same thing as she, but just as she met Groggle's stare, a forked lightning bolt hit the stage above. "Yah! I think I've seen enough!" Groggle spun about, crawling faster than Kristane thought possible, and the others skittered after him. Kristane literally caught the tail-ends of the medicine crew as they broke from the opposite end of the hideaway, and she followed suit with her friends, not daring to look back again.

BONG!

A Trick of the Light

Rellion laughed out loud at the thought of the shadow in the Tunnels that rang bells accompanying each theft. "Far be it from me to have believed you dead, Master Fool! Your timing is impeccable, as always!"

Flinging open the doors of the Chymist, he found that the exit was barely visible from the outside as the sky slowly turned black. Only the arcing blue light of the towers that powered Kairos afforded some light as they illuminated the canopy of clouds that was forming. He'd lingered too long; he had to get back to the Attic. Holding his hat in place with his free arm, he broke into a sprint.

The ominous tone of the Celestial Orrery hummed with every footfall as he took the stairs leading to the Abbey, two and three at a time. Within, the monks stood in groups around the Saint's Coffin, whispering worriedly to one another, foregoing their vows of silence. Rellion didn't bother to acknowledge them, not even with a tip of his hat. Reaching the top of the highest staircase, he slammed through the doors of the Attic.

The Rogue was deep into the hysteria of what was being felt throughout Kairos, they all shouted at once. "Rellion where have you been?" "Did you see it?" "The orrery… it's… it's making a terrible sound!" "Rellion… what's happening?"

"Silence!" Everyone went quiet. Rellion marched to the center of the room. He looked intently at the faces before him. *They're scared, and rightly so.* Only the bubbling of potions and the ticking of the clocks on the walls could be heard. There was something else, too; something familiar…?

A fearful realization gripped Rellion. He moved towards Kristane, reaching out for the pulsating necklace about her neck.

"How long?!" Rellion hissed menacingly. Kristane stepped back from him, confused and fearful, until her necklace was taut from his grip to where the chain laid on the back of her neck.

"I… I… I don't know," she mumbled feebly as she looked at the glowing thing within his hand. Xander stepped to his sister in a protective stance.

"Think quickly, my girl, our lives depend on it!"

"I don't know… It never has before… You said it was just a worthless trinket…." Kristane's face was a mingled mask of wide-eyed fear and astonishment, too scared of how Rellion was acting to let out more than a squeak, the pulse of the glowing light of the clockwork heart casting sinister lines on his features.

Stepping back from Kristane, he let go of his grip on her necklace and growled, "Put it away, hide it!" Kristane stumbled backward until she bumped into the broad chest of Xander, and unconsciously tucked the necklace below her collar, the heavy material obscuring the pulse of light. Xander, also shaken by Rellion's uncharacteristic actions, placed his hands on his sister's shoulders to steady her and himself.

"Listen to me, all of you! We are out… of time…" Rellion stopped mid-sentence, his gaze turning from Kristane to high within the rafters, where Purdy the Faerrian hung. Purdy had turned a deep red, and his sleek body quivered with some apprehension. Rellion stood silent, apparently at a loss for words, his head cocked, listening to something only he could hear. Kristane followed his gaze upwards. Rain had begun to patter and splash on the roof of the dome. There were long, low rumblings of thunder as the storm increased in intensity. *Crack!* A bolt of lightning bent randomly across the sky, bringing a sharp relief to the exterior of the dome.

Was it just a trick of the light? Maybe a reflection of all of us on the glass from below? Kristane swore to herself that she had just seen cloaked figures standing above, and she was gripped by the realization of what she had seen at the Celestial Orrery. There was barely another moment of silence, and no time to think more of it, before a large portion of the dome violently splintered into a rain of glass upon their heads. Dropping with a heavy strike that sent tremors of force through her body, the figures that Kristane thought she might have imagined proved themselves to be only too real. Rising from bent knees, they grabbed for those closest to them. Prya and Creff were within arm's reach. Kristane watched, horrified, as the shadowy figures clutched the pair from behind, the bones in the arms of their victims cracking audibly. Creff kicked out at the wraith that had ahold of Prya. The attempt was feeble, and Creff grimaced with pain, his obviously broken and restricted arms taking his weight as he assailed the bob-haired girl's attacker. But his bid to free her was enough; Prya fell limply to the wooden floor, holding her crushed arm with her one good one.

Arcing white bolts came from somewhere within the folded sleeves of the cloaked wraith that restrained Creff. They ran up his arms, causing him to convulse violently. With a bewildered croak, Creff's struggling ceased, and his body dropped ominously to the floor, his limbs splayed out at unnatural angles, his chin cocked and chest resting against the wooden floor so that he was looking up at Kristane. She thought for a moment that maybe Creff was just knocked out… but the vacancy in his eyes made the truth clear.

"No! Creff!" Kristane feebly held out her hand, clutching at the air. Xander's grip on her shoulders tightened, preventing her from surging forward. Stricken by fear and by what they had just witnessed, the other members of the Rogue stood wide-eyed and unable to move. As the intruders moved to claim their next victims, with Prya still cowering bellow them, Rellion become a blur of motion. Stepping forward, he brought his cane to bear. Brandishing the large pommel of his shillelagh as a club, he struck the advancing wraiths headlong. His first underhanded swing caught two of the wraiths mid-temple, their heads lolling to one side with the impact of it, just as they grabbed for Groggle and Cayson.

Unfortunately, Cayson did not escape unscathed. As one of the wraiths fell from the blow, something had ripped at his thigh, leaving a substantial gash through his pants through to his skin. Rellion, spinning with the momentum of his body, brought his club down hard in a crushing blow upon the head of the entity that loomed over Prya. The wraiths, stunned by Rellion's sudden onslaught, fell back.

"Run, my Rogue! The demons are at the gate!" Rellion eyed Groggle, and the young boy nodded back his understanding. Trembling, Groggle motioned for those nearest him to follow. The barking of orders by Rellion and the frantic waving of Groggle brought everyone in the room to their senses — including the deathly wraiths, who once again began to press forward. Those that had fallen, struck down by Rellion's cane, rose to their feet and joined the assault. Rellion, seeing their movement, clutched his cane before him double-fisted. A wind began to whip about the room that did not come from the gathering storm outside. The top of his cane glowed with a steadily increasing light. Suddenly, a wave of energy burst from where he stood, accompanied by a ring of fire that reached to what was left of the ceiling above, encircling everyone and knocking them all to the ground except for Rellion. The flames had created a perimeter holding their attackers at bay. Potions housed within their glass vessels along the shelving and upon the fireplace mantel began to explode with the heat, their contents splashing upon the cloaks of the wraiths, setting them aflame. Kristane stared up at Rellion from her place on the floor. His eyes blazed with a look she had never seen before as his long tresses danced about his head, thrown around by the wind the consuming fire created. *He's enjoying this,* she realized.

Kristane looked behind her. Groggle had pulled back the area rug and opened a section of flooring, exposing a trapdoor. *How long has that been there, and why didn't I know about it? And what the hell is going on with Rellion's cane?*

"Don't just lay there gawking, my Princess! Get out!" Reaching down to her, Rellion pulled her to her feet. Purdy, still a dark red in color, swooped down from his perch and wrapped his tail about her neck, his talons biting into her shoulder. He nuzzled into the crook of her neck, his body poised defensively and snarling at the wraiths. As she passed, Rellion pulled her in closely with his free arm, whispering in her ear. "You must not allow them to have it. He must not be awakened."

Kristane, her mind racing from terror, only managed a feeble, "Allow what? Who?"

"Head for the Tunnels and the Bizzarre; there is safety there." She looked at him, confused, but nodded out of habit.

Xander stood near the exposed chute, beckoning her to follow. The rest of the room had already emptied. Rellion paced backwards, the circle of fire retreating with him. "Go; she's right behind you!" Xander nodded, disappearing into the unknown below.

Kristane climbed into the chute, but held tight with her fingers upon the flooring. "Well, my Princess, what in the King's name are you waiting for?"

"But... but what about you?"

"By the Blessed Tree, what's this?" He peered down at her, smiling broadly. "How many ages have passed since anyone has given a second thought as to my well-being?" He laughed out loud. "Quite the contrary, if the truth be known! How gracious you are, my Princess!" And with that, Rellion gave Kristane a push with his foot, and she slid down the chute as he kicked the trapdoor shut.

No Honor Among Thieves

As she began to slide downward, the trapdoor splintered with an explosion of light, and then a heavy thud extinguished it. Kristane found herself in complete darkness, falling with the steep incline of the chute, the only noise her own heavy breathing rushing in her ears and the banging of her elbows on a metallic surface. Without any sense of where she was headed, the ride abruptly ended; she spilled out onto a hard surface with the taste of something similar to a mouthful of copper paupers in her mouth. She'd bitten her lip, and maybe her tongue.

Kristane pushed herself up with her bruised arms and elbows from the face-down position in which she had unceremoniously landed. She spat out the metallic taste, and a splatter of blood dribbled out of her mouth. Xander was already at her side, a slight cut across his cheekbone, pulling the debris of the trapdoor off her. As she steadied herself and looked skyward, she felt heavy rain cascading upon her face. A continuous rumble of thunder beat at her chest, but she could also hear the sound of retching to her right. Cayson was doubled over, his pants ripped and heavy with blood from a gash to his thigh. Purdy, his dripping fur still slightly red but now beginning to return to his normal white, hovered above Groggle as he sat against a wall, rocking back and forth with his face in his hands, murmuring to himself. Lathan seemed to be the only one none the worse for wear, supporting Prya with her good arm draped over his shoulder, the injured one limp to her side. Lathan stared contemptuously at Cayson.

Kristane looked at Xander again. Sensing her unspoken question, he wiped a hand across his face, shedding the water from his eyes, and answered, "Most everyone must have scattered. It was just these three, plus Cayson and the ginger twins, when I fell out." He pointed to the large tube that hung three feet above the ground, protruding from the wall. "The twins saw that he was hurt and left him."

"Just like you taught 'em — every man for himself, right Cayson?" Lathan spat out the words. Clutching his leg and looking pale, Cayson just turned his head and vomited.

"Rellion?" Groggle stopped his murmuring, and everyone looked to Kristane for an answer to Xander's question. She shook her head in response, the memory of the flash of light and heavy thud replaying in her mind.

"We have to keep moving. Whatever the hell those things are, they didn't look like they were going to stop." Xander's tense but calm voice pulled her back to the present. "It's stopped now." He indicated the clockwork necklace about his sister's neck, which had fallen out of her collar. "What did it mean, Kris?"

She was about to explain her ignorance when Groggle's mutterings returned and became clearer, his voice carrying over the storm's punctuated blasts. "The time has come, the time is now. For walks the land the ones most foul. All before was not as such. Beware the Forgotten Ones' foul touch…"

Still rocking back and forth, his hands pulled away from his face. Kristane could see the terror that lay there. She stared at Groggle; that old nursery rhyme meant to scare kids all of sudden really *did* scare her, and by the looks on the others' faces, it had had the same effect on them.

"All I know as that I need to keep it away from them," she declared, answering her brother's question. "Get him up; we'll head for the Tunnels and the Bizzarre." She pointed a shaky finger in the direction of the injured Cayson. "Lathan, help him. He goes with us." Her voice quavered at the memory of Creff's vacant expression. Creff wasn't all that bad, and he was a member of their little dysfunctional family, after all. She found herself caring more than she ever thought she would, especially since his last act was one of selfless heroism for Prya.

"Are you friggin' crazy? I am *not* helping that piece of …!"

"I don't care, he comes with us!" Cutting across Lathan's outburst, Kristane was hard pressed not to agree with him; but as obnoxious and deserving as Cayson was, he was hurt and he too was family of a sort. *More likely I just don't want to watch anyone else to die tonight,* she thought. Purdy swooped over to her shoulder and did his best to push himself into her neck in an effort to avoid the rain. Lathan looked like he was about to further protest, but seeing the determined look in Kristane's face, he shrugged it off. Cursing under his breath, he proceeded to kick water at Cayson from the gathering puddles as he hastened to assist him.

"Let's go, Groggle, now!" Kristane marched towards him and bodily forced him onto his feet. "Get it together! We're going to make for the Tunnels." He nodded meekly, and she felt a twinge of guilt for being rough — but she needed him moving.

Rotten Luck Remy

It seemed like it was taking them hours to get there, and mostly likely it was. Cayson had slowed their progress. Xander had bound his leg, reporting that the gash was long and most likely needed to be sewn up, but mostly looked worse than it was. Cayson didn't go as far as outwardly complaining, for fear of being left behind; but he was intent on making a production of it. The streets were empty, but the small group kept to the shadows of the alleys nonetheless.

They passed behind Wyndom's Iron Works, the building silent besides the hiss of the large bellows pumping air into the furnaces and the crackling of coals with each successive blast. The giants kept the furnaces always burning, needing the intense heat to forge the many things they crafted.

Market Street ended abruptly at Serpentine Lane and became Misery Lane. The Tunnels and the Bizzarre laid due northeast from this point along Burden Way. The interlocking clunks of the elevated cable car's cogs drew their attention upward as Kristane and the others passed under a support trestle. The Gripman was the only one aboard, his attention drawn more to the cloud-covered sky than below. The high-stacked apartments and rundown brownstones became denser the farther one traveled from the city's center. Little flashes of light shone in the occasional window as their apprehensive occupants peeked through already-drawn curtains.

Prya spoke for the first time since their escape from the Attic. "Kristane, I'm really cold… Not the way I thought today was going to end, and Creff… why did he…?" Prya cried as she looked down at her broken arm, still limp at her side.

Kristane could see by her pale face that she was suffering from cold and shock. She came over to her friend, careful not to touch her injured arm. "I don't know why he did it either." *Is it bad that I feel glad that he did?* Kristane thought guiltily. "It's not much farther… I'm sorry, I promise we'll find help." Kristane gave her friend a smile, and put her own wet and soaked arm around her friend, trying to warm her.

Prya returned her smile with one a little soupier. "I find my love in your eyes…" she sang, holding the last note a little longer than Eidolon had earlier that day. She tried to laugh at her own joke. Both girls giggled, but in a sad kind of way as their eyes misted. Prya sighed deeply, a little too hard; she caught her breath and grimaced in pain. Kristane knew she needed to find her friend help soon.

The large, gaping mouth of the Tunnels lay tucked within a small valley that rested at the foot of a high precipice. Trees and overgrown vegetation had taken over the site, making the old shafts and abandoned mining buildings all but invisible from the view of those who lived higher up and could afford to. Still, there was a faint glow coming from the treetops, emanating from below as the band of kids approached. Along the cobbled path of Burden Way, there was more activity than they had seen in the last couple of hours.

Raucous laughter came from just inside the arched entryway. Smartly dressed people oblivious to the earlier intensity of the storm balanced on the edge of the entrance, deciding whether to brave the light rain and head home or head back into the Bizzarre and continue the day's debauchery. Most, it seemed, had begun to opt for more debauchery.

"Ugh! You frickin' idiot!" Cayson and Lathan laid heaped in a pile, splashing about in a puddle. It appeared that Cayson had stumbled and pulled Lathan down with him, his foot catching on an old train rail that laid rusted and bent in a channel cut into the cobbles. Lathan continued to swear at Cayson, who normally would have let loose a similar tirade, but instead lay there grasping his injured leg, face gray and blood beginning to ooze through his clasped fingers and the makeshift bandaging Xander had wrapped it with, making it look all the worse.

"Lathan, shut up!" Kristane hissed at him. The revelers had seen the fall, and stood laughing at the pair. Xander reached down and hoisted Cayson up, supporting him with one arm draped across his shoulder. Lathan grew quiet as he saw that they were getting more attention than they wanted. The revelers, seeing that the show was over, went back to their bleak gaiety.

Xander, being taller than Cayson, stood stooped, water dripping from his curly dark hair. "Groggle, these two need help; is there anyone?" Xander did a slight heave, adjusting Cayson's weight upon his shoulder.

"There is someone who might, I think, but he won't do it for nothing."

"It doesn't matter. Let's find whoever it is." Kristane gave Purdy, who had remained perched on her shoulder, a stroke across the bridge of his nose.

At the topmost part of the arched entrance, etched into the wedged-shape keystone, was the name of the founder of the played-out mine: Theodore Bizzarred. It was doubtful that the prim and proper former owner of the mine would have consented to its current use. In fact, he was probably literally turning in his grave now that it was known as a sinful derivative of his namesake.

"What is that awful posting?" A well-dressed young woman carrying a parasol addressed her escort as they and several other couples passed Kristane and the others by. Pasted almost on top of one another, and over still more layers and layers of paper, were advertisements for upcoming and past events. The tunnel walls, especially near the entrance, were wallpapered with them. Kristane even recognized the toothy grin of Doc Fatterpacker peeking out underneath an advertisement for unicorn oil. "Can you imagine, a midnight carnival? Really, at that hour? Look at the oddities," the woman remarked indignantly. "A bearded fairy? I mean, that's not pretty. And what are those curly, sharpened blades that look like a pinwheel that man is holding?"

"Oh, come now, Therese, I quite think it would be great fun! If only you were allowed out at that late hour more often," her escort chided. Therese spun her parasol upon her shoulder, giving a fake and dejected pout. The laughter of her friends died away as Groggle led the others further into the mine.

A great expanse opened up before them where the old tunnels intersected. Though each of them had been here on occasion, the number of people who walked about due to the festivities of Hallow's End surprised them. Gambling halls, alehouses, fine drinkies, and any number of shops that sold mostly stolen or illegal wares squeezed in against each other, some literally on top of one another. All had been given a shine that was meant to suggest respectability but still a little bit of naughtiness, so that the patrons would feel they were getting away with something. A small city within a city, it was. To the left was a theater, whose performers staged acts of burlesque. A man hawked to the crowd about him with promises of things they had never seen before, his voice mixing with the general din of noise, music, and flashing lights. Everywhere, a sort of giddiness permeated the gathering. It was in steep contrast to the solemn aura on the streets of the city, but then again, most of these people had been in here all day.

To the right, where Groggle steered them through the crowd, was nothing less than a glittering palace of debauchery. The Bizzarre, around which all the rest had sprouted, was the pinnacle of illicit money mixed with showmanship. A pair of giant men flanked the double doors that led within. They looked odd in the oversized jackets and accoutrements of proper gentlemen. Kristane imagined that they were each as tall as two of her. As they opened the doors for patrons of the gambling hall, cheers erupted from one of the many craps tables. A low-hanging cloud of smoke was wafting about, pushed around by slow-moving ceiling fans.

"Hold it, young ones, the establishment has a dress code. You won't be entering here tonight." One of the giants had spoken and held his hand up to Groggle and the rest as they approached the doors. Groggle waved the man down to him. The giant bent at the waist, and still his head was not quite low enough to reach Groggle. Standing up on his tip-toes, Groggle whispered something in the man's ear and handed him something in his already-extended hand. The giant straightened up and peered down into his palm. Kristane could tell that he wasn't overly pleased with what he saw there, but he regarded Groggle with his bright smile and gave a "hmpf," and nodded his head towards the door.

"You guys will have to wait here, but I'll be right back." Still squishing in his wet shoes, Groggle brushed the front of himself unnecessarily and adjusted the goggles on his cap, making them even more crooked than they were before. He then walked purposefully through the doors that the giants held ajar for him.

It was just a short wait until Groggle returned with a tall, handsome man wearing a blood-red bowler hat in tow: Remington Symmes, or as he was known about the Bizarre, Rotten Luck Remy. Remy was anything but unlucky, though; in fact, he was the opposite in his dealings, especially as it came to gambling. Remy spoke like a gentleman, but was not unkind in his tone.

"What is a ragged troupe of Rellion's Rogue doing on my doorstep this evening, and where is your enigmatic leader?" He pretended to scan over their heads, as if Rellion would appear out of nowhere and surprise him. "Though Groggle has said it, I can certainly see for myself that you have had a time of it." Pulling a monocle from his vest pocket, he held it up to his eye, the lens adjusting itself like a camera shutter as Remy's eye was oddly magnified. "Possibly a bit worse for wear than Groggle has said." His monocle eye lingered on Prya.

"Please, Mr. Symmes, we need your help. We have nowhere to go and we… Rellion…" Kristane said in a rush, but was suddenly cut off by a disturbance just behind Remy. Another giant dressed in similar fashion to the doormen was escorting a man from the gambling hall. *Escorting* wasn't quite the right word; grasped by the back of his coat, the man was lifted a few feet in the air. More like *dangling*, Kristane thought.

"Beg your pardon, Mr. Symmes, but this gentlemen has… *insulted* Lord and Lady Orton." Giving the man a bit of a violent shake, the giant handed Remy a wallet and ring.

Rotten Luck Remy's demeanor changed in an instant. While he continued his verbal politeness, a decidedly violent layer lay just below the surface. "I see that you are not from Kairos, and in honor of Hallow's End, I will be generous in that you will live to not make the same mistake. Mr. White, please attend to this matter and send this gentlemen on his way with a polite handshake, thank you."

Kristane figured the handshake probably wasn't going to be overly polite.

"Mr. Black, if you would, arrange a bottle from my personal reserves for the Lord and Lady, and return their misplaced items. Please tell them I will be along directly to greet them." Remy handed the purloined items to Mr. Black as he bowed and went off on his errand.

Remy's mood changed almost as quickly as he returned his attention to the Kristane and the others. "Please forgive the interruption. You may call me Remy; there is no need for such politeness among friends... but where are my manners? Your story can wait for tomorrow. You and your friends need attending to; Rellion would be much aggrieved had I not shown you proper hospitality." The double doors opened again and Mr. Black resumed his post. "Ah, good, Mr. Black. Now that you have returned, please see to our young friends."

"The back room, sir?" He looked at Rotten Luck Remy inquisitively.

"No, no, no, Mr. Black, these are friends. Please escort them through the back to an open room and have the house doctor come by." Remy smiled, but Kristane thought that his idea of hospitality did not include direct association. *What exactly happens in the back room?*

Kristane decided that she was glad that she wasn't that kind of guest.

"Now I must return to business. I wish you all a good night. I must impress upon each of you, though, that you know the rules of my Bizzarre; there will be no practicing your trade within the boundaries." Without another word to them, the doors were flung open by the doormen, and Remy returned to the excitement inside. The last Kristane heard was Remy's voice trailing off as the door closed. "Ah, Lord and Lady Orton...!"

Shouldn't You Sterilize That?

Mr. Black had taken them to a second floor room at the back of the gambling hall. The room was cozy enough, though sparse; it was hard to determine whose room it was or what it was used for, but at least it was dry. There was even a window that overlooked the trash heaps in between the building and the smooth wall of the mine tunnel.

Shortly after Mr. Black had closed the door, there came a faint knocking. The person did not wait for a response, but entered without invite. "I'm the Doctor." It was a good thing that he had offered his profession, because otherwise, Kristane and the others would never have guessed it. The Doctor looked older than he probably was, with blood-shot eyes, and the smell of Scotch exuded from him. His hair in the front stood on end, as though he had just been awakened. One could imagine that he had been passed out at a table, his head crooked within his arm, balancing a bottle of liquor in the other. In fact, he still had a bottle of brown liquid attached to his hand. He took a blurry-eyed look at the kids, but was surprisingly stable on his feet.

"We'll handle this one first." He motioned to Cayson with the bottle in his hand. Pulling up a stool next to the couch on which Cayson had been deposited, he undid the wrap that Xander had done earlier and unceremoniously ripped back Cayson's trouser leg where it was already torn. Reaching into his breast pocket, he pulled out a spool of thread and a well-worn leather billfold that contained a number of sized needles.

"Damn, usually only sewing up giants around here." The Doc pulled out a very long and thick needle that looked as though it would normally be used on leather or thick canvas. Cayson gave out a slight whimper and nearly fainted. Eyeing the needle, the Doctor put it back and pulled out one half its size, but still oversized for the job at hand. Taking the end of thread, he ran it against his tongue and closed one eye, attempting to thread it through the eye of the needle. The Doc's hands began to shake, and he kept missing the eye. "Dammit!" Grabbing for the bottle he had set to the side of his stool, he took a long, drawn-out swig. It had the desired effect; the Doc's hands steadied and he hit his mark the very next attempt.

"Wait, wait, don't you have to sterilize that or something?!" Cayson pulled back on the couch with his elbows as the Doc leaned in to begin sewing up his leg. In response, the Doc spat on the needle and upended his bottle over Cayson's leg. Cayson went wide-eyed and gave another little whimper just before he passed out.

"Good, that will make this easier," the Doc grumbled. Kristane, while shocked at the Doc's bedside manner, stole a glance at Lathan, who was grinning from ear to ear. Admittedly, she had kind of enjoyed it too.

The Doc made quick work of Cayson's leg, the stitches nicely even and perfectly spaced. The man worked like a fine seamstress handling the finest of silk for a ballgown instead of a bloody gash of skin.

"Now, let's have a look at you, young miss." Scooting about on his stool, the Doc turned his attention to Prya, who, having seen the Doc's style of medicine, instinctively pulled back. "Easy now, missy, we'll take this easy; here, take a swig of this, it helps." He took another long swig of the bottle himself before handing it over to her; she took it by the neck. There was a moment when the Doc had not quite released his grip upon it but caught himself and let it go. Prya looked apprehensively down at the mouth of the bottle, shrugged her good shoulder, and swigged down a fair amount. Smacking her lips, she gave a little cough as her eyes watered.

The Doc felt about Prya's upper arm with a surprisingly light touch. Prya winced once or twice, but didn't seem to be in too much pain as she was examined. Completing his exam, the Doc sat back on his stool, took another drink from his bottle, and said, "It's not good, young miss. I can patch you up, but part of the bone has been crushed, and you'll experience some loss of sensation. We'll splint it for some support, but it will take more than what I can do to make you right."

"What do we need to do for her?" Kristane asked worriedly.

"Take her up to one of those fancy Doctors on the hill around High Street." The Doc pushed himself up off his knees, eyeing his nearly empty bottle. "Right. I've got things to get back to, so let's finish this up." Taking the three-legged stool he had just been sitting on by one leg, he slammed it to the ground and gave it a good stomp. It was no great feat — the stool was nearly matchsticks already — but it did make the kids jump at the unexpected destruction. Purdy gave a little squawk and glided over to a mantel on the opposite side of the room. Pulling a couple of the legs that remained, almost the same size, he set them along Prya's upper arm. "Give me that tablecloth there, son." Lathan pulled the threadbare cloth from the only table in the room and handed it to the Doc. Tearing the cloth into strips, he secured the broken chair legs and wrapped her arm up, immobilizing it against her body. "There you are. No gushy goodbyes, now." Kicking the remaining pieces of the broken stool under the uphol-stered chair that Prya was sitting on, he scooped up his bottle and bounced out the door, leaving the Rogue speechless and staring after him. Prya began to laugh, and the others joined in. After all they had gone through, they could hardly stop.

Cayson awoke from the noise. "What in the hell are all of you laughing at?" Looking over at him trying to sit up, they all laughed that much harder, to the point of tears. Cayson stared back at them, put out, then laid back down.

Kristane wasn't sure how long they had laughed, but she knew it was something that they all needed. Mr. Black returned to their room at some point and dropped off some fruit and cheese, along with something to drink. Things became quiet in the room, and Kristane began to replay the events of the Attic in her mind. Standing and looking out the window, listening to the din that echoed off the high, rounded ceiling of the Tunnels, she found herself just staring at shadows. Absentmindedly, she fiddled with her necklace, which she had tucked away at some point in the evening, almost scared to look at it again.

"Kris?" Xander had approached her from behind, trying to keep his voice in a low whisper. She did a half turn towards him, resting her hand on the sill of the window. The others were quietly feigning sleep, but she knew they were listening. "Kris, can I talk with you? I think we're still in real danger. Your necklace has something to do with them, the Forgotten Ones or whatever they were, and Rellion knew it. He knew it all along. I'm not so sure we should hang onto it." Xander paused, looking at his sister. "Rellion is dead, as far as we know. We don't even know what to do now…"

"I know. I'm scared too, Xander, but I'm not getting rid of it; it's all I have. It's all that *we* have. There must be a reason Rellion let me keep it." She found herself tearing up despite herself, but he had to understand: the necklace meant that she was somebody, that they both had a past. That, maybe, someone had loved them deeply once. "Please, Xander, we have to know."

"Kris, there are things happening that are beyond us…I'm not sure we should…" Xander saw the tears welling in his sister's eyes and his resolve weakened, as it always did when it came to her. "All right, Kris, I know." Xander pulled his sister to him, giving her a hug. She buried her face in his chest and cried a little more. Slowly, he let her go and went to lie down. Kristane returned to her unfocused gaze out the window. She knew that what Xander had said made sense, but she just couldn't bring herself to accept it. She had to find out what Rellion meant by his cryptic message: *You must not allow them to have it. He must not be awakened.*

'Kristane dried her cheeks with her hands and moved to close the window. As she did so, she thought she saw the shadows move just below. She stared intently at the place where she thought she'd seen something, but nothing moved. She grabbed hold of both sashes, pulling them closed, when she heard a distinct TINK, TINK, TINK. She hesitated, and returned a watchful eye towards the shadows. *Just being silly…someone's bell-collared cat rummaging in the trash, or maybe Rellion's Wee Folk.* Kristane chuckled a little at her own joke, but her mood turned somber with the thought of Rellion, and she clicked the window latch closed.

ROSE PLIESEIS

PRYA'S GOT A BOYFRIEND

Overnight, the crowd from the night before had thinned dramatically. Still, there were those who were just now making their way home to their beds, or to one of the many inns that were filled to capacity during the festival. The Rogue had awoken early, or at least so the cuckoo on the wall had said. The lighting in the Tunnels never really changed from one hour to the next. Kristane had a funny feeling that the cuckoo that had chimed and chirped the time was possibly the only clock in the entire Bizzarre.

It had been decided that Prya's need was the greatest. Her arm had swollen, and the bruising had taken on a much deeper blue and black in the outline of fingers where she was grabbed. They had no idea how they were going to help her, but they were going to go with the Doc's suggestion and head for the north end of the city. Cayson, being immobile and no one wanting to take on the duty of carrying him again; he didn't really have a choice, so he was going to stay put. Kristane, figuring that it would keep Purdy busy most of the day, instructed Cayson to leave the room window open so that Purdy could hunt the many rats that scurried about the back alley.

As the small group exited the mouth of the Tunnels, they encountered groups of people who were extremely overdressed for that time of the day. With blurry eyes, loosened collars, and hats askew, they waved halfhearted partings to each other. Some entered coaches that were pulled by automaton steeds, or strange carts that puffed with steam.

"My, my, what are you about, pixie?" A tall, young, handsome man who was about to enter a carriage spoke to Prya as he consciously covered his vest pocket and watch with his hand. Realization of who the man was donned on her, and she gave her best sly smile, which was no easy feat with her arm still throbbing from her injury. "Not out collecting valuables this morning, I hope?" The man pointed the pommel of his cane at her playfully, but lowered it as he caught site of her slung and bandaged arm.

"Come on, Ridley, hurry up, my head is splitting open!" one of the men in the carriage who looked especially green said, leaning out the door.

"Go on without me. I will catch another." Ridley pushed his friend in and closed the door. There were a couple of muffled laughs as Ridley tapped his cane against the coachman's step, signaling him to go on. The brass-plated steeds pranced forward with the crack of the driving whip.

"Not the work of the Briggers, I hope?" Ridley looked concerned as he removed his hat.

"Um, long story… kind of an accident… but no." Prya held her hurt arm steady with her good arm, giving the man a doe-eyed expression. Kristane and the others had remained silent, standing about Prya, watching the exchange. Kristane had recognized the man only just now; he was their mark from yesterday afternoon.

"Well, that in itself is good." Ridley regarded the others and their shabby appearance. "And here I thought my friends and I had a long evening. I would ask as to this story of yours, but I see this is more of a 'best not to know' tale." Prya merely smiled, and he returned it.

"The bindings are competently done, though a bit unorthodox. Is there a loss of feeling in the fingertips?" Ridley's question and demeanor had taken on a decidedly professional manner. Prya nodded at him. "My office is closed today, but all the better for this kind of accident of yours. Come to this address in a couple of hours, and we'll see to it, pixie." Ridley handed her a card, and turned to open the door of a carriage that had pulled up while they had been talking.

Prya held the card up, and Kristane looked over her shoulder to also read the title there.

Steven Ridley, MD

201 High Street, Kairos

Ortho- and Exoskeletal Manipulations

By appointment only

"But I don't have... anything." Prya lowered the card and looked at the back of Ridley's retreating head.

With one foot poised to clamber aboard the carriage, he turned to her. "No matter, pixie. You returned a favor from a lady who is most dear to me; and she, my grandmother, would be put out indeed if she knew I had not helped out another lady in need." He smiled at her, and Prya flushed. It was the first time she had ever been called a lady, and by someone who actually seemed to mean it. "Oh, just if you ever do happen upon my friends again, I would hope you won't share the part about where that favor really comes from. I would never hear the end of it!" With his quick laugh, the carriage door closed; and with a rap on the roof, Dr. Ridley rode off.

They just stood looking at each other, not knowing how to react to Prya's turn of good fortune.

Well, most of them didn't. "Prya's got a boyfriend! Prya's got a boyfriend!" Groggle was beside himself with mirth as he made faces and kicked his feet about in an awkward dance. Apparently, *he* knew how to react.

Prya flushed again, and gave him a good punch in the chest with her unbandaged arm, but smiled and laughed with the others. Groggle rubbed at his chest but continued to smile and make fish faces. Lathan was the only one who didn't seem amused. He watched closely as the carriage disappeared around a corner and rumbled across the cobbles of Burden Way. Kristane, looking at Lathan and following his gaze, heard the metallic clops of the horses' hooves against the stone roadway, but she caught something else also. In between the hoof falls, there was again a TINK, TINK, TINK like the night before, coming from somewhere in the dense underbrush that lined the road. *That cat sure does get around*, she thought.

Groggle still had a few crawns and paupers left in his pocket that hadn't been tossed in the air during their great escape the previous day. He deposited them into the collector next to the Gripman's post. Each coin turned and clanked against the counting mechanism inside of it. The Gripman kept his gaze forward, listening to the noise of the coins. As the others boarded the cable car, Groggle stole a look at the Gripman, and wondered if he would notice if he shorted the fare. The Gripman, not hearing the clanks that had become second nature to him, turned to Groggle and tapped the collector with his finger. Groggle smiled ruefully, dug deeper into his pockets, and pulled out the necessary coins.

They had backtracked to the elevated cable car station at Market and Serpentine. As they had some time before they needed to get Prya to Ridley's office, Groggle had suggested the Drunken Chymist. "Kristane, really, I didn't mean to listen… well, I mean everyone else was listening to you and Xander last night, and maybe, you know, we should get some information like you said. So I was thinking Rellion would go to the Chymist a lot… before, you know, what happened and all." Groggle stammered his way through the suggestion as Lathan and Prya tried to find something to do, intentionally not meeting Groggle's pleading looks.

"It's all right, Groggle, we know you all could hear. It affects all of us, if we're planning on staying together," Kristane said.

"You wouldn't leave us, would you? I mean, we're Rogue…" Groggle said excitedly.

Up until that moment, Kristane hadn't really considered whether they would all stay together or not. Deep down, she couldn't bear not having her family around, but something else had also gripped her. As she looked down into Groggle's eyes, the weight of the previous night's events seemed to well up in her all of a sudden. She saw Creff's lifeless eyes reflected in Groggle's questioning look, and the final moments she'd had with Rellion replayed in a flash. She knew it was the shock of fleeing for their lives that had kept the emotions from hitting her before, but now that they seemed relatively safe, it was another story. She knew her desire to know more was leading her into danger. She felt it wasn't for her to lead the others into the same, and that included Xander — but she also knew they would never willingly be left behind.

"Would you?" Groggle, not sensing an answer coming forth from Kristane, had turned to Xander. Kristane still stood silent, lost in her own thoughts. She slowly became aware that Prya and Lathan were no longer pretending to do something else, their full attention focused on Groggle's unanswered question.

Xander walked up to Groggle, grabbed off his cap, and gave his hair a vigorous rub, tossing his greasy locks into his eyes. "The only reason we'd ditch you is if you continue to refuse a bath! Come on… to the Chymist, you said?" Xander stuffed Groggle's hat back onto his head. Groggle looked up at him, smiling his infectious grin, obviously placated.

Kristane knew her brother only too well; they were of like minds and hearts. If things did get to the point of endangering the others, they would certainly venture off on their own. She smiled as genuinely as she could at Groggle and the rest of the Rogue.

Off for a Bit of Fishing

Back in the Attic, as Kristane slipped from view and the trapdoor slammed shut, the circle of flames began to wane as the ring collapsed inward. With a final effort, Rellion pulled his cane closer to his chest and flung his arms up. He directed the resulting blast outward and upward at the same time. What remained of the glass dome and rafters fell to the floor, blocking his Rogue's retreat. Dodging the falling debris, he made for the door, not bothering to look back.

The Attic and its attackers were now consumed in the burning ruins that used to be home. His long coat flapped behind him as Rellion, foregoing individual stairs, jumped from one landing to the next along the spiral. Reaching the curved grand staircase of the Abbey near ground level, he did a short hop and slid down the well-polished banister on his backside. The monks, now cowering in small groups, stared feebly at him, their gaze shifting from the unseen turmoil above to Rellion. He paid them no mind. Slowing his pace, he cantered up to the large, rigid doors of the Abbey. Pounding his cane to the floor, the doors unhinged themselves as they erupted outward.

Rellion paused on the threshold. Turning back to the anxious monks and tipping his hat, he announced, "Lord Monks! Your accommodations are longer required!" Despite the situation, he couldn't help himself; he just had to get one more insult in. He smiled and turned to go.

A small and wary crowd had begun to gather at the steps of the Abbey. Frightened by the atmospheric light show, they had come seeking solace. The smoldering top of the Abbey and its doors, dangling precariously from their hinges, had discouraged them from entering as they had intended. Pulling the lapels of his long jacket up about his neck and the brim of his hat farther down, Rellion pushed his way through the crowd and disappeared into the spattering rain.

It had begun. Many would have to unite for protection; old prejudices and misgivings, some not without reason, would have to be set aside. He had now become the hunted. If they only knew what really stood in their way, the Forgotten Ones wouldn't bother with him. "Time to visit an old friend," Rellion muttered to himself. "Hopefully he has forgotten… but then again, what fun would that be?" He chuckled out loud.

Cold drops of rain pooled about the brim of his hat as Rellion traipsed across King's Way. Intermittent flashes of the now-dying storm mixed with the cold blue arcs from the power coils bouncing off the clouds and reflecting in the puddles at his feet. Above, the darkness was complete; not even the crescent red of the Devil's Embrace could be seen. The heavy cloud cover hid that which now moved across the Brothers' faces in the reverse direction. Market Street, as it continued downward to the South, led to the twin bays of Merrow and Mererid, where long lines of row houses jutted up precariously along the rocky coastline and the bustling commerce of Traders Wharf, their inhabitants concerned more with fishing and trade than were the elite of the city proper. The normally bright and colorful exteriors of the row houses, which shone for miles from the bays, were dramatically muted by the gloom.

Rellion's footfalls soon fell upon the planking that held the seagoing vessels moored there. The shadows of the tall masts and booms could be seen swaying with the ebb of the tide in the sparse lighting of the piers, their rigging tied down and the spring lines taut against their hulls in response to the storm.

As intense the storm was, wouldn't it figure that a few grizzled and hardened fishermen would be standing along the pier, smoking and sharing a bottle in the light rain? "Lord Mariners!" Rellion called cheerfully. "I wish to inquire as to passage!"

A stooped and gray-bearded man replied, "Such a proper title for us salts, isn't it, *sir?*" The last bit pronounced with a bit of contempt.

"Ah, but the toils of the everyday man do make you fine gentlemen indeed," Rellion said as he raised his top hat slightly in salute, his face catching the little bit of light there was. "My travels take me very near the Isles of the Dead and the Manor Hall, and then back."

"Off for a bit of fishing, then?" The old man eyed him warily.

"In a matter of speaking, yes, yes I am," Rellion replied heartily.

The Manor Hall, despite its regal-sounding name, was the home of the consigned and otherwise damned prisoners of the realm. Oddly enough, the fishing was very good around the Isles of the Dead. Located south of the Bay of Merrow where the Sea met the Ocean, the water was extremely turbulent. Escape from the Manor Hall most certainly meant death. Centuries of castaway corpses, from those abandoned prisoners who had finally found freedom, kept the sea life teeming and the few surrounding isles littered with their skeletal remains. The Isles of the Dead were appropriately named, for no one living went there willingly.

Silence was all that greeted Rellion's wolfish grin; the small group of fishermen had no intention of such a venture. "Come now, there must be one of you looking to fill your pockets? For a quiet sail in the... well, I was going to say moonlight, but we seem to be without tonight. Just a quiet sail and a bit of fishing, then?"

From the shadows a booming voice spoke out: "I will take you, if our cargo back is nothing but fish." Towering a full head above the elbowed arm of the dock light, a giant of a man stepped into their midst, his upper dark-skinned torso and head still obscured by the lack of light. So large was he that one could have easily mistaken him for a mast of one of the docked boats.

"Taff, it's mad to sail there on a good day, and with all that's happened this night, even more so. And begging your pardon... sir." The old fisherman, hitching a thumb in Rellion's direction, could have easily taken lessons from him in the contemptuous use of titles. "Can't say as I like the looks of him, neither. Nobody travels there by choice."

Rellion smiled, but did not protest.

Taff stepped farther into the light, bringing his full frame into view. "My sluice is small, but I am an able sailor. It is a very long swim should the fish not be biting." It was less of a threat than a pointed fact; Taff was a very large giant.

"You have my word, Master Taff!" Giving a slight bow and tip of his hat, Rellion said, "I can think of no better company than a Brobdin man like yourself."

Taff was as good as his word on both counts. Firstly, his sluice was indeed small; with the giant's substantial weight, combined with Rellion's, the draft of the boat lay very low in the water. Yet Rellion quickly saw that the giant was more than just an apt sailor. He navigated each trough and crest of the agitated roll of the Cerulean Sea expertly.

The journey to the Isles of the Dead was a long one. Dawn had arrived by the time the sluice approached the Manor Hall. The steep cliff faces of the three islets, which formed a triangle, held back the crashing waves. A stone dwelling standing upon the plateau of the largest looked as though it had weathered countless storms. Once the summer home of some long ago noble, the Hall had been repurposed almost as long ago into many a person's final destination.

Taff moved to trim the jib of the small boat, bringing the telltales streaming straight back. As he pulled at the rope, his bare forearms peeked out from his threadbare pea coat. With the sun rising, it was hard for Rellion not to notice the scarring that patterned Taff's arms. "Master Taff, those are interesting markings you have there."

Seeing his exposed forearms, Taff consciously pushed the sleeves of his coat back down. "Rope and rigging burns from when I was younger... not that good at sailing at first."

"As you say, Master Taff, rare it is to find your like upon the water. In my not-so-uneducated opinion, though, you seem to have many years before the mast." Rellion met his eyes briefly, and then turned his attention to the Isles.

"Umpf... you forgot your fishing pole." Taff's deep voice resounded matter-of-factly in an attempt to change the subject.

"So it seems; how careless of me. If you do not mind, I believe I will just borrow one from the Master of the Hall, then." Rellion grinned coyly. "It's just through there, if you please."

Whiskeys of the Manor Hall

Rellion pointed to the closest inlet created by the islets' formation; here the sea was much calmer. Taff eased the boat within the natural cove without another word, carefully eyeing the back of Rellion's head. Looking over the side, Taff could see the reef formed there, the brightly colored sea life a stark contrast to the sun-bleached bones and skulls imbedded in the vibrant coral. Dropping the main sail and jib slack, Taff steered towards the largest isle and a mouth-like opening, allowing the natural current to draw them. A tarnished and barnacled bell hung at the entrance. The clapper smacked against the sides of the tarnished dome as Rellion yanked on the crank. Clang! Clang! Clang! Clang!

"Was that wise?"

"Indeed, my very large friend! Best to herald our visit. We will be honored guests… well, we will be guests, at any rate. If I may again ask for your indulgence, and have you grab hold of the guide rope there?"

Taff grabbed for the thick rope that hung by large, rusted rings hammered hard with iron pegs into the rocky surface; slime oozed through his fingers with each pull. Light from interspersed lanterns pitched a dim aura, and as they rounded a corner, there stood a collection of men and women with swords drawn — Warders, the jailers of the Manor Hall. Long ago, they were the elite of the Royal Guard, the Whiskeys, so named because they were once partially paid with the finest drink in the land, the moniker a source of pride. Greeting Rellion and Taff here this morning, though, was a mere shadow of their predecessors. The once-pristine uniforms of crimson and royal blue-trimmed coats were now replaced by frayed cuffs and purposely ripped-off sleeves. Mismatched tarnished medallions of the seven realms were pinned on lapels haplessly and without knowledge of meaning. The only theme unifying the old and new guard were the long swords that were the Warders' primary weapons. While their outward appearance had taken on the vestiges of lethargy and a small amount of corruption, each held a well-cared-for and well-sharpened steel blade, its tang and cross guard sculpted with the insignia of a long-ago throne.

"You, those in the boat, call out your business! There was no word of guests today! Of course, there is always room for more!" a particularly ornamented Warder called out from the outcropping, on which a half-dozen of them stood and laughed at their apparent leader's joke.

"Greetings, illustrious Whiskeys of the Throne! I seek an audience with the Master of this fine Manor Hall!" Rellion said this with a contemptuous smile and his arms outstretched in greeting. Taff gave a final tug, and the bow of the sluice hit the rocky edge that served as a dock.

"Whiskeys of the Throne, are we? Precious little of that drink makes its way here anymore, and those we answer to, though they think they're royal, have little nobility about them." The leader chuckled again, nodding to his cohorts, who nodded and smiled in return. "Possibly you bring some more favorable drink than the rotgut brewed here, possibly for safe passage?"

"Ah, but I simply use the prestigious title of your bearing, no matter who it is you choose to serve, or whose oath is ignored." Rellion continued to smile as the Whiskeys grew silent at the poorly-veiled insult to their heritage. "Alas, I am not prepared to barter today. Hopefully, this will suffice to gain an audience?" Rellion hooked his staff under his arm and turned a platinum signet ring that he wore on his forefinger face up. Slowly, he moved his hand across their field of vision, ensuring the embossed side of the ring could be seen. Each of them tensed and gripped their swords a little tighter, but still something deep inside the oath of their posts spoke to them. Like the swords they held aloft, this ring held the seal of the old throne.

One by one, they lowered their guard.

"I am ecstatic to find that not all aspects of loyalty have been abandoned." Rellion, whose wry smile had not faded, regarded them with a bit more liking than he had at first sight. "Master Taff, if you would please remain here with our fair transport." Taff merely grunted as he tethered a line about a rock as a makeshift cleat. The lead Warder pointed to two of the men, instructing them to stay. They eyed Taff with apprehension. Rellion stepped from the boat and clapped his hands together, "Shall we, then?"

The dock opened up into a cavernous expanse with a series of tightly wound stairs and terraces carved into the living rock. Salty bands of white marked where the tide had risen on occasion, and then receded. Rellion licked at his lips; he could taste the briny mist that filled the Hall. Stone balustrades lined each successive level, their newel posts capped with scalloped half-shells retrieved from the surrounding sea. A dim phosphorescent light emanated from the curved interior of the shells, lighting the path upward. The leader stopped abruptly on a large terrace and motioned one of his men to him. Speaking quietly into his ear, the man nodded his understanding and ran ahead of them.

Rellion took the brief respite to gaze over the balustrade, careful to avoid the slimy wetness that accumulated and dripped from every surface. Above him, natural skylights, formed through erosion, let in the muffled sound of the breaking water outside and spotlighted a canopy of treasures from the deep. Conchs, scallops, trident shells, and blown-glass bulbs completed a majestic chandelier, its beauty wasted on the few able to see it.

The Warder, noticing Rellion's gaze, said, "Use to have real fancy dances here a long time back; all the nobles must have had a real good time. Not much dancing here now." Rellion ignored the Warder as he looked thoughtfully at the woman depicted in the mosaic tiling of the ballroom floor. "Pretty, ain't she?" The Warder indicated the floor with a sweep of his hand and laughed. Rellion remained silent, as if he were listening to some faraway music, but the Warder soon became impatient and, pointing to a grand staircase, said gruffly, "This way to the Master of the Hall."

Reaching the surface, Rellion found himself directly within the Manor Hall, its opulence still apparent despite its repurposing. Bandings of black, gray, and white marble, with thin lines of silver excavated from below, walled an opulent and vaulted hallway that led back to a bank of windows, their protective location from the ever-raging elements being on the lee side of the three islets.

The subordinate Warder who had run ahead earlier now stood to the side of a set of double doors, his facial expression noncommittal. The lead Warder gave a single tap upon the doors and then opened them, allowing Rellion to enter first. Staying the other guards with the raise of his hand, he entered and closed the door behind them.

Sitting behind an immense wooden desk with a series of bookcases behind her sat the Master of the Manor Hall.

Hardly a Guest of Consequence

R ellion was slightly taken aback by the appearance of the woman before him. It was hardly unusual for a woman to be a member of the Warders, but the young age of the raven-haired Master of the Hall made him wonder. Taking in her bearing, Rellion quickly understood that this woman was very much in charge. Unlike her subordinates, her poise and dress were far more in line with the nobility they had lost. She immediately met Rellion's eyes as he entered the room; this woman did not suffer the inadequacies of self-importance. She did not pretend to be working on some meaningless paperwork or stand prone to a window, pretending to be thinking of something else. Rellion knew that she was attempting to read him; he already understood her.

"I am Lieutenant Riley Blackmore. Have a seat, sir." Taking command of the introductions, she pointed to a wooden chair set in front of her desk.

"Very gracious of you, Lady Whiskey." For the first time in a long time, Rellion actually did mean the title as a slight compliment. He took the seat indicated and balanced his cane to the front of the chair and floor as he sat. "I am known as Rellion."

"What business do you have here at the Manor Hall?" the Lieutenant asked without any inclination of who he was, remaining warily polite until she understood more.

"If you would, I am here to see one of your guests." Rellion tapped the signet ring he wore upon his finger against the wooden arm of the chair.

The tapping was not missed. "I'd ask where you gained such a prize, but I hardly expect it would be the truth. It has gotten you this far without your being clapped in irons but your time here as a 'guest' is as I deem it."

The Lead Warder behind Rellion shifted his weight just a little to let him know he was still there.

With a flourish of his hand, Rellion said, "Dear Lady Whiskey, today I promise to speak only truths... but if you must know, it was a gift given to me by the fairest of ladies a very long time ago." Rellion smiled and maintained eye contact with Blackmore.

"And tomorrow?"

"Let us not speak of what has not happened yet. Tomorrow, by your leave, I shall be off on yet another errand and others, unlike yourself, will have to be bothered as to my veracity."

The Lieutenant continued to look at Rellion in silence, her brown eyes not giving away her thoughts as she contemplated him. As if coming to some internal decision, she broke the long silence. "Which prisoner is it that you wish to see?"

"Hardly a guest of consequence, really... but I wish to see the one who occupies the stateroom," Rellion said airily, and for the first time since their encounter, the woman blinked.

The Warder behind Rellion whispered under his breath, "Ix."

"Sargent Banes, give us a moment."

Banes began to protest, but was held silent by the lieutenant's look. He gave the back of Rellion's head a scowl, but obeyed the command.

Blackmore rose from her seat and turned to the series of bookshelves behind her. Pulling one of the leather-bound tomes from its place, she proceeded to file through the yellowing and flaking pages. "You must know the laws concerning the stateroom and those that have been interned there." It was a statement as opposed to a question, and Rellion did not bother to answer. The signet ring that he wore granted him unrestricted access to many places both wondrous and malevolent within the realms, or so once it did.

"I make it a habit of understanding the situations I find myself in, but I will admit this one eludes me. The prisoner in the stateroom proceeds me and all of the other Warders posted here."

"Be very careful of such curiosity, Lady Whiskey." Rellion replied calmly.

The lieutenant regarded him for a moment, then continued. "Those who make their way here are generally pasty elites who have fallen out of favor with the Stewardship for one reason or another. They don't last very long. This Hall has long been a place where one is sent to be forgotten, but none more so than those sentenced to the stateroom." Blackmore turned another page or two, and placed the book at the edge of her desk nearest to Rellion. "There is no date of internment and no charge recorded, just the scrawled signature of the prisoner."

Rellion leaned forward in his seat and looked intently at the signature before him, if it could be called a signature. A misshapen pair of letters were scratched upon the decaying page. The quill used, heavy with ink, had dripped and blotted in areas. Dried blood was also imprinted by fingertips and a half-palm that the writer had placed to steady the paper. Rellion just smiled at the scrawl and the pair of letters: "I" and "X".

"Since when has guilt, real or imagined, ever been a prerequisite for a suite here at the Manor Hall? I have taken a liking to you, so let us speak more frankly. I would remark to you that it is not only the *guests* of this Hall that are sent here to be forgotten." Rellion leaned back in his chair, waiting for a response from Blackmore. She merely returned to her chair and returned his gaze. "Long that sword of yours has passed within your family. It has become your birthright to a promise made to a long-ago throne. Much of that loyalty has been lost to time by many of your kind. They serve a Stewardship that has grown corrupt and blind to its many citizens. Your very presence here as Master of the Manor Hall tells me how in fact your heart truly beats." Leaning forward in his chair, Rellion continued, "I put it to you, Lady Whiskey, that as long as you hold that sword, the code and oath of your forefathers still holds as well."

Blackmore contemplated him again. Leaning forward, she opened a top drawer of her desk and pulled out an ancient set of keys. "Access to the stateroom is but twice a month, always during successive full cycles of the moons — but you knew that already, didn't you?"

Rellion just smiled in response.

Buried deep within the islet of the Manor Hall was the circular cell of the stateroom, with a solitary door that ticked around like the hand of a clock, exposing itself only when the space in the exterior stone wall and it aligned. Blackmore escorted Rellion to the lower levels of the prison, bypassing several heavy wooden doors that he supposed held other "guests" until Blackmore finally stopped at a door along a long hallway. She handed the set of keys to him. "The trinket you wear gives you the right to speak with whoever is there, but does not afford me the same. I will go no farther."

Rellion took the keys and opened the door, closing it again without a backward glance. At the end of another short hallway was a door with thick bars. A keyhole on the surface of the door had already began to disappear with the rotation of the cell, just a small bit still peeking out at the edge of stone. Rellion glanced down at the keys in his hand. Even had Blackmore given him the final key, which he supposed she most certainly had not — if she even had access to it — unlocking the door would be impossible at this point.

A shadow stirred along the bars that served as the prisoner's only window to the outside. "Ix, is it now?" Rellion asked. "I must say, that is very morbid, even for you."

The shadow immediately stopped moving at the sound of Rellion's voice.

"Oh, good. For a moment there, I did wonder if it was actually you, my friend." Rellion waved at the air about his nose. "If I were you, though, I would call for the chambermaid a little more often."

"We are not *friends*." The hard raspy voice, cracking from little use, dripped with malice at the utterance of the word *friend*.

"Come now, Richard, once…"

"You will not call me that! That person died! He no longer exists!" Ix shouted in anger, and then panted heavily with the exertion.

"Very well, Ix, since our present time is short and you obviously have better things you need to get back to — bathing not being among them — I will do my best to make this brief."

"There is NOTHING I wish to hear from you!"

"I see that having only yourself for company has not improved your disposition. One would think that after a century or two of brooding and self-loathing… but as it is, I bring you word of hope."

"There will be no talk of hope in here, priest!" Ix's voice cracked with the effort to keep making sound, so long had it been that his vocal cords had done more than whisper in the night to himself.

"Rich… ard." Rellion stumbled upon the name. "They have returned; it is time. You know for what they search and whom they hope to awaken."

"I've done my part. I failed, and so did you. We all did. Hope died with the King and Queen!" Ix leaned against the wall of his cell, staring at the scratch marks that covered nearly every inch of the circular wall space, one for each rotation of his door.

Rellion's voice took on an uncharacteristic pleading tone. "The blood-line survived, Richard. They are the hope we have been granted."

"Take your ministering somewhere else, priest. I care not for it." Ix, pushing himself away from the wall, moved away from the door.

Knowing the conversation was over, Rellion spoke to the retreating shadow. "Only a fool thinks he can live forever by avoiding the fight… and in our case, forever is very long time indeed, my friend."

Ix listened for the withdrawing footsteps and the click of the hallway door. He moved to pick up a rock to scratch yet another cycle upon the wall. As his eyes adjusted to the half-light of the phosphorescent shells that made up parts of the high ceiling, he took in the seemingly unending number of marks that he had etched into the walls. Of course, he knew exactly how many there were, having counted them many times. Looking at the stone in his hand, he allowed it to fall slowly from his fingers. When it hit the floor, it echoed about the walls with the dull thud of stone upon stone.

FAT CHERRY POPPED FIZZ

The Drunken Chymist was filled nearly to the brim this morning as the group of kids entered. Groggle had accompanied Rellion there on occasion for whatever errand he thought was important, but the others were a bit out of their element. Count Bobo was leading his band and the crowd in a raucous drinking song, apparently a favorite of everyone there.

The pope and the drunk were one and the same
If only different in name
Both did come to the Chymist round
For their sorrows to be drowned
In whiskeys and scotches all golden brown
They spoke the good word to those all around
Hey! Drink! Drink! Drink! Till the King is crowned on high!
Drink! Drink! Drink! For the end may be nigh!

The chorus was punctuated by the patrons singing along with raised glasses and mugs in salute. Kristane found herself smiling despite herself at the jovial atmosphere. Xander even seemed to drop his serious countenance and was looking around curiously.

Said one to the other will you go to heaven or will you go to hell

Here at the Chymist we bid you all well

So they drank, drank, drank till the sounding of the bell

And blessed everyone they met fare thee well

Hey! Drank! Drank! Drank! Till the King is crowned on high!

Drank! Drank! Drank! For the end may be nigh!

Taps were pulled wide open with a constant flow of liquor, bartenders rotating mugs underneath struggled to keep up with the demand.

The pope and the drunk did declare out loud and clear

Drunk we are both on whiskey and beer

All did shout out, without any fear

Your reckoning day is near!

Hey! Drunk! Drunk! Drunk! Till the King is crowned on high!

Drunk! Drunk! Drunk! For the end may be nigh!

"Groggle, what are you and this lot doing in here?" Kate, the auburn-haired barmaid, shouted over the bar with two handfuls of mugs. She gave Groggle an inquisitive eye and looked Kristane and the others up and down. Groggle gave her a sheepish grin. Kate spoke to the other barmaid next to her. "Jess, cover me for a couple of minutes." Jess smiled her ascent and strode off with several tankards in her hands to a group of drinkers opposite them. Nodding to Groggle and the others, Kate indicated a draped area just off from the stage. "All of you meet me over there."

Drink! Drank! Drunk! For the end may be nigh!

The Count had just reached the final chorus, and with a final cheer of appreciation, everyone chugged down whatever was left of their drinks and slammed the mugs down.

Kristane thought that the woman seemed nice, but she gave Groggle a questioning look; he just waved her and the others on in response. The Rogue traipsed through the crowd, dodging flying arms and drinks to where Kate had nodded. Kristane and the others had never been inside the Chymist before. Rellion had warned them off from seeking *donations* there. Kristane could see that Xander had once again resumed his usual demeanor. He nodded to a group of Briggers that they had just passed, but the lawkeepers were so enamored with their drinks they never even looked Xander's way.

Kristane still had the oddest feeling that they were being watched, though. Turning her attention to the stage, she immediately met the eyes of the automaton piano player. While he continued to bang out a song upon the keys and sing out loudly, a chill ran up Kristane's spine, and she suddenly had an uneasy feeling about how intently the Count was looking at her, as if he were really "seeing" her. His eyes were not like those of the mechanical beasts of burden that she was used to seeing throughout Kairos. He seemed to be a great deal more alive than they were.

Shaking off the uneasy feeling, she turned her gaze away and quickly squeezed through the curtains and a small door tucked in behind them that the others had already passed through. The Rogue was met with a small study that was comfortably furnished. Cushioned couches and armchairs were placed in a half-circle about a low table and a small, curtained stage. Of course, Groggle and Prya had already made the place their own, Prya lounging in a chair with her feet up on the table and inspecting a wallet that she had lifted as she had passed through the crowd, and Groggle perched on the edge of a couch cushion, shoveling chips and treats that had been left out into his mouth. Crumbs fell from his mouth onto the floor, and in between the plush leather cushions. Kristane was jealous with their ease, and embarrassed at the same time. Pointing at Prya's feet and at the crumbs scattered before Groggle, she said a little louder than she had meant too. "Can you two, please! She'll be here in a minute!"

Groggle stopped mid-shovel, his hand poised in front of his mouth. Prya sighed and dropped her feet to the floor, tucking away the wallet she had stolen. She often bragged that she was so good that one day, she would even get something off of Rellion. Kristane agreed with her being good, but never thought it very likely about Rellion — and even less so now, she reminded herself sadly.

"'eally, Kristane, Kate es 'ine. Rellion introdu her efore." Groggle had not bothered to swallow before he started talking. Instead, his mumbled response just sprayed even more crumbs onto the floor and himself.

"I don't care, Groggle! You did see the Briggers out front, right? And the rest of us don't know her..." Kristane's rant was interrupted by the closing door as Kate entered the room. She carried with her bright cherry-red drinks that frothed and bubbled over the lip of each mug. Groggle was almost beside himself with his rapturous stare.

"Now, I know Rellion keeps you lot on a ration of whiskey, but here we go, a Fat Cherry Popped Fizz for each of you. Groggle's favorite, if I remember right." Groggle was already sucking on his striped candy straw; Kate, sensing their unease, motioned to them to go ahead. "Come on, the rest of you, sit and enjoy. Then we can talk of what brings you to the Chymist."

Xander and Lathan sat precariously on the arm rests of the furniture, each with one leg on the floor holding them in place. Kate took a seat with her hands clasped in her lap before her, and Kristane choose one near her. Kate was watching each of them with a contained delight, waiting to see their reaction to the drinks she had brought.

Kristane took hold of the straw with her lips, and already the effervescent bubbles of the drink tickled her nose. As the Cherry Fizz was drawn up the sugar-coated straw, with cherry and vanilla flavoring, it melted into the concoction. It was like every sweet sensation Kristane had ever had popped in her mouth at once. Not like eating a spoonful of sugar, but something far more explosive — like fireworks on King's Eve, and you wanted to scream *Oooh!* and *Aaah!* at the sight of it! Only this was in a glass mug, and you were drinking it!

"So, what do you think?"

Kristane just stared; she wanted to shout out her approval, but didn't know how to say it.

Groggle, though, did not come up short for proper wording. He screamed as loud as he could. "Yahoo!"

Kate smiled and laughed. "That's what I thought, too, the first time my grandfather made it for me!"

Count Bobo Mahoney

Kristane found herself more at ease, and started looking about the room as she enjoyed her drink. She was startled by a black-and-white picture whose occupants suddenly moved. Well, moved would be the wrong word; it was a series of successive pictures that flipped or spun within the wood frame like a toy zoetrope. Kristane remembered her fascination with one in the Attic when she was younger; the quicker she spun it, the faster the horses would run. Only this picture was not hand-drawn stick horses but actual people, all laughing and cheering with mugs in their hands as they sat atop casks. A fireman would run past the foreground of the scene every once in a while, and then a fire hose that had gotten loose would spray all the revelers. The scene would then reset itself, and the laughing and smiling faces began to cheer again. Kristane felt like she could almost hear those within the frame.

"Introductions first. I'm Kate, and this is my place. It's been in my family now for fifteen generations. My many greats-grandfather first opened the Drunken Chymist over three hundred and fifty years ago. The wonderful concoction you're enjoying was originally his idea.

"Now, I know Groggle here, but the rest of you … I'm guessing you're also part of Rellion's bunch?" Kate looked at each of them in turn, and they simply nodded. "There have been many stories whispered of yesterday's happenings… by your appearance here, some of them might be true." Kate did not wait for their response. "And where is his lordship Rellion, anyway?" Smirking and peering over their heads in jest at that last question, Kate looked expectantly toward Kristane. Kristane wondered why everyone always seemed to be looking for Rellion in such a manner, like he was some spectral ghost who all of a sudden appeared out of thin air.

Kristane looked to the others, but they were also waiting for her to respond. She had only just met this woman, but Kristane thought instinctively that maybe she could trust her. Kate had a kind face, and there was a sincerity that reflected in her eyes. Deciding that she could, Kristane started with the storm that they had witnessed, all the way up until the attack in the Attic, not knowing why but choosing to leave the part about the necklace out of her story. The others did not call her out on it. Only Groggle looked as if he might say something. As she came to the part about Creff and Rellion, Kristane found herself choking on the words, as she spoke of them and their sacrifice in keeping the rest safe. She was trying to remember the sound of Creff's voice; it seemed to be slipping from her memory faster than what he looked like. She hoped that that would not fade too. Kate sat quietly, never interrupting, only occasionally reacting with a kind smile or a sincere look of encouragement for her to go on.

"…And here we are now, with no place to go and no idea what to do next," Kristane finished, staring down at her hands that would not stop wringing in her lap.

Kate stood from her chair and kneeled before Kristane, taking the girl's fumbling hands into her own. Kate's hands were warm and reassuring. She waited for Kristane to look up into her eyes, and then gave Kristane a bright smile that warmed her. Kate squeezed Kristane's hands and looked at the others, smiling brightly at each of them as well.

"I see that you've had a tough go of it, and I am sorry for your friend, and that some of what I've heard is true. I don't know what it is you should do, but as for Rellion, maybe I can help a little with that. I wouldn't count him out just yet if I were you. There are many strange things about that man that make very little sense, but what I do know is that his talent for self-preservation is remarkable." Kate squeezed Kristane's hands one more time and then stood. "I'd like to introduce you to someone who may help you in what you decide to do next." Seeing the uncertain look on Kristane's face Kate added. "Don't worry; he's extremely trustworthy, though fair warning, a bit chatty when he gets going." Kate chuckled and walked over to a tubed mouthpiece that disappeared somewhere down into the floor near the knee-high stage. "Count, when you have a moment, could you come into my office please?"

The Rogue looked around at one another, uncertain of what was coming next, and then back at Kate. Even Groggle had no idea of what was happening, despite having been here before. "My great, great, grand-father, Old Pope as he was known around here, had this office and stage built for private meetings and entertainment." As Kate spoke, a faint din of music and the rumbling of gears and wood could be heard, as the curtains slowly draped to either side of the small private stage of their own accord. A crack that peered out into the bar and the backs of the other members of the band was visible, and slowly sealed itself as the wall and part of the stage rotated into the office. There, in all of his splendor, sat Count Bobo Mahoney and his piano.

"I know this is probably not what all of you were expecting, but regardless, Count, may I introduce you to my new friends and some of Rellion's charges?" Kate motioned towards the kids and named each of them for the Count. He blinked appreciatively at them as they sat openmouthed. "Kids, this is my dear friend Count Bobo Mahoney." With a flourish of piano keys, the Count punctuated Kate's introduction.

Prya was the first to gather herself and say something. "But it's just the clockwork band leader… it just plays music…" She had said what the others were thinking, but the look of indignation on the brass- and silver-plated workings of the Count's face made the others glad they hadn't voiced it.

"I assure you, little moppet, that I am so very much more than that!" Again, the Count finished with a sweep of the keys.

"Prya, the Count is different," Kate began. "He is, in fact, very special; he's been very much aware of everything around him for a very long time… though there are very few who know of this outside of my family, and I must ask all of you to keep his secret for me and him."

"But why? That's really awesome! I mean, wow, look at him, he's great!" Groggle exclaimed while moving to the very edge of his seat and waving his hand across the Count's eyeline, like you would if you were checking for movement in a lifeless body. Groggle hadn't really caught what Kate had meant; he still viewed the Count as a particularly well-built gadget.

"While I do appreciate the compliment... Groggle, was it? I can see you just fine, young man; stop waving your arm about like a rabid monkey." Groggle's excited smile faded, and his arm slipped limply back into his lap upon Bobo's remonstration. "Though it is quite understandable, young man, for you to be confused. Do not be put out by my tone; let me have that gregarious smile once again!" The Count began a lively tune, and blew steam out of his ears while smiling broadly. Groggle looked at the others hesitantly, and then smiled again.

"You see, Groggle, the very perception of the Count and the members of his musical troupe is why we must keep their secret to ourselves. I'm afraid that it could be very dangerous for him and the rest of the band otherwise," Kate said as she returned to her seat.

"And not without considerable danger to you, Miss Kate." Bobo gave a sweep of his arm and bow to where Kate sat. She nodded back appreciatively.

"But how is it that he came to be this way... and *what* danger?" Kristane looked questioningly at Kate, trying her best to phrase her question so that she wouldn't further offend the Count.

"The story is his, and happened long before me. So I'll let him tell it; and as I said earlier, it may help you with what you decide to do next." Kate nodded to the Count to take the stage.

GUEST OF THE STATE ROOM

Lieutenant Blackmore sat at her desk, staring at the same piece of paper as she had for the past hour; she couldn't recall what it was anymore. The light cast by the scalloped shells that dotted the ceiling of her office weren't really enough to read anything by, just enough for one not to bump into the furniture. Through the doors of her office, the waning face of the Older Brother illuminated the hallway, yet the shadows seemed to be winning; the moon had had definitely lost the brightness of its full cycle. Blackmore's mind had been stuck on Rellion since his visit this morning, and the cycle of the moon only renewed her thoughts as to the mysterious occupant of the stateroom.

"Dammit!" she cursed to the room, breaking the hard silence that had permeated it for hours. Abruptly standing, she moved around her desk and headed for the door. There was very little reason to head there, but the stateroom was her destination nonetheless.

As Blackmore negotiated the steps of the grand staircase that led below, she thought of the twice-a-month duty of inspecting the "guest" of the stateroom. During the part of the cycle when the barred door was visible, she was to verify that her charge wasn't dead. As canvas sacks of dried salmon jerky and other non-perishables were tossed through the bars, she would call out for him to respond. She played back in her mind the usual exchange. "Prisoner Ix, this is Lieutenant Blackmore, Master of the Manor Hall. Respond as to being deceased." There was never more than a low grunt in response, and she would mark him as alive in her report, with a simple check next to his name.

Passing under the chandelier that was lit to its fullest this evening, Blackmore's boots scraped at the roughened tile that was meant to keep one from slipping on the mist from the ocean spray that found its way through the crevices above. The tile had a dull sheen about it, but at one time she supposed it had shined more brightly. The remnant shades of a colorful mosaic could still be made out amongst the broken and missing pieces. Worn paths of centuries of boots passing over it still couldn't eclipse the portrait of a very beautiful red-haired woman pieced together in shards of clay, shells, and smoothed coral. Blackmore had never wondered as to the woman's identity; she had just accepted it as the portrait of the long-dead lady of the house. Whomever the artist had been, the Lieutenant believed that they must have captured the living person relatively well, her smile so playful that it continued into her eyes.

Blackmore continued on her path to the curving hallway that led to the circular cell of the stateroom. Caught up in her own thoughts and the echoing sound of her footfalls reverberating off of the walls of the enclosed space, it was only as she fumbled for the ancient key within her coat that she noticed the door was ajar. Stepping purposefully back from the door, she immediately rested her hand upon the pommel of her sword. After long years of service, Blackmore was not one to panic or become fearful. Instead, her senses became acute, and she listened for any sound that might emanate from the other side. She contemplated the door, noting that its locking mechanism had not been forced, and remembering very clearly the click of the bolt as she had secured the door earlier.

Blackmore cautiously pushed the door wider, the sparse light of the hallway casting a faint glow on the solid wall where the cell's inner door had rotated away until the next cycle. She continued into the confined space, keeping a steady eye upon the remaining shadows. Placing her hand upon the rock surface of the rotating wall to assure herself it was really there, the heel of her boot crushed a small rock, the crack of it echoing. Sliding her hand down the wall and bending to the floor, she picked up a few other small bits of rubble. Holding them within her palm up to the light from the doorway, she wondered where the fragments had come from.

Brushing her hands against one another and standing, Blackmore knew that if anything was amiss with Ix, she wouldn't know until the next cycle. Resigned to patience, she retraced her steps to her office. There were still items that needed her attention, and she doubted that true rest would find her; the mysterious "guest" of the stateroom would occupy even her dreams tonight.

Blackmore paused, regarding the moon and what remained of a terrace outside the windows of her office, its balustrade decayed by years of neglect and the constant rhythmic crash of waves. A shade caught in the corner of her eye; something or someone had moved within the halo of the scant lighting. For the second time tonight, her suspicions had been aroused. She moved quietly, but *Dammit!* she thought. There was no approaching the interior unnoticed from her position at the window; her shadow stood out like a beacon across the threshold of the doors. She waited breathlessly for her chance to move. Finally, a cloud passed before the moon and Blackmore slipped into her office, her sword drawn.

"You make far too much noise, Lieutenant," a cracked voice stated. Blackmore stopped short. An intruder was standing with his back to her, hunched over her desk, as if reading or searching for something. "Your boots and stride have the unmistakable stomp of authority." The man answered the unasked question as he straightened and turned to face her.

Bringing her sword higher into a striking position, Blackmore pointed the tip of it to his face. "Based on the day that I have had, including a strange visitor, the suspiciously open door leading to the stateroom, and your clothing patched together from old canvas jerky bags, I would quite like to know how you in fact came to be here in my office, Ix?"

Blackmore took in the ragged man before her. His visage had the pale pallor of a long incarceration without the benefit of sunlight, yet his chin and jawline were chiseled, and his overly long hair didn't really hide the regal look of his face. Unlike so many of the pasty elites she was used to seeing, this man did not display any muscle deterioration and fatigue. He appeared to be quite strong and fit under the patchwork of cloth and braided canvas that he wore. Yet Blackmore knew she had the advantage. The intruder was unarmed, and despite his apparent fitness, she knew she could take him.

Chuckling to himself, which caused him to hack, Ix smirked at Blackmore. "I bet you would. It really is none of your business, though. Now, if you would leave me be for a moment, you may yet survive this encounter."

"It wouldn't take long to raise the guard," she said pointedly.

"Then you would just endanger your men as well. But this is a matter of curiosity for you now. You believe you stand a better chance at solving the mystery without their interference. I believe you to be no slouch with that weapon, but you do currently stand in my way, so I take no honor in harming you." With each successive word, Ix's voice grew stronger, the years of lethargy shaking themselves from his vocal cords.

"While I appreciate the compliment, I think I have had enough of your smugness." Blackmore moved quickly, mid-sentence, hoping to catch him off guard and subdue him. He was right; she *did* want to know the mystery behind him.

Ix was impossibly quick; as Blackmore moved forward, he somersaulted backwards over the top of the desk, one of his retreating legs making contact with her sword arm as she brought it to bear upon him. Blackmore barely managed to keep hold of her weapon. Ix stood on the other side of the desk a roguish smile upon his face, inviting her to make her next move. But he didn't wait for her; instead, he pounded on the corner of the desk with his fist, just above the pedestal. As Blackmore pursued him around the desk, first one way and then the other, Ix would repeatedly roll across its surface, pounding the corners of the desk in succession.

A silent rage built within the lieutenant. She knew that this man was just toying with her, and she moved to engage him again; but then a creaking rumbled deep within the oversized desk. Blackmore realized that Ix had been pounding out a pattern, each of his movements bringing him to where he wished to be next. She stared at Ix, who wore that same irritating smile, as the sound of rotating gears sequentially pulled what sounded like large pins away from their strike plates, and a trapdoor lowered itself, retreating into the confines of the desk — and a sword raised up on gilded supports.

LEGEND IT HAS BECOME

Abruptly Ix dropped his smile and rolled across the desk, seizing the sword as he moved, landing him within a foil's length of Blackmore's guarded stance. There they stood, the tips of their swords pointed at each other's hearts.

"It is time that I be going; stay your blade and allow me to pass," Ix demanded. "There is no reason for you to be harmed." In answer, she immediately crossed blades with him, her first strike resounding about the room as steel crashed upon steel. The two combatants whirled about, avoiding each other's offensive strikes, and it appeared that Blackmore was gaining some ground. Ix was being pushed into the corner, near the double doors to the exterior wall. He parried each of her lunges expertly, and kept up his pace backwards. She had no intention of killing him, but soon came to the conclusion that that might not be a possibility anyway. He was either drawing her in, or was toying with her as he had before.

The clashing of swords had alerted her men; she could hear hurried voices and footfalls as leather boots slapped at the stone floor of the hallway. Despite her pride in the matter, she found herself relieved that she would soon have help. "Your time is up, Ix. There's no escape from the Manor Hall. There's nowhere for you to go; you cannot hope to take on all of my men."

Ix, also hearing the approaching men, feinted a lunge forward, but twisted mid-swing and slapped Blackmore across her cheek with the fuller of his blade. Not hard, but enough for Blackmore to get the point. Being treated that way only enraged her more.

"You are well out of your league, Lieutenant." Then, feinting another lunge, Ix brought his sword backward beneath his other arm, the point making contact against the wall behind him. A pocket door sprang sideways, slipping into the wall; the cool smell of a burst of ozone just before it begins to rain filled the room. The terrace Blackmore had viewed from the hallway windows could be seen through the hidden door a large expanse of its platform eroded away. Ix grabbed hold of either side of the door frame and heaved himself across the deathly drop. He landed solidly on the other side as a few loose fragments of the terrace broke free and plunged to the waves below.

A bit of madness had taken over Blackmore; just as her men bustled through the double doors with swords drawn, looking about the room for the source of the commotion, she stepped back to her desk and gave a drawn-out yell as she took a running start for the obstacle that separated her from her quarry. She cleared the precipice easily as a light rain began to fall. The blade she held above her head with both arms came crashing down, just as Ix, at the last minute, raised his defense. Their blades struck with such force that a trail of sparks showered around them. Ix was momentarily taken aback at the viciousness of the lieutenant's attack, but the look of surprise on his face was quickly replaced by a grim countenance. He meant what he had said; he had no desire to harm the lieutenant or her men, but he would not be hindered in what he had set his mind to. The two battled ferociously, Blackmore's men yelling words of encouragement from their place at the open pocket door; the remaining terrace only large enough to hold the two combatants. With each lunge and counter-parry, the rocks and slabbing creaked and rattled perilously, and soon began giving way from the combined weight of the pair.

Blackmore's attack had reached a fever pitch, the blood lust of battle giving her the advantage. Ix could only hold his sword aloft in an attempt to stave off her high-handed blows. As he backed away from her advances, his back bumped into the stone railing of the terrace. The balustrade crumbled beneath his weight. The sharpened edge of the lieutenant's sword glided against his as it sought to reach its mark. About midway into the stroke, her blade caught on Ix's, preventing it from falling farther. Following the length of her blade with her enraged eyes, she saw an unmistakable notch in Ix's blade that her strike had caught upon. She stepped back from the fallen man, his chest heaving from the exertion, and her panting quickened as she tried to regain her breath. "The Sword of the Bristol Cree." Blackmore stood staring at Ix, her eyes fixed upon the blade within his hand. "How is it that the sword of legend comes to be here?"

"Legend, it has become? More of a nightmarish fairytale, if the truth be known," Ix said with a grimace.

"Who are you?"

"I am *you*," said he, pointing at Blackmore with his sword where he lay against the crumbled rock. "A few years removed… well, maybe more than a *few*. I am what is left of broken oaths, forgotten honor, and failure."

Blackmore took in again the man before her, realizing that the patchwork clothing she could not see clearly before was intermixed with colorful cloth as well. Within the moons' light and flashes of lightning in the distance, the distinct crimson and royal blue of a Warder's jacket could be seen stitched and patched together with canvas. Ix, noticing the Blackmore's gaze, gave her his best cavalier grin and said, "Let's hope that not all oaths are broken, and not all honor is forgotten. Remind me, Lieutenant, to not get you mad again." And with that, he rolled backwards and plunged feet-first into the briny waves some hundred or more feet below.

Blackmore rushed to the edge, peering over into the abyss. Ix had disappeared into the darkness; she couldn't see whether he had surfaced or not.

"Lieutenant?" Sargent Banes brought her back from her reverie, calling to her from her office over the crash of waves and falling rain.

"Dammit, Banes, don't just stand there gawking! Find me a plank or rope or something, it's wet out here!" Blackmore admonished.

A Tale of Heroics, Brave and True

Count Bobo gave yet another flourish of the keys and began his tale. "Now, here I am to tell a tale of heroics, brave and true. Of how once I was a piece of clockwork, and how I became like you. Years did pass, though I knew not the passing of time… until one day a catastrophe struck at a little half past nine. The revelers were drinking and laughing to their hearts' desire, when somewhere within these walls caught the grandest of fires. Many did joke at the gathering smoke and flame, but all too soon though they realized it was not a game."

The Count pounded out a bridge of ragtime and continued his tale.

"Run they did to the doors, and jumped from the windows on high. Some of them must have thought that they could fly." Bobo turned to the group of kids and gave a quick wink. "All about me and the band, we realized everyone was gone. Yet here was I and the band playing, on and on. The flames began to lick at my piano and stage. It was then I slowly became aware of my cage.

"Oh, how that day I wished that I was not like you! How that day I did sing the blues! How I wished it wasn't true! How I…" The Count's singing trailed off with the tinkling of the keys as he caught the poleaxed look of the kids and a bit of a smirk from Kate. "You get the gist of it, anyway… you must of course forgive my showmanship!" Recovering himself, Bobo gave them a broad smile and continued to play a quieter tune. Kate chuckled as Kristane and the others continued to stare at the "man" at the piano.

"That picture there beside the desk was taken some two hundred years ago, during the big fire that almost burned the Chymist to the ground." The Count pointed, while still playing with his other hand, to the picture on the wall which Kristane had been fascinated with earlier. "That was the day that I became very much aware of myself and the things happening about me. I do not know how it happened, or even why. Possibly it was from so many years of being around the many races of Kairos, listening to their stories of hope and woe, that I finally wished for some of my own."

Bobo paused talking, and looked intently at each of them. "What I do know is that day, I felt pain. The fire had reached me and the other band members, and as the heat began to blister and buckle the metal that makes up my body, I let out a very painful scream for help." The Count stopped playing for a moment, and pushed up the colorful sleeve of his jacket, showing them the warped and discolored bronze of his forearm. Pushing the material back into place, he began a somber tune. "It could be that Benny and the other band members took their cue from me, as they always had; but they too became aware of our impending doom. You see, despite the life within us, we were then and still to this day slaved to the mechanisms that give us movement. We each began to call for help, but no one came. Firemen had come by this time, and we could see them through the flames, dragging hoses and pumping water. We know that they saw us but maybe, I suppose, they mistook our pleas for just another song, a grand and punctuated performance, possibly. We were, after all, just an oversized music box only moments before." In almost a whisper, staring down at his now motionless hands, the Count concluded, "I cannot blame them…"

"How terrible! How did you… um, survive… sir?" Prya gasped, stumbling on her words as she had before, though it was clear that she and the others had begun to look at the Count in a much different light.

"Prya, this is the part of the story that I think may help all of you." Kate looked sorrowfully at her friend who sat behind the piano, knowing that the memory of that particular day was difficult. "Count, if you think you could continue…?"

"Of course, Miss Kate!" Breaking from his gloom, the Count began a grand sweep of the keys. "As I began my tale, did I not promise some heroics?" With a series of metal plates rotating and a burst of steam, Bobo once again gave his broad infectious smile, masking what lay behind his eyes. "We must continue the tale! Fear had now gripped me. Though I will tell you truthfully, I was not sure until later that it was that. I had no experience as to feeling, you see. I must say the many excellent feelings I have had since have made my first foray worth it, though!" The shadow that had occupied the Count's eyes cleared away at his reminiscing, and he smiled again with his eyes. "Just when I had believed all was lost, there was a man — long coat, long dark hair, and a top hat — standing in front of the stage amongst the flames. He spoke briefly to us and tipped his hat. *It appears that you are in need of service, Master Musicians!* He said no more, but spun on his heel and with something he held in his hand, blasted apart the copper water tanks that fed the distillery. The deluge tamed the fire just enough that the firemen could take command."

Each of the Rogue looked at each other. Too many times, they had heard a similar salutation from Rellion himself, and from what they had recently seen of their own harrowing escape, it was familiar… but how was it possible? That fire had happened a very long time ago.

"I see from your wonderment that you suspect that what I have said may apply to a person you think you know. I promise you that what you suspect is true. The man I speak of is the same, for I have seen him several times since, though we have only spoken on one other occasion. He has come and gone through the years, staying for a while but never for very long; and many years will pass before I see him again. Always, he appears just the same as the man who saved me."

"That's not possible! I mean, he's just Rellion! He…" Kristane was conflicted with what she thought she knew, and what she had previously seen in the Attic, and what she had just heard.

"I assure you, young one, that I am not mistaken; but fortunately, you do not have to take my word for it. Miss Kate, if you could please assist?"

Kate nodded her ascent to Bobo and stood from her chair, gliding over to the same picture that was so much a part of Kristane's attention earlier. The scene had just reset, and the many patrons were all laughing and sitting on barrels from the Chymist. The same firehose shot across the scene unattended, spraying the group once again. This time, though, just as the group raised their hands and ducked in protest of the spraying water, Kate pressed a button otherwise hidden in the scrolling design of the frame, and the picture stopped abruptly. She pointed to a spot just over the left shoulder of a gruff-looking dwarf; there a man with a long coat, long dark hair, and a tall hat could be seen glancing backwards over his shoulder. Kristane hastened from her seat with the others in tow, gathering about the picture. There could be no doubt in their minds: Rellion was the man trotting away in the background of the picture.

A profound silence filled the room.

Kristane looked questioningly at Kate. She looked back in a caring sort of way, and spoke to them. "There are many things in this world that transpire without us knowing how or why. You've all been introduced to two of them this morning. I have to believe that even more may be in store for each of you very soon. I can't help but worry for you. There are things happening beyond all of us, and they seem to center around this man." Kate paused as she gestured to the retreating figure of Rellion, and again looked at each of them in the same caring way. "As I said before, Rellion's knack for self-preservation is remarkable; but it goes much, much, deeper than just that."

Kristane was still having trouble in finding words. The shock of what she and the others had just been told kept her in wonderment, and flashes of her past interactions with the man she called Rellion kept passing through her mind. Xander was the first, this time, to find his voice. Turning back to the stage, he addressed the Count. "You said you spoke with him on one other occasion."

"Yes, we spoke. His statement to me was a simple warning." The count stopped playing and stared down at the keys of his piano for a moment. Looking back up and meeting Xander's eyes, he said, "You see, as unique as I and the band are, there have been others."

Not Welcome Anymore

There was really only one place for them to go, and the others had agreed: the one and only place they had ever called home, and the one place where all their uncertainty had begun. Prya needed to keep her appointment with the Doctor; Groggle kept teasing her that it was a date, and Lathan said that he would go with her. In fact, he seemed adamant that he was going. Kristane was glad Lathan had said so, as she had an uneasy feeling that none of them should be wandering alone right now. So she, Groggle, and Xander began their trek along the back alleys and rooftops of Kairos to the Attic.

"I'm sorry, I'm just not very good at this," Groggle whimpered as Xander grabbed the back of his pants and dragged him over yet another ridge of a roof line.

"It's okay, Groggle," said Kristane. "I guess I'm just being overly cautious. Let's take the low road; the festival is still going, and we're nearly there anyway." Xander nodded his assent, and pointed to a gutter pipe that ran down the side of Pendulum Timepieces, the building they were on. He held Groggle steady as he clambered over the edge and grabbed hold of the piping. Shimming down the old big-mouthed cast-iron pipe was the most progress that Groggle had made in the last hour, though he pretty much skidded down the smooth surface and had to be coaxed off of the last couple of feet where he'd finally gotten a grip.

"Come on, Groggle, open your eyes!" an exasperated Kristane pleaded with him. "I promise you can touch your feet from where you are!"

"No, no, just leave me!"

"God, Groggle! Seriously, martyrdom doesn't suit you! Just open your eyes!" Any pretense at being clandestine was pretty much lost at this point.

Random people, some walking their dogs — both mechanical and real— stopped and stared or just did a quick double-take over their shoulders and then hurried on. One particularly large bulldog stopped and barked incessantly until its owner dragged it away, its deep, pronounced woofs trailing down the cobbled road. The only bit of luck they had was that none of the Briggers seemed to be patrolling that stretch of King's Way. All the excitement was closer to the city center, as usual. Xander had joked, "Most of it, anyway, you have to admit was kind of entertaining." Kristane didn't find this as funny as Xander, but knew he was just trying to raise her spirits.

Groggle had taken to moping after the incident, pacing her and Xander a few feet behind, and she supposed it didn't help that she had threatened to tell the rest of their friends about it. *Not that I would, but it was the only thing that got him off that damn pipe!*

Still fuming, Kristane had hardly noticed that they were nearing the Abbey. The ragman was there near the corner of the steps, yelling his dire warnings and, as usual, occasionally stopping to have a conversation with his feet or some random spot behind him. Kristane did her best to shake off her annoyance with Groggle, and instead turned her thoughts to what Count Bobo had said: of how others the likes of he and the band had once been persecuted and destroyed, long, long ago, even before he had come to life — some because of atrocities they had committed, but mostly just because they were different. They had asked about the others, but the Count either didn't know or feared the answer.

Kristane looked up just in time to keep from bumping into Xander. A monk was busy sweeping with a broom of bunched up straw at small shards of wood upon the steps of the Abbey. The doors were both barely hanging from their upper hinges, and one appeared to be completely cracked in half lengthwise, only a few wood fibers holding it together.

"Wow! What happened to the doors?" Groggle had caught up and stood with them upon the steps, pointing at the doors.

"I don't know, but it probably isn't good," Kristane replied as she motioned for them to join a throng of people who were slowly meandering into the Abbey. She had already come to terms with the fact that they were never going to get Groggle up the back way, and that they would have to use the front.

Services were just starting, and the humming chant of the monks filled the high ceilings of the tabernacle. With the festival still on and the Saint's Casket still on display, the Abbey was at capacity. The trio broke away from the gawking crowd and headed for the grand staircase leading to the Attic. Turning back to look over his shoulder, as he often did, Xander noticed the odd behavior of the broom-sweeping monk. He had followed them in, and when Xander caught him observing them, the monk became decidedly nervous and started to sweep his own feet as he quickly looked off in another direction, occasionally peeking back and forth with one eye as Xander stared at him.

"Kris, I have this uneasy feeling that we may not be very welcome here anymore," he whispered into his sister's ear so as not to panic Groggle. He nodded back down the way they had come, and Kristane caught a glimpse of the broom-toting monk as he peered around a corner banister. Abruptly he dodged back, hitting himself in the head with his broom handle.

Kristane suppressed a chuckle. "Well, if that's all we're up against..." But she knew better; their time here was going to be limited.

Stepping over what remained of the scorched Attic doors, Kristane fanned wafts of smoke and the smell of the still-smoldering wood away from her nose. She couldn't help but notice the heat that was generated by them.

Within was more of the same ruin, only worse. The charcoal smell was mixed with the various concoctions that Rellion had brewed, as well as the briny stink from pickled jars of animals, most now broken on the floor. At least the shattered dome above allowed some relief as the vapors rose up and outward. Kristane walked to the center of the room, where she'd stood the night before. About her, she could see where the wraiths had dropped to the floor, the flooring buckled with the impression of something extremely heavy hitting it. She wondered if the wraiths had been armored beneath their cowls.

The others wandered about the room and kicked absently at items at their feet. Kristane could tell they were thinking about some of the same things. Xander was brushing through some of the ashes where Creff had fallen, but their friend did not lay there; someone had obviously been through the space already, most likely the monks. Tears welled once again in the corners of her eyes at the thought of Creff, but she brushed them away quickly. She needed to know more, and time was short.

"Groggle, is there anything you can think of that Rellion had said or done in case something like this happening? I mean, anything... you spent the most time with him." Kristane, in her desperation, knew she was grasping at straws.

"He told me stuff, but it was almost always just about how things worked and books and stuff." Holding his hands shoulder height to the sides and nodding his head, he said again. "You know... stuff." She did know only too well what Groggle was talking about; she knew a lot of similar stuff herself, but nothing important. She patted him on the shoulder and strolled towards the observation window at the rear of the Attic that doubled as the Abbey clock's face. Kristane almost thought she could see Rellion there, standing sentinel as always, looking out onto the city center. The uppermost face of the clock had the same brass and silver crescents and moon shapes as the other two faces that rotated about on scrolled arms. Some shapes moved across faster than others, intermittently impeding the view below.

"What were you always looking at, Rellion?" she said in a whisper, and then recalled the night before the festival. The night before her and the others' lives were turned upside down. His words came back to her: *It's called the Devil's Embrace, and it has not appeared in a very, very long time. The time is almost upon us...*

"Time?" Kristane continued to think aloud. "What else were you looking at?" She stared up into the sky, and then in and about the Celestial Orrery at the city center; and then she focused upon the arms of the Abbey clock directly in front of her as they ticked around and around.

'That had to be it! But which one or ones represented the moons yesterday?' she asked herself. "Groggle, come here a minute!"

Dropping a burnt book he was studying, he scampered over to her. Xander, noticing the excited tone in her voice, also came over to where she was examining the back of the clock face.

THE RELUCTANT MARTYR

"Groggle, you know about astronomy. Which one of these arms represents the moons yesterday afternoon during the eclipse… the rhyme… the Devil's Embrace?" Kristane could barely contain herself as she pointed to the many spheres and crescents that spun and overlapped one another; she knew this would mean something. Groggle first looked at her and mouthed an "Oh!" and then looked at the clock face.

"Which one, Groggle!"

"Hang on, I'm thinking…" Stepping back a few paces, Groggle stuck his thumb up in the air at arm's length and closed one eye. Focusing on first the sky and then the clock face, he did this several times, and then said. "Oh, yah! It would be in reverse! 'Cause it's meant to be seen from outside… you see?"

"Yah, yah, I get it, just which one?"

Taking a couple of pronounced paces, he sidestepped to the other side. With one eye closed and his thumb and arm still extended, he stumbled on some debris. Xander caught him and set him straight. He eyed it a couple more times and then said, "Here, these here would have been overlapping yesterday in this top position." He pointed to a crimson-patina copper sphere and an odd-looking black crescent that had moved drastically from where Groggle had indicated their position had been. So far, in fact, they were nearly passing from view and back into the rotation of the workings of the clock below the floor. Kristane supposed that if had it been an hour later they would have been gone, just as along the horizon before her, the real moons the spheres represented were retreating and being replaced by another sphere with a silver and black crescent upon the clock.

They crowded about the objects that Groggle pointed out. Now separated and following their own paths, the symbols didn't look particularly different from any other. After staring for several minutes, Kristane began to get disappointed; the more she looked at them, the more unremarkable they appeared to her. She stood and began to pace back and forth. *There must be something else, some answer here,* she thought.

"Hey! There's something here! Try finding a piece of paper and something to write with!" Groggle had remained squatted, examining the pieces; his curiosity had not waned like hers had.

"What? Where? I didn't see anything," Kristane said with agitation as she started to look about her for a piece of paper that wasn't already ash. But it was Xander who tore out a few of the mostly blank title pages from a book, their edges blackened by the fire.

Taking the pages from Xander, Groggle said. "Here! It's sort of a code punched through the metal. Still need something to write with." Keeping his eyes fixated on whatever it was that he had seen, as if in fear that it might vanish if he blinked, he grasped out backwards, his grubby hand opening and closing on nothing but air. Xander again was the one to provide something.

"Oh yah, yah, that'll work better anyways!" Taking his eyes away for a moment, he saw the charcoaled and cooled end of some bit of furniture that Xander had handed him. Taking the piece of paper, Groggle placed it behind the crimson sphere nearest the crystal glass face of the clock and began to rub the charcoaled tip back and forth against the metal facing him, creating an impression upon the paper. He handed the paper back to Kristane, who looked at it quizzically; it was nothing more than some short, random horizontal and vertical lines with curved symbols mixed in. Groggle then repeated the same process with the crescent symbol with another piece of paper. Handing this to Kristane also, he stood up, grinning at her.

Kristane stood there with the pages in either hand, staring down at the little lines and curves, and was at a complete loss. "What? I don't understand."

"You need to line them up like they were yesterday." Snatching the pages from her, he held them up to the glass, placing one page on top of the other. Using the sunlight that shone through, he twisted the pages around until he found the alignment he was looking for. "See?"

Kristane and Xander closed in on where Groggle indicated, and looked intently at what he had discovered. There, the curves and lines of the paper underneath bled through to the top page, spelling out an odd phrase.

"Broken was the heart, one half of virtue, the other of sin, strike the bearer upon the sword of sacrifice, then when blood reunited, will they be made whole again." Groggle repeated the phrase once more, slowly, and then handed the pages to Kristane.

"Groggle, does this make any sense to you?" Kristane hoped that he knew something, anything. Groggle was about to answer when there was just a barely perceptible TINK, TINK, TINK that came from somewhere above them.

Kristane quickly raised her hand to keep Groggle from speaking, and he and Xander followed her gaze to somewhere above the demolished dome. That bell and cat were now becoming a little too coincidental, and coming from the rooftop above them, very improbable, Kristane thought — but as she began to voice her concerns, another commotion drew their attention.

From the stairwell leading up to the Attic, several voices could be heard. Their first indication that the voices were close was a broomstick that appeared to bob up and down from someone holding it as they ascended the stairs. Kristane looked at Xander and stuffed the papers into one of her pockets; then they both grabbed Groggle by the arms.

Sprinting to the staircase that led to the rooftop, they dragged and pushed Groggle, shushing him every few seconds. As they triggered the door at the top of the stairs, an unearthly scraping echoed down the stairwell as the metal guardian slid to the side, exposing the rooftop. Well, if their pursuers had wondered where they were, there was no mistake now. Xander gave her a *can you believe it?* look and pushed Groggle out into the sunlight.

Scanning the rooftop, Kristane could have sworn she saw a glimpse of a short figure as it blended into the cover of one of the many spires of the Abbey. It was no time to be chasing shadows, though; the voices had been alerted, and their only-too-real pursuers were directly behind them. Kristane and Xander, still holding Groggle by either arm, contemplated him for half a second; he just returned their gaze, wide-eyed and full of apprehension.

"Well, there's nothing for it! Let's go!" Groggle set his jaw and grabbed the goggles upon his cap, placing them over his eyes. Kristane would have thought it comical in any other situation.

"What happened to your sacrificial martyrdom?" Xander said hurriedly, chuckling in spite of himself as he and Kristane rushed Groggle to the edge.

"I have since adopted a new philosophy of *live to fight another day*," Groggle panted with even greater anxiety.

"Do you really think those goggles will help?" Xander said, looking into the bug-eyed face of Groggle as he helped him over the edge of the rooftop.

"Can't hurt from this point, right?" Groggle said hopefully as his goggles briefly caught on the stone ledge. Xander straightened them for him, and Groggle dropped to a decorative outcropping just over the parapet wall. Xander clambered over as well, and steadied the teetering Groggle, who stood with his cheek pressed to the wall and his arms splayed out to either side.

Peering over the edge to where her brother and friend now stood precariously, Kristane commanded. "I'll distract them! Get him down!" Without another word, she sprinted to the stairwell, closing the distance between it and the rooftop ledge just as the familiar hats of the Briggers appeared. She hesitated a moment, ensuring that they had spotted her, and then sprinted away from where her twin was assisting Groggle from falling to his death. Fortunately, there weren't very many Briggers, and they all seemed to have taken the bait. Shouting the usual commands of "stop" and "halt" with a few foul words mixed in, they gave chase.

Kristane hurdled a series of low walls, her agility creating a greater distance between her and her struggling, less-fit pursuers. Reaching the outer edge of the Abbey wall, well away from Groggle and her brother, she checked for the ropes that she hoped would still be there. Sure enough, strung from the Abbey to several different buildings were ropes with festive, brightly colored banners in celebration of Hallow's End. Picking one that was relatively level, she jumped without hesitation over the edge, her feet landing surely upon the rope. Using it as a tightrope, moving one foot after the other, she descended the slightly downward pitch towards the building across Market Street.

Nearly halfway across, the elastic nature of the long rope became more pronounced, each step causing a greater wobble, and then the rope abruptly surged like a wave. Losing her footing, Kristane bounced down upon her backside; but using the slackened rope as a trampoline, she rebounded back up. Turning to see what had happened, she saw a pair of burly Briggers hung over the rooftop ledge attempting to unbalance her. Holding them from the back of their jackets were two others, yelling more obscenities and waving their free fists at her.

Swinging the rope back and forth from its anchor, they caused it to lurch one way and then another. With each swing, Kristane would simply bounce down and then back up again, adding in a backflip when they really got ahold of it at one point. Kristane's antics only enraged the Briggers further, and she had the distinct impression that this was no longer just a simple arrest. They wanted to do her real harm.

Deciding her time was limited until they either worked the anchor free from the wall or happened to notice Xander struggling to pull Groggle back over the edge of the Abbey, she somersaulted forward upon her shoulder and backside several times, causing the rope to steady until she reached the opposite side of Market Street. Clambering down from the eaves of the Enchanted Book, she gave a quick look back at her pursuers. Frustrated and angered with her escape, the Briggers had begun to quickly retrace their steps back across the Abbey roof.

Kristane ran to the broken doors of the Abbey, which Xander and Groggle were just exiting after making their escape thanks to Kristane's distraction. Xander had several scrapes on his forearms and face, and looked completely exhausted; no doubt it had been a herculean effort assisting Groggle back to the roof quickly and escaping through the Attic. For his part, Groggle didn't appear any worse for the wear, though his goggles were a little lopsided again.

"There isn't much time; they'll be coming after us," Kristane told them.

Xander nodded to a large, covered cart full of barrels that was making its way up the long strip of Market Street leading towards the Bizzarre, where they had planned on meeting Prya and Lathan, the cart being driven by a pair of monks. Kristane gave her a brother an appreciative nod and sly smirk. Each grabbed one of Groggle's arms and raced towards the slowly moving cart.

"Wait! Are you both mad!"

THE EYE BEHIND THE WATERFALL

Despite Taff's masterful technique of tacking against the wind, the trip back from the Isles of the Dead and the Manor Hall was taking twice the time it had taken to get there. The giant man sailed the small sluice close-hauled, with one massive arm on the tiller, working the lines of the single sheet sail first leeward and then to the reverse. Rellion sat at the bow of the craft, staring at the landless horizon as it ebbed with each arc of the Cerulean Sea. Nothing had been said between the two; Rellion had merely taken his present seat, and Taff had silently navigated them away from the Manor Hall.

Rellion could feel Taff's eyes boring into the back of his head with each successive luffing of the sail from port to starboard. "Master Brobdin, I shall ask that you take me to Kaer Kairos. There will be no reason for you to come ashore." Rellion spoke over his shoulder, addressing the giant by the realm of his origin as opposed to his given name. The realm and land of Brobdin lay to the far north of the city of Kairos, beyond the Strait of Goosh and the high mountains of Skookum.

"Not allowed to go there," the giant said pointedly, now staring off into the horizon at some unknown point.

"Why, Master Taff, I would never have mistaken you for such a law-abiding citizen!" Turning now to face Taff, Rellion continued, "But as you will not be accompanying me, you have little reason to fret." Placing his hand upon the rail, Rellion flashed the sunlight off his signet ring at Taff.

Ignoring the bit of light that caught his eyes, the giant replied, "Dangerous. That won't help you there," nodding to the railing and Rellion's hand.

"Why, I am quite taken aback that twice, in the span of two days, there should be yet another person concerned for my welfare! I find myself nearly speechless!"

"Doubtful," quipped the giant at Rellion's improbable loss for words. Rellion smiled; he was beginning to like this man more and more. "Don't care much, would be your end, your decision. Stories of what sleeps there, though; that is a concern." Taff broke from the point at which he was staring and met Rellion's smiling face.

"There are many stories and even more legends as to Kaer Kairos, the old seat of the throne, I assure you." Rellion paused briefly, contemplating something off into the distance. "I daresay some might even be true. To recite an old Brobdin proverb I once heard, though, *you cannot awaken someone or something that is pretending to be asleep.*"

Taff stared at Rellion, who had not dropped his smile, for a moment longer, and then with an audible "Umpf," he turned the tiller of the sluice to port and again fixed his gaze upon a point on the horizon.

Kaer Kairos was a centuries-old ruin that had stood longer than the city of Kairos and predated the Celestial Orrery. Rellion stepped from the sluice into the ankle-deep surf that foamed about his boots as Taff brought the craft in for landing. Taff barely waited for Rellion to step from the decking before he pulled a single oar from beneath his seat and retreated back into the surf. "Will wait for you out here. If you are not back by night-fall you're probably dead," the giant yelled back to Rellion in between the strokes that were taking him farther away.

"Again, Master Taff, your concern heartens me!" Calling back over his shoulder but still looking at the stone worked surface of the ancient castle, Rellion spun the ring on his finger with his thumb, with a touch of nervousness.

A deathly silence filled the spaces of the island castle; there was a noticeable lack of life. Even the gulls with their incessant squawking, infesting the skies above the twin bays of Mererid and Merrow several thousand yards away, stayed far clear of here. The crack of stones against one another as Rellion's boots dislodged them echoed unnecessarily loud against the ashlar- stoned walls that secured the castle and ran the entire length of the island around. To the east, the remains of an arched land bridge that had once led to the mainland crumbled slowly into the sea, each crash of the waves eroding away another piece of rock. Large gaps in the deck of the bridge made traversing it dangerous; gone were the days when an entire battalion could stride it from the island of the throne to the capitol city. Its pier supports and corbels looked more like lonely sentinels that jutted up from the surface of the water, ready to fall against one another like dominoes at any moment.

Rellion paced towards a section of the wall that had partially fallen in upon itself. The markings of heavy ballistic fire having once assaulted the walls blackened and pocked the area around the opening. Fragmented stone and shards of metal mixed to make the climb up over the debris difficult. Rellion warily eyed a rusting hulk of a cannonball whose fuse had failed as his cane inadvertently echoed against it, the resounding *ping* stopping him. It had no doubt laid dormant for the hundreds of years since this fortress was last assaulted. Rellion thought, *Truly, the very last assault there ever was.*

Breaching the summit of the rock, he scanned the terraced remains of Kaer Kairos, each plateau building to the pinnacled and magnificent castle that was silhouetted against the setting sun each evening that he so often viewed from the windows of his Attic. Rellion was relieved to see that the fortifying wall had fallen to both sides, leaving a slope he could transverse and not a long drop down.

A low rumbling filled the air, and Rellion could feel it vibrating up through his boots. "At least my arrival has been announced; best to get to this festive occasion and commence with the socializing." Rellion spoke to no one in particular, though he knew he was probably heard; he followed it by chuckling out loud with just a tinge of apprehension at a joke that only he would find funny.

Making his way through the labyrinthine walls and stairs that rose to each plateau, Rellion came to the royal courtyard, which on the scale of the castle of Kaer Kairos was more of a forest-like park complete with a lagoon, streams, and paths. Once, a small army of gardeners had tended to the royal courtyard; but centuries of overgrowth greeted Rellion now. Large trees sprouted up through the middle of the gray-rocked path, and creeping vines threatened to trip him with every step forward. Only here was there any sign of life upon the island; though mostly vegetation, there was the occasional quiet buzzing of an insect or the movement of the carpet of leaves as something scurried to an unseen hole.

Approaching the lake, a cascading waterfall fed into the pristinely clear water from an outcropping of a rocky ridge fueled by some aquifer far deep within the earth. Rellion gazed upon The Seven Falls, as they had once been called; eroded by time, the dense rock yet held. As the water splashed back and forth, pooling at each ledge, it was punctuated by countless mini- rainbows reflected within the misty water droplets.

"You stomp about as if you own the place, priest!" A low rumble emanated from across the lagoon at the base of the final fall, so loud and clear even the falling water did not muffle it.

"I am but a servant to those who long ago called this place home. My long absence should more than mark the fact that I claim no ownership to Kaer Kairos, your Lordship!" Rellion gave a graceful bow, removing his hat in a sweeping motion, but kept a steady eye across the lagoon, not for a moment dropping his gaze.

"Do you mock my tenancy?" The low growl gave an unmistakable warning. "From such a man of religion as yourself, who has long held his post in that monumental facade built upon the giving of others? What stewards have your efforts wrought after all these years?" A pair of eyes, one glowing fiery red, the other opaque white like a very large pearl, peered from behind the sheets of water that fell as Rellion returned to his prone stance.

"Your Lordship, I have not come to bicker and banter intellects or the failures of many, myself included. I come in search of understanding. No doubt your Lordship has seen what has transpired in the sky above just a night ago?"

"Those fairytales and nursery rhymes your kind hold so dear have reached my ears, and my one good eye still sees many things, High Priest Rellion. Isolation and solitude has given me a very clear perception of that which holds me here!" The voice behind the curtain of water hissed out his contempt with a quick flash of bared teeth and fangs. "Rel-li-on!" His Lordship drew out the name in a long hiss, as if his distaste of it was poison upon his tongue. "Your niceties do not hide your duplicity. I feel the derision you have for those you deem lesser than yourself!"

Just as the fading light of the sun was beginning to cast shadows upon the lagoon, Rellion began his reply; with a slight shifting of his weight, his one leg moved slightly backwards. He knew that the longer this parley progressed, the more his chances of walking away from it dwindled. He would need every fraction of a second he could get. The problem was that the beast that still lay hidden undoubtedly had sensed the movement.

"My Lord Thran, I quite assure you that those fairytales have in fact come to pass. The Forgotten Ones have once again risen, and it shall be the doom of *all* should they awaken him. Your part in this is of your own choosing; I take no responsibility for what is now your task. I only come to see your resolve, be it voluntary or because the sin committed and the curse of the sword of sacrifice holds." Rellion knew that he was treading upon extremely dangerous ground; but knowing where Lord Thran of the Dragons stood in the coming storm was vital.

"Meddle no longer, priest! My penance is my own and not for your contemplation!" The large snout and head of Thran rose through the curtain of water, revealing the darkened den of the beast. Thran's razor-edged fangs snapped at the air, the girth of his mouth large enough to swallow a pair of horses whole. Crouching lower, preparing to pounce, Thran menacingly whispered a cadence that was familiar to Rellion. "From a place unremembered and long forgot, will come the peril that others have wrought; there too grows the poisoned tree with its red-leafed cowl, where long ago did happen a deed most foul."

Rellion stared directly at the Lord of the Dragons and spoke quietly. "Evermore the King's grace will be sought…"A bit of a jab at Thran, but he could hardly help himself, at least now he was assured of what the answer to his question was.

"Enough, priest! This day, I will be your peril!"

Rellion had not waited for the threat to be completely uttered. As Thran's massive body and retracted wings burst forth from his hidden den, he had already broken into a dead sprint, retracing his footsteps back to the rocky beach where he had landed hours before. Rellion dodged along the gray stone path, avoiding the trees and vines that blocked a straight line, doing his best to stay within the long shadows being cast by the landscape. He could hear the pronounced splashing of Thran as he crossed the lagoon. His roaring voice shook the trees about him, and the strewn pebbles along the path vibrated with each ferocious outburst. "Priest! Priest!"

Scrambling up the embankment that marked the hole through which he had passed into the old kingdom, Rellion could feel the heat of the dragon's fire behind him as it burned indiscriminately at any surface where Thran issued forth his anger. His boots reached the edge of the water as the small waves lapped up and over the top of them. Quickly scanning for his escape, his attention was called back to the crumpled wall behind him. Thran had just breached the top of the debris, his winged hands grasping each side of the mortar wall, the span of his body filling the entire opening. Meeting Rellion's eye, he smirked with a confident look of triumph.

Rellion raised his cane, the pommel glowing in the dying light of the day, its energy building within. But instead of pointing it at Thran, he directed the fiery blast at the ancient cannonball he had nearly tripped over hours before. The reaction was delayed, but the accompanying concussive blast sent him flailing backward far into the surf. Rellion's last glimpse before he was submerged was of the great dragon writhing in and amongst the flames and stone debris, his last blast of flame, meant for Rellion, waving wildly in the darkening sky.

As Rellion's head broke the surface and he was buffeted backwards with the surge, there was the hollow sound of a bump against wood. "Sorry about that; was checking to see if you were alive."

Rellion shook his head and spit water out of his mouth. "Why, Master Taff, but you are dependable and a man of your word! Barely did I dare think that you would remain, with the many fireworks of the afternoon."

"You didn't pay me yet," Taff said plainly, offering his hand and pointing back over Rellion's head with the other. "Don't you think you should hurry?" Thran was in the process of dislodging himself from the heap of wall that had fallen further.

"Worry not, my good man, his wings were clipped long ago."

"You're thinking he cannot swim either?"

"No, no, there is something else that holds him there…" Rellion heaved himself further into the boat with Taff's assistance, the giant now grabbing him from the back and dragging him into the sluice. Rellion rolled over on his side, smiling up at the large man. "I will tell you, Master Brobdin, that serpent's temper has not improved over the years."

Grabbing a line and hoisting the sail, Taff replied, "Thinking you bring that out in some; last group didn't seem too happy to see you either."

"Ha! Why, Master Taff, you are quite the comedian! Truth be known, it is hard to say which meeting of the two was actually more dangerous."

Stoically, Taff took his seat at the tiller. "We headed back to Kairos now?"

"Yes, my good man. There are some wards of mine I must now attend to."

ROSE PLIESEIS

Your Privileges Have Been Revoked

Kristane and the others dropped from the monk's cart, rejoining with Lathan and Prya at the elevated street car station near the Tunnels where they had first embarked that morning. Prya had been to see the doctor; Steven Ridley had turned out to be quite the benefactor. She held up her arm, showing the others the shiny, plated articulations of gears and pins that formed a framework about her fingers and continued up to her bare shoulder, her shirt having been cut back for the apparatus to be molded to her olive skin.

"Can you believe how pretty it is? I mean, look at it, Kristane!" Where others might find the situation difficult or unappealing, Prya was positively excited. She flexed the exoskeletal musculature around and around with barely a whisper of the mechanics creaking. "And look, look, he really ratcheted it up!" Striding over to one of the cast-iron benches, she lifted it effortlessly, the pedestals scraping against the cobbled pavement with the upward motion. "He said a lady should be able to defend herself!"

"Wow! That *is* amazing! I bet it's the levers along your forearm that make the elbow act like a fulcrum, but… Wow! It's precise; there can't be any friction!" Groggle was nearly as gleeful as Prya. He had ran up to her as she sat down the bench, his eyes just inches from her arm, taking in the entire apparatus. "The effort force is minimal to the actual resistance. I wonder how much…"

"God! Groggle, don't slobber all over me!" Prya gave the boy a little shove back, his face so close his breath was steaming up the metal plates of the connections as he quoted yet another book he had probably read somewhere.

Groggle gave an enthusiastic apology. "Sorry, it's just, wow!" Kristane had to agree with Groggle; she was amazed by the display of strength, and the Doctor had obviously outdone himself in the overall craftsmanship. The brassy-colored metal looked like it could withstand any punishment, and really did suit Prya.

Kristane looked over at Lathan as Groggle goggled at Prya's arm and continued to ramble on. Lathan stood slightly apart from them, and looked decidedly dejected. She wondered as to his temperament, but then, as always, she caught the look that Xander was giving her and realized that they were lingering too long. "Come on, everyone, we need to get back to the Bizzarre."

The crowd of revelers had not dissipated in their absence. They still found themselves pushing through as onlookers watched yet another display of something fascinating. Ambling towards Rotten Luck Remy's gambling hall, they were met by the sight of Cayson sitting on the steps, his leg outstretched before him, his head in his hands. Purdy the Faerrian buzzed around Cayson's head, his fur reddish with agitation. Kristane looked up to the top step to find Remy looking back at her, flanked by the giant men who tended the door to the Bizzarre. Purdy, noticing Kristane, quickly fluttered over and perched himself upon her shoulder, humming into her ear oddly, his attitude still put out and directed at those standing above them.

"What's happening here, Cayson, Rott… I mean, Remy?" Kristane caught herself mid-sentence as a shadow passed over Remy's polite smile. She figured — most likely correctly — that just maybe, while most people *referred* to him as Rotten Luck Remy, no one really ever called him that to his face. "I mean, I'm sorry, Mr. Symmes, but what's going on?" She motioned with her hands in Cayson's direction.

"I am afraid that your privileges as my guests have been revoked. A great deal has transpired since we last spoke; it appears the events of last night and the disappearance of your most esteemed mentor have set things in motion. Pieces are moving among the leadership of the religious and political game boards." Remy hitched his smile back in place and continued his polite rapport. "Your friend is not harmed, and all manner of etiquette was followed; I owe Rellion that much." Though his smile did not waver, Kristane could tell that Rotten Luck Remy did not enjoy owing anyone anything.

"But I still don't understand… and what about Rellion?" Kristane replied pleadingly.

"Word has been given that those who craved power have taken this opportunity to seize it. While I do not cater to their precepts normally, how should I say it? Hmm... our relationship is symbiotic." Remy straightened his jacket and brushed at some imaginary specks of dust as he took a few steps down nearer to Kristane. As his men began to follow him, he held a hand up, stopping their descent. Motioning for the Rogue to come nearer, Remy leaned into them, eyeing a point over their heads. "Rumor would have that Rellion was seen leaving the Abbey with a great deal of fanfare." Kristane and the others gave a little gasp and started to say something, but Remy quieted them. "He has not been seen since." Rotten Luck turned his attention to the group eyeing each of the Rogue in turn. "While your association to Rellion has never been without its risks, the danger is closer at hand than you might think. There are those who wish to ask you a number of questions, and I believe none too politely. So much so, a large portion of *tithing* has been dedicated to it." Remy indicated back behind them with his eyes. "No, do not turn around!" Clenching his teeth, the words just an undertone, Kristane heard the unmistakable roll of large barrels along the stone — the monks delivering their wares of whiskey.

Straightening back up, Remy grabbed hold of his jacket lapels with either hand and pushed out his chest pompously. "The rules of the Bizzarre stand. There will be no outside business conducted within its boundaries, but that is where my influence ends." Pausing briefly, Remy pulled his monocle and a handsomely colored handkerchief from his vest pocket and began to slowly polish its lens. "Now, if someone were looking for me to answer some questions and I wished to refuse their companionship, I would go where they would not follow." Speaking airily, Remy turned his gaze to the darkened tunnels that branched off of the main hub in which they stood.

Kristane looked about herself at her friends. "Thank you, Mr. Symmes. We understand."

"Please, it is Remy; there is no need for formalities among friends." Again giving them his polite smile and returning to his perch on the topmost step, he made it clear that they had been dismissed.

Together, Xander and Lathan hoisted up Cayson; he seemed to be able to stand on his own, though he was still a little wobbly. Kristane did not need to look around to understand the eyes that were watching them. Each of them had already felt the slight prickling at their necks, a sense developed over a childhood of stealing and avoiding being caught. Remy's message of a bounty upon them was clear, but Kristane wondered at his cryptic message of 'a tithing.' *The only tithing I know of comes to the Abbey, but how could they be involved?*

Raising his hand and snapping his fingers, Remy interrupted Kristane's thoughts. "Oh, I almost forgot one more thing. If you would take charge of this pair...? They have had a fair run of it, but the dice have not been kind to them this morning."

Mr. Black came through the gambling house doors with his back to them, carrying something in each of his hands. Whatever it was, he was having some difficulty holding onto it. Turning to face the assembled group, Mr. Black held up two small boys by the scruffs of their jacket collars. The pair were kicking and swinging as the giant man held them just out of range of personal harm, not that that was a concern.

"Frickin 'unster! Put us down! U' dalcop arse!" The Kressley brothers, Markyn and Munse, were unmistakable despite them being adorned in brand new suits. Their ginger hair even looked washed and combed for a change, but they had retained their old cap and bowler, which sat lopsided on their heads from the violent tantrum they were throwing. In between the insults they were casting, puffs of smoke came from the boys' cigar and pipe, still clenched tightly in their teeth.

"Wotcher, mates!" Cayson's fierce outburst startled Kristane and the others, mostly because it had been so long since they heard more than groaning and moaning from him.

The Kressley brothers instantly stopped their frantic swinging, and fell silent and limp in Mr. Black's grasp. Pushing their hats out of their eyes and then looking shyly at each other, they turned in unison and gave Cayson a timid and downcast look. "Oh, hey, 'ayson, we're 'orry. We were 'fraid...."

The Cat That's Not a Cat

"You're sorry? You were afraid?" Cayson yelled at the pair as the giant tossed the brothers down the stairs and they landed in an unceremonious heap at his feet. Even with the din that echoed in the cavernous Tunnels, Cayson's reprimand had drawn some unwanted attention. People had begun to give the reunited members of the Rogue and the spectacle they were causing a wider birth.

Xander grabbed hold of the delinquent brothers as they attempted to run back at Mr. Black and extract some form of revenge for their treatment. "Leggo, 'ander! Goin' to mess 'em!" Markyn yelled, while his brother Munse resorted to his favorite insults and was spitting and flipping double fingers at Mr. Black. The giant laughed boisterously and turned and followed the already retreating Rotten Luck Remy into the interior of the Bizzarre. Without a focus for their tirade, the brothers quickly calmed themselves, and once more took a sheepish stance in front of Cayson as he stared vehemently at them.

"Come on, everyone, we stick together." Kristane waited for some form of protest from at least a couple members of the group, but to her surprise, none came. As they traipsed across the length of the great expanse, an occasional pair of eyes would unexpectedly follow them. For a group that was used to walking in shadows, barely being noticed, they all became slightly unnerved by the scrutiny.

"So, which way do we go? I mean, how many are there, and then what? Eeny, meeny, miny, moe…." Prya closed her eyes and pointed randomly in the general direction of the gaping tunnel mouths before them.

Kristane was at a loss; though Prya had made light of their predicament, she wasn't wrong. None of them had any idea what to do next. They were taking the advice of someone they barely knew and whose motives were questionable. Kristane looked at Groggle, and he gave her a little shrug; he and the rest of their band seemed to be waiting for her to make a decision. She mused that decisions had been a lot easier not even two days ago, when all she worried about was liberating enough money to get something to eat and a place to sleep. When a mistake only meant an uncomfortable night sleeping outside atop the Abbey roof, or at worse, being chased around the city by Briggers. Here, standing before the unknown, scared her; making a decision that would possibly harm any of the people with her terrified her. There was so much they didn't know; so much so that if someone would just *tell* them, could they even understand? She found herself longing for Rellion to just yell at them to *Hurry up and get out of bed!* for the day. *Could he really be alive?*

"Pardon, little ones, before you embark." The booming voice of Mr. Black startled Kristane and the others, a testament to how out of place they all must be, that such a large man could approach any of them unawares. "It is the wish of the proprietor of the Bizzarre that you should accept this parting favor." The giant man held forth several motheaten packs, each with a ratty blanket secured with twine.

The Kressley brothers promptly went into a recitation of offensive insults. "Consarn u 'onster! U tallowcatch beast!" Mr. Black gave a sort of bemused smirk and tossed a single pack at the brothers. "You two are very small, you share." It was all Xander could do to hold the two back from rushing forward. Mr. Black just stood there with the same bemused look on his face.

"Ah, thank you, Mr. Black. Favor?" Kristane asked.

Glancing over his shoulder and lowering his voice so as not to be overheard, the giant replied, "A gift, young miss. Mr. Symmes wishes you well, and hopes your courage will hold. Only should there come a time that you might remember his graciousness." Kristane looked down at the well-worn pack and gave him a quizzical look. "I did say graciousness, young miss, not generosity." Grinning broadly and without another word, he turned, and shortly all they could see was the back of his head moving away, high above the pack of revelers.

Kristane slung the pack over her shoulder and decided to pick the tunnel directly in front of her, reasoning that this one seemed to smell the least. The rest followed her lead, with Xander giving the Kressley brothers a bit of a shove.

The tunnel was musty, but not overly damp. Some of their packs contained oblong cylinders of glass that glowed a radiant green. The small amount of light they generated gave everyone a sickly complexion, but it was enough to keep them from tripping over each other and the ground in front of them. Groggle had rambled on for several minutes about glowing mushrooms sealed in glass bulbs by glass blowers, and how the old miners had once used these same makeshift lanterns to get around. Kristane thought by the look of the one she was holding that it most likely was the very same one that some long-ago miner had used. The glass was dark with age, and a minuscule crack leaked something, giving off a weird trail of dusty light as it waved back and forth in her hand. It was only when the Kressleys became agitated at hearing about mushroom-cap varieties and which scales gave off the most light that a small shouting match broke out, and Groggle shut up.

The group trudged into the depths, and as the pitch of the floor began to decline, it seemed as if they were falling forward with each step. At this level, the rails and ties of the abandoned mine were twisted and broken from some long-ago tremor. Not once had they found another branch leading off the main line. In any case, Kristane had already decided to herself that they would not risk any detours that would cause them to lose their way. She hoped this was just a temporary hiding place, and planned to go only so far that no one followed them.

It was just as Groggle began to grunt and groan that they reached a connection point where serval other tunnels led off into impenetrable darkness. Standing just beyond the threshold of the tunnel into the widened hub, their feeble lights couldn't find the ceiling above. Kristane felt very lost in the void. A sense of vertigo grasped at her chest, and she had to turn her eyes downward to the floor to keep from stumbling. Prya gave a little gasp, and she had to steady herself against Lathan. Directing their lights, they barely illuminated the other connecting tunnel branches to either side of them.

"Smell that? Must be an air shaft up there somewhere." Groggle was peering up into the darkness. Kristane hadn't noticed just how bad the air smelt inside the tunnel they were walking in until he said something. A slight cool breeze passed across her face, giving her skin a chill and causing the small hairs on the back of her neck to stand on end.

Kristane was exhausted, and she imagined, though she couldn't see it, that the sun had about set for the day. Shaking off the chill and the apprehension that had been mounting, she made an executive decision. "This is it for now. We stay close to this tunnel. Lathan and Prya, take the brothers and grab some of those busted up rail ties for a fire. Prya can yank out the stuck ones." Markyn and Munse eyed Prya and then gave Kristane a defiant look, but quickly complied as Xander stepped closer and peered over Kristane's shoulder at them. "No one strays far from right here, and no one goes anywhere alone." Of what Kristane could see of her friends' expressions, the warning probably wasn't necessary.

"Kris, looking through all the packs, we've got a little food and enough water to last a day or two, and if we're lucky we won't catch anything from sleeping on these blankets." Xander gave one of the blankets a quick shake and a little more than dust fell to the ground. "Doubt that anyone would follow us here, but I'm not so sure we're completely safe. The bounty that Rotten Luck talked about only adds to the number of those hunting us."

Kristane's hand moved to the pendant that hung about her neck, and then she gave Purdy a little pat from his perch upon her shoulder. "I know. We just need to lie low and make a plan. If what Remy said was true and Rellion is alive, he's the only one who can give us some answers."

"That's if he *will* give them to us, Kris… after all we've seen and heard, there are secrets upon secrets, and Rellion has never been known for his ability to share."

"It's different now…"

TINK, TINK, TINK. The words stuck in Kristane's throat as the sound that had become all too familiar to her echoed from somewhere in the darkness. Purdy gave a little shudder and snarled softly as his wide eyes swiveled about. Wide-eyed herself, Kristane said in a hushed whisper. "Xander, that's not just a cat. Someone has been following us."

PRETTY GIRL, PRETTY NECKLACE

Kristane told Xander of all that she had observed and suspected, their conversation going relatively unnoticed by the others as the fire crackled and popped. Groggle and Lathan were occupied with Prya's feats of strength as she bent a steel rail into a circle, the creaking resounding about the cavern as the rail buckled. Opposite of them, with their heads bunched together, Cayson whispered to the Kressley brothers, occasionally giving Kristane a furtive glance; but she had too much on her mind to worry about whatever it was they were plotting.

Xander nodded to Kristane as she stood to address the group. "All right, let's try and get some rest. We need to take the watch in shifts. Cayson, you're up first, Lathan next; I'll take the last one."

Cayson grumbled something under his breath, but hobbled over to the opening of the tunnel and gingerly slid down the curved wall, keeping his injured leg straight. One by one, the rest of them shook out their blankets and took places about the blazing fire. Markyn settled onto his blanket, his head on one end, his brother Munse's at the other, their legs kicking at each other, trying to win more space for themselves somewhere in the middle. It wasn't long before the crackle and pop of the fire was punctuated by the snoring of the exhausted deep sleep of the entire group.

Cayson sat looking about himself as the fire slowly died, the embers giving off a small circular glow about the others as they lay sleeping. He pulled the miner's light from his pocket and stared at the faint green glow it emitted. He knew he should get up and throw some more wood on the fire, but his leg was stiff, and he told himself that stupid pointy-ear Lathan could take care of it when it was his turn. "Ugh, we'll see what happens when we find Rellion and my leg is better. Kristane won't be so bossy then," Cayson muttered under his breath. The glow of the light in his hand was fading. He blinked himself awake once or twice, but slowly his head fell forward, his chin to his chest. The light rolled out of his hand into his lap, and he was fast asleep.

A small figure watched from just outside the shadows of the dying fire. He had waited patiently as they fell asleep, silent as a mouse. He had been watching them for a number of days: the pretty blonde girl with the pretty necklace, the thing with wings, the one with the pointy ears, the foul-mouthed ones, the little strong one that had scared him, the smart one, the big one, and the complainer. He counted them off on his grimy fingers, which were long and tapered. He counted them three more times. He moved cautiously toward the pretty girl with the necklace, slightly hunched over, his legs bent, which masked his height. Reaching the halo of light that barely shone from the popping embers of the fire, he dropped to the ground and began to crawl on his belly, wiggling closer. She was breathing softly, her eyes fluttering as if dreaming deeply. He counted each ragamuffin one more time. He could see the chain of the pretty necklace, which he reached out for very slowly.

"Ahhh! She's awake, she's awake!" Kristane had popped her eyes open, wide awake, and seized the wrist of the intruder. Xander came rolling off of his blanket and pinned the thief's skinny body to the ground with all his weight. "No, no, he's too big, he hurts its!" Scrambling with a quickness that Xander hadn't expected, the slight figure rolled and squirmed out from under him, but Kristane hadn't slackened her hold. "Let go, pretty girl, let its go! Only wanted to see!" The intruder started to pull at his own wrist with his other hand, dragging Kristane along into the darkness. Purdy swooped in towards him, beating him about the head with his wings and scratching at him with his talons. "No, flappy-flappy, fly away! Leave its alone!"

The rest of the group had awakened at the commotion. Cayson tried to stand too quickly and just fell over. The brothers got tangled up in each other, and started rolling around punching each other. Groggle and Lathan stared around, rubbing the sleep from their eyes; it was only Prya that seemed to see what was happening and take action. As she ran to help, Xander had gotten hold of the invader's upper arm, and she grabbed the other.

"Owwwww! Owwww! Why little girl so strong? You are hurting its!" At this, the intruder's body went limp, and he began to blubber and sob uncontrollably. "Plee-ease! Don't hurt its!"

Lathan gathered himself and threw more of the splintered wood rails on the fire, stoking it so that the flames burned bright. Kristane relinquished her hold on their captive as he dropped to his knees, both Prya and Xander having a good hold of him. She bent down to better see his face, and he meekly looked up at her. His hair was matted with dried dirt and some kind of slime, and she could barely see his face from all of the mud that was caked there; but his eyes, a light blue-gray, shone brightly and danced with firelight.

"Why have you been following us?" Kristane began in a demanding tone, but at the meek look on the intruder's face and the tears washing away some of the mud in streaks down his cheeks, she finished her sentence a little more kindly.

"Pretty girl, pretty necklace," he replied quietly, his eyes still glistening.

"Who are you? What's your name?" Kristane took in the rest of the young man subdued in front of her. Though it was tough to see through all the grime, he couldn't be any older than the rest of them. His clothing was ratty and frayed and just as dirty as the rest of him, but there was a certain nobility to the tailoring and muted coloring. The embroidered half-coat was cut with differing shapes at the hems, and adorned with tassels of varying hues and jeweled necks.

"Name?" His eyes took on a faraway dreamy look, and his brow furrowed in consternation.

"Yes, what are you called?" Kristane thought he really was quite pathetic.

"Its is called… Pip." Kristane nodded at him encouragingly; he seemed to be fighting some internal battle as he struggled to form the word. "Its is called… its name is Pip… Pipkin!" Both joy and relief washed across his face. "Yes, Pipkin!" Pipkin gave the biggest smile, and with a childish voice, exclaimed, "Pipkin! Pipkin, Pipkin!"

"Okay, Pipkin, good, good, now calm down a little," she said, holding her hands up to calm him. "Why are you following us?"

"Why follow?" Kristane again nodded encouragingly and returned his smile. "Pretty girl, pretty necklace!" Pipkin again gave a huge smile, and awkwardly clapped his semi-restrained hands together in front of himself, fingers splayed and with his palms together, like a small child who was celebrating an accomplishment. Kristane stood and gave an exasperated look at him; Pipkin continued to grin at her with joy.

"Kris, we can't just let him go." Xander loosened his grip a little on the young man and looked intently at his sister. He knew that she was already feeling sorry for him.

"I know, but I think he could be of some help. He surely knows his way around down here, anyway." She looked down at Pipkin and was struck by some inspiration. Donning a caring smile, she said. "So, Pipkin, we're going to play a little game. It's called Briggers and Thieves. You're going to play the thief, and I'm the Brigger, so I need to tie you up for just a little bit. Okay?"

"Pipkin likes to play games! He likes games very much!" Clapping his hands together, Pipkin bounced up and down on his knees exuberantly.

Soon after, Pipkin sat restrained next to Kristane at the edge of the fire, the twine from their packs wrapped about his wrists and ankles. He was swaying and serenely humming a tune to himself that sounded oddly similar to the drinking song at the Chymist that Count Bobo sang.

"What do you mean, we're taking it with us?" Cayson seemed to have found his voice again. "You can't trust that thing! He's gone around the turn, and he's completely cuckoo!"

Kristane couldn't argue with that one; Pipkin was in fact more than a bit off-kilter. "I don't care. He needs our help and we need his. He obviously knows his way around down here. What were you expecting? We'd just parade through the middle of the Bizzarre and dance along King's Way? And stop calling him a 'thing' or 'it'!"

"He calls himself that!" Markyn and Munse chuckled out loud at Cayson's outburst and puffed on their tobacco, adding to the rising smoke of the fire. They and the rest had given up on sleep with all of the excitement, and were now watching Kristane and Cayson exchange barbs like a game of hot potato.

"Well he doesn't anymore, do you, Pipkin?"

Pipkin stopped humming and turned to Kristane. "Pipkin thinks that one complains a lot," he said, pointing his tied hands in the general direction of Cayson. The others did their best to stifle their laughs.

"Oh and that's not crazy?"

Kristane half choked back a chuckle herself. "We have bigger problems, Cayson. We need to find a safer place and some food and water."

"Eats? Eats? Pipkin shares with his friends!" Pipkin smiled broadly about the circle at everyone, but gave a disgusted look to Cayson as his eyes fell upon him. "Well, Pipkin will shares, anyway."

A MEETING WITH THE ESTEEMED

The sun inched its way across the land bridge that led to the ruins of Kaer Kairos, separating the twin bays of Merrow and Mererid. Rellion gazed out at the high rolling hills that greeted travelers to the city of Kairos; the brightly painted row houses that were muted the night that they had departed were now glistening in their full splendor this morning. Purples, blues, reds, and yellows, no two houses the same shade. The silence between the two men in the sluice had not been broken since leaving the island castle of Kaer Kairos. *How many years has it been since I've seen the bay from this perspective? Far too long,* Rellion mused; but then, had he ever really looked at it? *Funny how one could get so full of the path before them and not really see it.* "What say you, Master Taff? Is it not a sight to behold?"

The giant man grunted and said, "Seen better."

"In your many travels?" Rellion, turning away from the landscape, pointedly looked at the markings that dotted the man's semi-exposed forearms. Taff gave Rellion a look, but this time did not bother to cover the intricate scrolling. Breaking from the smiling stare of Rellion, Taff looked above Rellion's head to the docks of Mererid Bay.

"Seems like you have some more admirers," Taff indicated with a nod of his head.

"And what makes you believe they're here for me?" Rellion did not bother to turn around; he had already anticipated what might be waiting for him upon his return.

Taff shrugged his massive shoulders, "Lucky guess. You going to be needing some help? Could for a few more coins."

"No, Master Brobdin, no need for you to be detained or harmed on my account." Taff gave Rellion an incredulous glare. Rellion laughed out loud. "All right, all right, let's say there is no reason for harm to come to all of these men, then. There will come a time when all must choose a side against the gathering storm, and not all of their hearts are corrupt just yet." Rellion turned his attention to the throng of Briggers and garishly dressed others that lined the docks, a placid-looking man in long robes seemed to be giving them instruction. "Though some may be farther along than I thought." Rellion contemplated the man; even at this distance, the weak-shouldered and lanky man was easily picked out amongst the others. "It is merely a necessary diversion from my appointed task. Besides, I am all out of money." Rellion patted the exterior pockets of his jacket.

"Doesn't sound like it."

"You have keen hearing, my very large man, so listen carefully to this. I will ask that you take this trinket into your safekeeping and pass on a message to the Dame of the *Lady's Grace*." Rellion motioned to remove his signet ring, but the ring was not budging over his knuckle, so long had it been worn. "Your markings, Master Taff, are unmistakable to those who know them." Ceasing his tugging for a moment, he pointed at Taff's arms. Unconsciously, the giant took a quick glance at his arm and looked as though he might say something, but remained quietly watching Rellion. "I know who you sail with, and that your assistance was not just about a few extra crawns in your pocket. Return to your Captain; she will most sincerely wish to know where it is that I have traveled." Rellion smiled and returned to tugging at his ring. Taff's expression did not change.

"Now, if you would assist me with this, my good man." Presenting his hand, he gave the giant an expectant look. Taff reached into the cuff of his boot, brandishing an otherwise unseen long knife. Half-laughing, Rellion said, "Thank you, but I believe just a quick pull will suffice, Master Taff.

I am quite fond of this finger, and will be needing it later so that when I retrieve my ring, it has a place to sit." Taff eyed the point of his knife a moment longer, then stuck it back into his boot. With a quick pull on Rellion's finger, the ring came free.

So many boats were entering and exiting the harbor at this time of the morning that as the small sluice pulled up to the docks, Rellion's ascent onto the graying and barnacle-encrusted planks all but went unnoticed. Rellion watched as Taff's sluice pulled away and was quickly swallowed by the boat traffic within the bay. Turning to a company of Briggers that was in the process of searching boats and sailors, Rellion marched forward his arms spread wide and announced to those along the dock, "Gentlemen, I do believe that you will find that I am the man you're looking for!" Rellion tipped his hat and mockingly presented his arms with his wrists pressed together before him. "Master Lawkeepers, you may now take me into custody! Take me to someone in charge!"

Those along the dock, both Briggers and sailors alike, just stood and stared at the spectacle that Rellion was creating, so taken aback by his sudden appearance and declaration that they were unsure how to proceed. It was a rare occasion indeed when someone just surrendered to them. After a moment or two, though, one Brigger regained himself and, mustering those around him, they did in fact take Rellion into custody.

Rellion was pushed forward along the dock, his hands now manacled. A gathering of the Council of Stewards encircled the long-robed man along the promenade; each was listening intently to whatever that the man was saying. The half-dozen or so Stewards only broke apart as the man nodded to the approaching Briggers and their detainee.

"Ah, a gathering of the esteemed! Truly an honor to be so close to your Lordships! But how can it be that you aren't at each other's throats?" He eyed the robed man who had taken a position behind the assembled group. Rellion had already recognized the lanky frame of Cristobal Zekel, the priest from the Abbey whom he had repeatedly humiliated. "Of course, what else could bring such persons together but faith, and the promise of seemingly unlimited tithes from the devoted?"

"From whom we seek council does not concern the likes of you." A large, portly man, nearly comical in appearance, addressed Rellion first. His jowls quivered with the effort of speech, each word uttered at great cost, as if every breath he took in between words might be his last. Rellion knew of the man: the well-named Lord Oscar Piggleback. His reputation for deceit and masked treachery amongst his own had a storied past. "We are told you are responsible for the destruction at the Abbey."

"Since guilt has been established without due process, and I see that you are acting as judge, jury, and presumably executioner... then, why yes, your Lordship, in a way, one could say that I am responsible."

"You do not deny your complicity with your trained band of thieves to undermine the Council of Stewards and spread discord amongst the populace through heresy and trickery?" Piggleback pointed a chubby accusing finger at Rellion.

Laughing boisterously, Rellion replied. "Heresy and trickery, your Lordship? Though I do think much of myself, my influence in such matters is not as great as that of others." Cristobal, for the first time, peered over the handkerchief he was dabbing at his nose from his position behind the Stewards, making eye contact with Rellion with a self-satisfied smirk.

Rellion, his wrists still cuffed, made a circle with his arms and blew out his cheeks again, addressing the fat man before him. "Your Lordship's immense significance far outweighs mine."

Lord Piggleback nearly popped the gold buttons off his bright-pink patterned vest, which was already taxed near to bursting trying to hold in his tremendous girth. His face turned varying shades of red as he blustered in anger, "You dare! You dare! Lock this... take him away...." Piggleback never quite got the rest of his tantrum out before being overcome by a fit of breathlessness, but the Briggers got the general idea of his intent and marched Rellion away. Rellion noticed, in passing, Cristobal's searching gaze at his hand, specifically his ring finger.

Sing All Day and Play All Night

Pipkin, the boy that they'd found in the lower tunnels, sat singing a tune over and over. Kristane believed he probably did it because it annoyed Cayson the most. She had tired of it too, but all the same, it was sweet. It spoke of friends and love and was never the same tune twice. "We sing all night and play all day, we have fun right from the start; we are the one and the other, and you hold the key to our heart!"

They hadn't gotten any information out of him other than his name, and he seem not to understand how he had gotten down into the mine. Pipkin had led them through a series of tunnels to a rusty fan vent, which was creaking and slowly turning as it pushed out the deadly gasses that seeped up through the rocks. A single blade was three times the size of Kristane. It was there that they found a passage that led further into the darkness.

Take the fun way, yes? Pipkin likes the fun way! His childish voice played back in Kristane's head.

Pipkin hadn't waited for them to answer; he'd just jumped down into a tube-like slide, worn smooth by water that flowed from the surface. After a brief discussion as to whether they might make it back without their vanished guide, they had decided to follow Pipkin. Xander had had to grab Groggle and drag him kicking and screaming into the gap, and the others reluctantly followed. Kristane had brought up the rear; she could hear the mixture of nervous laughter and whooping interspersed with Groggle's screaming echoing back to her. Tucking Purdy into the front of her jacket and whispering soothingly into his ear, she pushed off from the tunnel lip.

It was hard to say how far they slid into the darkness, but soon the sounds of the others' voices were replaced by falling water. Kristane barely got a glimpse of the cavern into which she was falling. Purdy had struggled loose, and took flight just before she hit the water. As her head surfaced from the large pool she had fallen into, the darkness gave way to a semi-lit cavern. Purdy continued to swoop around her head in circles; the others had already begun making for the edge of the water. The cavern was lit from several air shafts that couldn't have been as far from the surface as the other cavern. Groggle speculated that they were a great distance east of Kairos, within the mountain range that made up the old mines.

"You hold the key to our heart!" Pipkin brought Kristane back from her musings with a long, drawn-out rendition of what she thought was probably the chorus to his little song.

"Would you shut it! You are driving us mad with that noise!" Cayson was having a hard time holding it together around Pipkin. They had been here in this secluded cavern for what seemed to Kristane nearly a fortnight. She had tried to count the days as the light disappeared from the shafts above, but she wasn't really sure anymore. Being idle for so long was raking on everyone's nerves.

"Pipkin likes the noise… *And I don't think it's very nice for friends to interrupt friends!*" Kristane shuddered a little at Pipkin's response. He had started to occasionally drop from his child-like temperament into someone completely different, usually about mid-sentence. Always very quickly, though, he would once again return to his innocent behavior, not seeming to be aware that anything had taken place. "But Pipkin will stop if his friends want him to." Pipkin looked slightly dejected, and just hummed quietly to himself, muttering occasionally and peeking up to where Cayson and the Kressley brothers were in conversation. "Pipkin is quiet, Pipkin is like a mouse…"

She had insisted on setting Pipkin free from his straps, mostly because he had escaped from them several times and had wandered off. Oddly, though, when they least expected it, and when Kristane heard the now familiar *"Tink, Tink, Tink"* — though she still couldn't figure out from where — he would return and tie his wrists back together and sit there smiling at them. She had told him that the game was over and they didn't have to play anymore, but he only stopped when she told him that she would think of another fun game to play.

Pipkin had been as good as his promise; he shared what turned out to be as safe a place as any, and extremely comfortable. Once they had shaken off the water from the "fun way" and traipsed out of the underground lake, they could hardly believe their eyes. An ancient locomotive with a several passenger cars and a caboose lay upon a set of tracks. Though dusty and filled with cobwebs, the old iron horse was lavish. All the compartments had been renovated into someone's personal traveling palace. A plaque on the engine named it as the property of Theodore Bizzarred, the long-ago wealthy owner of the mines. How long it had lain here forgotten was anyone's guess.

Groggle had been euphoric ever since laying eyes on it, expounding upon what a marvel of engineering it was. He had managed to get some of the lighting going after a couple of days, and all of them together had done their best to clean up the interior. Canned food and dried meats were found in what resembled a kitchen pantry, and each of them had had their fill. Xander and Lathan were busy starting a fire. Kristane could see by the fading streaks of light that the sun far above must be setting for the night. The cavern would soon turn cooler.

"Hey, come on, let's sit around the fire." Prya had walked up to where Kristane was sitting with her arms wrapped around her legs, on a ledge above the pool of water. She had come here most days listening to the water swirl below her, hoping to drown out some of the bad thoughts she was now prone to. Though they had all compared stories over the course of their respite and had even told Cayson and the brothers most of what they had learned, holding the group together was becoming more and more difficult. Mostly she came up here to think about what to do next, but being relatively safe had caused the really bad memories to rush in upon her. *Creff and his lifeless eyes.* The swirling noise that had captivated her came from the circular laid-stone spillway that sat just below the surface of the lake. Groggle had explained that this cavern was built to drain off excess water to keep the mine from flooding, and that through a series of channels like the one they had slid down, water would accumulate here and be flushed back out somewhere else through the bell-mouth spillway. "You know, like a big toilet, swoosh!" Pipkin liked the word "swoosh" so much after Groggle's story that he ran around for a couple of days yelling it. Kristane smiled to herself at the memory of Pipkin running up behind Cayson and the Kressley brothers, and screaming it in an attempt to scare and annoy them.

"Hey, I said come on." Prya nodded her head back toward the fire. She held out her hand for Kristane to take, smiling down at her with her endearing look. Kristane returned the smile despite her mood, brushed her hands on her pants, and stood up with Prya's assistance.

"Where do you go when you're up here?"

"Not sure, really. I guess just, well, you know… thinking."

"Yah, I suppose I do, but it's your job to worry." Prya gave her another smile and locked Kristane's arm into hers. "By the way, you come up with a plan yet?" Kristane just shook her head. "Well, you will," Pyra said as she squeezed Kristane's arm with her own.

The two girls were giggling as they sat down at the fire, and Groggle was telling the others about his success and failures with the old locomotive, his face smudged here and there with what looked like grease.

"Jeez, Groggle I am so tired of your tall tales!"

Lathan came to Groggle's defense as Groggle gave a sheepish look. "Leave him alone, Cayson!" Everyone's nerves and fears of the unknown were at a tipping point.

"Shut it, Lathan! I've had enough stories and talking. What are we going to do? Just hang out down here the rest of our lives and someday end up like *him*?" Cayson hooked a thumb over his shoulder towards Pipkin, who beamed back at the group.

"Tales? Stories? Pipkin knows stories and rhymes: The Two Brothers, The Poisoned Tree, The Dragon, The Saint, and the Broken Sword."

Pipkin counted the stories off on his fingers and, with his brows furrowing, in concentration, continued, "Some funny, mostly happy, a few a little sad *… and I know some that will break your very heart and make your ears bleed from the telling.*" Silence fell amongst the group as Pipkin's face dropped back into the carefree look of a small child. Purdy cooed dolefully from somewhere off to the side.

"Um, maybe a little later, okay, Pipkin?" Kristane said finally, and Pipkin clapped his hands together, his face alight with joy.

Cayson Grumbled, "You need to tell crazy here to go away, there's obviously something wrong with him." The Kressley brothers nodded fervently at Kristane, not daring to turn around to face Pipkin, both staying uncharacteristically quiet for a change.

"He's helped us, Cayson. You weren't complaining when he shared his food. Remember that we could have just left you, cut leg and all. Besides, I think it would break his heart if I told him to go."

Massaging his nearly-healed leg, Cayson frowned and mumbled under his breath, "Hate to have him be brokenhearted."

"Broken heart? Pipkin knows the Tale of the Broken Heart!" Pipkin could barely contain himself as he ran up very close to Kristane, placing his hands lightly upon her knees. "Pipkin has told it over again and again! It's about a pretty princess, and dancing, and lots of funny times!"

Kristane smiled at him pleasantly, but then a thought occurred to her. Reaching into her jacket pocket, she pulled out the two sheets of paper from the Attic with their cryptic wording. The papers had suffered since that time, and it took her a moment to open them and then align them correctly, but she felt that she could probably remember what it had said regardless of the smudging. "Pipkin, does your story have anything to do with this heart?"

Pipkin went very quiet for a moment as Kristane watched him silently mouth out the words upon the papers: *Broken was the heart; one half of virtue, the other of sin, strike the bearer upon the sword of sacrifice, then when blood reunited, will they be made whole again.* Screwing up his face, first in contemplation and then in a range of emotions varying from fear to anger to sadness, the young boy, tears forming in his eyes, spoke in a quiet voice. "Pipkin thinks it's same story, but different... Pipkin is happy..." He seemed confused by his last sentence. Squeezing tightly upon Kristane's knees, the tears were suddenly replaced by a fire in his eyes, and he descended into the personality that was so beginning to unsettle Kristane. *"But it also ends in sadness and pain. I think you should listen to the tale."*

PULL HARD, YOU INCOMPETENT DOGS

Lieutenant Blackmore sat at her desk, staring at the empty space of the pocket door that led to the crumbling terrace. They still hadn't figured out how to close the damn thing, and the breeze off of the ocean flapped at the papers on her desk. Blackmore contemplated the events of that stormy night a couple of weeks ago, and the pair of enigmatic figures who had set her to wondering, and how one of the pair's unlikely escape had affected her every thought. Her memories wandered to the morning after. Sargent Banes had just left her office, reporting that a dinghy had gone missing — that they had not caught the disappearance the night before because they thought no one would be crazy enough to cross the Cerulean Sea in little more than a rowboat. She recalled her response to the slack inspection: "Dammit, Banes! You saw his crazy ass jump off the terrace, didn't you? Didn't seem to care much for the rocks; it's doubtful he cares much for some little waves!" She still wasn't sure if she was madder at him or herself. She'd had had Ix dead to rights, after all.

Blackmore had followed protocol, and a report had been sent by pigeon to the Stewardship immediately. She thrummed her fingers on the surface of the desk, staring at the gilded arms that had held the sword that night. She slammed her fist down hard in anger and frustration.

Something in the desk started clicking, and slowly but surely, the support arms descended back into the desk, leaving with no evidence that they had ever been there.

"By God, doesn't that figure?" She stood from her desk and stared down at the surface; nothing was visible. Well, she had left that little bit out of her report anyway; it was just a concise, *Guest of the Stateroom escaped; please advise.* Damn birds couldn't carry novels anyway, she thought, attempting to placate herself.

A return pigeon was long overdue, and this fact did not bode well. The lieutenant strolled from her office to the windows in the hallway, scanning the horizon for some glint of the red-dotted plumage of the otherwise white bird. Little chance of seeing it unless it crashed into the window, but Blackmore was anxious for a reply. Just as she was turning her gaze from the hopeless search, she saw the unmistakable white sails of a large, fully-rigged ship emblazoned with the crest of the Council of Stewards bobbing up and down with the swells.

For her to see it from this distance, she knew that it was nothing less than a warship of Kairos, and probably carrying a full contingency of conscripted Marines. Blackmore's mind raced with the meaning of such a large company arriving here at the Manor Hall for the escape of a single prisoner. Granted, it *was* the Stateroom and it *was* Ix, but until she had taken the post, he was just some ghost the old Warders talked about late at night over too much drink. The lieutenant looked down at the pommel of the sword that laid harnessed to her side. The markings of the old throne and the position that the bearer of such a sword was given ran through her mind. Warders of the Throne they once were; the elite, the personal guard of the crown, the most trusted, the Whiskeys. Like her, those who did not fall in line with the Stewardship were resigned to either guard duty upon this barren rock for generations, patrolling for pirates, or the front lines of some unnecessary skirmish with some kingdom or another. Her sword, like those under her command, was passed down to her by birthright, hers presented to her by her grandfather who had served, his stories of honor and long-ago heroics filling her impressionable mind as it had not her father's or brother's.

"Dammit, Banes! Where are you?" Blackmore yelled down the hallway from her office. "Banes!"

Blackmore stared down with her hands behind her back, and Banes stood at her side as the magnificent pride of Kairos, the *Tonn Bris*, lay anchored just outside the eastern channel that lead into the islets of the Isles of the Dead. Several longboats were entering the natural enclosure, each carrying twenty or more men, the distinct profile of muskets pointed to the sky among those not manning oars. The lieutenant gave Banes a sidewise glance; he nodded in response and turned on his heel, his footsteps echoing off of the stone walls and flooring as he went to greet their visitors.

Blackmore had prepared herself for the consequences of losing a high-profile prisoner, but an armed invasion, such as this was, seemed to mean more than just a severe reprimand. It wasn't long before she heard the scuffling of several pairs of boots outside her office door, the clatter becoming more pronounced as they drew nearer. Banes entered first and attempted an introduction, but was pushed aside by a man the lieutenant did not recognize. He did not wear the trappings of the navy or Steward-ship, but was costumed in a long, burgundy cape that his weak shoulders could not hold. Blackmore noticed a wisp of sickly-sweet incense that accompanied the man into the room as he continued to prance forward.

Taking a handkerchief from within his robes, the man wiped at his nose and addressed her. "Lieutenant Riley Blackmore. I am here as a representative of the Council of the Stewards. My duty is to assess the contamination that you and your men have caused."

The man's voice had a pompous tone that grated on Blackmore's senses. She continued to assess the man as a troop of Marines filled the back of her office, and more stood in the outer hallway. "Contamination? First off, just who the hell are you?" she demanded, omitting her usual politeness. This man's demeanor had rankled her from the moment he said her name.

Squaring what little shoulders he had, the man said. "I am High Priest Cristobal Zekel of the Abbey." Blackmore could tell that the man had been waiting with anticipation to make this declaration; this man, this priest, was very proud of titles.

"High Priest? I don't remember there being such a position within the Church." Blackmore took in more of Zekel's attire, and the things he wore upon his hands. Here and there she noticed the crossed insignia of the church, especially upon the clasp of his cape and on the rings that adorned his fingers. He had the thatched haircut of the monks and was slight of frame; truthfully, he looked like an oversized marionette, but Blackmore had the eerie sense that no one was pulling this man's strings.

He nodded and gave a knowing smile. "The ineptness of this Manor Hall garrison and other events has set in motion the need for a more righteous council and an enlightened leader such as me. This proclamation should explain the need for you to extend every courtesy to me that you would to any of your superiors." Blackmore could see the man's eyes twinkle at his announcement of superiority as he snapped his fingers and a Marine quickly stepped forward, placing an official-looking parchment upon the desk.

Glancing at the swooping lettering and the embossed crest on the parchment before her, Blackmore found she had just about lost all manner of politeness. "Inept? Superior? The day…"

"Lieutenant Blackmore!" The High Priest cut across her statement with a shout that did not seem characteristic of his slight frame. The anger in his voice was that of someone who demanded to be held in high esteem of those around him, any affront to his perceived prestige taken personally. Those Marines in the room tensed at the outburst, and Blackmore noticed the slight movement of their hands towards their swords and stunning sticks. Calming himself slightly and giving her a smile that did not continue into his eyes, Zekel continued, "Has the escape been verified?"

"I and my men can provide a detailed account of the escape." Blackmore decided that feigning politeness with this man was her best course of action for the time being. "High Priest Cristobal," she added as almost an afterthought.

"That's better, Lieutenant, but forgive me if the word of eyewitnesses such as yourself and this band of malcontents doesn't fill me with certainty. *I* require a firsthand inspection of the Stateroom. By what I have been told, our arrival should coincide with the Stateroom being just about open. If you would fetch the keys."

Blackmore bristled with indignation at the imputed slight, but turned and retrieved the keys. Giving a slight nod to Banes, she marched from the room.

Blackmore marched quickly through the hallways and stairs of the Manor Hall, the High Priest and his contingent doing their best to keep up. She could see Banes trailing behind the armed guard, occasionally motioning to one or more of the Warders who patrolled the grand ballroom and lower stairwells. The hallway to the Stateroom being narrow, it only allowed for herself, Cristobal, and a few of the higher-ranking Marines to traverse it; as it was, the area became extremely cramped.

Reaching the rotating door of the Stateroom, Blackmore could clearly see that there was no need for her second key. What greeted them was an open and shadowed maw of twisted iron and crumbled rock distinctly bent inward. Stepping over the bent steel threshold, she was met with the answer as to how the cage had been broken. A long, thick rope made of canvas bags had been meticulously braided together and strapped about other solid objects in the room. Blackmore bent over to inspect a frayed end of the canvas roping that was still attached to the steel bars of the door. The braiding had given way to the pressure, but not before providing a way out. Standing again, Blackmore looked about the room, still holding the frayed rope; this was no spur-of-the-moment escape. Years had gone into this. Ix had used the rotation of the room itself as a fulcrum to bend the steel bars and leave. As her eyes adjusted to the diminished light, she saw that His Eminence the High Priest was in the process of hiking his legs and cape up over the doorway, a decidedly agitated look on his face.

"I see that in your incompetence as guard of this institution, you were correct in one matter. You certainly *have* allowed this prisoner to escape." Blackmore ignored him. Cristobal's tone, though contemptuous, was also slightly higher-pitched than before. His eyes darted about the close quarters, not remaining focused on any single thing for too long. Being battle-worn, Blackmore knew the signs of fear; this man only liked cages that he wasn't in.

"Tell me, Lieutenant Blackmore, do you find that as a woman you may have overstepped your abilities by accepting this post?" the snot-nosed High Priest asked imperiously.

Blackmore ignored this as well, too busy looking at the countless markings on the walls. It slowly dawned on her, as she looked again at the braided rope in her hand, Ix could have left here at any time.

Tentatively, a pair of the Marines who had followed them peeked within the room and entered. Cristobal seemed to garner some measure of strength with their presence. "I will take your silence, Lieutenant, as an affirmative. You need not worry as to this quandary any longer; you are forthwith removed of all duties." For the first time since entering the room, Blackmore looked directly at the High Priest; there was that same smug smile, but this time the glee carried to his eyes. "Tell me again how is it that you were unaware of this escape? Possibly there was some interaction between you and the Stateroom prisoner?" The High Priest folded his hands before him in a mock prayer, his ever-present doily hankie clutched between his fingers as he eyed her over his fingertips. Blackmore knew where this was headed already. "I am afraid the contamination may be greater than the Council expected; interaction with a Stateroom prisoner is strictly forbidden, punishable, of course, by death. As High Priest, it is my given duty to cleanse this Manor Hall of this infection that threatens our very salvation. Your and your men's sacrifice will be a testament to your life of service."

"Life of service? Too right! You damned pompous, self-righteous… I'll wipe that snot right off your sour…!" Blackmore did not bother finishing her thoughts aloud, closing the distance between her and the priest. Cristobal realized his mistake too late. In hopes of isolating the Lieutenant from her men, he had underestimated the woman before him — seeing only that, a frail woman. From his world within the Abbey, what more could she really be? The Marines within the room were not so inclined, though they were slow in their response. Being taken aback by the abrupt-ness of Cristobal's threats, they had come to the Manor Hall expecting a fight. They quickly raised their guard about the priest as he cowered behind their drawn swords.

Blackmore never troubled herself to draw her sword. If she and her men were going to make it from the Isles of the Dead alive, there was no time for individual battles. She turned her back to the priest and his guards and sprinted to the exit. A commotion had broken out along the passageway leading into the Stateroom; the Marines who lined the hallway had turned their attention to the noise behind them. *Thank God Banes finally got something right,* Blackmore thought as she sprinted the length of the corridor, none of the gathered Marines giving her more than a fleeting thought. Reaching the end of the hallway, she knocked aside the last few Marines barring her way. Banes stood there within the confined area with a half-dozen of her men keeping the soldiers from forming any kind of ranks, as shouted commands trailed behind her.

"Move it, Whiskeys!" Though Blackmore's men held the Marines here, at some point they were sure to be overwhelmed. "Get to the lower level and the boats. Now, Banes!" The lieutenant, drawing her sword, bodily shoved Banes and her Whiskeys down the stairs, turning at each landing to slow their pursuers.

The Marines didn't have much stomach for fighting; an occasional cut across a wrist or jab to an arm kept them from pushing forward. Reaching the sea-level grotto, Blackmore marshaled her full company of men, which had waited for her there, into the long boats that the High Priest had arrived in. Banes had scuttled all but three of the craft.

"Go on, we will defend your rear!" Banes and a couple of the others stood at the threshold of the grotto, the shouts and the crackling of the stun sticks of those stalking them becoming clearer.

"Get in the damned boats! We are *all* leaving this hellhole today! You will retreat, soldier, that is an order!" Sergeant Banes looked incredulously back at Blackmore; it wasn't in the makeup of a Whiskey to retreat, but nonetheless, Banes quickly followed her into one of the boats. Grabbing one of the oars, she yelled at her men, "Pull hard, you incompetent dogs!"

The stolen longboats were halfway through the water tunnel when the pursuing Marines reached the underground dock. A few of the more ambitious among them dove into the water in a futile attempt to catch the Warders. Reaching the tunnel's opening, Blackmore ordered her company to occupy a single longboat. Taking a musket from her belt, she fired into the bottom of one of the unoccupied boats and ordered Banes to do the same to the other, sinking them both and blockading the entrance with their busted hulls. Making for the second of the islets, which was blocked from the view of those aboard the *Tonn Bris*, Blackmore and her men boarded a small schooner there that was prepped and harbored. The boat was the largest the Warders had access to; it had been made ready on her orders earlier that day. The schooner was slow in comparison to the *Tonn Bris*, but the makeshift obstacles they had left behind for the High Priest and his contingent would buy them some time. She hoped that would be enough.

"Where do we sail?"

"We need refuge, Banes, far from the reach of those who want us dead, and answers, Banes — we need answers." Though not apt sailors, Blackmore's men knew enough to get the boat pointed toward the mainland, so she turned her attention from them and looked at Banes. "We go looking for the Ward."

"The Ward? That's just a legend. There is no secret haven for the Warders."

"After all the fairytales and legends we've just recently seen, Banes, I'm willing to go on a little faith with this one. Mark our path as the mouth of the Cynabell, where the eagles fly!"

A Tale of the Broken Heart

"All right, Pipkin, I would like to hear your tale." Kristane felt it best to placate the odd boy, as he seemed very insistent. The boy's smile became broader and broader, and the fire faded from his eyes. Pipkin stood as if he were upon a stage, and they were his audience to be entertained. Kristane had to admit that it didn't seem to be a very willing audience, but Pipkin didn't seem to notice or care.

"Once upon a time, a pretty, pretty Princess was sad and very lonely, for though she was around many people of the court, none of them played games or danced silly or dressed up like funny people. They were all too far grown-up for such nonsense. So her father the King called for the clock-maker to make her a friend, someone who would always play and dance and sing." Pipkin stood to his full height and did a silly pirouette until he stumbled and fell to his knees. Kristane looked on as the atmosphere lightened, and everyone seemed to be listening intently to Pipkin's story. Prya was smiling, and Groggle sat with his mouth slightly open while Cayson scowled, but she could tell that he was captivated as well.

"The clockmaker toiled and troubled and did a little bit of magic that only he knew, and so a princely boy was made to be the Princess's friend. They became very good friends indeed, and were never, ever apart. They played and danced and made up ridiculous stories. The clockmaker gave the pretty, pretty Princess a word of caution, though, to always guard the boy's heart, for she was to be the holder of it. As long as there was love between the two, then she would hold the key to his heart, and they would always be friends." As Pipkin embraced himself with a big hug and closed his eyes, Kristane was all of a sudden reminded of the little song that Pipkin had been singing. *You hold the key to our heart!*

"One day, the King met with some very bad men in his castle, men who had been telling lies and doing all kinds of bad things over here and over there." Pipkin dramatically pranced from one side of the campfire to the other, pointing into the distance and holding his hand above his brow, as though he was looking off into a faraway place. "They shouted and hollered to one another and to the King. They just didn't want to be friends, so they stomped out of the castle calling the King some very bad names. Now the pretty, pretty Princess and the boy who was her friend were playing all sorts of fun and silly games just outside of the castle. Their very favorite was hide-and-go-seek." Pipkin stopped recounting his story and counted backwards from ten with his hands over his eyes, then continued.

"The bad, bad men saw the friends playing and saw where the Princess hid, so they decided they would do something to upset the King. They had long swords and bad tempers and shouted at the Princess until she began to cry. The boy who was the Princess' friend heard her cry, and he wanted to be brave and true, so he ran very fast to her rescue. The boy was very, very strong, and he was gallant too; swords clashed and clanked and metal rang against metal." Pipkin grabbed for a tin cup and, standing in a fencing pose, one arm held high above his head, clanked his cup against the one Cayson was trying to drink from, its contents slopping all over Cayson's lap. Cayson protested, but Pipkin ignored him and went on with his tale.

"He saved the pretty, pretty Princess from the very bad men! But the boy who was the Princess' friend was hurt badly on his face from one of the long, long swords. The King thanked the boy, and the clockmaker was called to give the boy a new face. The clockmaker was very busy, and while the mask of metal he made the boy was very handsome, it just was not the same. The pretty, pretty Princess did not care, because they were great friends, but the courtiers and servants of the King *did* care, and whispered behind their hands and pointed their fingers when they thought he was not looking." Pipkin placed his hand in front of his mouth and pointed at the Kressley brothers. They gave a mingled look of shock and fear at being singled out by Pipkin.

"Time passed, and the pretty, pretty Princess grew into a beautiful lady and she became a Queen and she did not want to sing and dance and play silly games anymore. But the boy who was the Princess' friend *did* want to play and dance and sing. He became spiteful and jealous and vengeful towards the Queen and those who had called him names behind their hands. Soon his games became pranks, and his stories became lies, and before long he was worse than the very, very bad men who had once tried to hurt the Queen. The beautiful, beautiful Queen became sad and tried to talk with her friend, but his heart had hardened and he would not listen. The Queen called for the clockmaker to help set things right, but what he told her made her sad. The Queen cried for the boy who was her friend, who had once been there when she was happy and sad or even scared. There was only one way that she could stop her friend from doing bad, bad things. She could no longer guard his heart; it would have to be broken. So one very long day after her friend had done something very bad and the moon gave off a reddish glow, she broke his heart and maybe just a little bit of her own. And as the boy who was the Queen's friend watched, so too was his heart broken, and he never did any bad, bad things ever again."

Silence met the end of Pipkin's story as he took a gracious bow before them. Kristane unconsciously fumbled at her necklace below her shirt. It was Prya who broke the quiet; she began to clap slowly, looking around as she did so. She gave Kristane a look and a nod towards Pipkin in a way of *come on, help me, and is this right?* Kristane joined in as the others gave a halfhearted smattering of applause, but Pipkin did not care; he bowed several more times, and looked ecstatic at the attention.

"That was very nice, er, good… well, it was something, Pipkin." Kristane was at a loss for what Pipkin's story was, really. She wasn't sure how she felt about The Tale of the Broken Heart. She knew that she felt sad, but was confused by what else she was feeling. For a moment, her thoughts went back to their decimated home of the Attic and their search for answers. A charcoaled etching that lettered a broken heart, Pipkin's tale, her amulet... could all of these things just be coincidence? Kristane looked up to find Groggle staring intently at her, his mouth forming words silently to himself, debating whether he should speak them out loud or not.

"I thought it was a prince in that story. That's the way I heard it, anyway..." Groggle trailed off as Pipkin turned his attention to him.

His demeanor hovering between playful child and something else, Pipkin said, "Pipkin says it's the same story. Pipkin thinks Groggle is very, very smart, but Pipkin thinks too that he does not know everything."

"That was ruddy stupid! Broken hearts and a fairy princess or prince or whatever!" Cayson burst out all of a sudden, his patience worn thin.

"Pipkin did not say fairy Princess! Pipkin say pretty, pretty Princess!... *You should listen to the story, Cayson!*" Pipkin began to advance on Cayson; it was the first time they had seen Pipkin act in such a physical way. This time, Pipkin did not quickly drop back into his youthful and benign behavior, and did not look like he was going to. Cayson, realizing his error, dropped his cup with a dull thud and held his hands up before him, cowering behind them.

Buffoons and Idiots

The High Priest Cristobal Zekel sat at his new desk atop the Abbey, scanning several parchments in his hand. Craftsmen of all sorts worked about him, repairing the damage that had occurred during Hallow's End. Cristobal had insisted on taking up residence in the space immediately, feeling that his attained position deserved nothing less, despite the fact that the space was barely habitable. He did not see the smoke-streaked walls or the broken glass above, but the delusional throne of his power.

Before him stood several overdressed people, one very large one and having trouble with the prolonged wait for an audience. Lord Piggleback wore a plum-colored outfit this afternoon and was sweating profusely. His ensemble reminded the High Priest of a large piece of fruit that was overly ripe. He had purposely ignored them, savoring his new-found influence over them.

"Excuse me, Cristobal, will we be starting this encounter before the sun sets today?"

The High Priest cringed at the use of his name, and not his proper title. Madame Ridley was one of the only members of the ruling Stewardship to refuse to sign the proclamation that gave the High Priest ultimate authority in matters dealing with the faithful and those acts recently witnessed, which by his interpretation meant everything. More irksome to him, though, was the fact that she was the only member before him who refused to stand, having brought her own chair. "I am sure you will excuse an old woman's impatience, but time, you see, is best wasted on the young."

Cristobal gave a frown of irritation at this and thought, *This old woman is more likely to outlive all of those standing before me, and most certainly will dance on Piggleback's grave... unless something happens.* The matriarchal Madame Ridley, unlike many of her counterparts, was popular amongst the commoners. She did not adopt the gaudy and haughty dress and attitude of the others. Her simple but elegant all-black bustle dress showed her position without being ostentatious. If all went as planned on this day, though, he could at least push her to the side for the time being.

"Forgive me, madame; when the interpretation of the divine takes me, I must of course listen." Cristobal tossed the pieces of parchment carelessly onto the surface of his desk along with a tattered and frayed portrait of a red-haired young woman and pocketed a ring that had been among the personal effects of the escaped "guest" of the Manor Hall.

"Is that what you were doing? I imagine I have the same look on my face in the morning when it comes upon me to have a movement. Ba ha ha!" The old woman gave out a joyful laugh and slapped at her knee. Her attendant, who stood a few paces behind her, disguised a chuckle by pretending to clear his throat. The other Stewards and the monks that flanked Cristobal fidgeted with some nervousness.

"Madame's capacity for bluntness and levity is unparalleled. It is no wonder that you are held in such regard amongst the masses. I pray that it never leaves you." Cristobal wiped at his nose, smiled, and bowed with his hands clasped in prayer, but never dropped his gaze from Madame Ridley.

"Would that I could laugh at what has taken place. As for bluntness, this lot might be afraid of their own shadows, but I am not. Your counsel of dire consequences to this group of twits and the unilateral decisions being made without anyone's leave is not written out in that pretty parchment they signed."

"Now, Madame Ridley, there was a majority vote of this council..."

"Snap that fat lip, Piggly, or I'll stick this cane up your backside again!" Madame Ridley pointed her cane at the Lord and jabbed at the air several times in the general direction of his buttocks. Oscar Piggleback involuntarily rubbed at his backside and looked dutifully shocked and worried. "Don't try and school me on protocol. I've been at this since long before you grew your third chin. I know full well the dictates of the majority."

"Madame Ridley, how apropos. This is exactly why I have asked the council here today. We can ill afford another disruption of the faith such as what transpired at the Manor Hall and the dereliction of the Warders and their subsequent traitorous behavior." Cristobal, though incensed at first with the escape of both the prisoner and Warders, had cunningly flipped the events to suit his narrative. "To better serve the faithful, I believe that forming an executive court of this council would better cut through the minutiae." Cristobal spread his hands out before him, indicating the gathered members. Some nodded fervently in agreement, while others became apprehensive.

"My, what an inspired idea, High Priest…" Piggleback began to say, but was interrupted by the tapping of Madame Ridley's cane upon the floor. Piggleback silenced himself quickly and again grabbed for his backside.

"I highly doubt that story you have woven concerning the Warders, but what really chaps my arse is who, Cristobal, do you believe will sit on this court of monkeys?"

"Why of course, Madame, the very most devoted of you all."

"I'll bet! No doubt they will additionally need to be deaf, dumb, and blind as well, and as I am none of those things, I believe I shall be going." Madame Ridley rose nimbly from her seat, surprisingly so for someone of her age, as her attendant folded the wooden chair she had sat upon into the shape and size of a common umbrella.

"Good day to you, Madame, and many blessings. I shall think upon the thoughts you shared today with much relish." Cristobal smiled broadly and addictively wiped at his nose.

"Do not think this a victory, and for God's sake, man, do something about that condition. It is nothing less than revolting, and here I thought old Piggly's flatulence was repugnant! Ba ha ha!" Without a further word, the Madame marched out of the room with a scowling Cristobal and an indignant Piggleback in her wake, and a few other of the Stewards following her lead.

Madame Ridley marched down the stairs of the Abbey to her waiting carriage. It was a fine carriage, all in black, drawn by a pair of steam-driven horses, the finest the smiths at Wyndom's could craft. A handsome young man stood holding the reigns of the chestnut- and bronze-colored steeds, as the driver was busy checking the back wheels that, in comparison to the front, stood twice as high and nearly as tall as the driver who was inspecting them.

"Everything go well, Gram?"

"Buffoons and idiots; turds the lot of them, nearly to the last one." Madame Ridley turned as she approached the door the young man was holding open for her, and gave a single wave to a couple of other Stewards who had vacated the Abbey at the same time she had. "Went about as I thought it would. Oh, Steven, wipe that concerned look off of your face; you know it will freeze that way if you're not careful." She gently tapped upon his cheek, giving him a caring smile.

"Gram, do you think it wise to incite the new High Priest?"

"*Incite* is a bit strong. I assure you I was my usual polite self, and used the proper decorum for those in attendance. Ba ha ha!"

Steven turned to the giant man who was his grandmother's attendant and gave him a questioning look. The man looked first to the back of the Madame's head and then back at Steven, giving him a shrug of his enormous shoulders. "Gram!"

Madame Ridley tossed her cane into the carriage, grabbed the handhold bar, and ascended the drop-down stairs that had unfolded as the door opened. "Steven, you worry too much. Such a good boy." Turning on the first step, she bent over and gave kissed him on his forehead. "I have told you it is far worse to sit and do nothing as evil prevails. You are expected for dinner tonight at eight sharp; I see you have the pocket watch I gave you, so do not dawdle. We have a great deal we need to talk about."

The giant man took this as his cue, and as Steven stepped aside, he pushed himself through the door and took a seat opposite the Madame.

The carriage dropped noticeably and creaked upon its axles with the man's tremendous weight; the driver was again looking at the wheels and shaking his head. Mounting his perch, the driver gave a quick snap of the reins and shouted *"Giddy up!"*

Dr. Steven Ridley watched from the stairs of the Abbey as the carriage turned north onto High Street and disappeared behind the buildings.

Madame Ridley looked blankly out of the windows of the carriage, not focusing on any one thing in particular, and spoke softly to the giant man as she held her cane in front of her, both hands gripping the pommel tightly. "Jackard, you would look after him if something were to happen to me, yes?"

"Madame, that most certainly will not be necessary for a long time." The deep voice of Jackard rumbled about the cabin of the carriage.

"I am an old fool, but I am not that foolish. The High Priest is still testing his powers, but there will come a time when he will embolden himself further, and my grandson will need your assistance much more than I will." She turned to the giant man and held him with a steely gaze, awaiting his reply.

"Yes, Madame, I will indeed take care of the doctor. Gladly."

HEAR, SEE, SPEAK NO EVIL

The High Priest waved off the remaining Stewards who had lingered to do nothing less than prostate themselves before him, in a bid to be chosen as a member of the executive court. Turning to one of his attending monks, he said, "Bring him to me." The monk nodded his understanding and ran off to do his bidding. The High Priest didn't bother to wave out the other monks. They had already sensed their dismissal, and bowed themselves out the doors of his office. With a click of the latch bolt brushing the strike plate, Cristobal tucked back his arms and pulled the knob of the top drawer of his desk. Removing several pieces of parchment, yellowing with age, he added them to those littering his desk, proclaiming his recent edicts. Fanning them out, he slid the one he wanted toward him.

Someone with a fine hand had scrolled out an accounting of the Blessed Tree, complete with a detailed sketching of it. Thick roots twisted and braided about themselves above and into the ground, leading up through the trunk and into the crown of the tree. Long, broad boughs that tapered into wispy ends were adorned with ivory-colored leaves as big as one's head, and dotted here and there with delicate flowers. He caressed the corner of the parchment, where the writer had drawn a single heart-shaped fruit. Presented in cross section, it depicted the interior of the plump and fleshy skin, with a pit that was also heart-shaped. The pome was described as *pure white, that to look upon it would be as if to gaze upon the purity of the ages,* and promised the miraculous gift of immortality. This was Cristobal's divine path, the prize that would grant him the ability to see his vision through.

His thoughts were disturbed by a quick rap on the door. "Enter!" The High Priest did not bother to put away the papers he had been studying.

Rellion had passed the time idly, counting the days by the number of bowls of gruel- water garnished with rancid pig fat that were shoved through the small pass-through at the base of his cell door at the Bastille. He had sat silently waiting for the summons he knew would come, and hopefully a few answers.

And now a pair of Briggers escorted the shackled Rellion into the Attic, halting him at the edge of the High Priest's desk. With a wave of Cristobal's hand, the Briggers placed Rellion's cane and hat upon the desk and retreated out the doors. "I must admit I had expected to be here a great deal sooner, Brother Cristobal," Rellion said as he entered the man's office. "What possibly could have kept you from the chance to gloat?"

"It is High Priest Cristobal now," Cristobal replied in an unctuous tone, wearing his new station like armor, apparently unafraid of the prisoner before him. Gloatingly, he continued, "I was detained by a bit of administration at the Manor Hall, and I have been deep in prayer."

Rellion, ignoring the bait of the island prison, glanced down at the parchments littering the High Priest's desk, and then at the section of flooring that had been removed in front of the Abbey clock, exposing the gears and arms of the lunar movements that had rotated out of sight. Cristobal, noticing his gaze, said, "Yes, that was the missing piece I had been searching for. *‹Broken was the heart, one half of virtue, the other of sin, strike the bearer upon the sword of sacrifice, then when blood reunited will they be made whole again.'* So, which of them is it, then, and where are the halves?"

Rellion made no reply, but tested the flooring just under his boots with a tap.

"Nothing, then?" Cristobal dabbed at his nose with a lacy kerchief. "I often wondered why those decrepit fools had granted you your lofty perch up here with your motley 'Rogue' of misfits, but the scrolls have enlightened me much."

"You mistake ancient events for modern reality, Cristobal." Indicating with a nod of his head the parchments littering the desk, Rellion continued, "The Blessed Tree is not as it was, and never was what you imagine it to be. You would know that, if the elder monks hadn't met with such untimely deaths."

The High Priest gave a slight twitch, but composed himself with a shake of his head, as if shooing off an irksome fly. Regret was something he had no time for; he buried it under his surety that his vision was enlightened. "We will see," he said, pointing to an arrest statement.

"Awakening him will not be as you imagine it, either." Moving to his left, Rellion again tapped his boot heels on the flooring. "Besides, you will never catch my Rogue."

"Oh, always the pompous one. Granted, despite the ineptness of the Briggers and lack of any discrimination, they have rounded up several youths already. Surprising, really, the level of infestation. We will just cut them all until we find the correct one, then."

The gravity of the statement was not lost on a shocked Rellion, and he was reminded again of not seeing the path before him, so busy with the destination that he had not guessed the lengths to which this man might go.

As Cristobal nodded his head smugly at Rellion's dawning comprehension, a dull scraping drew both men's attention to the Attic rooftop access. "And those that the Briggers cannot catch, well, maybe *they* can — my heavenly angels."

Striding down the staircase was a pair of Forgotten Ones, their heavy footfalls and black cloaks unmistakable. Rellion had heard all that he needed to, and much that he wished he hadn't. "This has been very enlightening, but be wary, Cristobal. There are fates waiting for each of us, with far worse blessings than we can imagine in this life if we choose them." Reaching forward, Rellion grabbed for his cane and hat. "I bid you farewell for now."

Startled by the sudden movement, the High Priest pushed himself back into his chair and gave out a high-pitched screech. Rellion slammed the brass ferrule of his cane to the floor at his feet, collapsing the newly repaired flooring.

He quietly thanked the laziness of the laborers for just covering the hole and not filling it in as he dropped into the Attic's escape shaft.

FRIENDS OF A SORT

Rellion was reminded of bread crumbs as he scanned the rocky tunnel, holding his glowing staff before him. "Master Fool, once again you have out done yourself," Rellion said out loud to the walls. The light of his staff shone briefly across an ancient marking just at the break in the tunnel where it veered to the right. The same crest that adorned his ring had been scratched discreetly upon the rock surface at differing intervals. Absentmindedly, he fingered his ring finger with his thumb, spinning an imaginary ring around and around. So many pieces moving across the board, yet so many more that must come into play before this all ended... he wondered, Will there be time?

Rellion could hear a voice or two in the distance, echoing back to him from the darkened tunnel as small bursts of light flashed along the walls. He extinguished the pommel of his shillelagh and strolled into the cavern.

"I believe that that will be enough, Master Fool. Master Cayson, I am sure, will listen intently to your next tale. Will you not, Master Cayson?" Rellion paraded into the ring of campfire light, startling everyone with his unexpected appearance. Pipkin turned quickly and bowed in greeting, but the others started to shout at Rellion all at once.

"What?!" "'ere you bin?!" "What's going on?!" "You're not dead?!"

"My apologies, my young Rogue; answers will come, all in good time. I have been detained longer than anticipated. If it had not been for my most charming rapport, I believe I may not have been in time to keep Master Cayson from learning a valuable lesson."

Kristane almost felt like running up and hugging Rellion, so glad she was to see him, but then she thought better of it; it was Rellion, after all. Despite this, she couldn't help but sit there and smile up at him. Occasionally she glanced at Pipkin. Neither seemed surprised to see the other. She had about a hundred questions running through her head, but decided to go with what was in front of her first. "Rellion, how did you find us, and how do you know Pipkin?"

"Pipkin? I have not heard him called that in a very long time, my dear, but I am pleased that you know him by it. Pipkin and I are old acquaintances; one might even say that Pipkin and I are friends of a sort. It was with his assistance that I followed your trail here." Rellion gave Pipkin a slight nod in thanks and Pipkin bowed, one arm across his front, the other to his back. "I did in fact tell you to come here to the Tunnels, though, so bearing in mind that for a change you had adopted a sense of obedience, then me finding you was only a matter of time," Rellion said as he gave Kristane a quick wink.

Xander spoke up. "Unless you were dead," he said softly, and the others went very quiet, all looking to Rellion for his response.

"Master Xander, you cannot imagine how true a statement that is… but it is a task that is very hard to achieve."

"How hard exactly, Rellion?" Kristane almost whispered the question, so stuck it was in her throat at the fear of the possible answer. She had always been slightly intimidated by Rellion, but never fearful up until this moment.

Rellion turned his gaze from Xander to where Kristane sat, meekly meeting his eyes. "I see… my Princess, let us just leave it at *very* for now, but not impossible." Rellion took in a deep breath and looked to each of the kids in turn. "There is more reason to fear than you can possibly imagine, but none of you have any reason to fear me. I must ask all of you, my Rogue, to take my word for it until it can be made clearer."

Rellion nodded to the group of kids, then turned his back to them to take in the steam engine. With his hands upon his hips, he looked at it appreciatively. Thanks to Groggle's ministering, the engine now sat alight, with its subdued violet running lights glowing. Embedded within the frame, luminescent cables ran concentric circles about the boiler seams and along the wheel hubs of the engine and accompanying passenger cars. Though the accumulated dirt of long abandonment sat upon the black gunmetal that made up the exterior and the large mushroom-shaped stack, Rellion could see places where its polished surface still shone through.

"Always wondered what became of old Lord Theodore's train. Bit of an unbefitting end, really."

"Pipkin finds the choo-choo!" Pipkin yelled, while pulling down an imaginary whistle. "Woo! Woo!"

"Well done, Master Fool. As I remember it, the Lord Bizzarred enjoyed his comforts!"

So use to defending Pipkin from Cayson and the brothers, Kristane felt irritated by Rellion's moniker for him. "If you know each other so well, why do you call him a fool?"

"Not all titles are meant as slights, but if you prefer bard or jester, do not doubt the respect I have for your new friend Pipkin here. His abounding talents are unlike any other's." Rellion strolled closer to the campfire and took a seat upon a large stone. "Master Pipkin's flair for spinning a tale and entertaining is befitting for royalty."

Pipkin clapped his hands together and smiled broadly at Rellion.

Kristane, finding Rellion in a mood to uncharacteristically answer questions and mollified by his depiction of Pipkin, decided she would press her luck. "Rellion, who are those hooded figures that attacked us?"

Rellion contemplated Kristane and the others for a moment, then answered. "Nursery rhymes and fairy tales, you will find, often have a ring of truth to them. Often they merely teach us a lesson or entertain, but that is because someone once learned a lesson." Rellion paused a moment before pressing on with his response. "I think one more story. Master Fool, the Seven Ballerinas and Their Danseurs; the short version, though, if you would. The day wanes, and I find myself longing for one of old Lord Ted's comfortable beds."

"Oh, oh, I know that one too!" Groggle was raising his hand in the air in an excited manner, as Pipkin's shoulders sagged, giving him a dejected look.

"Very good, Master Groggle, but let us allow Master Pipkin his moment."

Pipkin immediately straightened himself, spun about with a quick pirouette, and in a singsong voice spoke:

Seven beautiful ballerinas danced 'round and 'round the clock,
Forever bound to the rhythmic tick, and the resounding tock.
Seven beautiful ballerinas, partners had they,
wrought with conflicts;
One wished for the others, and then there were six.
Six beautiful ballerinas all had cravings of great size;
One took in too much, and then there were five.
Five beautiful ballerinas, very selfish, each wanted more —
One gave into avarice, and then there were four.
Four beautiful ballerinas danced to the chimes,
wishing for inactivity
One sat down and became idle, and then there were three.
Three beautiful ballerinas, fury and hate was all they knew;
One fell to vengeance, and then there were two.
Two beautiful ballerinas, resentful of each other,
not wanting to be outdone…
One took the rivalry too far, and then there was one.
One beautiful ballerina, full of conceit and pride,
thought the day won;
She lost herself in self-love… and then there were none.

Pipkin finished his story and gave bows all around, but the only one giving a polite clap was Rellion. The others just stared at each other. Kristane began to say something, but Rellion held up his hand to quiet her. "As I said, the old rhymes we know have lessons to be learned. This one tells each of us not to fall and lose ourselves by giving into the sins of this world, but it also tells us of those who *did* at one time fall. Long ago, when Kairos was still a young city, the Celestial Orrery was shaped into the wonder that it is by many artisans and a Master. Much like other grand clocks, this one was adorned with clockwork figurines; but very much unlike the simple cuckoos you have seen, these clockwork mario-nettes were beautifully intricate. They were not clumsy or awkward, but would emerge at certain events and sway and waltz with great grace, to the delight of all the citizens of Kairos."

Rellion paused, eyes distant, as if viewing something that only he could see. "As time passed and the novelty of the dancers abated, people took less and less notice of them. Though as the rhyme speaks, upon the sound of the chimes, the dancers would emerge and perform their duty to entertain. It is beyond even my understanding of how or why, and it is unknown when exactly it happened, but at some point the clockwork dancers became aware of themselves."

"Like Count Bobo!" Groggle exclaimed excitedly.

Rellion smiled at him and looked at the others as they nodded their heads. "You have been busy, have you not? Yes, Master Groggle, in fact *just* like Count Bobo and his excellent troupe; but unlike them, the dancers had the mobility that the good Count does not. It began slowly at first; a dancer or two would go missing and then return upon the next chime of the clock. Most thought that they were just broken, a cog out of place or a spring sprung, so long they had danced; but the truth was far more nefar-ious. You see, someone *did* notice that there was something very different about the clockwork marionettes, and I am not so sure that he was not the one responsible for it." Rellion again paused, and adjusted himself upon the hard rock he was sitting on. "Often, he was seen dancing about with them, whispering to them each in turn, telling them the lies that would ultimately be their undoing and giving them the attention that others had ceased to.

"One day, as the clock chimed and it was time for the dancers to once again perform, they did not. They had heard the lies of the deceiver and had chosen to take them in. It was because of this deceiver, with the help of the dancers, that a great war began; and while this war did in fact end far too long ago for any to even remember, it was with a heavy price."

As Kristane considered what Rellion had just told them, she felt herself filled with an uneasy, almost all-encompassing fear that she could not understand. It was with a dry throat that she mumbled to Rellion, "But that still doesn't answer why they are after us… or does it have something to do with this?" Fumbling in her pocket, she took out the smudged papers that they had etched out in the Attic.

Rellion glanced briefly at the pages without taking them, and smiled proudly at her. "Never one to let a question go unanswered, are we?" Kristane blushed at that. "It is not me that they are after, but what they suspect I possess, and what they cannot be allowed to recover. For with this item, they would be able to reawaken the deceiver. You see, it is that clockwork heart; that trinket, the one that means so much to you, that they desire most of all." Rellion pointed to the necklace about her neck as the eyes of the others were drawn to it.

As Kristane looked down at the necklace that she had always worn, the words of Pipkin echoed in her memory: *pretty girl, pretty necklace.* She clasped it in her hand, and for the first time she felt as though she wished to rip it from her neck and throw it away — like it was something evil, and not the one thing she associated with a mother she never knew and a love she desperately longed for. "But you said it was nothing… nothing. How is this mine?"

"I will not ask for any forgiveness for the deception; I have my own reasons for keeping this truth from you. The story of how this necklace has passed to you is a long one, and tonight is not the night for the tale." Rellion looked over at Pipkin. "By your word, Master Fool."

"Pipkin listens, Pipkin understands…" Pipkin stole a guilty look, with his head bowed at Kristane.

"We are being hunted. It will not be long before the Forgotten Ones again find our trail, and another enemy I have unfortunately ignored has a head start already. Our only hope is that he has not yet solved the riddle of what you hold in your hand and where the other half lies. Prepare yourselves, my Rogue, for tonight, though we are hunted, we too must go on the hunt! We must return to the Abbey to steal a holy relic!"

WEIRDLY, CREEPILY, AWESOME

The archway opened up into a long hall with seemingly no end, and a high ceiling that reached into complete darkness. Lighting the shadows were interspersed bands of crystal, the source of illumination hidden deep within the walls by the ancient architects of the Abbey. The little arcs of light cast by them gave a funereal and disheartening pallor to everything, including the arch-carved recesses, the length and shape of bodies, stacked one upon another and rising far into the support columns and beams of the catacombs, identifying how deep the Rogue had come.

For the briefest of moments, Kristane hoped that the recesses might be empty, but there was no such luck. Full-bodied corpses, laid out in their complete decrepit majesty, were dressed in finery and wore masks of either plaster or some shiny metal. For some of those that wore plaster, only pieces remained — a bit on a forehead, a fragment covering an eye socket or a scrap across a chin, the rest of the lime-and-sand mixture decayed or in the process of flaking and blending in with the accumulated dust of ages. For those with the heavier brass and gold masks, the opposite was true; many of the ancient skulls had given way and had been crushed by the veils of metal, the death masks resting nearly on the stone base of the tombs, mixed with shards of discolored skull, jawbone, or errant teeth.

When Rellion had declared that *"we"* were going on the hunt for a holy relic, what he had meant was that his Rogue was going. *Of course, you are going on your own. I have important matters to attend to here with Master Groggle and Pipkin.*

"God, what is that smell?" Prya waved her hand in front of her face in a futile attempt to clear the air before her. "I can taste it in my mouth, blah!" Kristane watched as her friend spat a very unladylike glob of spit onto the floor and smirked as the boys, not to be outdone, began spitting every few paces. The Kressley brothers took it a step further by making a contest of it, seeing who could spit the farthest. It continued until one of them nearly hit Cayson in the back of the head.

"Really, what is that smell?" The putrid but sickly sweet smell felt like it was emanating from the actual rock of the tombs themselves.

Cayson, who had been put in charge by Rellion, trudging ahead with an air of self-importance that had begun to irk all of them, called back over his shoulder in answer. "It's the dead folks here, from before the Death Dressers. They just use to stick 'em down here without taking out their innards or basting their skin in those smelly alcohol rags. Guess when they started to rot, it leaked into the rock." To prove his point, Cayson pointed to the long-dried stains that had discolored the robes of the cadavers and collected about the bodies, trailing over the edge of the open crypts to the floors, where it had pooled.

Kristane found herself side-stepping the gruesome dried puddles like they were still fresh. Noticing a slight movement to her left, she peered at the corpse interred there as its chest began to move up and down, as if filling and emptying with breath. Clasping her hand to her mouth to stifle a scream, she bumped into Prya, pointing at the moving ribcage under the ripped and torn cloth of a silk robe. Curious, Prya poked at the robe with her finger. First a pair of twitching little noses peeked through the tear, followed by whiskers and then several beady eyes. Purdy gave a hungry growl from her neck.

"Oh, aren't they cute — but really gross, of course." Prya tried to hide a smirk as she looked back at her friend. Kristane dropped her hand with embarrassment as Prya pulled back the rest of the robe to reveal the rodents that had taken up occupancy, having built a nest in the chest cavity of the deceased. Being brought up traversing the back alleys of a large city, rats were nothing new; but still feeling a bit self-conscious, she choked out a relieved laugh.

To deflect from the masked snickers of her companions, Kristane tried to change the subject. "How much farther, Cayson?" His familiarity with the Abbey's catacombs was why he had been put in the lead, and also because of what Rellion had called "his enlightenment." She had no idea what this meant until they had started talking about holy relics and what they were. The ensuing conversation about differing body parts being lopped off upon death of saintly persons had reached a level of vulgarity that Kristane assumed only young boys could reach.

Cayson didn't answer directly, but stopped and pointed smugly. Sculpted into the living stone was a vestibule set back into the cavity where the bricking of the Abbey ceased at bare rock. There was no door, just a black space, arched by the arms of a regally dressed kneeling man and woman glowing with an unknown dim light. Maybe "regally" wasn't the right word, Kristane thought; the stone figures were adorned in some sort of religious habits, but the scapulae were ribboned just below the shoulders, trailing nearly to where they knelt. The presence of swords strapped to their waists could not be missed; nor did they seem odd for the obviously religious figures.

Inscribed above all of this in a curved eloquent script was, *Enter those faithful, retreat those of dissent, all are welcome, apostate or penitent.* Kristane searched for the source of light and found lurking between each of the lichen-covered crevices, where stone shoulders met necks and the small places in-between fingers, thousands of glowing insects. They dimmed and fired and then flitted away to another perch, giving the sculptures an eerie sense of movement.

"God, that's weirdly, creepily, awesome," Prya whispered, regardless of the fact that the only obvious company that the stone figures had had in many long years were the bugs. None of her companions seemed to think it odd.

"What does it mean?"

"It's a warning and a path," Cayson said matter-of-factly to Kristane, as the Kressley brothers nodded in agreement.

"What? How do you know?" she asked disbelievingly.

Cayson bristled at her tone, but then continued sheepishly, "Me and the boys use to sneak down to the gatherings at the Abbey once and a while. We figure it best to have you know our souls cleaned up a bit every once in a while." The brothers steepled their hands before their faces and nodded solemnly in agreement.

Kristane couldn't disagree with that. If anyone needed cleaning up, it was these three; but then she remembered that she was a thief as well, and so she nodded to Cayson. "You said a path."

"Rellion says that the monks of the Abbey aren't what they appear, or at least they didn't use to be." Cayson considered his statement for a moment, trying to decide if it made sense to him or not, but decided it was good enough and continued. "The monks use to be peaceful warriors a long time back, or so he said. This is their path to enlightenment."

"The monks, peaceful warriors?" she repeated back doubtfully, and thought, *all they ever do is chant and pray.*

Cayson replied as if he had heard her thoughts. "Well, I did say *use to be*. The tabernacle used to be more than a place of prayer." She gave him a questioning look. "Under all the pews, did you ever look at the floor?" Cayson pointed upward for emphasis to the Abbey, probably some hundreds of feet above.

Kristane thought on this for a moment. It was rare that she'd ever left or returned to the Attic any way besides the backdoor, but as she pondered further. There were times she remembered, as a younger version of herself, that the chants and prayers of the monks had piqued her curiosity so much that she had peeked down from the balcony. Through the balusters, as a curious little girl, she had seen the bedizened and patterned floor of the Abbey, and the strange procession the monks had made. Though sloppily and with singularly basic side-to-side steps, the monks had done their best to only step within the light side of the triangles of the floor, which now that she thought on it, looked unquestionably like their practice circle within the Attic.

Feeling as though he had made his point, without another word Cayson turned and stepped over the darkened threshold, the moron twins tight on his heels. Prya shrugged her shoulders and followed with Lathan, leaving Kristane and her brother to stare up at the stone guardians.

"You good?" Xander asked.

"Yeah. Just, did you know anything about any of that? I mean, Rellion never said anything like that to me."

"No, but it doesn't surprise me. You know Rellion and his secrets." Seeing the dismayed look on his sister's face, Xander continued, "Look, Kris, it bothers me just as much, but he tells us as much as it suits him. Before, I suppose it didn't matter so much, but now… well, I don't know." Kristane knew; she thought of Groggle and the escape hatch, her necklace, Count Bobo's declarations, and now this.

Following after the others, they were greeted by a small domed expanse, its height decidedly greater than its diameter. Even Cayson seemed hesitant to take too many steps deeper within. Along the circumference of the dome, columns hewn from the rock walls rose up and then gathered at the center of the cupola, like the spines of an inverted weaved basket. Spreading out to the sides of him, the others tried to take in the space that was lighted by the same kind of bugs as at the entrance, but thousands upon thousands more. The Rogue's movement set off large patches of the bugs as they fired and then extinguished, making the next grouping do the same. The effect was wave-like as it patterned itself across the walls and up onto the curved ceiling. Kristane was thankful that they appeared to want to stay where the lichen accumulated on the rock, but this thought didn't stop her from scratching at an imaginary itch or swatting at her arms.

Cayson, looking fixedly ahead, said, "There's something at the center of the room." It was difficult to tell with the shadowing and the firing of the insects in the background, but a strange, focused spotlight at the apex of the cupola shone down upon a stone plinth.

Cayson took a tentative step forward. The swoosh of a closely-passing projectile was followed by the resounding twang of the force of impact into the wall near them, the only prior warning a creaking of metal joints. Kristane turned to where she thought the initial movement had come from, just in time to see a shadowed figure as the insects' light faded across its shoulders and head. Startled by what she had seen, she was about to call out a warning when other forms were highlighted all along the wall line. She recognized them as the same statuesque man and woman as before, their serene faces repeated again and again. Only instead of being carved of stone, these statues were made of metal, much like Count Bobo; but more importantly, what kept her from her warning was that they lacked that spark of life in their eyes that she had come to recognize as to being *alive.* These seemed like nothing more than the vending machine idol that guarded the entrance to her old home, the Attic.

"Dammit, that was stupid." Cayson shook his head in dismay.

Kristane turned to look in his direction, and saw a circular blank area like a hole in the wall where there was no light. The tiny lighted bugs must have scattered with the violent jolt. As the bugs slowly returned to light the area, the metal shaft of a spear appeared. There was no telling how far it had gone into the stone, but a good portion of it still protruded. It was as long as she was tall, or so it seemed from her vantage point. The thing looked as though it could have pierced all of them together, but instead it had only skewered a black bowler hat.

"Frickin' hat! Consarn it!" Markyn trounced over and extracted his hat by sliding it down the end of the spear. Puffing on his pipe, he fingered the not-so-small holes that now adorned either side of his bowler. Kristane was shocked that all the older Kressley seemed to be bothered by was that his ratty hat was run through, not that by fortune of stature, his skull hadn't been just a few inches higher.

"Damn warning." Cayson was obviously only concerned as to his forgetfulness, not that one of his friends could have been hanging from a metal rod like a piece of meat above a cookout fire. "Penitent." Cayson trailed off in thought, then again hung his head in dismay as Markyn walked over and gave him a pat on his shoulder in an attempt to reassure him.

"Maybe you idiots should stop walking around," Prya said with a deadpan calm that Kristane, with difficulty, also found herself trying to maintain.

Cayson ignored her, deep in thought, but Markyn crammed his perforated bowler onto his head and flipped her a finger. Kristane almost laughed when Prya returned it with a blown kiss.

"So, penitent... means we should show humility. Being a servant to our beliefs, and to others. Don't stomp in all proud and such." Cayson pondered a moment more on what he had just said, then dropped to his hands and knees and began brushing at the layers of dust and dirt that covered the floor. Soon his fingers fell into an etched groove. Tracing the outline of it with both hands, it appeared as though it formed a double halved-diamond pattern. Growing visibly more excited, Cayson knelt down lower, took in a big breath, and blew hard along the lines he had uncovered. The Kressley brothers fell to their knees, and with the same enthusiasm started blowing and swiping. The misplaced powdery cloud caused Kristane to sneeze, but she almost choked from trying to hold her breath in, fearful that any movement might trigger another thrown spear. As her eyes adjusted to the diminished light, she looked again at the serene female face that had thrown the spear, silently hoping it was just the throwing arm that had moved.

"There, look!" Cayson said triumphantly, kneeling up with his arms spread in presentation.

Pulling her gaze away, she moved to Cayson's side and looked down at what he and the brothers had uncovered. With a respectful nod that she felt at odds with because she still felt like smacking the arrogant smugness off Cayson's face, she knelt down and started to swipe at the dirt. Quickly, with the determined efforts of everyone, the beginnings of a circular space was uncovered, reminiscent of their practice ring.

ᴄTHEIR FIRST ᴅDANCE

"There's a problem; this isn't right." Kristane was thinking the same thing as Cayson said it, and by the looks of the other Rogue members, they too had realized the same. "It's too big."

Instead of a single circle, Kristane could see a series of concentric circles outlined in the dust leading to the plinth at the center. "So what do we do?"

"I think I know." Lathan called them over from where he stood observing the walls.

Reliefs of over- and under-demarcations ran along the walls in between the columns and statues, depicting both men and women in the same religious habits as the monks Kristane knew, but so different from the doddering old fools she had grown to ignore. The forms were poised in differing stances in what seemed to be an attack, some holding spears above their heads, some swords, and others longbows with nocked arrows; but despite their aggressive stances, their faces were serene and peaceful. Instead of single fighting poses, the figures were depicted in pairs and even trios: a hand joined here, a leg hooked there, their stances a reverse mirror of the other in some, or a combination of their partners in others. She recognized many of the stances, especially the foot placements, just not the accompanying weapons or the pairing with someone else. She *should* know the steps, she thought; Rellion had literally beaten them into her head.

Now listen well, my dearest waifs, do not giggle and do not gaggle! When you wiggle when you waggle, till it jingles till it jangles, don't mess up your angles when you're tripping the triangles! Kristane found herself smiling at the memory of the silly rhyme, despite Rellion's use of a stick on her calves and backside when she had missed a step, or the intoned chime of a bell when her foot found the proper placement. She had always laughed along with all the other kids when Rellion slapped his own butt on each cheek as he reached the line about *it jingles and it jangles,* but now, as her smile faded, she thought only of her growing uncertainty towards her mentor.

"It's just like our practice circle, but in a sequence." Trailing his hand across the carvings, Lathan explained. "Do the first sequence of movements in this circle, then the next sequence, then in the third circle, that!" Raising his voice and pointing back, indicating the third and top line of the etchings, he said, "Until we make it to the center!"

Kristane didn't know why she was doing it, but she looked over at Cayson for some sort of confirmation. Meeting her eyes, he begrudgingly nodded. She could tell that it was costing him to admit that he wasn't the first to solve this problem. Then he said something that shocked her even more. "Right, you'll have to do it, Lathan, you're the best of us."

If Lathan was just as surprised as she was, he only showed it for a moment; but Prya caught her attention and mouthed out a shocked, *What the hell?*

Prya stood shoulder to shoulder with Lathan, studying the etchings. Kristane watched as her two friends nodded to each other, and then laughed at something one had said. She knew that it was the best decision. The sequences were meant to be done with at least one partner, and Prya and Lathan were the best matched; but that didn't keep her from feeling a little jealous. She didn't like Lathan that way, of course, but she sensed that the two of them together were moving farther away from her.

Lathan confidently aligned himself to where the carvings and the first ring began, and turned around to face Prya, his back to the center plinth, taking her hand in his. Kristane watched as the pair stared down at their intertwined fingers, and the thought struck her that she couldn't remember the two ever doing that before. She could tell by their body language that they had just realized the same. Lathan said something quietly to Prya as he stepped backwards onto the circular triangle mosaic. With his first step, there was an accompanying and hushed ringing, as if someone had struck a small bell that reverberated around the dome. All of a sudden, Kristane felt extremely anxious for her friends and the weight of what they were trying to do. She quickly scanned the statues around the perimeter for movement, and laughed nervously when nothing happened. Lathan took a couple more slow steps, his feet falling exactly where they should, the bells continuing to resound with each footfall. Still holding Prya's hand, Lathan guided her along with him, the pitch changing to another tone with the placement of her feet.

Soon their movements came quicker and quicker as they twirled around the first circle and leapt into the second. The inflections and tones filled the domed room, echoing from the cupola, and built into a melody — a beautiful thing that swayed like the wind and evolved like a summer storm breaking across a quiet plain until the tempest struck into its crescendo. Kristane found herself lost in the moment as her friends landed in the final circle; the whole of the world had disappeared, and there was only the two of them. The two looked so confident in their movements that Kristane now wished for it to never end for them; but as quick as it had come, it was gone. Lathan and Prya stood in the center next to the plinth, with the trail of quiet chimes like raindrops floating down and around from the dome. They dropped their hands awkwardly, far too quickly. Kristane thought that they must be embarrassed by the realization that others were watching something so intimate.

A droning rumble saved them all from the uncomfortableness, though, as the floor below the pair started to fall away.

WE GOT WHAT
WE CAME FOR

I t didn't fall apart into pieces, and only that portion that made up the mosaic of concentric circles moved; but it lowered all at once, rotating down like a screw being driven into wood. The plinth became a column that the round table of rock spun downward on. Kristane kneeled down to watch Prya and Lathan disappear below the floor level.

"Come on, you lot, let's go!" Cayson didn't wait for a response or protest from the others, but just jumped to the lowering platform, stumbling a little with the spin of it. Kristane and Xander followed, but the Kressleys stared down at Cayson apprehensively.

"No, 'rickin' 'ayson, 'ot doin' it!" Both boys stood there with their arms crossed, determined not to budge.

Cayson, exasperated and angry, shouted back. "Oi, get down here now, or do you want to stay up there alone?"

That seemed to have the desired effect. The boys looked around at the domed room and then began pushing at one another, trying to make the other go first. In the end, one ended up pulling the other over as Cayson rushed to break their fall.

As the rock platform dropped lower and lower, shadowy lumps appeared far into the dark of another opening below the room above, making it impossible to see what was there. The space was void of the bugs, the only light being the thin shaft that struck the top of the plinth and feebly poured over its edges down into the darkened abyss that they were descending into. Instinctively, the group backed away from the veil of darkness, their backs to the pillar at the center. The platform came to a grinding halt; the crush of small stones caught below its weight echoed out into the silence, along with a clicking, like the aperture of a camera, from the center column. A flash of light poured into the area from a band of crystals in the pillar at about chest height, the thin light above somehow being reflected internally down its length and then magnified at the now-exposed band. Though the light would have been considered subdued at any other time, with the long hours with solely bugs providing their only illumination, it was blinding for the group. Turning from the source and shielding their eyes, the haze of brightness that crept at the edge of their vision slowly lessened as their eyes adjusted.

Greeting Kristane and the others was a sight to delight kings and thieves alike. In a circular room identical to the domed one above lay mounds of jewel-encrusted armor, shields, weapons, crosses, and chests filled to overflowing with coins and gemstones. Halberds, bows, spears, and ornately topped crosiers were stacked indiscriminately next to each other, on end, in bunches of triangular towers, so precarious a slight nudge or stiff breeze would have caused it all to tumble over. Tapestries, rugs, and banners, all from antiquity, draped haphazardly across piles of treasure, with some rolled with obvious care. A fine layer of silt covered it all, but it couldn't completely cover the lambent radiance of lifetimes of wealth and memory.

"Don't touch it!" Cayson moved to grab for the ginger brothers as the sight of such opulence brought out the inbred greed in them. They were all thieves, after all. She could see that Prya even had focused on a necklace and matching earrings that she imagined her friend thought would look better on her than here, buried in dust.

"Frick it, wee 'aking it!" Markyn shoved Cayson's hand from his collar and spun on him, giving him a defiant stare. Puffing on his pipe, he dared Cayson to say otherwise.

Kristane was surprised that Cayson didn't rise to the challenge. "You can't take it. It's like the proverb says: *Casting away those material things*," he simply said, and that alone deflated the boys into a humbled shaking of their heads. "Oi, it's all right, boys, remember what's said about forgiveness? *You never learn anything by doing right!*" Kristane played that last part back in her head to make sure she had heard it correctly, but Cayson seemed to be self-assured of that particular quote. Regardless, the moron brothers seemed brightened by it. She shook her head; Cayson's supposed "enlightenment" seemed to need a little work, she thought.

Joining the rest as they left the platform, Kristane took a step down. With the transfer of their weight, there was a grinding of rock upon rock. Looking around in a panic for whatever was about to fall on their heads or skewer them, she saw an opening materialize in the wall to her left. "It's just the way out," Cayson stated matter-of-factly as if he knew it was there all along. "That platform there is just counterbalanced to the door... probably the floor, too."

"What do mean, the floor?" Staring down at her feet, reassuring herself that they hadn't moved, she took in the others and saw the brothers marching around without a care in the world. "Again, maybe you idiots should stop walking around," Prya said with the same deadpan calm as before. Markyn and Munse responded with a cheeky scowl and started jumping up and down in circles. "Idiots."

"No, not that floor. Where all the treasure is, where the monks cast off their physical burdens." Cayson indicated the treasure with an arrogant sweep of his arm, as if the answer was obvious to anyone over the age of five. Kristane found her newfound respect for him waning with the desire to smack him, and not just for the normal reasons — or maybe it was, again, Rellion she wished to slap.

Looking about the room, she found her gaze being drawn to a particular object. It wasn't floating in a jar in some murky fluid as she had half expected, yet she knew instantly that this was what they had come for. Upon a cracked stone podium, its surface befouled by nasty stains, laid a very familiar heart-shaped curio. Kristane couldn't explain it, but something that made her skin crawl was emanating from it.

"It looks just like yours… well, sort of, anyway," Prya said uneasily, looking over Kristane's shoulder.

Kristane clutched reflexively at its mirror around her neck, and Purdy hissed menacingly in her ear. Possibly she was just imagining the feeling, but as the others gathered around, she sensed that it affected them as well. While it looked much like the pendant hanging from her own neck, there was something decrepit about it. The spiderwebbed pattern of fractured and tainted stone that radiated out from the tarnished metal and smooth wooden heart made it look as if the trinket had bled out.

Kristane wasn't exactly sure if she was relieved or fearful that it hadn't turned out to be some odd body part of a moldy old saint. "I'm not so sure we should touch that thing."

"Well, there's nothing for it, then!" She didn't even have time to gasp as Cayson grabbed for the heart and quickly stuffed it into a pocket. "Better get out of here fast!" He didn't need to even grab for the Kressley brothers; they were already three paces ahead of him, heading for the slowly lowering stone that opened out into the only exit that they knew of.

Lathan and Prya didn't hesitate either and nearly outdistanced the ginger twins as the circular podium began to rise back up to the dome above in a counterclockwise motion. Kristane, in a state of shock, gaped at the backs of her retreating so-called friends as a couple of squeaky, *buts* and *what's?* trickled out of her mouth. Grabbing her hand, Xander spun her around so quickly that it made her head spin, and it took her nearly three dragged steps before she found her legs working like they should. Recklessly, she followed her brother as he made for the ever-smaller opening.

Just when it looked like they might make it, the unthinkable happened: Xander stumbled. Trailing behind him as she was, Kristane's forward motion tripped him even further, and the two went down in a symphony of grunts, gasps, and wheezes accompanied by a spray of dust. She choked on the cloud and then gagged at the intake of the silt-misted air. Rising far too slowly under the circumstances, upon bruised knees and scrapped knuckles, she could see, through the haze, the wide-eyed astonishment mixed with fear on the faces Prya and Lathan, not necessarily for themselves but for her and Xander. The aperture was now only a half of what it had been as her two friends knelt within the opening, waving their arms frantically.

Prya, with a look of steeled determination, raised her mechanical arm to the descending stone. The screech of stone and whatever mechanics controlled the circular rising platform heaved ominously, filling the treasure anteroom with a biting echo. Peeking through the opening and around her, Kristane could see the apprehensive faces of the moron brothers staring back at her. *God, I'm going to smack them and Cayson too,* she thought to herself. *That is, if I make it out of this, anyway.*

Through clenched teeth, sweat already dripping down her forehead from the effort, Prya looked at her with a pleading, *"Hurry!"* The platform shook violently, as when sprockets and gears catch on one another and there's nowhere else for them to go but to break off their teeth and spin wildly. She had seen an elevated streetcar do that once, and the outcome wasn't pleasant. Emboldened by the courage of her friend, Kristane hauled herself up, with Xander already by her side.

Ducking down under the closing door, they squeezed past the straining Prya, the articulated exoskeleton of her arm creaking. Kristane remembered Groggle going on about leverage and force, whatever that meant, but she hoped it would be enough. Letting out a defiant scream as they passed, Prya scuttled back and let go. The whir of gears and scraping stone from deep within the treasure room was suddenly silenced by the slamming of the stone door. Only a wisp of dust that escaped from below signified where the opening had been as it fell into place and melded into the wall.

Rounding about, Kristane eyed the Kressley brothers, her chest heaving from anger as they scurried to the sides of the room, trying to avoid what was sure to be an outburst. "Cayson, you idiot!"

"What? You're both fine! What does it matter? We got what we came for!"

"We could be stuck in there, or worse, *dead* is what is the matter!"

Cayson had the nerve to look indignant at her fury.

Just as she was about to go full stride into her tirade, Xander said to her, "Let it be, Kris, he doesn't understand." Rounding on her brother, she was still looking for an outlet to her anger, but pulled up short when she saw her twin's consoling expression. Yes, Cayson was an ass and deserved what she wanted to give him, but the real source of her rage, deep down, was Rellion.

FLUSHED DOWN THE TOILET

Kristane and her brother lagged behind the others as they traversed the last few turns of the ancient tunnels that led to their refuge within the mines of Kairos. She watched as Cayson ran to Rellion like a dutiful little sycophant, and while she felt ill, it was only with her own self-disgust for the lengths she had gone to try and please this man herself.

"Well done, Master Cayson, you do make me proud!" Rellion quickly pocketed the necklace and patted him on the shoulder appraisingly. Rellion turned to where she stood within the mouth of the tunnel and greeted her with a blank stare. Xander bumped her shoulder as he passed and said, "Come on."

Rellion gave a pronounced yawn that Kristane knew he was probably faking. "Well done, my Rogue, but the exposition of your exploits can wait. We must all rest, and in the morning we'll put some space between ourselves and them." She began to protest, and Prya joined in half-heartedly, but he quickly cut them off. "Enough! All in good time!"

Rellion faked another pronounced yawn and marched toward the train. Kristane turned to talk to Pipkin and demand from him further answers, but found that he had already disappeared into the shadows. She wasn't the only one frustrated; the others gathered in closer and took turns abusing Rellion, though admittedly not so he could hear. Even Cayson and the Kressley brothers joined in. "Bloody pile o' 'it! Bloody 'ellion 'ay friggin' nothing!"

It was several hours later that the others finally grumbled themselves to sleep. Groggle had retreated to the cab of the engine, where he seemed to be the most comfortable; but the rest of them decided to bed down around the fire. Only Kristane and Xander remained awake. They did not speak, but stared into the dying fire, occasionally looking at each other. They didn't need to exchange any words, each knowing that whatever came, they would face it together. Kristane felt lost; it was only Xander's presence that helped her to hold it together, and how could she possibly go through this without him by her side? Knowing her brother would not sleep until she laid down, she walked over to him and gave him a hug, and then picked out a stretch of ground that didn't look too hard, resolving herself to demand more from Rellion in the morning.

Kristane's sleep was fitful. A quiet splash of water awoke her; a stone had fallen from somewhere and broken the surface of the lake. Kristane turned over and saw the others laid out before the still-going fire; she mustn't have been asleep long, unless Xander had put some more wood on. Turning to her other side, she was shocked to see Pipkin just a few yards away, sitting in the crease of two boulders staring wide-eyed at her, a look of terror on his face.

"What's the matter, Pipkin?" she whispered quietly, not wanting to wake the others.

Pipkin was rolled into a ball, his arms clasping his knees tight to his chest, tremors of fear shaking his entire body, with the familiar TINK, TINK, TINK emanating from somewhere in his clothing. He tried to mouth something, but found himself unable to. With a great effort, he raised one hand and pointed his finger to Kristane's chest. With the light of the fire, she had not noticed her necklace dully pulsing. Fear gripped her; clutching the clockwork heart, she scanned the shadows, but the fire made it nearly impossible to see anything beyond the halo it cast.

"Pretty necklace glows… danger, pretty girl… danger." Pipkin had found his voice, but it was barely above a whisper.

Xander stirred, and his eyes popped open, taking in Kristane, the necklace, and Pipkin cowering in the background. Instantly he was on his feet, his attention focused on any possible movement around them. Kristane felt like she was dreaming, the blood rushing to her head and clouding her vision; she wasn't sure what she was seeing. A pair of darkened silhouettes seemingly floated amongst the other shadows, moving steadily forward. Suddenly, there was an intense squawk and a flash of feathers as Purdy dove at the approaching figures, his wings batting at their heads and his talons ripping at their hoods. All at once, the rest of the Rogue were awake and staring around for the source of the commotion. Purdy had succeeded in holding up the advancing figures, and had even pulled the hood off one of them. Kristane stared mesmerized at the shining metal face of the Forgotten One. She was beautiful, despite her look of rage as she swatted at the Faerrier, her features a combination of various finely-shaped metals. Her hair, of thinly spun strands of brass and gold, looked liquid as it bounced about her shoulders as if it were real. Purdy swooped in for another attack, but caught the backhand of the other Forgotten One, and was sent sprawling towards the drive wheels of the train.

"No! Purdy!" Kristane reached out, taking her hand off the necklace as if to try and catch him as he fell. Both of the intruders turned towards her shriek of despair, and their eyes were immediately drawn to the pulsing necklace about her neck. The other dancer dropped her cowl and the two looked at each other, their metal visages contorting with sinister elation. Deliberately, they moved for Kristane and the item that they so desired.

"Get to the train!" Xander commanded the others, and ran to his sister's side.

"No, no, noooo! Pipkin scared!" Pipkin hadn't moved a muscle; he sat cowering and blubbering to himself, rocking back and forth on his backside, his arms wrapped tightly about his knees.

"Xander, we can't leave him!" Kristane turned to aid Pipkin as the dancers came within arm's reach of Xander and her.

Prya ran forward, and with an upward swoop of her articulated arm, struck both Forgotten Ones in their chests, launching them backwards, the collision of metal against metal ringing hard against the walls of the cavern. The Forgotten Ones quickly regained their feet, and with twin looks of surprise that quickly turned to anger, they again strode forward.

"Come on, Pipkin, I'll protect you! Come with me!" Kristane held out her hand, desperate for Pipkin to take it.

Pipkin looked up at her, tears still welling in his eyes, but just stared at her hand. "Pretty girl protect Pipkin?"

"Yes, yes! Please just take my hand!"

Pipkin continued to stare, his features screwing up with some internal battle taking place. "No, Pipkin scared… *No, Pipkin protects*!" Kristane was taken aback by the sudden and determined focus within the boy's fiery eyes and fierce voice. Kristane thought that Pipkin was going to pirouette again, but instead, with a mischievous grin, he nimbly rose, reaching behind his back with both arms — and pulled from somewhere hidden within his jacket a pair of long daggers, each with fullers as broad as a sword.

"TINK! TINK! TINK! Fear no fear and fear no love, for I'll not die a coward's death, as I pray on high above!" Pipkin clanked the swords together before him in unison as he said the words *"tink"* and gave Kristane a wink. *"Run, pretty girl, this is my burden!"*

Kristane stood there, shocked; the repetitive *"tink"* she had thought were bells and heard so many times at Pipkin's comings and goings were the concealed weapons he now held menacingly before her. Xander grabbed ahold of his sister's shoulders and pulled her aside. Without another word, Pipkin launched himself forward at the oncoming Forgotten Ones, his initial onslaught so fierce that they retreated, holding their metal arms before them like shields. It quickly became clear that Pipkin, though deadly with the twin daggers he flashed one way and then the other, never giving the dancers a purchase, was not going to do them any harm.

"Here, my Rogue, to me! Master Groggle, get this piece of ornate scrap moving, now!" Rellion had emerged from the passenger cars of the train, waving to all of them. Kristane watched as Groggle shouted back something incoherent with Purdy held carefully in his arms, carrying him to the cab of the train. Rellion gave an exasperated grimace and ran towards him.

"Come on, Kris let's go!" Xander urged his sister forward.

"But what about Pipkin?" Kristane was still having trouble shaking off the shock of the past several minutes, her head clouded and both her legs as heavy as stones.

"Hurry! Something tells me he can take care of himself!" Xander continued to prod his reluctant sister along as the sound of metal on metal resonated about the cavern, loud as an ironsmith forging a piece of hardened steel.

Rellion reemerged from the cab of the train just as a tremendous creaking of joints and the rumbling of boiling water stunned Kristane back to the present. A large plume of steam billowed out from the train engine's mushroom-shaped stack, the domed cap directing the burst of heated water vapor downward, disturbing the fine silt that lay upon the ground and throwing it into the air. Suddenly, the old steam engine was alive, and illuminated from front to back with a glow that gave it a ghostly look against the cascading dust. The great beast picked up speed, shattering small rocks against the rails with its immense drive wheels. As it moved, Rellion pushed the others into the cab. Xander and Kristane, bringing up the rear, stumbled into the cab, winded from chasing down their hopeful salvation.

"Step aside. Master Groggle, one more blast should suffice!" Rellion, brandishing his cane, set it aglow and directed its energy into the open tinder box of the train. With earnest, the iron horse surged forward.

Kristane, heaving and breathless, clutched at the stitch in her chest; something was missing, and panic struck her at the realization. "Oh no, my necklace, it's gone!"

Xander spun about, and looking back along the tracks from where they had come, saw the necklace lying not far from where he and Kristane had boarded. Without a thought, he jumped from the train, stumbling slightly as he regained his balance, and ran to retrieve it. The sounds of the continuing battle and the shapes of Pipkin and his combatants were occasionally visible in the dusty background.

"No Xander, leave it!"

"Master Cayson, Master Lathan, hold her!" The boys grabbed for Kristane as she attempted to follow her brother.

Rellion peered back out of the cab. Xander was already running back, but something was wrong; he moved with a lopsided gait, his ankle obviously sprained, or worse, from his jump from the train. Kristane joined Rellion at the open-sided cab, and the others gathered about as well, all craning to see, yelling words of encouragement.

Their anxious voices drew the attention of the Forgotten Ones, though, and Pipkin, seeing Xander's predicament, bodily shoved them backwards with a series of kicks. Running all out, Pipkin reached Xander, who had succumbed to his injury and exhaustion at the edge of the precipice that jutted out over the mine's spillway, before the metal women could right themselves. Taking the necklace from Xander, he spun around twice and gave it a mighty heave, throwing it towards the retreating train. Rellion extended his cane and skewered it by its chain, swinging it about and allowing it to slide back along the shaft.

Xander saw the Forgotten Ones coming determinedly at them, their faces contorted into masks of rage; he thought that this was the end. At least Kristane was safe, and the necklace too; he resigned himself to accept what seemed inevitable.

Pipkin sheathed his daggers and grabbed Xander by both shoulders, turning him to face him. "Hold your breath!" Pipkin said to Xander with a mischievous smile.

"Wait, what?"

"Pipkin says *swoosh!*" And without further warning, he shoved Xander backwards. Xander's feet caught on each other in surprise, and he unceremoniously toppled backwards, headfirst, over the precipice and into the flushing spillway.

Rellion and the others watched from far off as Pipkin yelled "Yippee!" and did a cannonball into the gaping mouth of swirling water. Kristane was nearly in hysterics as the train entered the mouth of a tunnel and left the cavern, the pair of Forgotten Ones still in pursuit. Cayson and Lathan kept a tight grip upon her to keep her from going to her brother. Rellion picked a spot somewhere behind the caboose just as it cleared the tunnel entrance, and with his cane, blasted the ceiling of the cavern until it crumbled behind them, their escape sealed from further pursuit.

Kristane dropped her head and sobbed as the last little bit of light that had filled the cavern with dawn was extinguished by the collapsing rock.

"My Princess... Kristane, you must not give into despair," said Rellion, lifting her chin with one hand. "Trust in your brother's abilities and those of Master Pipkin; there is still hope for their well-being. For now, the danger has passed for all of us."

"How do you know we aren't in any more danger?" Kristane responded angrily, choking on her tears. She was furious with Rellion for telling her to be calm, and terrified that she was never going to see her brother again.

Rellion approached and knelt down to her. "I know that we are safe for now; your necklace confirms it." Kristane looked down through blurry tears as Rellion placed the clockwork necklace in her hand. It no longer pulsed with light at her touch.

A Boy and His Horse

Xander awoke to the pattering of rain upon his scratched and muddy face, lying half in and half out of what seemed to be a river. The pebbled beach of smoothed river rocks on which his upper torso laid pressed against his already-bruised muscles. A mixture of blood and mud stung his eyes as droplets of water fell from his damp hair. Grasping at the rocks about him, Xander slowly pulled himself along the stony bed with his elbows until he reached some tall grass. With a great effort, he rolled onto his back and let the rain fall upon his face again. Opening his eyes, he found it difficult to focus on the canopy of trees and the grasses above and to the sides of him. He only dared to move his head slightly, due to the throbbing in his temples.

Glancing toward his feet, he could see the mountain range that must be the Effervescent Peaks in which the Bizzarred mines were located — and which he had abruptly vacated, thanks to Pipkin. If this was the Effervescent Peaks, then the river that gurgled and rushed past his feet must be the Cynabell, which was far east of Kairos. Xander wondered whether he should thank Pipkin the next time he saw him or not — and if he would ever see him again.

Xander closed his eyes and imagined the dark and twisting spiral that was the ride down and out of the mines. At times, he'd felt as though he was going to drown, and other times his body had bounced back and forth against the smooth rock surfaces so hard that he wondered even now if something wasn't broken. He ran his hands along his chest, putting pressure on his ribs; while painful, he didn't think anything was fractured. Tentatively, he moved his legs about, and they seemed to be in working order as well, except for the sprain in his left ankle, which had been the result of the bad landing from the train. His thoughts turned to his sister and the others, and he was filled with a sense of dread. Had they gotten away? Was Kristane safe? The fear of it was enough to overwhelm him, and a bit of panic rose up in his chest. He tried to sit up, but the aches and pains left him breathless, and he collapsed back into the grass. Taking a few slow, deep breaths, he calmed himself, knowing that in all probability his situation was worse than hers. She was with Rellion and the others; they had to have gotten away. They'd look after her.

The light rain that pattered on his face began to smack harder as the droplets increased in size and intensity. Xander felt a coldness run through him that chilled him to the bone; he began to shake from head to toe, and knew he needed to get under cover. Slowly pushing himself over onto his stomach, he drew his knees up underneath himself, then paused from the exertion of it. A moment later, on hands and knees, Xander crawled toward the cover of the trees. Occasionally a small rock bit into his kneecaps, shooting pain through his legs; but each time, the pain helped to clear his head to the point that he almost wished for the next one. Finally, propping himself against the rough bark of a densely canopied tree, Xander closed his eyes and let the sound of the rain wash over him as he drifted off.

He awoke with a start. Somewhere in that place between sleep and wakefulness, he thought he'd heard the familiar *Tink, Tink, Tink* of Pipkin; but all he heard now was the rushing of the Cynabell. "What happened to Pipkin, and how did I get to the bank?" Xander wondered absently.

Looking about, he found that he'd slept till nearly dusk, and while the rain had stopped, there was a misty fog hanging within the valley. His clothes hadn't dried, and as he rubbed his hands together, they didn't feel like his own hands, but more like something dead. Blowing on them for warmth helped a little, but Xander was keenly aware that if he didn't find better shelter soon, it wouldn't be long before he succumbed to exposure. Scanning the ground, he located a dead branch that looked like it might hold his weight. Pushing himself up the trunk of the tree, he winched himself into place with the makeshift crutch. Teetering slightly, he took a couple of tentative steps, and found that his ankle didn't hurt as bad as it had. Xander wondered whether it was actually better, or if he just couldn't feel it any longer.

Having no clue as to where he was, he decided that staying within sight of the river and following it upstream was as a good a decision as any. He stumbled and fell several times, adding more bruises to his already pain-wracked body, but was determined not to give up. Dusk was soon upon him, and the temperature was dropping quickly; moonlight was his only guide as he meandered one way and then another, listening for the gurgle of the river. The fog had a murky haze that made him wonder more than once if he was dreaming; he waved his free arm in front of him as the wisps of mist seemed to cling and coil around his fingers. Not paying attention, so transfixed was he by the wavy spirals of mist he was creating, he lumbered into a series of brambles and fell headlong into a copse. He swore to himself for becoming so distracted. Within this thicket, the gloom was less, but a heavy cover of it floated above his head and up along the incline from which he had just fallen. He supposed that it was once a streambed that fed into the river, but was now dried up.

Turning his head toward where the water might have run, Xander was startled by the sight of a huge, ghostly figure that stood silent and unmoving. A monstrous metal stallion was poised there with its head bowed. Again, he wondered if he was in a dream; it was so unlikely that such a large beast would be here, abandoned. The stallion was unlike anything Xander had ever seen, being used to the weathered mechanical beasts that pulled carriages and carts all over Kairos. This iron horse put them to shame. The body of this magnificent animal was plated in the battle armor of men: breast plates, helms, greaves, and gauntlets, its rear haunches and flank affixed with ancient round war shields and decorated in scrolling and etchings that Xander didn't not recognize. Age and the elements had tarnished the metal, but certain pieces shone brightly even in the diminished light. Xander imagined that the stallion must easily stand twenty-one hands high to its withers, and it looked as broad as a small cart. He approached it slowly, limping forward on his crutch. The animal did not stir, its eyes closed. Xander had an overwhelming urge to pet the horse; reaching his hand to its muzzle, he gave it a gentle stroke. The plates were smooth to his touch, and gleamed in the moonlight.

He continued to stroke the stallion. "You are an amazing horse. Wish you could come with me, or at least give me a ride." He gave it a final pat and started to turn away, resigned to move on, leaving the horse to its eternal slumber.

Abruptly, a blast of steam blew from the horse's nostrils, tossing Xander's hair back across his face with the force of it. The stallion's eyes shot wide open, and it reared its head upward, neighing as Xander stepped uncertainly back, in fear of being trampled. The horse's large hooves rattled with the chainmail that draped them, and each pawing of the thicket's ground was thunderous. Xander held up his free hand in defense, peeking through his splayed fingers and making eye contact with the great horse. The initial anger within the stallion's eyes subsided, and it stopped its tramping and waved its head from side to side, flinging the leather straps of its mane. Xander dropped his hand a little lower, but not his eye contact. Slowly, the horse calmed and bowed its head, allowing him to stroke its muzzle and forehead.

"Wow! And here I thought you were something when you were asleep." Xander shivered, his hand shaking as he touched the metal snout. "Don't suppose you know where there's any shelter, do you?" He chuckled to himself at the absurdity of holding a conversation with a metal horse. "I must be delirious if I think you understand me, eh?"

The great horse dropped to a single knee, the joints of its leg creaking ominously as the accumulated corrosion of ages broke free, and whinnied softly as it nodded its head backward.

"So I *am* crazy. Well it's not like I'm getting a better offer anytime soon."

Xander did his best to scramble onto the broad back of the stallion as it patiently held its position. The back of the horse was wide, but Xander found sitting there comfortable. He gave the stallion a pat on its neck, and the beast rose. Turning around, it walked slowly into the brush, away from the Cynabell. Xander didn't remember how long he rode before he began to drift off again, but the slow up-and-down gait of the horse was soothing in comparison to stumbling around on a crutch. All he remembered was that the leathery mane was surprisingly soft as he laid his head forward across the stallion's neck and fell asleep.

I Am Nobody, If You Must Know

Xander awoke to the smell of something awful.

The best he could tell, it was the heavy blankets that covered him. The odor was so foul that he half-expected to see the rotting body of a dead rat lying on his chest, which thanks to Purdy had happened on more than one occasion. If it hadn't felt so good to be warm again, he would have thrown them off himself. Instead, he laid there trying to guess where he was and how he'd come to be here.

"Awake? Wondered if you were going to. You were in pretty bad shape, boy."

Xander turned in the direction of the rough voice to see a dark-haired man sitting with his back to him, wearing a piecemeal uniform of canvas and faded blue cloth. The man didn't bother to turn around, instead continuing to poke idly with a fire iron at the flames in a hearth.

"Where am I?"

"You, boy, are within the grand walls and refuge of the Ward. Though they're not as grand as they once were." The man gestured absently with the fire iron, in a sweeping motion. "Mean anything to you?"

"No. How did I get here?" Xander shuffled his body and raised himself up on his elbow. The door of the place, or what was left of it, stood propped up against the door frame. The stone walls were cracked from the building settling in many places, and chunks had fallen away.

"Wasn't for that horse of yours bringing you here, doubt you would be alive."

"My horse?" Xander thought back, trying to remember; yes, he remembered mounting the metal stallion he'd found, and a few semi-lucid moments when he'd found himself draped across the horse's back, staring down from a precipice high above a mountain trail, and the clinking sound of chainmail as the horse traversed a narrow path. "It's not my horse. I found it."

"I assure you, boy, he *is* your horse. Aldebarron doesn't just awaken and grant pony rides like some carousel puppet."

"Aldebarron?"

"Yes, pride of the many realms both old and new, glorious steed of the house of nobility, warhorse of the last great war... and most assuredly yours." The man spoke in a grand and slightly contemptuous manner, punctuating each title he gave to the horse with a flourish of his poker, yet never looking away from the fire.

"Warhorse... mine... how do you know his name?"

"Stories, legends, and mostly the fact that his great deeds are etched into the shields that make up his body. Can read, can't you, boy?"

"Yes, I can read, just not those markings... and I have a name." Xander said this last bit in an undertone, being in no shape to respond if things went badly, but he was tired of being called *boy* in the unctuous way the man was using it.

For the first time, the man turned around and stood looking at Xander, the poker held loosely in his hand. "Do tell then, boy. What are you called?"

"My name is Xander."

"Xander." The man slowly repeated the name, giving Xander a penetrating stare as he did so, holding his gaze as if searching for some meaning in the name. The man broke the hard look first, and glanced down into his hand holding the poker, grasping it once, twice; then, giving it a little shake, he tossed it to the side of the hearth with a clank. "All right, boy, you have a name."

Xander pushed the smelly blankets off and, with an effort, sat up on the cot on which he had lain. He could see that his ankle and hands had been wrapped, and when he went to brush his hair back out of his eyes, his head was bandaged as well. "I have you to thank for this?"

"I mended you," the man confirmed, his hand now resting on the hilt of a sword sheathed at his side.

"Do *you* have a name?"

"My friends call me Ix, though I don't have any of those." Ix laughed out loud, though it seemed more of a croak then any sort of mirth, and then went on. "Ix, pride of the Manor Hall, inglorious failure in the extreme, cannon fodder in times of war; and most assuredly I am nobody, if you must know." Ix laughed even harder at this declaration. Xander couldn't help but notice that this man, this Ix, spoke of himself with a great deal of self-loathing. Xander sat quietly while Ix continued to chuckle to himself. He needed to get moving, though where to he didn't know. He stood up from the cot, testing his weight upon his leg; it seemed fine. He was still stiff and sore, but he needed to get back to Kristane and the others.

Ix stood there contemplating him. "Where do you think you're going, boy? You've been at death's door for going on a week, and you think you're just going to up and traipse off?"

"Wait, what, *how* long?" Xander's stomach tied itself in knots at the thought of being asleep for so long. "I've got to go — my sister, my friends!" The anxiousness and panic was more than apparent in his voice.

"There were others with you?"

"Yes, and well, no, we got separated in the mines, and my sister Kris…" Xander stopped himself mid-sentence. This man had helped him, but he knew nothing about Ix. Ix was a complete stranger, and he had almost, in his panicked state, told him everything. For all he knew, Ix could be one of the Briggers; he had on a misshapen uniform on after all. He eyed Ix warily, lingering on the faded crimson and blue.

"This tattered veneer you're eyeing is nothing more than my cloak of shame. What lies beneath it died long ago." Ix pulled at the lapel, flapping the jacket he wore outwards, and pointed at his chest. "It stands for nothing more than that, but I wonder as to why you're so leery of it? Suppose you've had a little trouble with the established rule?" Ix fiddled with the pommel of the sword that hung at his side. "In that we have something in common, then."

"Are you a deserter?" Xander looked the man in the face, waiting for his reply, hoping to detect some slight movement that would betray a lie.

"I'm of a mind you can say that, but recently, very recently in fact, I have come to hope for a bit of redemption." Ix looked at Xander and gave an embittered sigh. "Listen to me, boy; you will be going nowhere for the time being. Both you and your horse need tending to. As for your sister and your friends, they are beyond your reach at the moment; but when you are able, I will point you in the direction you wish to go." Xander began to protest, but Ix cut him off. "The Ward is well-hidden. I would say that the two of us — well, three, counting the horse — are the only ones to seek sanctuary here in a great long while. You will not find your way out of here on your own, and as I said, your horse needs tending to. As strong as Aldebarron is, time and stagnation have taken its toll."

Xander gave Ix a mutinous look and resigned himself to leaving at his first opportunity. He didn't care what this man said, he was going to get back to his sister as soon as he could figure out how.

"Now, boy, if we're done here exchanging pleasantries, you have some work to do." Ix pulled a tattered rag from a pocket and tossed it at Xander. "There's a bucket, and the well is in the courtyard. First use it on yourself, and then tend to your horse. There's an oil can in the stables with him. That should take care of some of that pent-up energy."

OTHER FRIENDS OF A SORT

Xander stood just outside of the stables in a large holding pen, looking at the swirled calligraphy and etchings that appeared as he polished the large shields of Aldebarron's flanks. So many of the strange markings had been hidden under dirt and corrosion that with each swipe of the rag a new character emerged. He still had no idea what any of it meant, but the pictures of various creatures and persons seemed to tell a story. Xander's arm ached, and not just from the exertion of cleaning this magnificent horse. Though he wouldn't admit it, Ix had been correct about his overall condition. It had been several days before he was able to stand erect for more than a couple of hours at a time. Ix had also been right about not being able to see a clear path out of the Ward. On the few occasions he had wandered around, he was greeted by sheer cliffs to all sides of the natural enclosure.

The Ward was decrepit and rundown; the stable in which Aldebarron was housed looked as though it could board nearly fifty horses, but the back half of it had collapsed in upon itself. There was a gathering hall for meals that still remained in fairly good shape, complete with large, burnished pots and pans for cooking that hung around a central kitchen hearth. The grounds had individual quarters for housing those seeking refuge, all in varying degrees of decay, and natural-looking parapets atop towers that blended into the landscape, looking out to every side. Xander had watched Ix ascend these high towers a couple of times and give a strange whistle or humming sound that he made with his hands held to his mouth, the sound of it eerily hanging on the breeze longer than it should have. Xander was surprised when, after a few days of this, an enormous bird of prey — an eagle with white feathers atop of its head and brown plumage covering the rest of its body — had circled in closer and closer to inspect Ix, though it never came closer than a stone's throw. On the occasions that the yellow-beaked predator visited, though, Xander was treated to either fish or rabbit for dinner that night, which was a marked improvement over the stores of extremely dried meats from the kitchen pantry that Ix said would never go bad but tasted as rancid as it smelt.

Xander stood back from Aldebarron, admiring the sheen that now graced the hide of the great metal horse. Hardly any traces of the corrosion or dirt that had covered him were visible; the burnished patina of the diverse alloys gave the horse an even more handsome look. Aldebarron, seeing that Xander had halted in his chore, nudged him with his head and snorted out steam in a playful manner. "Hey! I know, but I think you might be good for now. There isn't much more to groom; I'll start rubbing off metal if I keep it up." He gave the horse a pat and Aldebarron threw his head up and shook his mane. Xander laughed and gave the horse a stroke along the bridge of his nose as it dropped back down to his height. Pulling at the horse's jaw, indicating he wished him to come lower, he whispered into the horse's ear. "Besides, I need your help, my big friend. We have to find my sister and the others soon."

Xander was about to say something more when he heard behind him the labored breaths of Ix and the slapping of the man's sword against the wooden and armored body of the self-articulated manikins that were stationed about the courtyard. Ix had taken to practicing for hours a day, swiping and dodging expertly at the clumsily creaking appendages of the animated conscripts. One morning when he didn't think Ix was watching, Xander had wound up a couple of them, and with a long stick he had found, tried his skill at it. He felt he had held his own pretty well until an unseen extra arm shot out and hit him in the gut, knocking him to the ground, breathless. To Xander's chagrin, Ix had appeared at just that moment; he had merely shaken his head in disgust and traipsed back into the gathering hall without a word.

Xander involuntarily rubbed at his right butt-cheek at the memory of the bruise that was his wounded pride from hitting the ground.

"Come here, boy, and bring your stick!" Xander was taken aback by being addressed; he hadn't noticed that Ix had dispatched the manikins he was practicing on.

"My name is Xander," Xander grumbled under his breath as he grabbed a stick that was leaning against the pen's fence and strode to where Ix was.

"Let's see how you handle yourself, boy." Ix brandished his sword at Xander.

"Little unfair, don't you think?"

"Fine, we'll trade." Ix flipped the sword around and handed it to him hilt-first.

Xander grabbed the hilt and tossed his stick to Ix. The weight of the sword was substantial, though not so much that he couldn't handle it; but it surprised him nonetheless. The grip was hardened wood that looked as though it was fused into the metal of the cross-guard and pommel. Well, *fused* was the wrong word, he thought; *growing* into the metal was a better description. In fact, the wood looked like it had sprouted roots and was growing into the length of the entire blade. Xander held the sword up before himself with both hands, the tip pointing straight up; it was then that he saw a notch in the blade. "It's broken."

Xander could see Ix staring at him in a menacing stance as he adjusted his focus from the blade to Ix in the background.

"Yes it is, but the blade is still sharp, and is almost without equal. Now come at me, boy!"

Ix didn't wait for Xander to move, though; he rushed forward and slapped the long stick down on one of Xander's forearms, causing Xander to drop his guard and the point of the sword to stick in the ground in front of him. Ix swung around and whacked the stick across Xander's shoulder blades with such force that he could feel a tingling of pain shoot through his lower back. Incensed, Xander swung aimlessly with the sword at Ix, who casually sidestepped his enraged blows, occasionally poking him with the end of the stick as Xander over-extended. Tiring quickly, but still infuriated, Xander put everything he had left into a rush towards Ix; with the sword held aloft, he yelled and pressed forward. Again Ix sidestepped him, and double -handing the stick, smacked him even harder than before across his backside. The point of the sword dropped again into the dirt as Xander clutched his butt with his free hand. Of course, it was the already bruised right cheek, thought Xander, as he knelt there panting, bent over with his forehead resting on the pommel of the sword.

"How is it exactly, boy, that you expect to be of any help to your friends or your sister?"

"I've never used a sword before!" Xander shot back at him vehemently, but do not rise; instead, he drooped down a little further and looked sidelong around the wooden grip of the sword at Ix as he hovered above him.

"You think anyone who is wearing a real one of these," Ix tugged vigorously at the lapel of his jacket, "is going to give a damn about that?"

"No, but I *am* going to find them and help them if I can!" Xander couldn't remember ever being this angry; he was always the one who remained calm and in control, but that was not what was really bothering him. Despite his talents as a member of the Rogue, Ix had pointed out with this little demonstration of his prowess that Xander was unequipped, in fact woefully so, to handle everything, and it made him very afraid. Afraid that as much as he wanted to protect Kristane, it might not be enough, and that he would fail.

Ix, sensing that his message had found its mark, spoke a little more kindly. "Very good, boy. Now let's try it again, a little slower."

Ix took a few paces back and waited for Xander to stand, but before Xander could do so, there was the slightest shuffling of feet and a very familiar *TINK TINK TINK*. Ix grabbed for his sword and Xander at the same time, hauling him over the short wall that fenced the stable pen.

"I think...." Xander started to explain his suspicions to Ix, but Ix silenced him with a barely audible *shush*.

Peeking back over the solid wall, both men saw that a fair-haired boy had come around an outcropping of stone, through the arched entryway, and was taking very long, deliberate strides as he seemed to count to himself. Every few paces, as he pointed to individual fingers from one hand to the other, he would bend down and draw something in the dirt with a short branch.

Aldebarron gave a snort from back behind them, and the boy looked up from his musings and smiled broadly at the horse. "Big, big horse, so handsome, so big." The boy clapped his hands together, and Aldebarron gave another snort and neighed loudly in what Xander imagined as recognition.

Xander was about to offer an explanation when Ix, with a tone of surprise and the look of menace dropping from his face, said, "The Fool?"

"What, you know him too?" Xander said incredulously. "How do you know Pipkin?"

"Pipkin… and I are friends, sort of… well, we know each other."

"I thought you said you didn't have any friends." Xander was reminded of a similar explanation of friendship between Rellion and Pipkin.

"I didn't know I had any living friends!" Ix stood abruptly and leapt over the short wall, marching deliberately at Pipkin, Xander scrambled to keep up, to make sure he didn't miss this odd reunion.

But Ix didn't speak as he approached Pipkin; he stopped short of where he was standing and just stared at him. Pipkin returned his gaze with an affable smile and did not speak either. Xander looked back and forth at the two. Ix's look was hard to define; he seemed to be searching for words, but was unable to find them.

Xander decided to break the awkward silence. "Pipkin, where have you been? Did you see what happened to the others?"

"Pipkin sees friends, friends ride choo-choo! Woo! Woo!" He pulled at an imaginary whistle in the air. Xander felt a knot in his chest lessen just a little. "Pipkin forgetting the Forgotten Ones, and Pipkin goes finds more friends to help!" Xander wished he could forget the Forgotten Ones too… or did Pipkin mean something else? He was about to ask when he was interrupted by Ix, who had snapped out of it at Pipkin's declaration.

"What do you mean, Fool? What friends did you find?" Ix's voice had taken on a concerned and wary tone.

"You see, you see, friends coming soon!"

Xander looked down at the ground where Pipkin had been scratching with the branch and saw the scrawled image of a giant arrow. Following Pipkin's path backward with his eyes, he saw a series of arrows several paces apart, all pointing forward to where they stood.

"For the love of it, Fool, what have you done?!"

Ix didn't have to wait for a reply from Pipkin, though, due to the company of uniformed men and women led by a determined-looking raven-haired woman marching into the courtyard.

"Been looking for you, Ix. Damn if it hasn't been a merry chase," Lieutenant Blackmore said, with an extremely satisfied grin as her men spread out behind her.

Pipkin clapped his hands and jumped around. "Pipkin finds friends! Yahoo!"

A Happy Troupe of Thespians

Groggle and the others were all standing, staring out the windows of the bi-level carriage above from where Kristane sat. They had rushed up there as they had approached the Effervescent Peaks to better see the phenomenon that Groggle was now explaining with his usual awe. Kristane couldn't find the energy to be as excited as they were; her thoughts were on her brother and Pipkin, and whether she would ever see them again... even though the thought of what Pipkin had done frightened her slightly. The others had tried to comfort her as the locomotive rattled along the rails higher and higher into the Skookum Mountains. Each of them, she knew, was also upset about Xander, and each dealt with it in their own ways. Even the moronic redhead brothers were despondent and wouldn't meet her eyes.

"See, the gases bubble up from the hot lakes, and then are frozen, causing the bubbles... and due to the gas being lighter...."

Kristane could see the bubbles as they floated lazily down from the higher elevations above. She remembered when the weather was cold enough and the wind just right, some of the translucent multicolored air balls would fall all around King's Way. When they were younger, she and Xander would run down from the Attic and pop the bubbles as they drifted down; they would explode in a flash of color and sparkly droplets of ice. She smiled to herself at the memory, but then Rellion's voice called out from the past and intruded into her happy feelings. *What are you doing? This is the perfect distraction, pockets full, everyone's arms up in the air, get to collecting; we have expenses, you know!*

Rellion had kept to himself for most of the journey; he was forward in the cab of the engine while Groggle rested. The few times she had seen him over the past several days was when they would have to stop to clear overgrowth off the rails, which was becoming more and more frequent as the engine trudged slowly upward. Kristane wanted more answers to the revelations that were making her head spin, but there was a certain comfort in just sitting here in her own self-pity. This always led her to become angrier with herself as Xander's voice called out to her, *Come on Kris, this isn't you, we have to keep moving!* Even when her brother wasn't here he still was, pushing her in the right direction.

She focused on her own reflection within the pane of glass. Purdy cooed softly from somewhere behind her as she contemplated the person mirrored in front of her. It was time to stop with the despair. Nodding to the person she saw reflected there, she vowed to find the answers and her brother.

Suddenly, Kristane was thrown forward along the cushions of the leathered couch as the screech of the drive wheels grabbed at the rails below. The chandeliers swayed back and forth, their lead crystals and pedagogues tinkling against one another. Above her. Kristane could hear her friends attempting to disentangle themselves from one another.

"Get off me, you long pointy-eared..." Cayson's voice was silenced by a thud and a gasp for air. Kristane assumed that it had been Lathan who had quieted him. The close quarters and the long anticipation of the unknown had intensified their bickering to the point that it was only a matter of time before the group's old rivalries surfaced again.

"Just get off of him!" By the sounds of the swearing and the litany of insults, the Kressley brothers had joined in the fray as Prya yelled at all of them. "Leave him alone!"

"May the King's grace and the Blessed Tree grant me the discernment that afforded me the likes of all of you! Masters Cayson and Lathan and the rest of you, get down here!" Rellion hollered up at the observation deck of the passenger car from outside the carriage. "There is more than enough work down here to satisfy that pent-up energy!"

Righting herself, Kristane peered over the cushions of the long couch, looked out the window, and met Rellion's eyes as he looked down from the domed top of the car. He held her gaze for a moment, then turned and marched back to the front of the engine.

The others came scrambling down the staircase, led by Lathan, who was sporting a bloody lip, and Prya, shaking her head in disgust. None of them spoke as they meandered past her, and she fell in line behind Groggle as they opened the door, slid the tailgate aside, and clambered down the iron stairs. As she hopped from the final step to the ground, Kristane's boots met unexpectedly with a hard surface that she could immediately tell wasn't just dirt. Kicking at the soil, she could see the metallic plate of what Rellion had described as a switchback turntable. They had run across another one a number of days back, when they had to stop and adjust it slightly to align the rails, a warning signal-post alerting them to the danger. Looking around, she could see where the vegetation had stopped its growth in a large circular pattern where the table was, making a good-sized clearing.

It didn't take long for them to ascertain what Rellion was on about, and why he had stopped the train. Broken down upon the rails was an extremely large wagon and about a half- dozen other vardos of varying sizes surrounding it. Plastered to the wooden side panels of the wagon was a portrait of a man with a big, toothy grin, and emblazoned in large colorful letters across his tall hat was *Doc Fatterpacker and Peg-Leg Noodle's Traveling Medicine Show.* Kristane smiled in spite of herself as Fatterpacker screamed instructions from the foot board he was perched upon. His disgruntle- ment was focused at the dwarves who were in his employ, his face nowhere resembling the happy look that adorned the side of his wagon.

A couple of them seemed to actually be listening, while the others stood in a circle passing a bottle around and rubbing their hands together for warmth, all of them apparently oblivious to the fact that a large train had stopped just short of them. Noodle, wearing yet another colorful wig that Kristane could not truthfully say was the color of anything she could recognize, was excitedly pointing from the cracked wheel on the wagon to the team of metal oxen that a pair of dwarves were attempting to unharness. Noodle tramped back and forth on his prosthetic leg, occasionally cupping his hand to his ear, trying to catch what Fatterpacker was yelling.

"I said… brin… adder!" It was no use; Fatterpacker's rants were lost on the wind, and Noodle stood shaking his head. In exasperation, the Doc threw his hands in the air, but then bent down and reached into a jockey box from under the driver's seat, pulling out an oversized purple- and-gold megaphone. "I said bring me the ladder, you obtuse bunch of play actors!"

Noodle rushed to the back of the wagon and pulled hard on something underneath the wagon. A long, rigid ladder slid from its storage place, three times the length of Noodle. The dwarves who had been fussing with the broken rear wheel came to help him, and in a comedic episode where Noodle found himself on the ground more than once, the ladder was finally propped up against the side of the wagon so that Fatterpacker could descend. Missing the last couple of rungs as he came down, the Doc stumbled over his own feet and those of the dwarves who had been steading the ladder. Still holding onto the megaphone, he took a swipe far above the heads of the dwarves, and then tossed it to the outstretched arms of Noodle. Straightening himself and brushing at his long purple coat, the Doc spun on the spot and went immediately into character.

"Salutations and welcome! There can be no doubt that you have heard of my miracle elixirs and contrivances that make everyday chores a pure joy!" Fatterpacker addressed Kristane and the others, swiping his arms to the side and pointing to the visage that adorned his wagon. "Broken down as I find myself to be, let it never be said that Doc Fatterpacker did not first attend to his patrons even in these wilds! You there, grumpy one, go and grab me my medicinal satchel!" The dwarf took one look at the ladder and turned and spat at the Doc's feet, just missing his boot — which was something, since the sheer amount of spit could have filled an entire beer mug. Fatterpacker pretended not to notice the large puddle that was slowly moving toward the sole of his boot, but eyed the dwarf beadily from a sideways glance.

Noodle moved closer to the Doc, and cupping his hand to his mouth, in a not-so-quiet whisper said, "Um, Doc, these are them kids from Kairos — you know, the ones under the stage and in the show back during Hallow's End."

Fatterpacker contemplated the throng before him, titling his head to the side, listening to Noodle's explanation as a sly smile adorned his lips. "Why, of course they are! Knew it the moment I laid eyes upon them!" Dropping his arms back down and opening them in greeting, instead he said, "Come to join our happy troupe of thespians, have you, then? Cannot say I am surprised, and your timing could not be better; we do find ourselves 'short' a man or two." He again gave the grumpy dwarf an eye and kicked at the dirt where his boot was in danger of becoming spoiled by the puddle of spit.

"No, um, that's not what we are doing. We, um, well, at the moment we really don't know what we're doing." Kristane stammered for an answer due to the sudden realization that she really hadn't a clue, and hadn't for a while. As much as she wanted to demand some answers from Rellion, she realized again how far she had lost herself in her own self-pity. Looking to the others, they looked as lost as she felt. They were all caught up in the whirlwind of events, mostly just trying to survive before the next heavy wind came along and blew one of them away.

"What we are doing is attempting to make haste while this monstrosity impedes us!" Rellion came trouncing toward them with a disdainful scowl, motioning towards the medicine man's cart with his cane. Kristane was almost fearful that Rellion planned on blasting the cart with it, such was his agitation.

"Why, good sir, I can hardly be blamed for the fractured wheel of my transport; such is the luck of things." Fatterpacker swept his arm to the side, indicating the wheel. Kristane imagined that Fatterpacker was a man very much use to others in his face, for his smile never wavered as Rellion approached, and the dwarves too gave him about as much notice as they had to the appearance of the train. "Dear sir, entrust that this is much more of an inconvenience to me than it could possibly be to you." The Doc traipsed over to the wheel. "As it is, certain events concerning atmospheric phenomena and the shortsightedness of one particular merchant have caused us to move on earlier than expected for Brobdin and the Festival of the Hunt. Let it not be said that Doc Fatterpacker remained where he was not wanted!" Fatterpacker gave the cracked wheel of the cart a quick tap with the toe of his boot.

An ominous splintering sound emanated from the remaining spokes and the circular wooden felloes that held them in place. As the top of the wagon swayed, the flat steel banding that wrapped the wheel shot out unexpectedly at high speed. While everyone in the vicinity ducked instinctively, the group of dwarves, who were still passing the bottle amongst themselves, barely noticed the deadly projectile that passed just over their heads. Only the reverberating twang of the steel as it flexed in flight caused them to briefly look up, but thinking it no more than the warning of an incoming storm, they immediately went back to their drinking.

As the wagon collapsed upon itself, the axle trapped by the rails cracked loudly, like a strike of lightning. Rellion said with no pretense at feigning sarcasm, "No doubt a lesson in absurdity, but I don't suppose that you have a spare?"

"Well now, that is a very amusing story in the telling, but never you mind — my commendable troupe will have this repaired in no time!" This happened to be the one thing that caught the attention of the drinking dwarves. The Kressley brothers could have taken a lesson or two from their vulgar response. Fatterpacker ignored the outburst, and purposefully walking towards Kristane, said, "Now, let me tell you of the calming properties of my miracle elixir with a touch of vanilla and today, today only, I am prepared to offer it to you a two-for-one deal!"

Clan of the Dead Fairies

Reluctantly, the realization that they were just as stuck as the igno-minious troupe of the medicine show had dawned upon Rellion as well. Despite his threats to burn it to ash, the fact was that it would take just as long to craft a new wheel. Fatterpacker was so distraught at the threat, though, that he had gone as far as prostrating himself. The dwarves, on the other hand, responded quite differently, producing several lethal looking instruments that Kristane imagined were not for fixing the wagon.

Once a verbal treaty was made and the word was given that they were not going anywhere, Fatterpacker and his troupe became magnanimous hosts. The decorated vardo wagons that the nomadic dwarves were famous for were quickly circled, forming an encampment that helped break the colder winds that had started as soon as the sun had set. The dwarves' craftsmanship was not spared for the wagons and carts they called home. Pitched rooftops complete with chimney stacks sat atop gilded window frames and multicolored stained walls of mahogany and walnut wood inlays, their shapes depicting many things in addition to the particular clan the dwarves claimed to be a part of, such as the Dead Fairies, the Tinkers, the Headless Unicorns, and the Kingship of Log Walkers.

"Oh my, not fairies!" Prya gasped as Groggle pointed out to her the clan name emblazoned on one of the vardos. Though the dwarf language was more pictorial in nature than any written word, Groggle knew enough about it to decipher.

"Begging yer pardon, miss, but no, no, these are good men." Noodle said in response to Prya's exclamation of dismay at the clan name of the Dead Fairies. "They're not the ones responsible for the killins way back when. That's just the name their forebears took when they did their duty. You sees Beezy here?" Noodle pointed to the grumpy dwarf that Kristane had now met a couple of times. "He's descendant of them that stood toe to toe 'gainst that what was tryin' to do them fairies in.

"You're all too young to know nothing about that, me and Beezy is too young for that tellin' too, but sure enough it did happen." Noodle paused for a moment and took a big swig from the tankard he held, spilling some of its contents from the corners of his mouth. Smacking his lips and wiping the dribbles from his chin with the back of his hand, he continued. "I'm not sayin' it's a good moniker by our standards, but you see, they was damn proud there wasn't more dead ones." Beezy took a bite out the blue reptilian creature that he had been barbecuing on a stick; though charred around the edges and quite dead, the chameleon continued to change colors. He gave Kristane and the others a hard stare with the tail of the lizard hanging half out of his mouth.

Kristane found herself wondering about the stories behind some of the other names of the dwarf clans, and if each of them held the same sort of heroic tales as the Dead Fairies. Sure, she had seen the other races of Kairos walking about the city square, but having no contact besides the insides of their pockets and snatching their belongings, she again found herself woefully ignorant of the world she lived in. So separated were the races and creatures of Kairos, with only the fringe of those denizens ever venturing amongst each other, she supposed she hadn't gotten a very good impression of any of them nor possibly them of her, whether they had known it or not. Just an audible curse when they found that something had gone missing.

She had never even seen a fairy, and the only unicorn she had ever seen was one that was dead and trussed up by its legs across a long pole being carried into the Black Kettle by a pair of giant men fresh from the Festival of the Hunt. Kristane remembered, as a young girl, she and a slightly younger Prya crying for the rest of the day after they saw it, even as Rellion had instructed them in the finer arts of crime. Rellion had tried to placate them by saying that it had died of *natural causes,* but the long shaft and distinctive feathered fletching of an arrow still embedded in the breast of the beautiful creature had ruined that lie.

Noodle interrupted Kristane's thoughts with a question. "Miss Kristane, beggin' yer pardon, but where's the tall boy that was under the stage witcha? Just now realized I hadn't seen him."

With the corners of her eyes tearing slightly, she replied, "My brother Xander? Well, he, um, got lost…."

"Now, I shouldn't worry; bet you'll find him soon enough, right?"

"Yes, I'll find him…" Kristane couldn't complete the rest of her thoughts aloud; she just forced a slight smile, which Noodle happily returned, and Prya gave her a one-armed hug.

"Come now, that's enough campfire stories. Give us a song, Ed!" Fatterpacker, who had busied himself with other things while everyone else had set up camp, mostly with his feet up on a barrel, paraded into their midst in grand fashion, holding a strange-looking instrument. "Look there, Ed, you and this grumpy one here have gone and put frowns on our guests' faces, and unhappy guests are less inclined to purchase things."

"No, no, it wasn't that, I was thinking of something else…" Kristane was taken by surprise; she supposed she must have been frowning as the Doc pointed a finger at her, and she quickly dried her eyes.

"Now, now, Ed always goes on about the old days and ancient history! I ask you, makes you wonder, were there ever any good times?" Fatterpacker held the instrument aloft, with his exaggerated way of speaking, from one of its multi-stringed necks, its oblong body twisted to one side like a misshapen pear. "A happy tune, Ed, none of your usual brooding pieces that depress me and put everyone to sleep!" Tossing the instrument to Noodle, he stood expectantly with his hands on his hips.

"All right, Doc, all right, there's one my ole granddad use to play. Not sure where it comes from, but it's merry." Noodle strummed at one of the many sets of strings and fiddled with the tuning pegs on a couple of the necks. When he felt satisfied, he began to thump at the hollowed out wooden body of the instrument, setting a tempo that the dwarves around the fire stomped out with their feet. A few of them pulling out instruments of their own to play along, including an odd-shaped flute, a fiddle, and a palm-held squeeze box. *"There's a land long ago, Where a rooster did always crow, The jolly old king could not sleep, And told the rooster to take a leap…"*

Noodle had started slow, but by the fourth line the tempo of the song really picked up, and the dwarves' footfalls became more pronounced. By the start of the chorus, most of the dwarves had jumped to their feet and were dancing around the fire, alternating between slapping and punching and hugging each other. Groggle had already joined in, crowing like a rooster as he jigged around with the dwarves, who stood only a little taller than himself; and the Kressley brothers were tailor-made for the tough love exhibited by the dwarves. They were smacking each other so hard it was a wonder they were still standing. Kristane found herself enjoying the entertainment, and looked over at Prya, who was smiling but had a strange, surprised expression on her face at the same time. Noodle started up the second verse, and if possible the tempo quickened even more. *"Hand me down your polished crown, Hand me down your polished crown, Hand me down your polished crown, we are throwing it to the ground; in the dirt goes the crown, in the dirt goes the crown, in the dirt goes the crown, we crow cock-a-doodle-doo all day."*

"Did you hear him?" Prya whispered to Kristane.

"Well, yeah, he's right there, hard to miss him." The revelers were still whooping and hollering at the conclusion of Noodle's song, Fatterpacker stood just behind him, clapping vigorously.

"No, not that, did you really *listen?*" Kristane looked sidelong at Noodle again, who was smiling broadly, tipping a mug to his lips, his toupee nearly falling off of the back of his head. Prya continued, "He sounds just like…"

"Eidolon!" Kristane didn't mean to say it so loudly, but once the shock of what she had just realized hit her, Noodle spat out the grog he was drinking and stared back at her.

"What's this?" Fatterpacker, who had partially caught the girl's conversation, bowed his head down to their level. "Of course, this is Eidolon Noodle! Just Ed to all of us, though!"

"But on the stage at the festival?" Prya leaned into the conversation, but Doc just looked at her quizzically.

"See, miss, I can sing real pretty, but it's no great secret that I'm not one to look at —might say I look better going than coming," Noodle said, catching onto Prya's meaning as the Doc remained blissfully unaware. "Doc says that we make more coins if we sell it up a bit, and I reckon he's right. Spend as much time under the stage singing into a can as I do up on top, sometimes, but it's all good, miss." Noodle sat up straight and pushed out his chest. "Important thing is that folks hear it, makes me real proud that folks feel so good about my songs." Turning to Fatterpacker, he then said, "Doc, they mean Bufford."

Fatterpacker, finally shaking off his obliviousness, slapped Noodle on the shoulder. "What, that prissy, fancy fool? Could barely string two words together! Only time he said more than 'give me another drink' was when he demanded more money for moving his lips and staring flirtatiously at the crowd. Let it not be said that I don't think that it's not a talent, and that he wasn't good at it, but it was absolute thievery, what he was asking for! Had to be done with him after Kairos!" Both Prya and Kristane stared at him with utter looks of shock on their faces. Misunderstanding their looks, he continued, "Don't be concerned, my fine young ladies, we will find us another pretty boy! The show must go on, after all!"

Kristane wasn't sure how she felt about the deception. A little sorry for Noodle, though he didn't really seem to care; maybe disappointed… or was it something more? Nothing in her life right now was real; everything seemed coated with a thin veneer of falseness.

Still not catching on, Fatterpacker continued. "Oh, he's fine; no doubt he was able to acquire another benefactor. That boy had a real flair for earning the sympathies of old and lonely dowagers." Fatterpacker laughed heartily and slapped Noodle on the back again. "Give us another one, Ed!"

Nevertheless the Deed is Done

The sun had set by the time Noodle started up his fourth shanty, his voice booming across the crisp cool air. "Mrs. Lorry took a stroll in the village, she was a woman of great privilege, everywhere that she went, she dragged along her cat crooked and bent, singing oodle doodle oohm papa…." The rest of the Rogue had joined in with the dancing and howling. Kristane hadn't seen any of them smile and laugh this much in a very long time. She caught herself smiling too, and once or twice Prya and Lathan had tried to pull her up from her seat to dance with them; but she was too intent on Rellion, stealing glances back at him periodically — watching for what, she didn't know. Most of the time, the only thing she got was a glimpse of the backside of one of the dwarves relieving himself along the tree line, his kilt hiked up above his head; but the last time she did, she found him looking directly at her. Holding her gaze for a long moment, he turned and walked back into the trees that encircled their camp. Believing the others wouldn't miss her, and figuring the festivities weren't going to let up for some time, she took it as an invitation.

Attempting to trace Rellion's steps, she pushed through a line of brambles, the din of the ongoing party fading slowly behind her. The cool air carried on it the smell of pine needles and the earthy scent of decaying leaves from the forest floor. Fatterpacker's wagon had broken down upon a narrow plateau that hugged the side of the mountain. Rellion hadn't wandered far; he stood looking down into the valley from whence they had come, the railway lost amongst the trees and the rock formations that jutted out to hide them from view.

"Good evening, my Princess… you are displeased with me," Rellion stated matter-of-factly as Kristane approached his side and refused to look at him, glaring instead straight ahead. No, "displeased" didn't even come close to how she felt. Angry, outraged, ready to grab his shillelagh away from him and rap him upside the head with it was more like it. Rellion seemed to guess her thoughts, and shifted his cane to his other hand. "After so many years, I have still not learned a single lesson, so intent on my own place in all of this that I literally have allowed time to catch us. Pondering on an evil that once seemed so distant, I neglected the one growing at our heels."

Kristane remained steadfast, refusing to look Rellion's way, but her ears had pricked up at Rellion's uncharacteristic tone. He continued. "I have prepared you for some of what is to come, but should have told you more, and sooner. You are no longer the little girl with a smudged face and tangled hair who cried every time you fell; you are a strong young woman, and the burden you must endure should have been placed upon you before this." Though Kristane remained silent, she turned to see Rellion with a sad smile on his face, his eyes glancing sideways at her. Turning and placing a hand on her shoulder, he said, "There are things that will happen that are inevitable, and we have not reached the level in which you will be less displeased with me. The Forgotten Ones know our trail; they will most likely pursue us rather than look for Xander and Pipkin. You must know in your heart that they are still alive, and are in far less danger than we. The clockwork heart you hold so dear, and this other piece… the dancers are drawn to them."

Rellion pulled the tarnished pendant from his pocket. It was the first time she had seen it since the catacombs of the Abbey. Kristane felt the same revulsion she had before. "Not like a beacon, but more like a lighthouse on a stormy night that flashes intermittently. They covet it nearly as much as they covet you; with it, they will resurrect their master, and it is the only thing that can. Should he be awakened, all of the realms of Kairos would be damned."

Clasping her own necklace, her fingers tingled with the impulse to rip it from her neck and toss it into the precipice below. Rellion, again sensing her thoughts, said, "I am afraid that hiding it or tossing it to the winds would only slightly delay them, for now that they are awake, there is nothing that will stop them from searching."

"So why don't we just destroy it?"

"I wonder, my Princess, could you? With the great amount of emotion that you have placed into it, *could* you destroy it?" Kristane looked down at the piece of metal and wood and wondered if she could. Rellion was annoyingly right again; it was her only link to an unremembered past, but if it meant the safety of those she cared for, she thought she could. "As it is, while in the past it has obviously been damaged, it is not within your or my power to do so…"

"So that's half of the heart like the one in the message, and broken like in the story?" Kristane said, indicating the tarnished pendant.

"Yes and no. These are but pieces of the whole; the answer is a great deal more complicated."

Finding a sense of courage born of her ire, she shouted at him, "Well, that's it, isn't it? You never really *say* anything! What are we doing, then, if this is all so hopeless?"

"Is that what I said? Did I say that there was no hope?" Rellion looked down at her, his steely gray gaze penetrating her. "We are in fact delaying, if that helps to enlighten you."

"Delaying? Delaying for what?" Her voice echoed with exasperation.

"If you must know, we are delaying in hopes that others will know of the Forgotten Ones and choose to aid in the battle before us."

"Fine! We just keep, what, running, hiding, until they find us or the Forgotten Ones kill us?"

"To put it bluntly, yes. Our only advantage thus far has been luck; they had not until very recently known that you were the blood-bearer.

Fortuitously, they may not yet realize that both halves of the heart are in our possession." Rellion put away the necklace he was holding.

"What does that even mean?"

"You asked me before how this trinket came to be yours." Rellion pointed to her necklace, paused for a moment, and softened his gaze at the young woman before him. "The Tale of the Broken Heart is only too real. Though lacking substance in some ways, the pretty, pretty Princess and her friend were not figments of some bard's literary musings. A very long time ago, an automaton like no other before it was created to act as the play-friend and protector of a young princess. How he became alive and aware is no less than the miracle that you have since seen with Count Bobo and his band. It is always tied to emotion, always; but they have all been born of free will, and much like the failings of their creators, are subject to that temptation. The Princess, later the Queen, loved her friend, and he was magic-bound to her by the clockwork heart with a single drop of her blood.

"The necklace would glow when she was in mortal danger, and her friend could always sense it and run to her aid. This is why the necklace glows for you, Kristane, and only you." Rellion paused and sighed. Turning Kristane toward him and placing both of his hands gently upon her shoulders, he continued, "It is *you*, Kristane, my Princess. You are heir to the ancient throne of Kaer Kairos; this trinket is imbued into your very being by your very bloodline. You are the blood-bearer of the Broken Heart."

"I don't understand… how *could* I be? I'm nothing more than an orphan… a thief." Kristane's anger was replaced by shock and disbelief; Rellion was speaking words that had no basis in anything she knew of herself. She felt very dizzy, and her legs wobbled under her.

"You are a great deal more than you think yourself to be; and let us be honest, you were never a very good thief." Rellion smiled broadly at her and gave her a little wink, the levity pushing away the haze that had started to form in her vision, steadying her. "That profession was never more than a pronounced training in the ways of the world. You and your brother were brought to me in secret for safekeeping until the day you were old enough to face the challenges ahead, for this is still a dangerous land,

and there are those who, had they suspected your heritage, would most certainly have done you harm."

"But Rellion, I still don't understand, I just can't be...."

"It is not for you to understand, but with time and the crucible before you, I pray that you will come to accept." Rellion smiled again at her and patted her once more on the shoulder as the snap of a branch behind them caused them both to turn quickly, Rellion placing himself in front of Kristane.

"It is not appropriate for gentlemen to eavesdrop, nor a lot such as ourselves either, but nevertheless the deed is done!" Fatterpacker's toothy grin peeked from behind the bushes as Noodle, Beezy, Groggle, and the rest of the Rogue pushed their way through the line of briars, all staring at the pair, a bit wide-eyed.

Noodle kicked at the dirt feebly with his peg-leg and offered a muttered apology. "Beggin' yer pardons, but we heard raised voices and was wonderin' what happened to the young miss..."

Remove Your Hats, Bow Your Heads

Kristane's friends had yet to broach the revelations of the night before, but Fatterpacker was certainly irritating her with all the bowing and calling her Your Highness every time she passed by. He even went as far as to make the dwarves remove their hats in her presence. They did so reluctantly, but she was surprised when Beezy started doing it without being prodded by the overbearing leader.

"Miss, the boys and me have just about got the new wheel fitted should have you all on your way by midday," Noodle said as he approached the spot where she sat near the campfire.

Groggle was seated across from her, looking at a tattered book, occasionally stealing a furtive glance over the pages. She didn't know where the rest of the Rogue had wandered to or, for that matter, where Rellion was, but she really didn't care; she was content in her semi-solitude.

Noodle smiled broadly at her and scratched at his wig. She returned his smile with a halfhearted one. "Thank you, but you should really be telling Rellion."

"Would, miss, if knew where he had got to… strange fella, if you don't mind me saying."

Kristane smiled and chuckled a little as she replied, "No I don't, and knowing Rellion, I don't think he'd mind much either. Probably consider it a compliment."

"That's better, miss, much rather see you smiling."

"Thanks, but I don't think there's been a lot to smile about for a while."

"That little fella Groggle over there, he's been telling me and Beezy something about it, figure you've all had a right bad time of it. Shame with all you so young and all." Kristane looked in Groggle's direction to see him pulling the book he was pretending to read up higher over his eyes. "Now, now don't be too put out with him, he's just a little scared and concerned for all of you, needed to get it off of his chest," Noodle said, trying to placate the glare she had shot in Groggle's direction.

Kristane turned her gaze back to Noodle and gave him a small smile. "I suppose it doesn't really matter anymore. No reason to keep any secrets. Do you believe the old stories of the Forgotten Ones and the throne of Kaer Kairos?"

"Heard some tell of it. My ole grandad was full of old tales and pretty songs he swore were from the courts of the royals. Can't say as to what I believe, but from what the young lad has said and what we saw back at that fancy orrery thingy, well, makes me start to think that ole grandad wasn't just drinking a bit too much of his homemade." Noodle pulled out a rag from his back pocket and wiped his face and neck. He motioned to sit down next to Kristane, and she scooted over to make room for him. "As for royals, should you be one, I'll tell you the truth: I wouldn't mind having to bow to one such as you." Pausing, he wiped at some of the grime on his hands with his already-dirty rag. "Been all over the realms of Kairos, met all kinds, you start to get a feel for how people are going to be, and I think that even if you're not what that fella Rellion says, well, you sure seem to have the heart of one."

Kristane felt embarrassed by Noodle's accolades, and her cheeks flushed. She wanted to say *thank you,* but words escaped her.

"Well, better be getting back at it." Noodle gave her a little pat on her knee and pushed himself up, stretching out his back and giving a little groan. He again smiled broadly at her and traipsed off in the direction of the broken-down wagon.

By afternoon, there still hadn't been any sign of Rellion, but the rest of her friends had wandered back once they started to get hungry. The ginger boys and Cayson had grabbed some of the brisket that the dwarves had been smoking over a low flame all morning and drifted back out of sight. She had thought it best not to ask from what type of animal the dwarfs were barbecuing, the unicorn from her childhood sneaking back into her thoughts. Whatever it was, it was a big; a pair of dwarves had had some difficulty hoisting the skewered slab of meat upon the makeshift spit.

Prya and Lathan had come back and sat with her as they watched the dwarves take turns spinning and basting the meat with generous amounts of their favorite brew. It was hard to tell which was being basted more, the brisket or the dwarves.

"So, royalty, huh?"

Kristane grimaced her embarrassment.

"Always knew there was something wrong with you." Prya gave her friend a hug, lingering with her arms draped across her shoulders. "Just so you know, I'm not bowing."

Leave it to Prya to make light of the situation. Kristane found herself feeling extremely grateful, as the rest of the afternoon was devoted to laughter with her friends, the main source of their levity being the dwarven cooks as the spit caught fire once or twice.

A commotion started somewhere behind them just as they finished off their second helpings, and the third for Groggle. Kristane could hear Fatterpacker shouting orders at his troupe, which had lined up, with half pushing the wagon from behind and the other half pulling on the reins of the re-harnessed pack animals. Mixed in with all the grunting of the dwarves, yelling of orders by Fatterpacker, and bugling of the beasts, there was a great creaking noise as the mammoth wagon slowly rolled over the rails. The top of the wagon shook precariously, threatening to topple over at any moment.

As Kristane and the others approached, the Doc spun around with his megaphone still held to his mouth. Doing a double take, he inadvertently shouted through the cone magnifying his voice, "Your Highness! We will have your path cleared most hastily!" Turning back to the sweating and groaning dwarves, he shouted even louder. "Remove your hats, bow your heads, you lowly bumpkins! Royalty is in our midst!" Again spinning back, Fatterpacker swept his hat behind his back in an elegant bow.

Looking over his shoulders, Kristane saw the struggling dwarves, who were already bent over from their task, saluting in Fatterpacker's direction, each with one finger held high in the air. Prya covered her mouth to suppress a laugh, and Kristane couldn't help but find their flippancy funny as well. Beezy in particular, his shoulders flush against the back of the wagon and pushing backwards with the force of his legs, was interchanging salutes with both hands; but as he met her eyes, he turned bright red and quickly removed his hat and nodded. She was instantly jerked out of her lightheartedness, and Rellion's words from the night before sat heavy in her stomach, along with a sense of panic and dread.

"Careful of the inventory!" Fatterpacker had gone back to his meaningless bellowing.

With a final scrape of the metal banding against the rails, the last wheel slid over the obstacle and teetered ominously. The faint, muffled sounds of clinking bottles could be heard as the dwarves retreated to a safe distance. Fatterpacker and Noodle, on the other hand, ran forward, their arms outstretched high in the air in a futile gesture to steady it by sheer will. After a few moments the wagon settled quietly, and the bugling of the metal-clad pack animals and cheers from all around filled the cool afternoon breeze.

Noodle turned to Kristane and the others with his infectious smile. "Well done, boys! Thought we was going to lose that one for sure! Right, Doc?"

"Yes, yes, quite an acceptable performance all around! But if there is a single bottle broken…" Fatterpacker halted mid-sentence, the color washing from his face as he ogled at something that had caught his attention somewhere behind her.

Squawk! Squawk! Squawk!

Quickly, the cheering of the group abated, and a lingering smattering of applause died with the ruckus that Purdy was making from his perch upon the mushroom-capped stack of the train. A cold chill ran across Kristane's chest, and the hairs upon her arms tingled with the fear she saw mirrored in both the Doc's and Noodle's eyes. Haltingly she turned to look; she felt absolutely paralyzed. For the longest of moments not a single person moved, each of them transfixed upon the figures that were moving deliberately towards them from the back of the train. The Forgotten Ones. The beautiful dancers had not bothered to pull the cowls over their heads, their vicious grimaces intent on their prey: her.

"Yawp! Yawp! Yawp! *Lare dayam isimun!*" A voice like a drumbeat startled the entire company.

Beezy, the grumpy dwarf that Kristane had never heard utter more than a loathsome grunt, erupted with a fearsome rallying cry. Immediately, the other dozen or so dwarves united in the whoop and rushed forward, forming a line between her and the oncoming wraiths. Brandishing some lethal-looking weapons and a soup ladle or two, they stood shoulder-to-shoulder. Of the four wraiths, three rushed forward. At first the line of dwarves held, their bodies so low and dense they seemed rooted to the ground; but with a coordinated set of swings of their plated arms, the Forgotten Ones tossed them about like heavy sacks of grain. One dwarf smashed into the cylindrical boiler of the train and slumped down against the drive wheels; another skidded and rolled across the ties of the track, and yet another flew entirely over their heads. Given the force of their impacts, Kristane was dumbfounded when the dwarves got up quickly and return to the fray. She swore to herself that she had heard bones cracking.

Closing ranks, the Rogue — including Cayson and the Kressleys — gathered about her, while Noodle grabbed a long pole and did his best to jab and push at their assailants. He did fairly well until one of the Forgotten Ones yanked the pole from him and leveled two of the dwarves with it, additionally catching one of the Kressleys across the head. Markyn fell with a thud in the dirt, his bowler hat rolling on its brim some yards away and his pipe still clenched in his teeth. His brother Munse, incensed at seeing his brother knocked cold, raced forward; but Cayson, intent on him not suffering a similar fate, held him by his collar.

"You there, get up, yes, hit that one!" Fatterpacker had not relinquished his bullhorn, and continued his useless instructions. "Now I ask you, ladies, is that good form? You, grumpy one… Ed, what's his name again?" Kristane, though scared, marveled at the Doc's cluelessness; you would've thought he was advising them as to how to best wash and label bottles.

Slowly, the dancers gained ground. The phalanx the initial three had formed gave room for the fourth to come at them unimpeded. From the corner of her eye, she saw Beezy with an enormous hammer, the head a large block of iron, with a handle that looked like a tree limb. Swinging it forward and back like the pendulum of a clock, he ran twirling it full-circle just steps from the lead Forgotten One, uppercutting her with the broad face of the hammer head and knocking her in the chest. The force sent the dancer flying backwards, the momentum of the swing lifting Beezy completely off the ground and landing him several feet away. The Forgotten One was slow to regain her feet, but the savage and brutal look she gave Kristane chilled her to the bone.

Running to her side, Prya placed herself in front of Kristane, her exoskeleton appendage pushing her away so forcefully that she was about to complain when she saw what was draped about her friend's neck. Prya met her eyes, and with a mischievous smirk that couldn't quite hide the fear she felt, said, "Told you I'd get something from him. Run; I'll draw them away." With a wink, Prya yelled, "Hey, over here!"

"What?" Kristane grabbed at the necklace under her own shirt; she didn't have to see it to know it was pulsing. "No, you don't understand! They already know it's me!" But the damage was done; the Forgotten Ones, drawn to the tainted heart, went for Prya as well. Kristane looked around for a possible escape for the both of them, or at least a place to go and draw away the dancers from the others.

The pack beasts, still attached to the wagon, bugled with alarm. Without someone to attend them, they were attempting to push through the bushes to escape the clamor of fighting. It was then that Rellion crashed through the same bushes; he seemed breathless and sweating, as though he had run a great distance. Pausing but a moment, he took in all that was transpiring and ran directly to the young women, pulling them back behind him. Focusing on Prya and the pendant around her neck, his face was a mixed mask of anger and pride at Prya's deception.

Kristane watched as he again raised his cane before him, and she was reminded of a gathering storm. That same fiery look was in his eyes, and a palatable sense of energy resonated around him, much like that night in the Attic — which now seemed like it had occurred during another life. She felt her knees begin to buckle under her as a resounding blast knocked everyone around them to the ground. Strange, arching energy played about the faces of the Forgotten Ones, and they twitched with spasms. Her friends, the dwarves, and the others lay silent and unmoving, some toppled upon each other. She stared worriedly at them.

"They are only unconscious, but it will not last long. Come with me now! We must find safety before they wake!"

"But the others…" Prya mumbled, her gaze lingering on the prone body of Lathan just a short distance away.

"They are far safer without the both of you here; come now!" Rellion spoke impatiently to them, and moved to take Kristane by the arm.

Batting away his hand, she shouted. "I'm not leaving them here like this!"

"If you care for them, you will leave them. It is you, your pendant, and now the other half of the heart that they wish to possess! The others will be safe enough."

"Safe enough? Safe enough? What does that even *mean*?" Though she herself had only minutes before contemplated drawing the Forgotten Ones away, her anger at Rellion's seemingly disregard for the others made her livid. She looked at a fearful Prya, pleading with her eyes to understand why her friend had done what she had done.

"Argh." Slight movements and groans indicated that the others were beginning to come to. Lathan was the first to push himself up and stumble drunkenly to them, his hands gripping the sides of his head. He was just about to speak when his eyes widened. Dropping his arms, shaking his head and pointing to somewhere in back of Rellion, he rushed forward. Unknown to them, one of the Forgotten Ones had awoken while Rellion and Kristane had argued.

"Master Lathan, no!" Rellion yelled, yanking Lathan aside forcibly. The Forgotten One grabbed hold of Rellion's arm instead. Rellion stiffened, his eyes rolled back in his head, and his fingers spread wide. The arcing energy that had killed Creff back on the night of the Forgotten Ones' first appearance in the Attic caused him to release his cane and the hold he had on Lathan, but not before the same striking energy was transferred to the boy. As Lathan slumped to the side of Kristane, she was reminded immediately of the old rhyme: *Beware the Forgotten Ones' touch.* She dropped to her knees to check Lathan. Feeling at his chest, she gave a sigh of relief as it continued to expand and fall with air.

Rellion, on the other hand, gave a shudder as the energy ceased; and his eyes, rolling back down, focused briefly on Kristane's. He gave an odd little maniacal laugh and fell like a marionette with its strings cut. She scurried on all fours to him and clutched at his chest, but unlike Lathan, there was no sign of him breathing. The visible skin on his hands and face had turned gray, and his normally icy gaze was vacant. Kristane felt herself beginning to tear up when the same Forgotten One that had ended Rellion approached Prya. Her friend struggled for a moment, lashing out with her metal arm, but was quickly subdued; a second dancer had grabbed her from behind. With the wrenching and bending of the fine levers of her arm, Prya screamed in pain. Kristane watched as the metal plates of the Forgotten One's face formed a triumphant smile as it placed a single metallic finger upon Prya's forehead. With a quick burst of light, her friend slumped over. Sobbing with grief for her friends and the mentor she both loved and hated lying dead, all Kristane could do was watch as the necklace about Prya's neck was yanked free, and another Forgotten One bent down to Kristane, placing a single finger upon her own forehead.

Kristane saw a quick burst of light, and then nothing.

Before You Wasn't Dead Anymore

"Beggin' your pardon, Mister Rellion, but we thought you dead… gave us all quite a fright when you sat straight up, eyes poppin', and all the groaning and such. Meaning, if you please, I had to tell the boys to stop digging a hole and all." Noodle was wringing his hands fretfully, having just handed Rellion a tin mug of whiskey.

"My dear man, you would find it odd how many times I have heard that." Through the trailing curls of hair that hung unhindered down his forehead and across his face, Rellion eyed the dwarves that stood back from Noodle. Most of them were bandaged with bloodstained cloth across their heads and limbs, some still holding shovels — in anticipation, he supposed, that they might just yet have to continue digging a hole. Looking back at Noodle, he asked, "How long?"

"Well, reckon it's been several hours, just about sunset."

"Kristane? The others?" Rellion sat hunched over on a log with a ratty blanket draped across his shoulders. Having foregone his usual banter, his tone was more of a command as opposed to a question; he wanted only the pertinent facts.

"Sorry, Mister Rellion, but they done took the young miss… sure enough think she was alive… Beezy run after 'em. Haven't seen him since, though. The young miss's bird-thing there did too." Noodle pointed to Purdy, who had taken a perch next to Rellion. "But he come back just before you wasn't dead anymore…" Noodle paused, clearly wondering if he had caused some offense; but seeing that Rellion was waiting for him to finish, continued with his tale. "Erm, well, the rest of your lot is just there. Some a little worse for wear, but all's good." Noodle pointed back behind Rellion.

Turning quickly despite the ache in his body, his gaze first caught the sheepish demeanor of Groggle, his head bowed and eyes lowered as if he had just quickly looked away; but next to him stood Prya, her mood apprehensive and guilty. Relieved to see her unharmed, he smiled at her but also raised his eyebrow in admonishment. "Well, my Rogue, did any of you shed a tear upon my passing?" Shocked, they looked up from their quiet reposes and gawked at him. "No one, then? I cannot say that I am not disappointed; I am becoming quite sentimental in my old age, I fear. The way you stare, though, I must look a fright; or is it that you wonder who you should fear more, myself or the Forgotten Ones?"

"Rellion… err, I… I mean we, err, maybe just me… we don't know what to think. I guess we knew something was strange about you, but I guess we just didn't believe it, really, until we saw, you know, it. I guess…"

"Master Groggle, I applaud your courage in finding your voice. Had things been different, you would never had known of, should we say, my condition. As it is, you now do, and I will not regale you of the whys or hows." Rellion still took a long swig of whiskey. As he began to speak again, Rellion looked above the heads of his Rogue at a delicate wisp of steam that emanated from a jagged cut running lengthwise along the boiler of the train. "What I said upon our last foray into this stream of colloquy stands even truer now. What we must all fear is what the Forgotten Ones intend to do with our Kristane and the necklaces." Pausing and looking at each of them in turn, he said, "I intend to ask from all of you more than you believe you can give."

"Oh, very good, you have finally awoken for the day! Nasty business, that earlier, but we must be on our way, of course! Late for the Festival of the Hunt; going to have to run the wagons through the night to make up time!" Fatterpacker trounced into the middle of the muted throng, addressing Rellion with a buoyant bounce to his step and a toothy smile.

"Doc, he was gone and dead!" Noodle threw his hands in the air impatiently. "An' the young miss has been taken!"

"Yes, yes, Ed. Well, I guess we *are* all a bit dead tired from our individual ordeals; we all deserve a long rest, but we must sally forth, as I said. As to the young miss, who are we speaking of again?"

"Kristane! *Her Highness,* Doc!"

"What, Her Highness taken? That will not do, Ed, we must muster our efforts and secure her royal personage if we wish to gain her future favor!"

"Been discussing it just now, Doc. The not-dead sir here was just goin' to say somethin' when you walked up." Noodle motioned to Rellion as Fatterpacker looked back and forth at the pair. Rellion straightened himself and shrugged off the motheaten blanket which was presumably to be his burial shroud and assessed those around him. Looking past the grinning Fatterpacker, he couldn't help but look up at the side of the medicine man's wagon that displayed, among other things, the man's toothy grin, purple top hat, and a balloon stenciled into the background of the banner.

"You have a balloon." It wasn't a question, just one of Rellion's usual statements.

"Why yes, but we haven't taken it up in years. Very amusing story, actually, never thought we would get Ed back down again. Started with this cat that got tangled up —"

"We will need use of it." Rellion cut off the showman, and turned to his Rogue just as Groggle was snapping his goggles down over his eyes with an ear-to-ear smile on his face. Giving him a wink, Rellion continued. "Masters Cayson and Lathan, please assist Master Groggle in making this transportation airworthy. Now, Master Noodle, tell me of our dwarf friend."

"Sure enough, Mister Rellion! He'll do what he can and won't quit. Beezy don't generally shine up to your likes, but he's taken a fancy to the young miss an' he can pretty much track anything. But if her pet bird there had no luck, not sure how he's gonna fare." Noodle sat near the fire across from Rellion, speaking a little louder than necessary, overcompensating for the loud banging and raised voices of the others as they bustled about at Rellion's instruction.

"This mountain is riddled with the shafts and tunnels of the abandoned Bizzarred mine, Master Noodle. I believe Purdy returned due to the Forgotten Ones taking Kristane underground… but his return is fortunate." Rellion poked with his cane at the ground, making a long jagged line with other swooping figures. "Purdy can track Kristane, but he can also track Xander, her brother. The boy has a great deal of strength, and he was lost along with another one of our companions. If others I have exploited and have set into play have done as I expect them, you will find all of them in this vicinity." Rellion pointed to a roughly drawn set of peaks east of a meandering line etched in the dirt. "There is one among them who will know what to do."

"Pardon, sir, aren't you meaning yourself?" Noodle was a little more than nervous at the idea of getting into a balloon with a twelve-year-old whose entire flight experience included what he had read from a book. Noodle scrutinized the dwarves that sat nearby, threading old pants, kilts, shirts, and even the ratted death shroud they had used for Rellion into the skirts and panels of the numerous rips and holes of the Medicine Show's disused hot air balloon. He flapped at his nose in a hopeless effort to wave off the stench that came from a slow-boiling pot of tallow the dwarves intended to use to further seal their stitchwork. He looked at the surface of the pot as a single thick bubble rolled to the surface and finally popped, tossing glutinous droplets in all directions, and gave the balloon's canopy a wary glance before looking back at Rellion.

"No, Master Noodle, I must pursue Kristane and her captors. With her in hand, they will not be as quick as they were to find us. While they do not rest, they do not wish to cause her harm until she is presented to their master. It is my hope to delay them further, until you and the others are in a position to assist."

Working through the night, the dwarves repaired and spread out the colorful patchwork balloon in the clearing near the campfire. The bright hues of dawn were climbing the range to the east by the time they were done. It was the quiet time of the day when birds were still nested down, and their morning singsong had not yet greeted the day. The only sounds besides the swearing of the dwarves was the *"humph"* of the intake and discharge of a large bellows that was set before the fire, breathing life into the hot-air balloon. The Kressley brothers had taken to helping, and jumped and swung from the handles of the oversized bellows, collapsing the ribs of the accordion-like fabric, each down-pull sending the peak of the fire higher and at a dangerous angle outside of the confines of the firepit. Being a bit overzealous in most things, they had to be bodily removed to keep them from setting everything ablaze.

Rellion walked amongst his Rogue, speaking with them quietly, patting an exuberant Groggle on the head, sharing a cigar with the gingers and even giving Prya a hug. Lastly, just as the balloon was about ready to take flight, he took both Cayson and Lathan aside together. The boys stood shoulder-to-shoulder, their heads bowed, as Rellion spoke quietly to them, his hands resting on their shoulders. With a quick nod from the boys and an affectionate squeeze and jostle of their arms, he folded himself into the underbrush and was gone.

"Hold up there, Ed! Best I'm with you when we greet Her Highness's royal brother!" Fatterpacker marched towards the hot-air balloon, which floated a few feet off of the ground now, with only the tie ropes keeping it from ascending. He was struggling with a large carpetbag, both hands tightly gripping the handles, his gait decidedly slanted to the opposite side, compensating for its weight.

"Doc, you sure that's best? Bit heavy already, you know, with all the kids. Then there's the Festival over in Brobdin and all." Noodle motioned to the interior of the basket.

"Nonsense, that bunch over there will go and set up and prepare for our arrival! Must put our best foot forward, Ed! Just bringing a few trinkets to show our commitment to this venture. You there, take this bag up in there!" Fatterpacker toiled with lifting it up to a dwarf already in the basket, and extended a gloved hand to Noodle, who reluctantly helped his friend up.

"Lift off! As we soar off into the heights of greater nobility, my troupe of players, I will think fondly of..." Fatterpacker was drowned out by the firing of a makeshift burner fueled by his own elixir, as Noodle and Groggle upended a pair of bottles into the contraption.

As the tie ropes were cut free from their tethers, the balloon bobbed once or twice but did not gain any height. Both Noodle and Groggle ran about the edges of the basket, looking for the impediment, when the large carpetbag that the Doc had insisted on bringing was tossed over the side by the dwarf accompanying them.

"No!" Fatterpacker's stricken exclamation sounded like it was coming from a tunnel as the balloon shot straight up from the loss of so much ballast. The crack of bottle against bottle could be heard as a tie rope dragged across the top of the carpetbag.

Unlikely Party
at the Ward

Steam trailed from the nostrils of the great metal stallion Aldebarron in the cool morning air that came at this elevation, no matter the season. The heavy fall of metal hooves kicked up a thin layer of dust, which rose higher and higher with each circuit of the horse as he ran about the paddock. A young man sat astride the horse, pitching his weight and balance into each of the close-cornered turns with a precision that belied his actual experience. In fact, Xander had, until just recently, never sat upon a horse before, much less on one as grand as this one; but Aldebarron wasn't just any horse, metal or flesh and bone. He was the steed of kings, and had seen a hundred hundred battles.

"Boy, it's the crack of dawn! Aldebarron can run until the dying of the heavens, but you can't! Give yourself a rest!" Ix walked defiantly into the path of the oncoming horse.

The stallion abruptly changed his pace, his head rearing upward; and planting his four metal hooves deep into the ground, he came to a sliding stop just before the dark-haired man. Ix hadn't even flinched as a plume of dust surrounded him like a funeral pall. Xander couldn't decide whether he had a death wish or was just crazy. Muttering under his breath he said, "My name is *Xander*."

Whether he had heard it or not, Ix ignored this, as he always did. Walking around to meet the eye of the stallion, Ix said forcibly. "You should know better!"

"Know better, what?" Xander slid from the back of the horse, dropping in front of Ix.

"I'm not talking to you, I'm talking to him!" Ix hooked a thumb back at Aldebarron and met Xander's eye. Xander had begun to notice that even when Ix didn't say *boy*, he *did* say it.

"You think he can understand you?" Xander demanded with an incredulous smirk. He almost felt like laughing, but figured the sinewy man would knock him to the ground if he did.

"He understands me just fine. I hear you whispering to him all the time; you think he can't understand you? It's you that doesn't understand." Xander just stood closed-mouthed, staring back defiantly, not knowing what to say next. "Ha! Maybe there *is* an ounce of understanding in that thick head after all. Clean up your horse and yourself!"

Turning his back on him, Ix marched off towards the paddock, where Pipkin sat upon the low wall. He started clapping excitedly as Ix passed. "Big horse very fast!"

"You know better too, Fool!" Ix replied, pointing his finger at Pipkin but not breaking stride as he went into the Gathering Hall.

"Pipkin still thinks big horse very fast… Pipkin knows." Pipkin was still dejectedly muttering to himself as Xander led Aldebarron to the stables, but started clapping and smiling again as they passed him.

Xander wondered why he was bothering to comply with Ix's orders, but then reminded himself that up until very recently, he could barely lift himself up onto the large steed's back, much less ride him. Benign compliance was best until he could formulate a plan. Turning back around, he was about to call to Pipkin, but found that he had vanished.

This had become annoyingly commonplace. Not that Pipkin didn't always just disappear and reappear, but it was as if the young boy somehow knew when Xander was about to ask him something. He had once, when Ix and Pipkin were together, broached the subject of Rellion and how they all knew each other, but at the mention of Rellion's name, Ix went

A Tale of the Broken Heart

into such a violent and hateful tirade that Pipkin had scampered off and hadn't returned for a couple of days. It was only after Ix had hacked all the limbs and heads off all of the training manikins that he'd finally settled down. Xander hadn't bothered to speak the name again, but at least it made it easier for him and Aldebarron to run close turns around the wind-up soldiers.

The sweat on the young man's body from the couple of hours of exertion was like little droplets of ice as his body temperature dropped back down to normal. Instead of reaching for the rag to wipe down his horse, he grabbed from a hook the midnight-blue cloak that he had found in a footbox under a bed in one of the dilapidated quarters. It was one of the few items he had found that hadn't become the ripped and frayed nest of some animal. Xander gave an all-over shiver as he swung it over his shoulders and clasped it in the front with a silver broach that had a strange emblem of a tree upon it. He fingered at the raised engraving, thinking how strange it was that the tree looked like it was glittering, almost alive; yet he knew it was just some trick of the metal and how it was burnished.

"Looks good on you." Xander was startled by the distinctly feminine voice of the raven-haired woman he had come to know as Lieutenant Blackmore. She stood on the other side of the pen gate, her arms resting on the top rail.

Xander stood stoically, with only the slightest of nods in acknowledgement. He thought that it was probably because of a lifetime of avoiding uniforms that he didn't trust this woman, and had very little to do with her personally. The moment they'd been led by Pipkin into the Ward a fortnight ago, he'd recognized her and her company as Warders of Kairos. Unlike the Briggers who patrolled the city center and the outlying villages and boroughs to the north and east — where a skirmish meant locking up a thief or a drunk, or breaking up a pub fight after they'd made their wagers on who would be the victor — the Warders were experienced soldiers. Blackmore was most definitely the latter.

Noticing his preoccupation with the emblem, she pointed to his chest. "It's a depiction of the Blessed Tree. That cloak must have belonged to one of the Knights of the Baennaith." Xander didn't look down, keeping his eyes fixed on Blackmore. "Not surprised you haven't heard of them;

they died out centuries ago. That cloak shouldn't even exist." Reaching over the gate, she loosened the latch that held it in place and gave it a push. The hinges scraped against their knuckles with nothing but bare and pitted iron between them. "Until I saw you with it, I doubted they had ever existed, much less a Blessed Tree."

Xander shrugged and knelt down, wiping the dust from Aldebarron's hocks. He truthfully had no idea what the Lieutenant was talking about; he'd heard of the Blessed Tree, of course, but had always thought it was just some form of blessing given from one person to another, or as Rellion used it in sentences, a curse like *dammit*. As for the Knights of Whatever, the most he knew was that they had nice cloaks.

"That is quite the stallion. Where did you get him?" Blackmore continued to be inquisitive, and had cornered him a handful of times since her arrival, asking him questions that he mostly didn't know the answers to. Ix had waylaid her several times when he noticed she was alone with him, and that usually ended in a heated conversation between the two — one where they both started with their hands on the pommels of their swords, and ended with one or the other storming off. Otherwise, a tenuous truce had been reached upon the arrival of her and her company of a dozen or so men and women. Xander imagined that it could break at the slightest word, but from what he could gather, Ix was a prisoner from the Manor Hall, Blackmore had somehow fallen out of favor with the Stewards or some holy man or such, and neither of them thought much of Rellion. Which was an understatement; since the Lieutenant seemed to have the same violent physical reaction to his mention as Ix, there were very few unbroken chairs or tables in the Gathering Hall anymore. None of which gave him much confidence in the company he was presently keeping.

"Found him," he replied without looking away from dusting the mail that wrapped the horse's hooves.

"Found him? Really?" Blackmore contemplated this for a moment or two, obviously trying to decide if he was telling the truth. Coming to a decision, she knelt next to him, and in a voice not quite as commanding as he'd heard her use before, asked, "Xander, who are you?"

Of all of the questions he'd been asked by Blackmore, this one shocked him the most. Not because of the straightforward bluntness of it, or because it was a request for identity, like "What do you do for a living?" or "What family do you come from?", but more like a plea. It was the tone of a person who had spent a lifetime in search of a cause that would make all of the sense of duty, the horror of conflict, and bloodshed worth it. It was a question and tone of hoping and searching.

Xander found himself wishing he could give her the answer she wanted, but instead he just stuttered out, "I-I'm just Xander… I'm n-nobody." The words echoed into his very being. Aldebarron whinnied softly and stomped his rear hooves, and for the first time in his life, Xander really thought he was nobody.

He felt tears welling in the corners of his eyes; he supposed he must look extremely forlorn, because the raven-haired woman placed her hand on his shoulder and said to him comfortingly, "Xander, everyone is *somebody*. I'm sorry if I upset you." While she was kind, he suspected he heard a bit of disappointment in her voice.

The silence that followed Blackmore's apology was broken by Ix thundering into the paddock, his voice cracking against the moment like lightning. "I've told you to leave that boy alone!" Seeing Xander's distress, Ix unsheathed his sword mid-stride, stopping short of the kneeling woman. "What has she said to you, boy?"

"I said nothing to him, you pompous jackass!" Xander was always surprised by how the Lieutenant always held her ground in the presence of Ix. Despite being a full head shorter than him, she stood and returned his venomous rage. "I do wonder, though, why the hell you're so protective of him! I'm just asking him the same damn questions you refuse to answer — how do you know of the Ward, why do you carry the Bristol Cree, who's the young sprite who disappears like a shadow, and why in the bloody hell does that boy there ride the battle stallion of the Kings?" Blackmore, hitching a thumb back at Xander without turning her attention from Ix, ended her litany of questions.

Xander had overheard all of these at least once in the last couple of weeks, and had started to wonder as to some of them himself, though he didn't understand half of what she was actually asking. He did wonder what she meant by Ix being protective of him; Xander believed him to be anything but.

Gritting his teeth, apparently in an attempt to suppress the anger he was feeling, Ix replied. "As I have said to you, *repeatedly*, the truth of these matters is far above your station or your ability to comprehend!"

"Why, you smug piece of...!"

"Yay! Pipkin sees, Pipkin sees!" Just as Blackmore was in the process of unsheathing her sword and finishing up whatever she was about to call Ix, Pipkin's exclamation and delighted clapping came from above them, where he sat peeking down on the proceedings from the rickety canopy of the paddock.

"Dammit, Fool! What is it now?" Ix peered up at Pipkin through the open spaces in the slats.

"Pipkin likes balloons! Pipkin likes parties!" The young boy was jumping up and down, pointing at something in the sky to the west. Dust and pieces of rotted wood began to sprinkle down from the canopy, catching in the hair and on the shoulders of everyone underneath.

"Dammit, stop dancing around up there or you'll fall through! What are you on about? Balloons?" Ix, forgetting the argument, trounced near the open gate and shielded his eyes from the rising sun, scanning in the direction Pipkin pointed in between his excited claps. Fixing his view at a single spot in the sky, he said, "Call your men, Lieutenant, we have guests."

NONE BUT THE KING COULD RIDE THE STALLION

"Banes! Get your lazy ass out here and bring your bows and my long musket!"

Xander followed Ix and Blackmore into the courtyard. Blackmore's men had already formed a row of archers, and the rest had taken up positions within the space, some behind low walls and others behind what was left of the practice manikins. Banes marched towards Blackmore, tossing her musket to her in a high arc. She caught it with a single hand, and with the fluidity of a dancer, swung the stock to her shoulder, planting her feet in a stance that would take the energy of any kickback from the heavy doubled muzzle.

"There is wording… Fatpac oodle-M show. It's difficult to read it. Looks like pants and kilts are covering most of it." Blackmore lifted her gaze from the telescopic eyepiece running the length of the barrels, inspecting the optics, then returned to her observation. "I see at least a dozen occupants. Several very short."

To Xander, the balloon looked like a speck that was slowly bobbing against the background of clouds. Had it been positioned a little farther to the west, it would have been lost in the Skookums.

Blackmore dropped her stance, cradling the musket's stock under her arm with the muzzle angled to the ground. "It's coming from the far north, riding the valley current and coming fast." Without the aid of the telescope, the Lieutenant contemplated it; and talking more to herself, she said, "It's not from Kairos, definitely not one of the military's, too far out from any villages that lie in that direction, and too coincidental to be just floating past us."

Reassuming her firing stance, she said, "Best to just figure it out afterwards." Thumbing back each of the hammers with a quiet click, there came the whir of cogs that were mounted along either side of the breech. A single thin, oblong cylinder that was mounted under the twin barrels made a sucking sound with the intake of air.

"Pipkin sees, Pipkin sees, pretty girl's flappy, flappy bird! Yay balloon!"

Pipkin was still jumping up and down upon the paddock canopy when what he said clicked in Xander's head. "Flappy bird? Kristane? Purdy!" Xander quickly scanned the sky. Blackmore was right; it was coming fast, and he could just see the broken-up wording that she was talking about. Orbiting around the patchwork panels of the balloon's envelope, he made out the distinct flapping of wings and a long tail with a tufted end. "Fatoodle Medhow, Fat-oodle-Med-how, Fatterpacker-Noodle Medicine Show!" Xander rushed at the Captain. "No, don't shoot!"

Tripping over his own feet in his haste to get to her, he just barely got a hand on the barrels of her musket as she squeezed the trigger. The reverberation of the silver tubes stung at his hand like an open flame. The resulting concussive blast from both muzzles coalesced into a small ball of fire. "What the hell?!" she demanded.

Xander watched apprehensively, his stinging hand grasped within the other, as the flaming projectile veered to the left side of the fabric envelope of the balloon, just missing it. He sighed in relief… and then a small flame took root within one of the panels. The fireball hadn't missed entirely, but had grazed the balloon. The occupants within the basket, close enough to be seen now, began to wave their arms dramatically. The exterior fabric of the balloon started to smolder with dark plumes of smoke, like a fire deprived of oxygen just before it sparks.

At the extreme angle the basket was falling, being dragged by the momentum of the smoldering balloon, Xander could make out a propeller mounted to the backside that was spinning furiously. Shouts of dismay filled the courtyard from all of its occupants, bar one. Upon a small saddle sat the determined and grim figure of a dwarf pedaling a stationary bicycle. As the gyration of the prop blades hit a fevered pitch, the bottom of the basket collided with the natural enclosure of the courtyard, sending the basket spinning counterclockwise.

"Take cover!" The booming voice of Ix rang in Xander's ear as he was brusquely pulled to the side. Blackmore and her company retreated a safe distance from the impending crash.

Twisting and rotating along the basket's bottom edge, the craft came to an uneasy stop… and then was slowly pulled over and slid several more yards onto its side as the cascading balloon burst into flames, with the skirt lying on the still-firing burner. Tumbling out the basket, a small boy, his flight goggles slanted to the side and under his chin, fell to the ground and looked like he was hugging it. The dwarf yanked off the crank arm of his bicycle and proceeded to beat the burner into submission as pieces of charred fabric caught on the breeze and floated around like confetti.

"Yay! It's a party! Pipkin likes parties!" Pipkin danced around from his perch on the canopy, trying to catch the falling confetti-like embers with his cupped hands.

Several occupants, having been tossed from the basket upon impact, stood uneasily. One wavered for a moment or two, and then fell right back down onto his backside, just staring straight ahead. Another brushed at his purple suit and bent over to retrieve a violet top hat. The feathers attached to the band were bent along the quill, making them droop oddly.

"Greetings, greetings one and all! We are on an urgent errand for Her Highness! Let me introduce myself; I am Doc Fatterpacker, and these are some of the members of my happy troupe!" The Doc gave a long bow and his signature toothy grin. "Now please announce my arrival to His Young Highness!"

No one moved or spoke. Blackmore looked the Doc up and down, her musket resting lazily on her shoulder, with a disbelieving smirk on her face. "Dammit, but I've seen it all now. Aren't you a pretty peacock?"

"Thank you, Madame, thank you! But I dare not tarry in the idleness of courtship. Where is His Highness?!" Fatterpacker peered about inquisitively while Groggle gave a low groan, attempting to roll up off the ground, and Noodle picked up his wig and attempt to dust it off.

Xander, seeing Groggle and his other friends, stepped forward. When Ix restrained him by the elbow, he said indignantly, yanking away his arm, "I know them!"

"*Squawk, squawk!*" Purdy, his screech agitated, dropped to a hover just in front of Xander, his wings beating rapidly to stay aloft.

Offering his arm as a perch, Xander spoke soothingly to the Faerrier. "Easy, Purdy, easy, it's fine. Where's Kristane?" he asked while stroking the flustered animal.

"Xander!" Prya, dislodging herself from the confines of the basket, rushed up to him and threw her arm around his neck. Seeing her articulated arm in a sling, he had a sudden sense of foreboding. Behind her, he saw Lathan smiling broadly, and the rest of the Rogue in varying stages of extricating themselves from the wreckage or picking themselves up off the ground. Even Cayson gave him a nod in greeting. Everyone was there, he realized… except Kristane. He looked at Lathan questioningly, and the smile faded from the young man's face.

"Ah, of course, Your Highness!" Seeing the slight altercation, Fatterpacker performed his most impressive bow, which would have rivaled any performed in any royal court, directing it towards Xander.

Ix trained his sword at the bowing man and asked in his gruff voice, "What is it you have to do with this boy?"

"Dear sir, I seek only an audience with His Highness to regale him with the adventures of his sister, *Her* Highness. You must, of course, be his valet or manservant, yes? If you would make the introduction promptly!"

Ix moved menacingly at Fatterpacker, his sword pointed directly at the showman's chest, and Noodle spoke up. "Beggin' everyone's pardon, but he means we need to speak to the boy about his sister, Kristane. Tall, odd fella told us to follow that bird thing there, said he could find Xander. Sure enough I had my doubts, but we're here." Noodle glanced at the smoking and sputtering burner of the balloon. "Course, it wasn't without an obstacle or two."

"Tall, odd fella?" Strolling forward, her musket still resting on her shoulder, Blackmore injected herself into the conversation.

"Yes ma'am, calls himself Rellion." Noodle gave her a polite bow as Xander stole a look at Ix. Ix had turned ashen, with an angry scowl, and Blackmore, he also noticed, seemed to have a disdainful line to the set of her mouth, like she had just tasted something bitter.

"But Doc's right, that's just by the by; the young miss is in real danger. Been stolen by the Forgotten Ones, and I don't mind saying they done got the better of us. Rellion told us there might be someone with the boy that would know what to do."

"Kristane? Where?" Xander was beside himself; he wanted to shake Noodle, but quickly realized that his thoughts must be mirrored on his face, given the alarmed look in Noodle's eyes, He reprimanded himself silently; they had just risked their lives to bring him this news. Taking a couple of calming breaths, he started again. "Sorry. When and where did they get her, and why didn't Rellion come?"

"Hold up a moment. I have seen more than my share of legends recently, including the one that's currently dusting my boots." The Captain stomped on a burning ember of balloon fabric, kicking up a small plume of dust for emphasis. "Now I'm to believe some fancy peacock and his merry band of misfits, no insult intended," Blackmore cocked her elbow at Fatterpacker but nodded politely to Noodle, "have crashed landed into the midst of an otherwise unknown and forgotten place to warn us that some fairytale creatures have now come to life and stolen *Her Highness*.'" Blackmore smirked, with more than an air of doubt. "And dammit all, while I'm on a horse, if I ever see Rellion again, much less hear the name, I will stick him with my sword from stem to stern!"

Noodle was literally taken aback by the last exclamation. Withdrawing by a pair of uneasy steps, he roughly stammered out. "Beggin' pardon, meant no offense, seems agreeable 'nuff he does, but after what them

Forgotten Ones did to him, not sure sticking anything in him would do him much harm."

Blackmore eased her temper and looked at Noodle questioningly. He continued, "I'm here to tell you, ma'am, that what them Forgotten Ones did to him, being dead and then sittin' up and chattin' and all, is no fairytale."

Xander looked questioningly at Prya as she let go of him, and she nodded. He didn't know how to feel about it, but all that really mattered was his sister.

"Come forth straight from the lips of my ole grandad or some fancy bard, they all have." Blackmore returned to her doubting smirk, but Noodle waved it off. "Now, I know I sound like I been drinkin' some of Doc's medicine or hit my head on the ground — well, did in fact do that — but truth being, we all seen the same thing." Noodle gave an encompassing gesture indicating his fellow ballooners.

Blackmore looked at him and the others hard, challenging the truthfulness of the statement. Not seeing any hints of a lie, she turned the same hard look at Ix. He answered by meeting her eye but staying silent and detached.

"Grandad use to call his odd type some fancy name. I forget — just remember it meaning 'The Undying.' Well, to answer the young boy there, Rellion run off after the young miss and those that took her. We set off best we could; we been comin' as the bird does for over a day."

Xander was shocked that Kristane had been in such danger for that long already. He felt the muscles in his shoulders tense, and clenched his jaw, biting back the tirade he wanted to shout out. He fumed at himself for not leaving and finding his sister sooner. If he'd been there, then he could have helped her. Maybe.

Xander was about to act on his impulses when his pending tirade was interrupted. "Amongst the fallen but not allowed to rest, Ordered by oath and the King's bequest, The failed Amaranthine blessed to be undying, Cursed to stand together, their behavior testifying..."

Ix spoke in a solemn voice, like he was reciting a prayer as parishioners would do to fortify themselves against the evils that besieged them.

"From a place unremembered and long forgot… They will take her there. We must go to Kaer Kairos," he concluded straightforwardly, as if he had just finished a particularly inspiring sermon and the proper response of all was *Amen* — which by the set of his shoulders and his resolute glare, it had been for him.

"We've already been given a death sentence with more than enough assistance from you and Rellion — but I'll be damned if I'm taking myself or my men into that rumored hell. What makes you think I'm going to follow you *anywhere*?!" Blackmore shouted.

Whatever presence was missing from Ix's brief sermon before was paid back with his response. The regality of several lifetimes shone through the rags of his tattered uniform as he declared, "I am Count Richard Manorlorn of the Amaranthine, one of The Undying, bearer of the Bristol Cree, Warder Commander, and sworn protector of the House of Alesdair!"

Blackmore didn't blink or twitch a muscle, her mind racing wildly as the pieces of what she knew and what she had just learned fell into place, even as Ix pointed the Bristol Cree at her. "Though the boy knows it not, he and his sister are descendants of the House of Alesdair. You wanted to know who he is, Captain? None but the King could ride the stallion Aldebarron! You will hold to the oath of your forefathers, Warder!"

FORTUITOUS CALAMITY

Kristane awoke with pains that made her wish she hadn't awoken at all. The dull ache that started in her head and permeated every nerve from there down made the slightest move of just her little finger send a shocking echo reverberating along her spine and rising back to the base of her skull. She laid there, very much feeling the hard surface she was lying on, only too aware of the jagged pebbles that were cutting into her cheek. She dared not to sit up or even open her eyes, the pain of it less than what it would mean to do so.

Through her eyelids, she could sense a difference in the light, rather than if it had just been dark. The twinkling there, just on the edge of perception, reminded her of the burst of light when the Forgotten One had touched her. For a moment, she debated as to whether she was dead or not; but she imagined that even death couldn't be this agonizing.

Abruptly, she felt a yank at the top of her head, and the tearing away of some of her hair from the roots. She wanted to scream, but her throat and mouth felt as though they were stuck together. She was so dry from lack of water that she barely recognized her own tongue in her mouth. Instead, only a muffled croak came out. Something cold in the shape of a hand was forcing her mouth back and open. Kristane didn't resist; even if she had chosen to, she just didn't have the strength.

Gagging and sputtering, she half-choked on the ice-cold water that was poured down her throat. The few swallows that reached the back of her throat burned like a fire against the dehydrated tissue. Nonetheless, it was a relief she wasn't expecting. Her chin drooped to her chest, and water dribbled from her half-opened mouth. She attempted to suck back some of the escaping liquid, every cell in her body demanding more. Chancing a look, she raised her eyelids slowly. There were a series of popping ghosts of light as she halted at half-mast, waiting for anything to come into focus.

What she saw was the delicate metal foot of a Forgotten One peeking from under the heavy fabric of her charcoaled cloak. Lolling her eyes to the right, she saw a very small fire that highlighted the tool-worked walls of a tunnel. Kristane knew that she must have returned to the Bizzarred mines… and with that realization, the corners of her vision blurred, and she succumbed to unconsciousness once again.

It took three or perhaps four more times of repeating this ritual before Kristane became lucid for more than a few minutes at a time. She believed that they had moved each time, though she couldn't be sure; the glimpses she had were brief and fuzzy. She choked up less of the water being given her, but with awareness came a desperate sense of fear that gripped her deep. By habit she reached to her chest, and found that her necklace was gone. Conflicting emotions rippled through her. She hated how the trinket had caused so much fear and grief, yet at a time such as this, she craved the comfort that it had brought her for most of her life.

The Forgotten Ones were silent, besides the shuffling of their limbs against fabric or a scuff of metal against the stone floor of a tunnel, yet Kristane slowly came to realize that they were communicating by a series of gestures and facial movements. She could sense that they were irritated by something. It was during one such time, when the Forgotten Ones' series of gestures became especially angered, that Kristane heard a low rumbling that grew in intensity.

"Hang on, Master Dwarf, I have you!"

Kristane's heart literally skipped a beat as she swung her head about, looking for the direction from which she'd heard the muffled but all-too- familiar voice. She turned at the approach of pronounced metal footsteps. Meeting the lowered brow and squinted eyes of the Forgotten One as its facial plates moved to a visage of anger, she struggled to cry out, "Rellion…!"

Kristane wasn't sure if she had even made a sound as the tip of the Forgotten One's finger touched her forehead, wiping away any conscience thought.

From a broken-away path that hung over the edge of a precipice, a tall figure, his head cocked oddly to one side, held tight with both hands to a dangling, much smaller man. "Come, Master Dwarf, your near-fatal calamity was most timely!" Rellion heaved at Beezy, securing him in a heap on the narrow ledge that they were traversing. "Ridiculous to believe that were not aware of our presence before, but thanks to our young Princess, we know we are not far from our quarry."

No Matter How Royal the Whelp

The revelations of the early morning had laid a heavy silence upon the Ward. It wasn't a natural silence, but one that holds to men's hearts with quiet whispers and furtive looks, the breeze carrying them from person to person, causing greater unease with each telling. Blackmore and Ix stood in the middle of the courtyard, speaking quietly, barely a hand-span between them, attempting a degree of secretiveness that only added to the silent anxiety of the others. Flickering torches highlighted the pair with sudden bursts, as the cold remains of Fatterpacker's balloon fluttered about them with the wind.

Xander watched them from the shadows of the paddock, Aldebarron masking his presence. He didn't need to hear the discussion; the heated argument from earlier in the Gathering Hall told him everything he needed to know. He and his friends were to be left behind.

Groggle and Noodle had done their best to give a complete accounting of everything that had happened, and at the conclusion, Xander had demanded that they leave immediately to rescue his sister. Ix had refused his *boyish impulse,* as he referred to it, and had gone as far to say that *some young whelp* was on no accounts going along with the small band that was to rescue Kristane from Kaer Kairos, no matter how royal the whelp.

Funny how all his declarations of servility to the old throne didn't seem to increase his opinion of me, Xander thought. Many times he had looked across the twin bays of Kairos, Mererid and Merrow, at the castle, hardly giving it another thought. As a young boy he, Cayson, and some of the other boys their age had dared one another to run at the sentries who stood guard along the entrance to the land bridge that lay between the bays, tossing rocks and doing their best to harass them. Even then, they knew the danger of such things. The ancient law was clear: enter Kaer Kairos under penalty of death. Though the decree was mercilessly enforced, there wasn't much need; superstition and rumor of what was there kept even the most desperate of thieves or heroes looking to make a name for themselves far away. Xander had almost forgotten that at one time, he and Cayson had been friends; it was hard to determine when they had started to drift apart, and all things became a competition. Well, at least as Cayson viewed it, anyway.

Royalty, kings... none of it meant anything to him. It was just the rantings of some madman he'd recently met, and an obstacle in the way of him helping his sister. *It would be childish foolishness to hand-deliver both of you to them.* Ix hadn't bothered to elaborate as to *why* it was foolish. Blackmore seemed to have taken Ix's proclamation as gospel, and Groggle had confirmed what Ix and Noodle had said, telling Xander of the conversation that he'd overheard when Rellion said the same to Kristane. For whatever reason, the Forgotten Ones had taken Kristane; and Xander didn't give a mad steward for whatever reason Ix and Blackmore had for just leaving him behind. He was going.

Xander watched as Blackmore and Ix traipsed back to the Gathering Hall and disappeared from view. Standing precariously on an old crate, he lifted a black leather saddle onto the back of Aldebarron. Xander had previously found a number of saddles in the stables, most of them spoiled and decaying to dust, but he'd managed to salvage this one. Admittedly, it was bug-riddled; from the horn to cantle, insects had created interwoven random paths of ingested leather. When oiled and buffed out, though, the patterns almost looked like they belonged. Aldebarron's girth was far too great for the straps and flank billet to buckle, but Xander found that just as the bridle did not attach to a bit, the great stallion had other points these could be connected to.

"Attaboy. I hope you know which way we're going, because I don't. We have to get to Kristane, though." Xander gave the horse a stroke along the crest of his neck, and Aldebarron whinnied softly. "I get it. You do understand, don't you? Let's get to the old ruins, then." Aldebarron shook his head from side to side and lightly stomped with his front left hoof, the chainmail tinkling against his lower leg. "Got it." Xander nodded in understanding. "Let's get those wrapped up for the time being." Retrieving some strips of the cloth he used to wipe down the stallion, he bent down and began to tie them around the horse's ankles, restricting the movement of the mail.

Startled by a noise he heard behind him as he stood, Xander spun around to find Groggle standing there with a dejected frown on his face. "You were going to leave without me and the others?" the boy demanded. "We're Rogue, right?"

The truth was, Xander had kind of forgotten about Groggle. This made him feel all the guiltier that he hadn't just decided to leave without him or the others, but had ignored the thought of them completely. Xander gave a heavy sigh, weighing in his mind the possibility that if he didn't take Groggle, he might alert the others, and then Xander would never get to his sister. "Don't suppose you would just stay here with the others, would you? Where it's safe?" he ventured. If possible, Groggle looked even more morose at the suggestion. "All right, climb up — but no whining when your backside starts to hurt."

Groggle smiled grandly and snapped his goggles in place.

As quietly as a metal stallion the size of Aldebarron could be, they skirted the perimeter of the courtyard, hugging the shadows, Groggle's arms wrapped tightly around Xander's waist, his cheek flattened against Xander's shoulder blades. The mistreated practice manikins afforded some direct line-of-sight distraction for anyone who might be watching from the Gathering Hall as they approached the entrance to the Ward. Abruptly, though, Aldebarron halted. Just ahead in the dim light cast by the waning gibbous of the Older Brother, Xander saw what the stallion had already noticed: a pair of Warders. Blackmore's men were positioned along the mountain trail leading off into the darkness. He couldn't help but wonder if they were there on his account, Ix possibly suspecting that he would do as exactly as he *was* doing.

A few pebbles tumbled down the carven stairs, which led to the parapets positioned to either side of the arched entry of the Ward. From step to step, they pattered faintly, but it was enough to make the guards curious. Xander could hear the near-inaudible tone of questioning as the sentries slowly began to ascend the rock notches. Following their path upward with his eyes, waiting for their opportunity to slip out quietly, Xander spotted the hunched-over form of Pipkin atop the high wall. His hand was clasped to his mouth and he swayed forward and back, clearly trying to hold in his laughter. Xander caught himself from chuckling at Pipkin's antics, and encouraged Aldebarron forward. He couldn't help but wonder if his group had just increased by one... *make that two*, he mused, as Purdy silently swooped in from the side and nestled himself just in front of the saddle horn.

DAMNABLE HORSE NEVER DID LISTEN

Ix paced the Ward courtyard like a caged animal, berating himself for not shackling the boy to his bed. Blackmore shouted orders in the background, her men hurriedly packing in the early morning light. The two sentries responsible for watching the egress during the night stood at uneasy and nervous attention, barely blinking as they took the full brunt of the Lieutenant's vulgarity-laden rebuke.

"You two ignorant frickin' asses! —Dammit, Banes, no, leave that! I said I want out of here within the hour! — If you two had half a brain between the pair of you... it's a wonder you can wipe your own... Banes!" Blackmore's diatribe shifted from giving orders to the dressing down of her men with the experience of a wartime trench commander. "Ix, I could use a hand here, if you're not too busy with your self-loathing and recrimination!"

Ix grumbled to himself. Being in the company of others grated on him after the hundreds of years of solitude, but he knew he needed the help of the Whiskeys. For one, the small schooner anchored near the outlet mouth of the Cynabell River, which the Lieutenant had outlined as part of the plan to get to Kaer Kairos, would take time to find without them, and he couldn't hope to sail it alone. Time was a commodity he had little of, especially with the disappearance of the boy, the Fool, the horse, the bug-eyed kid, and that squawking Faerrier. As it was it would take three days, more like four, to sail around the southern tip of Kairos. Meanwhile, Aldebarron could carry the boy and the lot of them for hundreds of miles in a straight line as fast as the wind.

"Damnable horse never did listen to anyone anyway, and the Fool, well, he was half- cracked long before this. There's little chance of holding him accountable for anything," Ix growled to himself, his hand gripping tightly at the hilt of his sword.

Secondly, he pondered bluntly, men were going to die. Ix thought hard on the *"such is life"* perspective he had towards using Blackmore and her men as fodder, but all else was trivial compared to the lives of the twins. Ix hated himself, that he should have lived so long that others' lives should mean so little to him. "Such is death, damn the Blessed Tree," he seethed jealously to himself, and he hated himself even more for being envious of their ability to die.

"Ix! Tell this frilly peacock and these kids to get outta my face and that they're not going with us!"

"Madame, I must insist! We will not be left to the wilds of this land! Doctor Fatterpacker must return to the ministrations of his adoring public!" Fatterpacker held his finger high in the air, and stomped his foot for emphasis as the Rogue shouted out their disapproval, which only enraged Blackmore further.

"There's no way in hell we're staying here while our friends are in danger!" Prya spat in anger as the rest of her companions nodded along fervently.

"See that archway there? I will hang all of you from it in irons, *upside down*, until your eyes bulge if you don't get out of my face!" Blackmore yelled. Fatterpacker looked appropriately astonished at the threat, but the Rogue only stared back at her defiantly. "Banes, bring me the shackles!"

Ix came marching into the fray, staring first at Blackmore and then the kids. Assessing them, he said, "We'll need a distraction. Keep up, or you'll be left to die," the former sentence being addressed to Blackmore, the latter to the Rogue and Fatterpacker. The Doc gave a triumphant smile, but it drooped a little as the understanding of Ix's remark sank in a little farther. Prya and the others were not taken aback by the threat. *Too stupid or too young to understand,* Ix told himself.

The mainsail cracked crisply against the salty breeze as it was rigged to catch the changing wind off the low end of Kairos. The schooner swung hard with the change in current to the western side of the headland. The efficiency and grit of Blackmore's men couldn't be denied. What they lacked in military decorum, proper dress, or seamanship, they made up for in toughness and complete fidelity to Blackmore. Even the medicine man and his pair of cronies weren't incapable of a bit of roughing it, Ix noted. In fact, the dwarf and the man with the peg leg were more than able sailors, having taken the helm each night as the others rested. The kids, on the other hand, were a menace; half of them were seasick, and the other half constantly underfoot. Keeping the little redheaded brats out of the rigging had become a full-time affair.

"Pardon, sir, don't mean to be waking you and all, but was a-wonderin' if we could talk for a bit." Noodle had been relieved from the wheel by the dwarf. Dropping the cowl of the worn cloak he had retrieved from the Ward, Ix could see, in the flickering of the deck lights, the dwarf precariously balanced on a barrel, peeking over the wheel handles. Ix still hadn't caught his name, but he'd learned that it was generally best not to know. Made it easier to forget them.

Undraping the trailing ends of his cloak from his knees, where it had covered him as a makeshift tent as he squatted upon the decking against the rail, feigning sleep, he looked up at Noodle's anxious face. He didn't spend much time belowdecks with the others. The long-established habit of keeping one eye to the horizon and the uneasiness he now felt about the confining space of the crew quarters kept him perched here on the thick boards of the main deck. He couldn't decide which of the two reasons the prevailing one was. "Not sleeping," he informed Noodle.

"No, s'pose not, you keep a wary eye; have been 'round fellas like you. My friend Beezy is the same. Tell him all the time…" Noddle trailed off timidly, realizing by Ix's hardened stare that he was rambling. "Well, by the by, not what I bothered you to chat about. Like I said, known a few fellas like you." Ix gave him the same hardened stare. "Meaning not all undying and such, but can see the same in your eyes as them. Don't think you have to live a long life, just have to see what you probably *have* seen to look at others the way you do." Noodle pulled absently at his chin, scratching at a scruff of beard that didn't exist. "Those folks down below, they know what they's in for, an' so do we, even the Doc." This drew a dubious smirk from Ix, just as Fatterpacker let out a loud snore from the quarterdeck, where he slept sprawled out like a gingerbread cookie — having been banned by Blackmore from further contact with the crew after attempting to sell them parts of the schooner. "Now, I know what you're thinkin', but Doc, he knows the people of all the realms. Can say he has a real hunch about most things, in his own way. He'd sell you your own shoes on your feet, but he hopes like all of us for better tomorrows and is willing to pay the price. Let me see if I can do justice, as my old grandad would say: *There's a price for making things better, and a price for letting them stay the same; turns out it's the same price.*" Noodle paused for a moment and scratched at the side of his head. "Good night, then, and won't bother ya any more, just wanted a bit of a chat."

As Noodle walked away, Ix contemplated the hobbling steps of the retreating man and called out. "Thanks... uhm?"

"Friends call me Ed, or Noodle if you like, and that's Percy at the wheel there."

"Some friends call me Richard...but I prefer Ix at the moment."

Noodle gave Ix a smile and an understanding wave and disappeared belowdecks.

A Good Game
of Pattycake

Madame Ridley pressed tenderly at the cheek just below her left eye, inspecting what she assumed was the beginnings of a very impressive shiner. "By the King's Grace, how long has it been since I was involved in a brawl?!" She chortled at the thought that a woman of her age should have a black eye from a fight! She eyed the pommel of her cane appreciatively; a smear of blood tarnished the otherwise shiny silver cap. They'd had to wrestle it from her after she'd cold-cocked a couple of them. The Brigger to the right of her had it stowed in the crook of his armpit as he nursed a bloody lip and pulled at his two front teeth, attempting to ascertain if he might still lose one.

This made the Madame laugh. "Ba ha ha! That'll make you think twice about messing with an old woman again, won't it?" She continued to laugh as the large sergeant of the Briggers gave her a hateful scowl. "Better off than those other two, though, aren't you? Doubt they'll wake up before breakfast!" She tapped her foot on the floor with glee, wishing she still had possession of her cane so she could use it on that damn priest when he finally deigned to show.

As if on cue, High Priest Cristobal Zekel paraded into his office with all the self-proclaimed pomp he could muster, with Oscar Piggleback riding his heels and sporting a greedy and triumphant smile. The ever-present simpering monks skittered around him like rodents, as if hoping for enlightened crumbs to fall from his robes. Admittedly, seeing the back of the frazzled gray hair of the old woman gave him a certain euphoria, and he couldn't help but don a smug smile as well. It was quickly wiped away, though, when Cristobal saw that they had given her a chair to sit on. The thought that she was once again *not* standing in his presence rankled him. With a flourish of his robes, Cristobal stopped a short distance from the Madame, facing her and the guards who surrounded her. The Briggers gave a curt click of their heels, and gestured with their hands the blessing he now expected from everyone in his company.

Madame Ridley looked from side to side at the Briggers. "Ba ha ha! What's with all this hand waving? Utter nonsense!" Madame Ridley waved her hands up and down and slapped them on her knees. "You teach them that one, Cristie? Haven't had a good game of pattycake in a long time myself!" She held her hand up to the Sergeant expectantly, but was met with a straight-eyed stare of purposeful avoidance which made her laugh all the more.

Straightening the hem of her dress, pushing at a few of the fabric wrinkles and tucking an errant stand of hair or two back into her disheveled bun, Madame Ridley stopped laughing and glared back at the High Priest. "Well, let's get on with it, Cristobal, looks like Lord Jelly Belly there might explode with glee if we don't."

Cristobal took a moment to savor the position the woman was in. Taking the parchment from Piggleback, he perused the piece of paper that meant incarceration or worse for those Stewards and their families who had condemned his holy edict. His gaze lingered appreciatively upon the first name to grace the list: Madame Ridley's. No wonder Piggleback was so exuberant. The High Priest was just as happy that he would soon be rid of the old thorn in his side. Scanning further, he saw the signatures of his handpicked executive court — chosen, like Piggleback, for their reputations for malicious acts against one another, lack of morals, and their uncanny ability for self-preservation. Cristobal then glared at Piggleback and tapped at the proclamation with his long, skinny forefinger.

"Yes, High Priest? Is there something amiss?" Piggleback nervously wiped at the sweat that had formed above his upper lip with the back of his hand. In response, Cristobal's glare became so intense and full of rancor that Piggleback wobbled on his heels. Tapping the proclamation once more with his finger, Cristobal continued to eye Piggleback.

"Of course, Your Holiness, merely an honest oversight…" The fat man clumsily reached for the quill offered by one of the monks and scrawled out his name. The crow-feather plume affixed to the shaft convulsed this way and that as his pudgy fingers trembled from anxiety and fear. "There, all official, Your Holiness." Piggleback stepped back away from the desk with a nervous chuckle, as if already attempting to distance himself from the proclamation.

"Ba ha ha! Come, Cristie, you know ol' Piggly isn't used to doing things so openly. Back-alley knifings by hired hands is more in line with his tastes. But as I said, let's get on with this. Ask me something so that I can deny you, threaten me so that you feel powerful, and then toss me down some hole until you have the intestinal fortitude to have me done in."

"Madame is always so colorful. Done in? How colloquial. I only wish for you to denounce the heresy you have spoken, accept the enlightenment that has been given to me, and then, yes, I will have you and yours *done in*, as it were. I do, of course, prefer the phrasing *cleansing of the faithful* myself."

"Good Lord, are you still playing pious, or do you really believe all that zealot shite you're spewing? Or is this all just show for your followers here?" The monks that hovered like a halo about the High Priest gasped out loud, and the guards around her fidgeted at Madame Ridley's remark. She watched their reactions carefully, as if just seeing them. "I see. I must be getting old. We have gone far beyond what you believe, and are now in the realm of what *they* believe and fear." The elderly woman sighed deeply, and for the first time in a long while, felt the weight of time pressing down on her. At least her grandson was safe, or Cristobal would have already threatened her with him. The thought buoyed her spirits. "I will give you this, Cristie, you've spread hysteria and fear like the words of a fine poet, and all in the name of a self-serving prophet."

The High Priest straightened his weak shoulders and reveled in his triumph as Piggleback quivered and panted with his own excitement. "The Madame surely needs time to reflect." He gave a dismissive wave with the back of his hand. "Take her to the Bastille." Then, clasping his hands before him, a bit of lacy fabric intertwined in his fingers, he said. "I will, of course, pray for your salvation in this matter, Madame."

Damn, Now I've Committed His Name

Sitting hunched over, his head nodding occasionally despite his determination not to, sleep was slowly beating at exhaustion. His racing mind was shocked at his body in its resolve to keep itself conscious, the physical manifestation being abrupt tense and terse movements of his head and arms. Suddenly, the man was on his feet, the wide planking of a deck swaying below him. In the distance, he heard the whistling of a fast-approaching projectile. Ix had missed the initial blast of the cannon, but the way the iron ball cut a path through the currents of the sea air was unmistakable. He had been upon many a ship that now lay below the brine, with this being the last sound they had heard.

Following his senses, Ix looked up just as the shell splintered the mainmast of the schooner, wooden fragments raining down upon him. Flames licked at the sail from the exploding shrapnel, highlighting the heavy mast as it swayed ominously about a quarter of its length up from the deck, held together by a single shard of wood, the rest of the pole all but disintegrated. The shard twisted with the motion of the mast, teetering counterclockwise as it swung to the bow of the ship, first striking the mizzen and then coming around full circle and colliding with the foremast. He stepped to the starboard railing as all three fell with a concussion that made the schooner bob low in the water. The dwarf was busy pulling the still-sleeping Fatterpacker away from the debris, his station at the wheel crushed under the weight of the mainmast.

Ix waited and listened, but there weren't any more of the singsong whistles of projectiles. Why bother? A single shot had effectively rendered the schooner crippled, he realized as he ran to the stern, scanning the dark horizon. This was no attack by the inept navy of Kairos; this was the work of experienced and professional seamen.

There was no reason to strain his eyes. The decorated prow of a galleon was already running up next to the schooner port-side. The delicately worked curves of a figurehead stood high above the waterline, dwarfing the little schooner upon which he and the others sailed. The few deck lights that hadn't been crushed flickered on a beautiful face and an outstretched arm that held a single pearl, the bronze of the statue showing the patina that only many years of saltwater crashing about it can give. Ix immediately recognized the siren's tails curling up on either side of the ship's bow as the double tailed mermaid of the *Lady's Grace*.

Something clicked in his head, and he turned to find out why, besides the dwarf and the Doc, he was alone. Turned out that Blackmore and her soldiers were trapped, along with everyone else, belowdecks. The butt end the mainmast was wedged into the hatch that led below. He yelled, over the sounds of grappling hooks taking hold of the decking and rails, mixed with the incoherent shouts coming from the topside of the *Lady's Grace*, "Dwarf... Percy! It's the Brigandborn! Help me with the others!" He silently reprimanded himself after his call to action. *Damn, now I've committed his name.*

The dwarf grunted his understanding, and rushed alongside him to the crushed-in decking of the stairwell. Percy wedged himself into the space where the mast met the main deck and angled up to the poop deck. Squatting down as far as he could, his shorter stature allowed him to get nearly to the broad end of the broken mast.

Pushing with his powerful legs, Percy let out a low groan, and the mast inched upwards. The splintering rails of the poop deck and main decking cracked like brittle twigs with the dwarf's backbreaking effort. Ix stared into the dark crevice left by the massive piece of wood, searching for any sign of movement. After a moment, a single hand shot up from the darkness, grasping at air, and he reached for it, heaving whoever it was up into the half-light of the remaining deck lamps. Percy rolled the tapered mast off his shoulders and backed away from the opening, the echo of splintering wood sounding as it crashed again onto the deck. Noodle met Ix's eyes with a fearful but grateful look, and Ix grabbed the man by the seat of his pants, pulling him the rest of the way out.

Noodle was about to give his thanks when the dwarf hit the deck with nearly the same force as the broken mast had. The sound drew Ix's attention from Noodle to where Percy lay. The last thing he saw before his head jerked back from the impact of the stock end of a blunderbuss was a figure descending a gang plank, her long, curly red hair framed by the black leather corona of a broad cavalier hat.

POCKET FULL OF WORMS

"Hurry up, Groggle." Xander had lost his patience with his friend. The thought of his sister in danger and in the hands of the Forgotten Ones had filled him with an almost debilitating sense of dread and panic. As swift as Aldebarron was, he hadn't realized how far east they were when they first started from the Ward. Granted, he had been unconscious at the time of his arrival, but it was only late last evening that they'd finally crossed the Cynabell River at a point that wasn't as wide as the rest.

Aldebarron didn't exactly swim across as much as he trudged across the bottom of the river bed. They had completely lost sight of the great battle horse about a quarter of the way across as his heavy metal bulk sank. The only sense they had of him was the tugging of the rope that Xander and Groggle hung tightly to as they were dragged across. As it was, the trip was extremely perilous, as the swift current swept them downstream from Aldebarron's location. Groggle had almost been swept away twice, and then he had to be carried out on the other side, his body convulsing from the cold of the water, which meant that they had to stop for a while and warm him up.

"Please, I'm trying, but my butt is bruised and aches," Groggle called from somewhere behind a copse of shoulder-high bushes. Xander could partially see him through the branches and leafy scrub, trying to squat and relieve himself. Had it been any other time or circumstance, Xander might have found himself smirking at Groggle's constipation. "I'm sorry," the younger boy continued. "I know it's important, and I'm worried too, but my butt has been pounded so hard from riding that it's been compacted and won't come out."

Xander found himself actually smirking at that one.

Looking towards the snowcapped Effervescent Peaks through a break in the canopy of trees, he attempted to gauge how far they still were from Kairos. Though the mountains looked close, he knew in his heart that they only looked that way due to the great height of the peaks. They were still several days and many, many miles away from their goal. After three days of nearly constant riding, Xander could barely remember the last time they ate, the small supply of rations they had liberated from the Ward kitchen being exhausted now. *Was it a day ago, or was it two?* Xander shook his head, trying to shake away the fog. He was having trouble focusing on the time that had passed. He was pretty sure that he remembered at least three sunrises… or maybe it was four. What he did know was that they were still deep within the wildwood. His scratched arms and the numerous tiny rips in his pants, from the needled branches of trees and dense bramble that Aldebarron tore through like it was nothing, was all the evidence he needed.

"It's all right, we're going to take a longer break here." Xander hated the words as he said them, but he could no longer see straight; and if he didn't allow them some rest and an attempt at finding some food, the hectic pace he had set for them would be in vain.

There was a heavy, audible sigh of relief that emanated from the bushes that Groggle inhabited, followed by an indiscreet and prolonged flatulence that made even the birds above give pause. Purdy, who had taken a perch in the limbs above Groggle, took a sniff at the air and then made a disgusted face, and swooped down to the horse's saddle, nuzzling his nose under his paws, doing his best to avoid the offensive smell. Shaking his head and allowing himself another brief smile, Xander ran his hand through his dark hair. His fingers crunched on the leaves embedded there, and a barbed twig pricked his finger, drawing a small amount of blood.

Xander began to scan the forest floor for something to make a fire with, when Pipkin sauntered out of the brambles to his right. The sudden appearance of the Fool didn't even startle or bother Xander anymore, Pipkin's silent comings and goings being so frequent that Xander had become conditioned to accept them. He wondered how the Fool was keeping up, but hadn't bothered to ask… not that he would get a straight answer anyway. *Pipkin follows horsy, must save pretty girl with the pretty necklace,* was what Xander imagined he would get in response, and he had other things to occupy his thoughts. There was no reason to worry after Pipkin; he always seemed to just show up whenever they stopped.

Pipkin smiled broadly at Xander, holding high in the air, by their ears, a pair of skinned and gutted coneys. Immediately, the Fool's smile faded to one of disgust as he held his nose high and sniffed at the air. "Pipkin doesn't like the smell the little bug-faced one makes," he groused, focusing his attention directly to where Groggle had just emerged from his repose, attempting to fasten pants that still seemed to be hovering about mid-hip. "He is foul, foul, the smell of his bowels makes the great wolves howl, dwarfs growl, and old ladies scowl!"

"Hey! It's not me, it two-hundred-year-old jerky of who knows what type of meat… and, and besides, the up-and-down on the horse!" Groggle did his best to defend himself, and looked embarrassed and disgruntled as he attempted to out-yell Pipkin. But Pipkin had already began to dance around in a circle and start on the next verse of his made-up song, gibbering and cackling with laughter something concerning a cow patty, a barn owl, and how it wasn't the size of the stink bug, but how big he stank.

Xander gave out a guilty laugh before he finally came to Groggle's rescue, calming the both of them down.

Later that evening, Purdy still sat upon Aldebarron's saddle, his eyes closed but his long ears twitching and turning from side to side. Xander knew that Kristane's faithful pet was on the alert, sensing every movement and scent carried on the cold breeze. Earlier, Pipkin had kicked away the twigs and branches that Xander had accumulated for a fire, complaining as only he could, *Pipkin is Fool, not foolish. Light and smells bad, but smoke bad, bad, bad!* The Fool had returned with some cleaved, very dense-looking limbs of a tree that barely gave off any smoke; and though the heat was strong, the coals emitted only a faint glow, barely penetrating the small ring the companions occupied.

"Xander, how far, do you think?" Groggle asked as he tore into the hindquarters of a whole coney he was well into polishing off.

"I don't know, but far," Xander replied as he looked at the speared portion of meat he had allotted himself. With a great effort, he took another bite. Not that he found the dinner provided by Pipkin unappetizing, but with every moment that he felt they delayed, he worried they would be too late.

Neither of the boys had ever ventured past the docks of the twin bays, and hardly as far as to the entrance of the mines; but here, they found themselves in the deep woods, where the pathways and Steward Roads only stretched north and east, and nowhere in the vicinity of where Xander imagined them to currently be. He had heard of the small boroughs of the outlaying lands of Kairos, where those who choose to discreetly hide from the tyranny of the Stewards, and he supposed also the church, made their homes. They only ventured to what was deemed civilization when absolute need demanded it. Not even the Stewards bothered with securing these wildwoods, feeling any enforced tax wasn't worth their time.

It was then, amid his thoughtful wanderings, that he realized that Pipkin had vanished once again. He knew that it was commonplace, but something struck him as odd this time. Pipkin's skewered and roasted coney sat upon a rock that had until very recently been occupied by the strange boy. Purdy gave a little grumble, drawing Xander's attention. The Faerrier had not opened his eyes, but his ears twitched and remained pointed in a particular direction.

"Peace, little brothers, I wish only a moment of warmth next your fire." A short, stout, dwarf-like man took a tentative step from the brush that just before had hidden him from sight, his hands held forward with fingers splayed through fingerless gloves.

"Ahh!" Groggle fell over backwards from the rotted log he sat upon, his legs kicking wildly as he tried to right himself.

Xander jumped to his feet in surprise. He looked the little man up and down and realized that the only thing missing from the person before him was the long, double-sided parchment sign that the man usually wore like a blacksmith's apron. *Hear me, unbelievers! The beginning of the end is nigh! So say the Wee Folk!* echoed in Xander's head.

Raggabrash nodded agreeably to Xander. "I see by your disposition that we are of like minds. We have seen each other before, have we not?" Not bothering to wait for a reply, he answered his own question. "Yes, yes, I've known of you since you were very little brothers."

The wild look in the man's eyes that had always caused Xander and his friends to give him a wide birth was still there, though greatly subdued. What surprised Xander the most was that he had never heard the man ever do more than scream short-sentenced rants and mumble gibberish, and that was always from afar. Now Raggabrash stood here in the middle of nowhere, speaking nearly complete sentences and seemingly, and impossibly, sane.

"Oh, fried coney, one of my favorites." The disheveled man skittered forward, pulling back his sleeve and hooking his arm downward dramatically, all in an effort to keep the dirtied fabric of his habit from touching the food. Funnily enough, thought Xander, he did not bother to keep his just-as-dirty hair from falling across his face, or worry about his blackened fingernails while he proceeded to gnaw the meat.

"Hey, that's not yours, that's Pipkin's." Having righted himself, Groggle mustered up his best authoritative and not-scared voice.

Raggabrash eyed Groggle defiantly, half the meat of the small rabbit already devoured, but then decided better of it. "Of course, of course, a trade then, little brother." Rifling through the many loose strands of his colorful habit, he finally found a pocket and traipsed over to Groggle and motioned for him to hold out his hands. "There. Compensation of the wildwood's finest!" Groggle looked down into the palms of his cupped hands to find an array of nuts, berries and rotted acorns, blended with bits of lint, assorted bugs, and an earthworm or two. Raggabrash stared at the pile for moment, and then took back an acorn and one of the long and slimy worms and placed them back in his pocket. Nodding his head in satisfaction, he returned to his meal.

"Uhm, thank you." Groggle looked at Xander and did his best to inconspicuously drop the contents of his hands on the forest floor before wiping the remaining dirt on his trousers.

As Raggabrash devoured the remaining meat, and was in the process of loudly sucking on the bones and alternately each dirty finger, he said slowly and deliberately, like it was the greatest gift ever given, "You are welcome. And thank you, little brothers, I was extremely peckish." Tossing the last of the bones over his shoulder, he continued. "Much to do, and we must not tarry. My parishioners wish to meet you."

"Parishioners?" Xander gave a wary look about himself, half-expecting other madmen to all of a sudden materialize from the bushes and from behind tree trunks; but Purdy, while now awake, gave no sign of warning, and did nothing more than stare back at him.

"Yes, yes, the Wee Folk, from before and after the Winnowing. You are far from your destination, and time is tocking; or is it ticking? Never mind, the beginning to the end is nigh!" For a moment, the old ragman seemed to slip back into his mentally-addled self, staring wildly at them without seeing them. But quickly enough, he gave himself a physical shake, as if shedding something extremely unpleasant, and continued. "You'll be needing their help after all, and it will only be open for a short time longer."

Xander looked over at Groggle for some sort of understanding, but Groggle just gave him a shrug. Nearly aggravated beyond words, Xander said, "Absolutely none of that made any sense."

Raggabrash gave him a once-over as if confused for a moment as to who he was speaking to. Then, as if an internal decision had been reached, he gave Xander a look that suggested that he was the most obtuse being the ragman had ever met, which struck Xander as strange in that this man, of all people, was somehow questioning his intelligence, or possibly his sanity. Raggabrash gave him another once-over, and just shook his head with exasperation and motioned for them to follow him. "Come, little brothers."

Xander had already convinced himself that there was no possible way that they were going to follow this lunatic, and that parting ways with him sooner rather than later was the best course of action… when Aldebarron whinnied softly, and began following the old tramp. Staring in disbelief at the disappearing hindquarters of the warhorse, Xander looked at Groggle, but he just shrugged and said, "Well, at least it's in the right direction." Holding his finger up towards the moons through a break in the trees, he added, "I think, anyway."

Xander cast a quick look behind, hoping to catch a glimpse of the ever-disappearing Fool. Knowing the attempt was futile, he quickly kicked dirt on the fire and turned to follow.

Boredom Was Their Lot

Those who stood sentry upon the entrance to the land bridge idly stared forward at nothing in particular. Boredom was their lot; no one ever dared to seek passage to the antiquated throne of Kaer Kairos. True, there was the occasional group of street urchins who would attempt to taunt them with thrown stones, or the drunkard who stumbled too close, but that was the extent of their excitement. All others gave them a wide berth.

A younger soldier stood fidgeting, not quite used to the complacency such a post afforded. It was either this or serve in one of Kairos' other military branches, but being a member of one the city's noble families, his father had bought him the honorary position of Praetorian of the Bridge. He wasn't like others, too desperate or too lazy — though in fact he *was* lazy — to take the coin of the Stewards and become fodder for the bands that attacked the borders of the Desolation far to the east. Nor did he have the constitution to fight aboard ship, keeping the waterways safe for commerce. Waves literally made him sick; just the thought of the up-and-down motion made him gag a little as he stood there looking sideways at those he silently served with. He knew that his father couldn't care less what happened to him, but hadn't gone so far as to sentence him to certain death in the military. Besides, his father had promised his mother that he wouldn't be responsible for killing him… directly, that is.

So here he was, in a fine, tailored uniform with more tassels than he could count, holding a spear twice his body length, of which he barely knew one end from the other, collecting fifty crawns a month for shifts totaling four hours at a time, three times a week… being bored.

The man to his right — he thought his name was Bartholomew, but he really didn't care — was nearly in the same situation as he. Youngest born, older brother in line to inherit, and all his sisters either promised or married off to influential people. Bart wavered uneasily on the back of his heels, still drunk from whatever it was he drank. Bart was always drunk.

"What you looking at, Piggy?" The young man ignored the slurred hiss of his fellow Praetorian, returning his unfocused gaze forward, only flinching slightly with annoyance at the derogatory use of his surname. "That's what I thought." The drunken man nodded to himself satisfactorily, the action causing him to stumble forward on his toes. The other guards chuckled lightly, but otherwise continued with their silent watch.

The young guard knew there was no sense pressing the matter with this drunkard. Though they were just figureheads, some still took the position seriously. Their Captain of the Guard was one such man, and any unnecessary conversation or break in protocol meant being fined. Hardly mattered with his overly generous stipend from this post, and the allowance his father gave him for staying away from the family estate; but he was content in his life of leisure. No sense causing waves. Besides, their shift was about to end, and he wasn't due back until after King's Day and the second Saint's Parade.

"What the bloody hell is that?" Bart blinked blearily, leaning hard against his halberd, his cheek pressed against the iron shaft, his double-handed grip the only thing keeping him from sliding all the way to the ground. "Are those them damn monks from the Abbey? They're not due until tomorrow."

The young man turned to look at Bart, then followed the man's gaze forward. The initial presence of the shadowed figures took him by surprise; no one ever approached them, yet here were four long-cloaked individuals determinedly marching directly at them, dragging along what appeared to be a young woman. He had heard about the scheduled reenactment of the Saint's Path from Kaer Kairos, but that had to be rumors. Nobody ever went there.

"All right, you lot, hold it right there! I don't care what vision of divinity has inspired you, you're not due here till tomorrow!" Bart, though drunk as he was, straightened himself and somehow kept some of the slur from his voice.

The figures did not pause.

Puffing out his chest and holding his spear in a menacing way, Bart looked sideways at his compatriots and in a voice tainted with laughter, said, "You believe this batch of loonies? What, you all deaf as well as mute? I said… Hey, whoa, whoa there!" Bart's exclamation caught in his throat as one of the hooded figures dashed forward.

The speed, from someone the young man had also come to believe was one of the monks of the Abbey, astonished him, and must have the others as well. They all just stood there transfixed. It was only Bart who began to stumble backward, as he seemed to be the object of the offended monk's ire, since the monk was making a line directly to him. Bart's bravado was much less loud than his voice, after all.

"Piggy" watched as if he were a faraway spectator looking at an interesting painting or picture. He saw without really seeing as Bart's blood sprayed across his face from a wound that ran just above the collar of the boisterous drunk's uniform all the way across his neck. Though "Piggy" knew it must have been much quicker, the slice seemed to take an eternity. First the thin line barely bled, until the deeper right carotid artery of the neck was struck, and the blood fanned out from the pumping of the man's heart. The warmth of it felt odd to him in the chill of the night's air.

He knew he had stopped breathing, the little puffs of steam no longer rose from his lips like they normally did this time of year. There was just this strange gurgle of fear that emanated from the back of his throat. A second of the misjudged monks grabbed the Praetorian ceremonial pole-ax from Bart's falling body, and impaled another of his fellow guards through the chest, the multi-bladed head slicing through flesh and bone and catching on the black cape draped across the man's back. Funny, "Piggy" thought absently to himself, he hadn't even seen that monk move forward. Sprayed crimson arched and then puddled at his boots. The only sounds besides the low crash of the waves behind him were the bubbled rasps and sharp intake of breaths as one by one, those who stood guard with him fell to the ground.

Standing as immobile as a granite statue, he watched as the last of the hooded "monks" breezed by him. He met the blonde-haired girl's eyes for the briefest of moments as she was dragged toward the land bridge and Kaer Kairos. He saw the pleading desperation there, and thanked the heavens that he was a coward.

Absently, he looked at the carnage around him, finally taking in a breath. He choked on the sudden intake of cool air mixed with the blood-stink of his comrades. The shock of the previous few moments left him wondering, as he looked down at himself, how he was going to clean himself up before the Captain of the Guard saw him and fined him for a soiled uniform. A single drop of blood dripped down the bridge of his nose and splashed on the toe cap of his squared and polished boots. It was then that a deep bellowing roar pierced the otherwise silent twilight, and no matter how many times he'd told himself that it was just the rumbling of some far-off thunder, his eyes still began to swell with tears and his body began to shake convulsively from head to toe. Lurching forward, bent over himself, he violently retched across the top of his boots and the cuffs of his pant legs; and still, all he could think of was that he was going to be fined for a soiled uniform.

I Was Hoping Not To Get Stabbed

"For the love of it, will you please just run him through, already, or just get on with shooting the rest of us, so we don't have to listen to his endless prattle!" Blackmore rolled her eyes at the astonished look on Doc Fatterpacker's face, made even more comical by the swaying and intermittent lighting of the deck lamps aboard the Brigandborne ship.

The Doc looked his ridiculous and animated self with his hands trussed up above his head on the mainmast of the pirate ship. Restrained as he was, he somehow still seemed to gesture with his hands from side to side with each over-pronunciation. "Madam, I will have you know that you are not helping in the colloquy process. The good captain here must come to understand that our quest of honor is of extreme importance and urgency, and will certainly expedite our..."

"You moronic primped-up peacock, she's just pushing you for information!" *Pushing* was the wrong word for it, thought Blackmore. The pirate captain hadn't spoken a word, and this idiot hadn't stopped talking since he regained consciousness. But with this outburst and the signal of a single rap of a sword against wood from the redhaired woman behind him, the Quartermaster clouted her across the face with the handle end of his whip.

This was her third such strike administered by the giant with the unique markings upon his arms. Banes reacted immediately by futilely rearing up, but was struck in the same manner. He had tried to whisper something about this man to her earlier, but that had ended in both of them being struck similarly before she could hear what he was on about. Giving a heavy whistle through her teeth, Blackmore gritted against the pain in her wrists, as the force of the blow pulled her against the heavy iron cuffs that were anchored to a metal ring in the deck railing behind her. Before righting herself, she spat a mouthful of reddish saliva onto the deck beside herself, and gave the giant a bloody smile as she continued to attempt to squeeze her hands through the iron cuffs that imprisoned her.

"Why now, sir, I don't see how that was necessary; the good woman here is in firm standing with their Graces, the Prince and Princess. Furthermore..."

"Just cut his tongue out, because I swear *I* will when I'm free of this, and yours too, you ginger-haired witch!" Blackmore braced herself for another strike that didn't come. Up until this moment, the Brigandborne captain had kept her back to them, just listening to Fatterpacker ramble on. When Blackmore looked around the giant Quartermaster's thigh, she saw the pirate captain smiling at her.

"My, but aren't you are a feisty one, even for a Warder. Tell me, Lieutenant, why do you counterargue this man's every babble with such vehemence?" The pirate captain strode a few steps closer to Blackmore and stood next to the Doc with her sword drawn. The giant yielded his position to give his captain full stage. Her orange hair flowed and curled nearly to her waist; only the black cavalier hat kept it from drifting near her face in the evening breeze as she went on. "Now, I am not one to fall into the ramblings of fools and their fairytales."

"Madam, I must protest. I am neither a fool nor a liar!" Fatterpacker looked indignantly from one woman to the other.

"Hush, sweet man, the girls are talking just now." The Captain gave Fatterpacker a lite pat upon his cheek and pursed her lips. "You're so cute. I promise I will be right back with you," she purred while emphasizing her grip on her sword.

It was when she turned her crystal-blue gaze back to continue their conversation that Blackmore was struck by the thought that she had seen this woman before. Was it a Steward's wanted notice, or something else? She felt like she should be able to place her, but just couldn't. It drifted on the edge of her memory like a long-forgotten song.

"I must ask myself, why is it that a troop of Whiskeys have abandoned their post at the Manor Hall?" The captain looked to her Quartermaster, who nodded in confirmation. "And are out and about sailing the high seas with no less than a dwarf, a peg-leg, a pretty man, and a gaggle of children so far from said post?" The pirate captain pointed to each respective individual and group with the point of her sword, but blew a kiss at Fatterpacker, causing him to look flushed even in the half light. "Is there a ring of truth to these silly stories?" she asked. Holding a finger to her lips as if in contemplation, she eyed Blackmore with a steely gaze.

Blackmore knew she had taken her protesting too far. She'd known it as it happened, but had hoped that the distraction might confuse the issue of their identities, or at the very least keep that stupid peacock from spilling too much. And though they had been warned, she'd hoped to keep the focus on herself, and not on the kids trussed up opposite of her along the starboard railing.

The knocking of the listing schooner, which was still lashed to the pirate's galleon —caused as the two hulls rocked together — reverberated through the otherwise silent night. Blackmore knew without seeing it that the schooner was no more than a floating barge now; she might get her men and the others to the two lifeboats if they weren't already scuttled, but that would mean incapacitating the Captain and her giant henchman at the very least.

As she continued to wrench at her wrists, hoping for freedom, she eyed the giant Quartermaster with the strange markings, wondering who he was that should know of their post at the Manor Hall. Banes had done nothing but stare daggers at him their entire incarceration. If she could just get to one of the confiscated swords or pistols that laid just out of reach, which the pirate crew had placed there in an attempt to demoralize the Warders, she might at least kill one of them…

Ix twitched a little at her side, and she wondered even more why he'd been so quiet. At first, she thought he was still laid out; but it was obvious that his attention was fully centered on the pirate captain, and had been for some time now. Despite his head being ducked far into the cowl of his motheaten Warder cape, Blackmore sensed the movement of his gaze.

"As it is, I honestly don't care. We have business in and around Kairos, and since you are all obviously deserters, that means you were not looking for us." The Captain swished her sword back and forth and strolled about in self-thought. The black skirting of her part-pants, part-dress flitted about a pair of elegant legs, looking more like a tapered ballroom gown than the garb of a pirate. Giving a little twirl, like she was actually dancing, she returned her attention to Blackmore. "Which is, of course, a bad news/worse news situation for you. The pretty man I'll keep for a while, and the urchins... well, there must be some scrubbing needing to be done somewhere around here. But for you... now, normally I would just sell you back for the bounty, but I just don't have the time. Truly, I do like Whiskeys, and you wouldn't believe it, but in another life I was even quite intimate with one of your kind... you know, girl-to-girl, what I'm saying, right?"

As the Captain gave Blackmore a little wink, she couldn't help but believe that this woman was actually sorry for what she was about to do; but she was just an apologetic viper, after all. She danced about them to a song that only she could hear, but inevitably she was going to strike.

In frustration and uncontrolled anger, Blackmore yanked and pulled at her wrists. She felt the gush of blood as the skin of her right wrist ripped upon the iron of the cuffs — and that arm came free. Lunging for the pile of weapons, hindered by the hand that was still cuffed as the length of chain ran its course and the empty cuff caught in the deck ring, she came to an abrupt halt — yet the effort had been just enough. Grabbing for a random sword in the pile, she swung it back around just as the pirate captain bore down upon her. The redhaired woman was incredibly fast. Blackmore wasn't even sure if she hadn't completely jumped the entire expanse that had separated them.

The women crossed swords before Blackmore had a chance to regain her footing. Her body, still sprawled out across the decking, her left arm still cuffed to the chain, gave neither means of defense nor the ability to regain her balance. Blood dripped from her injured wrist onto her face, and the weakened state of it signaled to Blackmore that she was never going to win this fight, despite her near-psychotic rage.

"That was beautifully done; and I am saying, girl-to-girl, that you have my respect, but…" In a single fluid motion, the Dame of the *Lady's Grace* swept her blade point through one of the holes of the Lieutenant's basket hilt, and with a downward thrust, skewered Blackmore's shoulder to the decking below her. The blade punctured the flesh and muscle right between Blackmore's collarbone and shoulder blade with agonizing precision. With the retrieved sword pinned to the wound and lying across her body, Blackmore, despite herself, screamed in pain.

As one, the Whiskeys surged up as much as their restraints would allow, shouting, trying to stand and get to their leader, but the Quartermaster had already stepped forward with his whip, snapping it across faces and chests until they were silenced.

The pirate dame stood above Blackmore, victorious, her sword embedded in the Lieutenant, looking admiringly at the subdued Whiskeys. "Such loyalty; magnificent. Really, my dear, my deepest respect. If it was but any other day…" The dame gave her a sad little smile that for the briefest of moments melted the hardness of her eyes; it was almost graceful as she looked down on Blackmore. For an instant, Blackmore imagined this woman from the perspective of looking down, seeing her next to her boots, in the cracked and missing mosaic tiles of an ancient ballroom.

As something impossible dawned in Blackmore's eyes, the Dame, catching the recognition forming there, looked closer at her and then turned her gaze to the sword with the notched blade laying across the woman's chest. "The Bristol Cree, as I live and breathe." It was a reverent whisper, intended only for Blackmore. The Dame looked at her, surprised, and said. "Impossible, unless…"

Immediately, the Dame looked back to the Whiskeys, searching for what she must have missed. Unceremoniously, causing Blackmore a great deal of pain, the pirate woman yanked her sword from the other's shoulder. Reaching down, she grabbed the Bristol Cree, brandishing a sword in either hand, and marched to the kneeling men. Scanning their faces more closely, it was but a moment before she stopped abruptly at the cowled man.

"Dammit, Richard! You ever-living bastard!" She was enraged, spitting out the words like venom as she screamed at him. Flinging back Ix's cowl with the tip of her sword, she crossed both swords across his neck, forcing his chin upwards so their eyes could meet.

"Hello, Polly, you're looking well." Ix gave a weak smile, and did his best to look everywhere but at the Dame of the *Lady's Grace*. Briefly, he met the eyes of Blackmore as she rolled over on her side to observe the commotion, her expression incredulous.

"By the Blessed Tree, why didn't you *say* anything before I almost killed these people?"

"I was hoping not to get stabbed this evening. You know your temper, Polly." Ix chuckled meekly as he gave a nervous smile to the siren before him.

"Slim hope of that you, dumb bastard!" With the same fluidity she'd shown handling Blackmore, she pulled back and plunged the Bristol Cree directly into Ix's chest, piercing him until the cross guard and hilt had nowhere else to go.

Spitting up blood as it ran down his chin, mixing with that of the wound in his chest, Ix drawled, "Feel better now?"

She leaned over and whispered in his ear, "Not by a long shot, my love." Ix's eyes rolled back in his head, his last sight being that of her smiling and somewhat gratified face.

The Whiskey Tea Party

Ix awoke with the same disquieted sense that he always had, for longer than he wished to remember. Was this the last time he would? A large part of him silently hoped every time that it would be; or better, he thought, that he had not awoken at all. He could feel the bite of the iron cuffs on his wrists, but could not sense that there were any others shackled near him; and by the heat and brightness visible through his closed eyelids, he knew that the sun had risen.

He never dreamt or had profound visions during the resurrections that the Blessed Tree had granted him. It was always just that moment of death to this. He wondered what it would be like if he was ever allowed to die. That son-of-a-bitch Rellion used to like to preach about the hereafter, but even he had shut up about those promises over the centuries... probably from the fear that, because of their own actions, they were all headed for the wrong destination.

There was no pain in his chest; he knew that the wound had already stitched itself back together. But he could definitely feel the hard, weathered decking of the *Lady's Grace* against his cheek, and the dried blood of his healed wound itching his skin. *Well, at least she pulled the blade out this time*, he mused.

Ix could hear the billowing of the wind in the sails of a galleon at full sail, and the rush of the water as the ship crested the waves. Nearer, he heard the work of the deckhands mixed with their gruff talk; always the same, as with all men at sea. *When was their next ration of liquor?* But closer still was the idle chatter and laughter of what sounded like a tea party.

"Stop pretending, Richard. I know you're back."

Ix opened his eyes to find the red-haired captain and the raven-haired lieutenant staring at him with tea cups in their hands. Both women were seated at a small table spread with dried meats and cheeses, with a lavishly hand-embroidered tablecloth adorned with mermaids and large sea creatures. As a center piece sat his sword, the Bristol Cree, cleansed of gore.

"I have to say it, I really like your new friend. *My* new friend, anyway." The Dame of the *Lady's Grace* raised her teacup to the Whiskey Lieutenant, and they toasted one another. Blackmore, using her left arm — the other being bandaged and in a silken sling — gave Ix a smug and dirty look, and up-ended the petite ceramic cup. The giant Quartermaster, who stood close by, quickly and with all the decorum of a royal cup-bearer poured her a refill from a large glass decanter of whiskey.

"When Mister Taff told me that Rellion had paid a visit to the Manor Hall, I didn't dare think that he could convince you to crawl out of your hole." The Dame indicated the giant Quartermaster with a sweep of her teacup, and he refilled it as it passed, emptying the decanter. Returning her attention to Ix, she said, "I mean, why would you listen to *him* and no one else?" The Dame's carefree voice descended into a bitterly jealous tone. "But here you are, and from what this beautiful woman tells me, on a quest no less."

Pulling against his restraints, Ix lifted himself into a kneeling position and stared back at the regal woman, keeping his silence.

Half-whispering into her cup, "Dumb bastard," she looked back at Blackmore and gave her a conspiratorial wink. "Oh! You're going to love this next one. It's from a ship that sank on its way to Brigandborne Cove near the Eye of Vedava some several hundred years ago. I'm telling you, that was no easy one to find." Setting down her cup, the Dame clasped Blackmore's knee with both hands in an excited and delighted manner as Taff presented the ladies with a barnacle-encrusted purplish bottle that turned iridescent with the sunrise. Taking his scabbard from its sheath, he held the bottle aloft and expertly struck the cork from the top. "Well done, Mister Taff!" The Dame politely clapped while the Quartermaster poured.

Closing their eyes, both ladies inhaled deeply, and then each took a very unladylike swig. Opening their eyes together, they nodded solemnly to each other.

Before the women could take another swig or begin to banter as to the smoothness of their whiskey, Ix said. "It's not a quest, Pollyanna. I've met a boy; he is of the bloodline, and his twin sister has been taken by *them*. You must take us to Kaer Kairos before it's too late."

"I must? I *must?!* I must do nothing I do not wish to do, especially what you tell me to do!" Slamming her fist on the table violently for emphasis, the Dame's ladylike demeanor faded, causing Taff to place a restraining finger on the tabletop to steady it. "And don't give me that look. You know damn well that we're not married anymore!"

Blackmore, shocked by the statement, sputtered out some of her drink. "*What?!*"

"Oh, I'm so sorry, my dear; I've ruined tea, haven't I? Forgive me; but yes, I am Countess Pollyanna Crogan Manorlorn, Mistress of the Manor Hall, and this wretched piece of flesh *was* my husband once." Placing her free hand to her breast in a conciliatory manner, she emphasized the past tense.

Blackmore, trying to gather her astonished thoughts, replayed the vision of the decrepit and aged tiling of the ballroom floor of the place she had only ever thought of as a prison. Up until this point, she'd truly wanted to think that this woman only bore the *resemblance* to some long-deceased person, and was not the actual person.

"It is quite simple, really. Richard built our lovely home for us, and it was decorated and furnished by my family with the treasures of the deep. It was so lovely… until he turned our home into a prison. In more ways than one, I will have you know." Batting her eyelashes at Blackmore, she sipped at her whiskey.

Thinking about it now, Blackmore had to admit to herself that the place did have a certain opulence that couldn't be explained away as being a common prison. As if reading her thoughts, Polly Manorlorn spoke fondly and distantly of some aged memory. "You should have seen it back then. The Spring Balls were divine; they went on for days on end… and so many people! You would have loved it!" With a sweet smile, she focused again on Blackmore. "Well, maybe not, but they always ended in some duel or other, and you *would* have loved that part."

"Still married, Polly, and they're going to bring him back if we don't do something."

"Shut it, Richard! I'll not have you ruin our enjoyable time with talk of a formality of signatures, or of him! Besides, my lovely friend here told me all about it while you were *napping*. So tell me why you think this time will be any different?"

Blackmore, finding her voice, interceded before Ix's reply. Setting down her cup, she made sure she had their attention. "Obviously there is a *long* history here, one that I cannot ever begin to understand; fairy tales come to life, legends that manifest themselves." The Lieutenant hovered her hand above the Bristol Cree, nearly fearful to touch it, afraid that it might disappear. "I have met and spoken to this boy, and he *is* a boy; no one can make a mistake about that. But there's a glint of something there. His every action thus far has been selfless, his strength being in his singularity of purpose, to protect. Purpose is a desire that beats within the heart of every Whiskey, and is denied us. Abandoned, betrayed, and now hunted, we are relics of some long-forgotten hope and purpose. If for no other reason than to see my end, knowing that for the briefest of moments there was hope again, I wish to help this boy." Blackmore looked fixedly at the Dame, with a beseeching determination.

Pausing to let the moment linger, the Dame absently rapped a ring upon her finger against the one-of-a-kind china cup. Blackmore, seeing the motion, knew immediately its origin, having seen only one other ring like it in her life — and recently. The Dame, noticing her attention, smiled wryly and quietly set down her cup. "Damn Whiskeys; you're all the same." Looking Blackmore straight in the eye with the steely gaze of the warrior, not the lady that she was as well, she declared, "I can see why you like her, Richard."

The Dame sighed deeply. "All right, my love, and Lieutenant, I will take you to your doom." She shook her head with a sad kind of understanding and stood. "Mister Taff, there has been a change of plans. I leave it to you. Oh, and dear, it was such a lovely whiskey tea party; you can't image how long it's been since I've enjoyed myself this much, you know, girl-to-girl."

Watching the retreating Dame, Blackmore asked Ix in a conciliatory but condescending manner, "What happened between you two? What did you do?"

Ix looked for a minute as if he might ignore the question, but then quietly answered, "We didn't realize that 'until death do you part' was going to last so long, and she's just mad because I wouldn't sign the divorce papers. We're still married."

Pollyanna Manorlorn stopped the conversation she was having with Taff and shouted from no less than half the ship away, "No we are *not!* And he's just pissy because I killed him again!"

Blackmore looked at Ix disbelievingly, and he offered as an explanation, "She has very keen hearing."

KING FROBLY WOBBLY

Watching Groggle from behind, Xander wondered if he himself looked just as helpless and youthful. Groggle held onto the back of Aldebarron's tail as if his life depended on it, his attention twitching from side to side with mostly-imagined shadows and noises. He'd even gone as far as lowering his goggles to his face, a sure sign he wasn't feeling comfortable in any way. Xander, though he couldn't see anything either, and granted, he was feeling just a little more confident than his short-statured friend, still had the distinct impression that their trek through the woods was being intently observed.

The ragman, Raggabrash, marched purposefully, far ahead of them. In fact, Xander was not even sure that they still were following him; but the great warhorse seemed assured of it, and Purdy hadn't raised an alarm, so on they marched. A breeze barely blew between the ancient limbs and trunks that stood as protectors of this area, so vigilant their watchful stance that the richly earthen smells of decayed flora and fauna felt as though it was seeping into his clothing. Oddly, the wildwoods seemed both more open and denser here. The canopy of vegetation above completely obscured the few stars they had been able to see earlier, but the meandering way in which the ragman took them was much easier going; they had barely brushed a single bush or bramble with a pant leg or sleeve. Xander couldn't see a trail; as he turned around to look where they had come from, there wasn't a single distinguishing mark that they had even passed, but the old kook was obviously following something.

He was thinking that this had gone just about far enough, and as if reading Xander's mind, Raggabrash's voice carried back to him. Then it sounded as if it came from above and behind, as well as echoing off of the ceiling of leaves. "Come, little brothers, not far now. My parishioners await us at the moonlight chapel."

"Uhm, Mister Ragman, sir, who exactly are your parishioners?" Groggle's squeaky voice bounced about just as Raggabrash's had.

"I told you, the Wee Folk!" the ragman said, without hiding his irritation.

"Oh, okay, that explains it, then." If Groggle wasn't feeling uncomfortable before, this was definitely enough to push him over the edge as he turned to give Xander a scared look.

Xander did his best to give him a nod of reassurance that he himself did not feel, but it was enough; Groggle trudged on, though his grip on Aldebarron's tail became tighter, and he'd pushed his shoulder right up against the great horse's hindquarters. So close, the movement of the horse's stride occasionally threw Groggle off balance.

Slowly, the trees and bushes parted to reveal an otherworldly luminosity. The muted glow encroached into the trees as if a battle of light and dark were taking place. Then, suddenly, it was there: a small clearing large enough to fit even the wide girth of Aldebarron and many more, though it was barely a pinpoint in the vastness of the woods.

The glow was, in fact, otherworldly, filtering down into the open area from the full moon of the Younger Brother and his crescent Older Brother to the East. Dew-dropped vines hung down from the canopy of trees, creating semi-circular walls, the beams of moonlight piercing through them into the darkness; what had looked ominous at their approach looked ethereal from this side. Wildflowers dotted the clearing in patches of pinks, blues, and golds. Interspersed amongst them were small benches and chairs that just happened to be rocks and branches that looked like furniture. It was nothing less than magical, much like a small child's secret garden, where one's imagination could live unbound.

"Here, little brothers, the moonlight chapel!" Raggabrash proclaimed proudly, his arms held worshipfully to either side. "Must hurry, they will be here soon, must prepare my pulpit." The crazy ragman ran off to the other end of the clearing, mumbling to himself.

Xander and Groggle followed carefully, picking their way through the poppies, marigolds, and daisies, the small flowers blooming lushly despite the crispness in the air. The small chairs and benches looked like they would only fit a person of ten inches in height at the most. Xander and Groggle were startled from their reverie by the clanging of metal and what could only be the whooshing of a bellows. Sure enough, as they approached Raggabrash's "pulpit," they found him busy lighting a small furnace with a stovepipe of old cans that made up a very crude foundry. The open-fronted stick shack looked as if a stiff breeze would knock it down. If it hadn't been for the limbs of the surrounding trees, which had grown and interlaced themselves, holding it together and supporting it, it probably would have fallen long ago. Dispersed on the tops of crude-hewn worktables laid scavenged and salvaged bits of metal, springs, pins, cogs, and wheels. Pots of grease, hand-levered oil cans, paint, burnishing rags, and a collection of fine tools made up the calamity of the "pulpit." Only a large magnifying glass set in an articulated arm seemed to be properly clean and cared-for. As the ragman bustled by them, fidgeting with a crucible, Xander looked more closely at the old crazy man's hands and fingers poking through the fingerless gloves he wore. They were not dirty in the sense of dirt, but stained and burnt by the heat, grease, and assorted lubricants from the workshop. They were not large and fumbly, but long, steady, and tapered, perfect for the use of precision tools such as the ones he saw here.

Ceasing his incoherent mumbling, Raggabrash cocked his head to the side and said, "Listen, little brothers, the Wee Folk have arrived."

Xander strained his ears to listen for what the ragman was hearing, and just as he was again about to write it off as the man's inherent madness, he heard it. Easily mistaken for a breeze that rustled a few leaves, there was the soft patter of movement; and then, emerging into the moonlight of the Chapel, walked, marched, rolled, and danced the Wee Folk, Raggabrash's parishioners.

Toys, they were; antiquated to be sure, but toys — and the likes of which he had never seen before: bears, ballerinas, horses, monkeys, knights, soldiers, and an assortment of every other creature imaginable. When he was younger, Xander used to long for the toys he saw displayed in the window of the Imaginarium, the bright little shop with the funny man inside. Of course, those were things denied to a small boy and his sister with little to no means. That is, other than what was granted by a tall, top-hatted benefactor whose only real impulse, until very recently, seemed to be the fleecing of others.

Groggle's timidness had all but evaporated at the sight of the complex and geared workings marching towards them. Yet he could tell that Groggle's enthusiasm was somewhat mollified, by what he supposed was the rebuke of Count Bobo back at the Drunken Chymist. He was about to place a restraining hand on Groggle as he rushed forward to get a better look, but he sensed the excitement and joy that emanated from the clock-work beings at their presence.

The ballerinas twirled, the monkeys skittered from one side to the other, and the soldiers and knights marched as if in an honor parade; but really, these "Wee Folk" were nothing like the toys he had once coveted. These toys were ancient and far more sophisticated. Their eyes sparkled with the glow of life and wonder, their little metallic faces were poised with euphoric broad smiles, and their mannerisms were all but random. They were filled with the emotion and "life" that he had come to know from their kind, minus the anger of the Forgotten Ones.

"Welcome, Wee Folk!" Raggabrash excitedly clapped and gave a welcomingly bow to each of his parishioners as they moved into the Chapel and began to sit at the rustic pews of rock and broken branches. "Yes, yes, we should take care of that immediately, that gear socket needs replacing." The ragman deftly examined a ballerina as she was helped in by the others. One of her legs was cocked at a strange and unnatural angle. Motioning towards his pulpit, not ceasing his ongoing dialogue of clinical comments towards similarly injured Wee Folk, like some healer in a battle triage ward, he abruptly stopped his ramblings at the appear-ance of a metallic bear that could not have come to more than calf-high on Xander.

"Lord Frobly Wobbly Bear! Welcome; too long it has been since you have graced the Chapel!" Raggabrash seemed beside himself to be in the presence of the timeworn toy that strutted wobbly into the moonlight.

The other Wee Folk stepped aside to allow the bear's passage as he ambled in with roly-poly legs that rotated oddly within their sockets. Xander thought the motion comical at first glance, but even with the farcical movements of his arms in tandem to his legs, the Lord Frobly Wobbly commanded a certain regality. It may have been the pointed and jeweled crown upon his head, that Xander supposed was truly made of precious jewels and gold, despite lying cockeyed; or it may have been the tattered fabric cape of deep burgundy that draped across his broad, tarnished brass and copper shoulders, but it went much deeper than that, really. It was this little bear's bearing; he was a king.

"Raggabrash, as always, your ministrations to the Wee Folk are welcome, and I give you thanks. My travels have kept me afar for too long, but my time away has been necessary." The Bear King's voice cracked through his internal voice shell mechanism, and he seemed to wheeze with the effort as he gave the ragman a slight bow. But the voice was deep and commanding, the type of voice that was used to being listened to. "The time has come, the time is now, for walk the land the ones most foul…" Deliberately pausing while fixing his gaze upon Xander and Groggle, Lord Frobly continued. "Or better said, soon the *one* most foul."

Groggle went ghostly white for a moment, his fascination with the clockwork beings tempered by a verse Xander had heard Groggle himself recite, which seemed almost a lifetime ago now.

"My manners, of course, of course; I beg your grace, Lord Frobly. The little brothers that were spoken of have come, as said." Raggabrash indicated Xander and Groggle with the sweep of his arm, but stopped talking and gawked at him. Xander could feel the wheels of the man's mind racing in the uncomfortable silence as the ragman hesitated. "Well, I must say I don't rightly know who the little brothers are."

"It is all right, Raggabrash, be bothered not by it." Diverting his attention back to Xander, the bear said, "Your Highness, you are most welcome." Xander cringed at the honorific, but clumsily returned the deep bow that the mechanical bear afforded him.

"I'm sorry, but who are you exactly, what is this place, and why were you expecting us?" Xander looked from the tattered form of Raggabrash down to the Bear King expectantly. "And it's Xander, please, not Your Highness."

"Your indulgence… Xaannder." Lord Frobly crept over Xander's name, but even though he had dropped the honorific, Xander couldn't help but still hear what he felt was the undue respect present there. "Much to explain and very little time, as such things always are." The bear gave an audible sigh that again rattled somewhere within his chest. "Time must be taken, though.

"We, the Wee Folk as we are known now, are the remnants and the abandoned from the long ago Winnowing that occurred during the last Great War. We have watched throughout the centuries for the Forgotten Ones and the Deceiver's return, in hopes of fending off another catastrophe. We watch from the shadows and crevices, and have seen you and your friends at the center of what is to come."

"Excuse me, uhm, Lord Bear, sir, but what is the Winnowing?" Groggle, finally finding his voice and somehow avoiding the urge to grab at the toys surrounding him to see how they worked, spoke up, voicing one of the chief questions that had begun to form in Xander's mind as well.

"It does not surprise me that even one as clever as yourself does not know that part of Kairos's history."

Groggle puffed out his chest with pride at the compliment.

"Much was done by the Abbey, and its then-High Priest, to obliterate what occurred during that time. The Winnowing is a veiled description of the genocidal killing and culling to separate the desirable from the undesirable of my kind. Though some of my kind are not without fault, the atrocities committed by the Forgotten Ones, the Deceiver, and their followers drove the panic and acts of violence against us all."

The old bear paused contemplatively, and then said, "Unfortunately, I and these few other survivors found ourselves labeled as undesirable."

"But you're just toys!" Groggle blurted it out so quickly he surprised even himself, then looked sheepishly about as he realized that he might have offended them.

"True, we are but toys, as you say, in appearance." If the King Bear was offended, he did not show it, giving Groggle a cheerful smile. "But fear of the unknown condemned those of us who found ourselves alive and aware. Even the Wee Folk who had not yet awoken and become sentient found themselves condemned for the crime of being what they were: simple toys.

"There is a part of me that wishes not to blame your kind and the other races for their fear of us. Alarmed parents afraid for the safety of their children I can understand, for it was that same kind of unconditional love… that awoke… many of… us, unlike… the Forgotten… Ones." The Lord Frobly seemed to lose himself. His voice stuttered and trailed off quietly, and the glint of life that was in his eyes was replaced by cold metal orifices as he slowly bent forward.

Xander found himself concerned that the King Bear might fall over, or worse, not awaken again; and he'd just looked to Groggle to see if he had a clue as to what had happened, when Raggabrash spoke up. "Don't be troubled, little brothers, all will be well in a moment."

A pair of knights marched from their positions behind the King Bear up to his bent back, and immediately steadied him. Afterward, it appeared they were turning something at his back; and only then did Xander notice, and wondered why he hadn't before, the key that protruded through the bear's cape.

With a jolt, Lord Frobly's body shook with tremors, like a clock alarm wound too tight announcing the intended hour, and his rotund legs and arms swiveled back and forth in their sockets. As the spark returned to his eyes, very slowly he began to speak, gaining speed with each word, his voice drawling out like a phonograph record at the wrong speed. "Iiiii muussttt beggg yourr pardon; not very kingly of me to become so unwound so early in the day. Like all of my kind, I am tethered to the workings of how I was built. I am very old, older even than the Forgotten Ones and my companions here. Very few of us remain from the time of the Winnowing, and only these few have awakened since." The bear gave an encompassing motion with his arms. "The mechanisms within me are not perpetual coils and springs, steam, or even electrical in nature. I am but a simple clockwork bear beneath all this finery." The Bear King indicated his crown and worn cape. "Raggabrash, in his time with us, has purchased me more life than I should probably be allowed; but even his fine craftsmanship will not keep this old spring from becoming un-sprung forever." Lord Frobly pounded at his chest with a chubby brass fist for emphasis.

"I'm sorry, Lord Frobly, but you said before... Well, you mentioned acts of violence against your kind."

"Yes," the old bear said quietly to the ever-curious Groggle, his voice the only sound within the Chapel; even the monkeys had gone quiet and had stopped their skittering. It was as if the whole of the world had paused for him to speak. "The memories of the crucible meltings in the middle of King's Way still weigh heavily with each of us, as our brethren both big and small were smelted to slag. The pleading screams still haunt me sometimes, but it is the looks from all the Wee Folk, those of despair and betrayal towards their keepers, some of whom were just children... that more than any other memory haunts me the most." Xander felt that in that moment, if Lord Frobly could shed a tear, he would have. The soft whinny of the great warhorse brought him back from his reverie. "Only the beasts of burden and a few others were considered desirable enough to avoid the crucible, but the dread that inflicted them afterwards drove them into themselves, and most are no more than the pack animals they were originally made to be.

"Myself, I would have been melted down as so many others were, had it not been for the love of the little boy who was my keeper. When his parents too became fearful of our kind, they made him take me to King's Way. I, being unaware of the finality of what such a trip meant, did not flee." Lord Frobly Bear stared off into a vision that only he could see, and again whispered out the remainder of his tale. "It was the noise as we approached the Winnowing that first alerted me to danger. Feral it was, full of fear and anger. The boy was scared too, and held me tight to his chest, his father and mother pushing us forward through the gathered crowd. A myriad of faces, crooked with hate, pushed forward and back at us and pointed fingers towards the crucible."

Lord Frobly gave a little shiver at the memory. "More than once, the little boy tried to turn around; but his father kept a steady hand upon him, despite the tears that fell from the boy's face. I don't know how it happened or how the boy got away, but there was a surge in the crowd, and suddenly we found ourselves being jostled around, and then we were running. My little boy held me tight, but he did not know where to go. After being bumped around, we found ourselves in an alley, almost quiet besides the roar and crush of people beyond the building edges. Seeing a sewer grate, the little boy pushed me down into it. It was the very last I ever saw of my little boy — his sad and tearful face as he turned and ran away."

Xander felt bad and maybe a little sad for the King's tale, and for the other Wee Folk with their downcast heads; yet he couldn't understand why the bear had believed it so important for him to hear it just now. "I'm sorry for what happened and the fear you must still have." Xander thought back to his encounter with Count Bobo, and the warnings and trust the steam-powered mechanical musician had put onto him and his friends. "But I really just want to get to my sister." Xander looked anxiously at the moons above, wondering how much time had passed since he'd followed the crazy ragman here. He was still on the wrong side of that mountain range in the distance, and even more so, he was very far from where he should be — with Kristane.

Lord Frobly followed Xander's gaze upward knowingly, and he spoke to him sympathetically. "You do not see it now, but my tale will become of great importance to you, and to your sister and your friends. You are all, like all of us, intertwined in this tale to some to degree or another, whether you wish for it or not." The King Bear gave a sigh that again rasped and rattled through his ancient voice-shell. "I know that your time is short, and more so than you can imagine. Raggabrash will show you the Wee Folk's trail to the city." Xander began to protest, but the bear, anticipating his reluctance, continued. "It will take you there much quicker than you can manage on your own, despite the gallant steed you ride."

"Thank you, Lord Frobly." Xander did his best to accept the help of the ragman, and even attempted an awkward bow to the King Bear.

While it lacked what Xander imagined was proper decorum, probably an inch too high or maybe too low, he felt it was gracious enough.

Lord Frobly returned the bow even lower, and nearly fell forward on his rotund legs, but with a sweep of his ragged cape recovered his gracefulness. "One more thing before you leave. We have gifts for you and your friends." The bear motioned forward the same knights that had assisted him earlier; both carried what appeared like books, pamphlets, and a few loose papers.

Marching directly before the wide-eyed Groggle, they stopped just short of where he was standing, and presented their outstretched arms to him. Groggle, hesitantly but excitedly, took the documents and began leafing through them. Xander peered over his friend's shoulder to look at some of the titles. *The Tale of Two Brothers*, with the depiction of the same two moons shining above, only with cartoonish features and wide grins. *The Dragon, the Saint, and the Broken Sword*, with a fearsome black dragon spraying flame from its maw. A dwarven children's coloring book of the Clan of Dead Fairies. The last was a graphic battle portrayal that only a dwarf child would find interesting, of decapitated fairies, dwarves, and shadowy figures with blood-spraying wounds and missing limbs. Each black-and-white lined picture came with suggested coloring choices. Xander wondered to himself why green would be a suggested blood color choice, and for whom it was meant for. He had never met a fairy, much less seen one bleed, and for that matter he didn't remember seeing a dwarf's blood, either. As Groggle began muttering to himself and running his hand across the book covers reverently, Xander shook his head at the nonsense that seemed to be nothing more than children's books, and returned his attention to King Frobly.

The little bear was holding out a short but thick piece of wood, measuring no longer than from the tip of Xander's forefinger to the heel of his palm — easily small enough to hide in a pocket. Xander took the proffered stick, hefting it in his hand, and was surprised at how heavy it seemed for its size. "Uhm, thank you Lord Frobly," he said with reluctance, and thought about the absurdity of yet another useless object. Forgetting his manners, Xander did not bother to wipe the smirk from his face; but then, seeing the King studying him, tried to salvage his rudeness by inclining his head slightly to the bear.

Frobly was nonplussed, returning Xander's smirk with one of his own, and said. "You're welcome, Xander. But if you'll give the staff a firm shake once, then twice more, and finally thrice more, and hold it away from yourself..."

Xander actually found himself counting out the bear's request in his head, and was soon glad that he had followed Frobly's warning, holding the small stick at arms-length. Upon the first shake, the stick doubled in size, and caused Xander to pause with surprise. It felt no heavier than it had, but a scrolling pattern now enlightened the surface of the wood. He shook it twice more, and the stick was now the length of a cane. Three more times, and on the third and final shake of this sequence, the bottom of the stick — now a full-sized staff — struck the ground of the glade. The ground trembled with the strike, and a stiff breeze emanated from the center of the impact. The King Bear's cape ruffled back from him, and the leaves and limbs of the trees stirred all at once, lifting briefly and then falling back into a gentle sway. Xander felt a pulsing sensation in his hand. He wondered at the strange feeling; was it the rapid beating of his own heart causing it, or did the staff beat with its own pulse? All along the otherwise smooth wood and wrapped about the length of the quarterstaff was the scrolling he had noticed before. In an odd way, it seemed similar to some of the same that he had seen along the flanks and shoulders of Aldebarron.

"It is a very special piece of wood," the King Bear noted, "granted to very few. But me calling it a piece of wood does not do it honor; it is so much more than that, and so is its source. A tale too long for now, but one you will find on your own."

"It is too much." Xander moved to lay the staff back at the King Bear's feet, as reluctant as he was to do so.

"It is yours, sire. The one it was first granted would want it so."

"Who?"

"One who long ago left the confines of this world," the little mechanical bear said cryptically.

Xander wanted to question him further, but the look on the King's face told him that he had received all he was going to for now. "Thank you." Xander gave what he thought a proper bow, and this time he really meant it.

Lord Frobly waved away Xander's thanks with what seemed a bit of embarrassment. "I but return what was already yours." Composing himself again and hurrying on before Xander could ask about that statement, the Bear King gave Xander further instruction. "When you wish to put the staff away, gently strike the end thrice upon the ground or other surface, and backwards-shake it twice and then once; know that any force you give it will be manifested through it even greater."

Xander did his best to tap the staff delicately on the ground, but there was still a rumble at his feet, causing small pebbles to skip across the surface of the dirt and fallen leaves. He could feel it wasn't so much the action itself, but a combination of things: his grip, his stance, but mostly his intent. With two shakes, and then a final shake, the staff once again fit in the palm of his hand, and King Frobly nodded agreeably. "Lastly, a warning: until your strength in its use grows, know that some of the life you borrow of the wood will be taken in return. Such is the magic of these things." Though not knowing fully what the bear meant by this warning, Xander nodded his understanding regardless.

"That leaves the last of your friends." Xander was attempting to figure out what the bear might give to either Purdy or Aldebarron when King Frobly directed his attention to a high limb among the drooping trees along the edge of the glade. "Come, young friend, you are welcome here in the glade of the Wee Folk." Lord Frobly beckoned with a metal paw.

Pipkin looked shocked at being addressed, and went stiff as a statue — much like a child who thinks that if they don't move, then you can't possibly see them. Xander had the distinct impression that, more than just being scared, the grubby young boy was struggling with himself, trying to determine whether he was truly welcome or not. Then Pipkin tentatively grasped at a lower branch and hung by his arms, the consternation clear on his face as to whether he should drop the few feet more to the ground. When he finally landed, he remained crouched down, making himself as small as possible, like a cornered and timid rabbit.

Lord Frobly wobbled closer to Pipkin in that comically regal way only the bear could pull off. "Come closer, young one." The King Bear took Pipkin by the hand, leading him into the chapel. Pipkin stayed nearly as low as the bear was high, his legs and feet making short little scrambling steps under his body, nearly hopping at times. "Now, then." The bear let go of Pipkin's hand and turned to him. Pipkin gave a quick and odd little nod of his head, but his eyes remained downcast, only occasionally stealing a furtive glance through his matted hair. "Where is that gift? Ah, of course, thank you."

This time, a pair of mechanical ballerinas approached Lord Frobly and handed him a handheld vanity mirror. Xander could just see the intricate looping of swirling vine-like shapes and heart shaped motifs that ran down the wooden handle and up across the crown. The mirror was small, and one would have had to turn it from side to side to see their entire face, only managing a small portion of a chin, forehead, or cheek at a time.

Lord Frobly held out the mirror to Pipkin, beckoning him to take it. His curiosity getting the better of him, Pipkin looked up, and seeing his reflection in the mirror, he grinned. Carefully, Pipkin extended his hand, and the bear placed the mirror in his palm. The timid boy wrapped his fingers about the handle with both hands, and continued to gaze at his smiling reflection.

Giving a pleased nod, the King Bear turned his attention back to Xander. "There is little time, and so much more to speak of; but the way will close very soon." Glancing at the two moons trailing across the night sky, he pointed to them. "Once a month and sometimes two, for a very short time, as the Older Brother mocks the Younger with his crooked grin, the waning crescent will shine the way, and a path will appear to the Wee Folk's glade. There may come a time when you will be of need of this; but for now you must hurry, before the Older Brother runs and hides with his waxing crescent." Xander stared up at the two moons, and understood that Lord Frobly was speaking of the moon setting beyond the horizon. The Younger Brother still shone brightly and directly above.

Raggabrash, having finished his work with the injured Wee Folk, ambled up to them and bowed to the Bear King. "Safe travels to you, Raggabrash, and to you all," said the Bear King. "The Wee Folk wish you success in the quest for your sister, Xander, and we will continue to help where we can." Xander returned the bear's bow and muttered his thanks, while Groggle gave a much more enthusiastic goodbye, shaking the King's hand vigorously and nearly upending him.

"Hurry, Little Brother is tocking, no time, no time!" Raggabrash, his wild-eyed countenance back in place, becoming more and more impatient and agitated, pushed at Groggle.

Aldebarron had already begun walking, the great horse's girth spreading wide the weeping branches of the trees, with Purdy sitting upon his back irritably twitching his ears at the leaves that tickled at them. Xander wondered if the great horse was headed in the right direction, but the ragman had Groggle by the back of his collar and was aggressively urging him in the same direction, so Xander followed.

After a short distance and some awkward turns that Xander swore were taking them in the direction from which they had just come, he called to the ragman. "How do you know the way, Raggabrash?"

Raggabrash looked up at the canopy of trees, inspecting them from side to side. Then he looked down at his feet, cupping a hand to his ear as if thinking that those appendages had addressed him; and after only looking back over his shoulder and realizing that he wasn't alone and it wasn't the trees or his feet talking to him did he answer him in an annoyed voice, "The fairy stones shine the way." Kicking at some leaf litter, the ragman uncovered a shiny stone that caught upon its lustrous, smooth surface the moonbeams peeking through the canopy of leaves above. Pinpricks of crystalline pale green light radiated just above the skin of the stone. The lunatic said something inaudible to the stone, and after giving Xander a prickly glare, trudged on.

Xander looked searchingly past Raggabrash; and as if his thoughts had summoned it, a cool breeze swept past him, flipping the dead brown leaves upward and then down into a cascade of brittle rain. Shining every few paces were the stones, blinking on and then off again like lanterns as they were covered and then uncovered again by the blanket of the wildwoods.

"Thank you, that was helpful," Xander said softly.

Raggabrash replied to Xander's thanks by cupping his hand to his ear and staring down at his feet again.

ABSOLUTELY NOT AS PLANNED

The young girl stared straight ahead with a vacant look. There was no defiance or courage there, and fear had left her mind days before. Her head rested loosely against her up-stretched arms. She was a trapped animal that only wished for an end to its suffering. To reveal that she had blonde hair would take half a day's worth of soaking, so matted and tangled by dried blood and mud it was; it clung lifelessly to her cheeks and neck. The rope that bound her wrists had dug deeply into the skin, which was raw from prior struggling, before she had given up. Even if the Forgotten Ones hadn't bound her and secured her to what appeared to be a horse harness tie-ring, she doubted she could have moved anyway.

It was this penetrating despair that caused her not to notice or even acknowledge the quiet, hunched shadow that lurked along the small stone wall next to her. Rough but powerful hands clasped hers briefly, and then went to work upon her restraints. Kristane cast her gaze sidelong and upwards to her left; through the knotted strands of her hair, she saw a grizzled face with a big, blunt nose. She knew she should know this person, but her mind was fogged with abuse and exhaustion.

"Thank you." It was barely a whisper, and her lips cracked and bled with the small effort, her tongue thick in her mouth.

The dwarf grunted in reply just as her restraints came loose. Falling into him, she winced with pain as Beezy grabbed hold of her wrists in an attempt to keep her from flopping completely over. Kneeling down, he cradled her, doing his best to brush the thatch from her eyes and mouth, but it continued to stick to her face. Quietly, he reached for a waterskin at his side and brought it to her mouth, only allowing a small drizzle to pass over her lips.

"Must leave. Quietly." Kristane found it difficult to understand the guttural, accented words, and as much as the dwarf tried to be quiet, his voice still carried. "Must hurry this way." With a sense of urgency, Kristane found herself yanked up by the dwarf's unrelenting arms, which felt like two stout iron rods under hers. The suddenness of standing nearly upright made her swoon for a moment, but the dwarf gave her no time to recover, instead gripping her about the waist, holding most if not all of her weight erect.

Kristane found herself looking at the world through blurry eyes; the light that fuzzed at the corners of her vision didn't look or feel right. It was like the sun had dropped from its perch in the sky, and if she just extended her hand up a little higher, she might burn herself. She thought she should be cold — wasn't it winter? — but why was she so warm? With the pain of lacerated and bruising skin and the side-long movement of her feet, as Beezy did his best to support her from his shortened stature, her head began to clear. A corona of light filled a deeply-bowled dale all around her, but she still could not understand why. As she looked further outward, to the limit of her vision, a curtain of darkness covered the upward-sloping hills and a series of stone walls. It just shouldn't be this bright or warm for what she assumed must be a winter night.

Slowly, with Beezy's urging, she shuffled one foot forward, occasionally dragging a toe as it caught in the crevices between the flagstone paving. Her head still drooped forward like a ragdoll's, the effort to support it upright going to the endeavor to move forward. Sweat beaded along her brow. She couldn't tell if it was from the physical effort or the intensifying heat.

A crackling noise to her right, as from a large bonfire, drew her attention. Corded lengths of wood that intertwined and wrapped about each other, in some instances growing into a single branch, spiraled upward and downward. Piercing and biting into the ground, massive roots dislodged flagstones of the courtyard around it. Disrupted stones from the surrounding retaining walls piled up against massively rotund roots, appearing no more than pebbles against the fleshy bark. Despite Kristane's damaged frame of mind and physical state, she couldn't but be awed by the sheer size of the braided trunk. She had to turn her head to see where one side of the trunk rounded out of sight from the other. Kristane couldn't fathom the number of years, much less the number of centuries, it had taken for a tree to grow this large; but while this was impressive, the fact that every inch of it looked like it was on fire shocked her even more.

With her concentration pulled from the task at hand — that of just struggling to stay erect — her toe caught on more than just a stone. A trailing root that hadn't found the earth below felt as though it had reached up and grabbed her ankle. Despite Beezy's best efforts to steady them, they both ended up in a snarl of limbs on the ground, with Kristane lying mostly on top of him.

As soundlessly as possible, and with as much careful deliberation — to cause Kristane no further injury — the dwarf moved her off of him. She found herself lying flat on her stomach, staring at a burning root as big around as her thigh just a few inches away. Placing her sprawled hand a little closer, Kristane could feel the heat radiating from it; but as she inspected it further, she saw that there was no charring of the wood, and no telltale wisps of smoke that would suggest it was being consumed. "The tree is on fire, but it doesn't burn," she said out loud in a weakly wondering voice.

Beezy gave her no further time to contemplate the revelation, other than a strained grunt and a quiet word she couldn't quite understand. "Poisoned," she thought he said. Brusquely, he heaved her over his head, placing her across his shoulders like a lumpy and unbalanced bag of potatoes. With a swaying trot, due to her legs dragging to one side of him along the ground and catching here and there on the exposed roots of the tree, Beezy resumed their escape.

Kristane did not need to turn around to know who approached them from behind. The distinct metal clanking against the flagstones was more than enough to renew her despair and hopelessness. To the dwarf's credit, he redoubled his efforts at the sound, leaping over roots that easily stood as high as his waist. She felt the air pushed from her lungs each time he landed. She would have screamed, as old bruises along her body were inflamed each time she bounced against the dwarf's shoulders, but it had become a struggle just to breathe.

With a quick and flashing motion that neither she nor Beezy saw, the dwarf dropped to the ground, and she with him. Immediately her head was jerked back, metallic fingers clasping at her scalp and hair. Where the hair wasn't bunched, single strands were pulled free from skin between the articulating joints of the Forgotten One's fingers. The oddly satisfied face of the automaton held her fast, meeting her eye-to-eye as she lifted Kristane up and around to stare back to where she had first heard the others approach.

"That went absolutely nothing like how it was planned. You must forgive me, my Princess." Rellion gave Kristane a sardonic and apologetic smile as he was forcefully pushed to his knees, a pair of the Forgotten Ones on either side of him restraining his arms. "My dear ladies, if you would please just loosen your grip a smidge, I would be most thank —"

Before he could finish his quip on the proper etiquette for prisoner treatment, one of the metal women tightened her grip about his wrist and yanked backward. The crunching of bone against bone overwhelmed the crackling of fire that otherwise filled the night air. Unceremoniously, the beautiful but horrid metallic woman let go of Rellion's arm, and it fell loosely to the side of his body. Taking a moment to recover, Rellion straightened himself, and in his most haughty voice, declared, "Now, my dear ladies, I'm not sure that was —"

That was the last Kristane heard of Rellion's unfinished exposition; it was interrupted by the grinding of his other arm as it too was wrenched backwards at an unlikely angle. His head sank forward, Rellion unconscious from the pain and shock, the rest of his body still held up by his disjointed arm by the Forgotten One.

Kristane thought she had no more tears to cry, but a single one escaped. It barely made it to her cheek before it was dried by the warmth of the tree that did not burn.

PARADE OF SYCOPHANTS

O n the early morning of King's Day, a procession of monks, laborers, Stewards, and recommissioned Briggers accompanied the High Priest across the land bridge. Despite the openings that looked straight down into the sea, his small army slowly maneuvered about the large, crumbled ruins of the walkway that led to Kaer Kairos. Occasionally, a broad-chested man wearing the newly stitched emblem of the High Priest on his Brigger uniform waved forward a group of workers bearing long, thick planks to span the open spaces.

The sea, unfettered by the protection of the bays and colliding with the support piers, shot up through the holes and planks like an uncontained fountain. The booming crash of waves, accompanied with the cascading drops of saltwater, drenched the workers. Cristobal Zekel walked and paused as necessary as his way was made safe. Such was his arrogance, he posed as if it were no less than a long, velvet carpet that was being laid before him in a great hall on his way to some throne — which, in Cristobal's mind, was exactly what was happening.

"Hold the umbrella aloft straighter! My robes are being spotted!" he admonished the monk whose attention had been drawn away by the precarious slip of one of his brothers, who, along with several others, carried the Saint's wooden casket. The tipped parasol had allowed a drizzle of the falling water to splash upon his High Priest's shoes and the hem of his robes.

"Yes, Your Grace," the chastised monk said feebly, steadying the shaft and handle with both hands.

Cristobal was nearly giddy with the thought of his goal almost within reach. He felt the palatable trepidation of those with him, and rightly so; blind obedience and religious fervor only went so far when faced with their own mortality, but they would see. According to the Gospel of the Dragon and the Saint, they would be safe. The High Priest had a moment of disquiet at the thought of the rumored beast, but then fortified his resolve with the fact that three of his angels accompanied him, and they had already placed the blood-bearer there. Posing as some of his monks in their long, hooded robes, only the slightest glint of golden metal at their feet gave away their true identities. *But how often does someone look at another's feet?* Cristobal asked himself.

"Can we not proceed at a quicker pace?" Calling out to the sergeant of the newly formed Holy Shepherds, handpicked from his congregation and many recruited from the Briggers for their near-zealous faith, the High Priest found himself annoyed again, and waved for his chair to be brought forward. A throne with a high cushioned seat tipped precariously back and forth as his monks attempted to manage the weight of it. Setting it just to the back of the High Priest, they waited as he delicately sat into it and extended his hand to the side, where another monk presented a bowl of grapes.

Cristobal plucked absently at the bowl with his brows knitted in irritation. The Stewards he had allowed to make this journey with him, including the blubbery Piggleback, stood somewhere behind him, whispering to themselves. The sound was like a gnat that hissed in his ear and aggravated him even more; but the Stewards were still necessary, if only in the short term. They had already been delayed earlier, as he had refused to parade through the carnage of the night before. Nothing was allowed to mar his ascension today. Cleaning up the spilt blood and bodies of the bridge guards seemed to take hours. Piggleback had not even seemed concerned that his youngest son, the sole survivor, was still in a mumbling and drooling stupor. In fact, he seemed disappointed to see the boy's head still attached to his body. Admittedly, the stray pair of heads that littered the bridge egress, their tongues lolling out and bloated, gave Cristobal a slight twinge at the memory; but to think that he cared one moment for the boy, the guards, or any of them would be a true leap of faith.

A large, brawny man hurriedly walked back to the High Priest and gave a low bow. Talking more to his feet than to the priest himself, he said. "Forgive me, Your Grace. The laborers are fearful, and the way perilous."

"Then by all means bring the lash to bear, Sergeant, and hasten my journey."

"Yes, Your Grace." The large man backed away with a succession of bows. Cristobal pushed off his annoyance and allowed himself a smile, which on any other person would look sickly. He reflected fondly at the loud shouting of commands by his new Holy Shephard and the crack of the cat-o'-nine. His Grace was enjoying himself very, very much. Finally.

"Your Grace?" The Holy Shepherd with the whip from earlier bowed and looked up from lowered eyes to get the High Priest's attention. So deeply intent was his gaze on the distance and the laborers there that Cristobal had missed what the man had said, much less seeing him approach. It had taken most of the morning so far to traverse just a portion of the land bridge.

"Yes, what is it?!" Cristobal asked testily, dabbing a kerchief at his nose.

"Your pardon, Your Grace. We have reached Kaer Kairos."

Snapping his fingers as he rose, signaling the attendant with the umbrella to scamper forward, Cristobal's eyes blazed with anticipation. "And none too soon." Parading forward, he smoothed out the fabric upon his chest, straightening his stole and chasuble, his hand trembling with excitement. As an afterthought, and as he passed, he placed his hand upon the man's shoulder. "You may rise, my son; you have done well. Make clear the way; I wish to be the first to set foot in Kaer Kairos."

Cristobal teetered on the edge of the land bridge. The broken stone of the path that led to the gates of the ancient royal throne lay just inches away from the tips of his toes. He was drunk with a fervent giddiness he had rarely felt in his lifetime. Already, he was fascinated by the twin high-spired towers that supported the Bridge of Paragons. Its arched expanse stretched high above what use to be the invulnerable gates; but now only rusted and bent metal bands, as wide as a pair of carriages end to end, hung from broken and bowed hinges, or laid forgotten across the threshold of the gate. Any timber that was once strapped into place by them had disintegrated with time. The portcullis hung to one side, bent as if a giant hand had grabbed it from the top and swung it wide like a door. Both towers showed signs of rubble and open crags in their walls, where the decimation of war had taken place.

Silence. The silence beyond the crashing waves sobered Cristobal. Even with fifty or so dumbstruck men in accompaniment, all hanging upon his every word, the land before him was far too quiet for his liking. Cristobal turned, doing his best not to let his nervousness show, motioning for the bearers to bring forward the Saint's coffin. They marched forward fearfully, their hands white-knuckled along the rod that was pushed through O-ring brackets along the exterior of the box.

After only the briefest of moments, spent fortifying himself once again with the thought that his path was divine, he strode impudently forward. The throng behind him trudged along reluctantly, most of them wide-eyed, their heads on a nervous swivel. They jumped at every scrape of a boot or misplaced step of their companions.

An attending monk walked beside him, holding a decaying parchment with a map drawn on it. Cristobal would occasionally slap at the man's fingers with a switch to encourage the monk to keep the map at the proper height for his viewing. Approaching a curved and high garden wall, Cristobal knew that they were only a few hundred paces away from their destination. Irritably, he struck at the monk one last time. "Enough; get out of the way! I wish to see it unhindered by your frightened countenance!"

Cristobal closed his eyes and raised his arms to either side. He wished to take this moment and greet his greater destiny, savoring it. Slowly, he paced around the curving wall, knowing that this path led to the ancient royal gardens where the Tree of Baennaith, the Blessed Tree, lay. Gradually, he raised his eyelids; but instead of seeing the ivory leaves and bark described in the scrolls, his gaze fell upon the flaming behemoth below. Shocked by what he saw, the High Priest steadied himself with a hand against the retaining wall. Flames licked at every individual leaf, each the size of a man's head, and coursed along its massive trunk and limbs, just a hair's breadth above each surface.

"What does it mean? What has happened here?" Cristobal whispered.

Curiosity had overcome his followers; and with the pallbearers taking the lead, the High Priest's minions began to wind around the stepped tiers and stone stairs of what must have once been vibrant flowering beds. Each gave Cristobal a respectful and shaky bow as they passed. The wonder of the spectacle before them replaced some of their fear; their eyes still darted from side to side with a twitch of nervousness, as if they were all as men walking to a known doom, yet they kept going with an eagerness not one of them could explain.

Cristobal followed the last of them absently, his mind now enraptured by the tree that spanned hundreds of paces high, and most probably more. The twisted and braided base of overlapping limbs could have easily dwarfed the Celestial Orrery at the center of the city, the enveloping canopy of leaves reaching seven times more than its width. Many of the leaf-bearing branches dipped low, not unlike a weeping willow, to the point that Cristobal felt he might be able to reach out and touch them; but he stayed his hand. Where fire met branch and leaf, there was a sparkling of pure ivory white as it was consumed and then again appeared, as though it immediately regenerated, only to be consumed again. The entire tree pulsed with it.

Cristobal repeated again and again, in a hushed murmur: "What could it mean? The old scrolls said nothing of this. It does not burn."

So engrossed was he with his own thoughts that the High Priest stumbled into those who brought up the back end of his entourage. Some stood on their tip-toes, trying to see over those in front of them to find the reason why they had stopped so abruptly. He was suddenly furious that these simple people now blocked his way. "What is the meaning of this? Make way!"

Murmured whispers of, "It's the High Priest," proceeded him as he began to push his way through startled faces. Instantly, a corridor of living bodies was formed as those who backed away or sidestepped trod on the feet of others next to and behind them, any protests of harm muffled by their fear of inciting His Grace.

"Make way! Make way!" Cristobal ceased his shouting abruptly and composed himself, brushing at the front of his robes and slowing his stride to one he knew to be more dignified for his station. Soon he was raising and lowering his hand in blessings, and his followers responded in kind by bowing low.

As the High Priest reached what had caused the sudden blockage, he nearly lost his composure. A rush of emotions and fearful thoughts made him catch his breath and stare. He could feel the eyes of those around and behind him looking to him for explanation. Here stood four of his angels, uncloaked, standing above that bastard Rellion, who was hogtied and gagged. The High Priest quaked with hate at the sight of him. A dwarf and a young girl lay nearby, both trussed up similarly; at least, as best he could tell it was a young girl, for her long and filthy hair fell before a slight and drooped posture, masking her face. *This one must be the blood-bearer*, thought Cristobal.

Many of his Holy Shepherds had drawn their swords and fidgeted nervously, their hands gripping and re-gripping the hilts. Cristobal could see the questioning in their eyes — a mix of fear, trepidation, and mistrust. Whether it was directed at him or the angels he could not tell for certain, but neither would do.

Thinking quickly and taking a moment to dab at his nose, Cristobal proclaimed, "Behold, our enemies are delivered unto us!" For emphasis, he raised his hands high and circled slowly around, meeting the upraised eyes of soldiers, laborers, monks, and Stewards. If there was a thing Cristobal knew well as a priest, it was the staging of a moment. "It is a sign of the divinity of our mission!" For the briefest space of time, Cristobal had almost said "my mission" as opposed to "our mission," but had avoided this near-gaffe just in time. "Lay low your swords and armaments; see how the angels of the One serve our cause! A miracle is brought to you this King's Day!" As if this were their cue, and Cristobal certainly meant it as such, the Abbey monks dropped to their knees with arms swung high, and gave their credo of thanks in low, murmuring tones.

Discomfort still marked many faces, but warily, the points of blades and firearm muzzles dipped toward the ground. The Stewards did not seem as easily swayed; a pair stood wringing their hands as if they were trying to rub off skin, and Piggleback had reverted to his new nervous habit of sucking on his knuckles. He had nearly his whole fist stuffed in his mouth, and was working on the second when Cristobal addressed them. "Doubters of this miracle would best be served by praying for deliverance!"

This had the desired effect, and Cristobal smiled broadly as most of the Stewards collected themselves, dropping their arms to their sides and giving him effective bows. It took an extra look from him for Piggleback to stop his incessant sucking, though. Finding the High Priest's attention focused upon him solely, Piggleback's eyes darted from side to side and then rested on his own fist. His eyes widened, as if in surprise at finding it in his mouth. Slowly he removed the chubby digits from his gaping maw, trailing drool down his many chins and giving an audible gulp as his only apology.

Finally satisfied, Cristobal began. "Let us give..."

Whatever it was the High Priest was about to say was drowned out by the shrieks of the terrified workers, followed by a roaring bellow that pierced through and echoed about the bowled dale. The resonating rumble dislodged loose stones from the courtyard retaining walls and made even the great tree shudder, yet not a single leaf fell.

LIKE A TOILET! WHOOSH!

Groggle was busy bouncing stones off of the circular tapering walls of the tunnel that they now found themselves in. His earlier apprehension had turned to nervous boredom. As the pebbles and small rocks skipped end over end, they rang against the metal sides of the pipe, sounding much like the tinkling of small bells or fine crystal goblets being clinked together in a toast. The sound would echo about the excavated expanse for a few brief moments, and then fall silent into the trickle of water at the tunnel's base. Xander had thought about telling his friend to stop once or twice, but if Groggle was garnering some sense of solace from the action, well then, Xander felt that his small irritation at the nearly ceaseless ringing — mixed with the clapping of the great warhorse's hooves — was probably worth it.

Raggabrash's reaction was quite the opposite, though.

With a particularly large handful of thrown stones, the lunatic's demeanor broke. "Little Brother! It is not respectful to traverse the Wee Folk road so! Besides, we may no longer be the only ones who walk this path. And no, we are *not* almost there!"

"What?" Groggle feigned an innocent demeanor, pretending he didn't understand what the ragman was talking about. Which, of course, caused yet another bout of bickering, much like all of the other ones thus far between the two. The most animated one had been the disagreement as to whether the storm pipe they now traversed was the magical Wee Folk road, or just the ancient underlying substructure of a large and highly elevated city's watershed. Xander thought that Raggabrash was going to lose his mind, or at least more of it, if he couldn't convince Groggle of the otherworldly properties of the tube.

At first, Groggle had been fascinated, explaining in his usual way — about things that he had only ever read about — all of the intricacies of the age-old sewer system of Kairos. But after the first few hours of seeing only metal pipe walls three times the height and width of Aldebarron, and always the same dark hole on the horizon, the discussion had lost its appeal.

The long, gloomy haul through the pipe had been uneventful so far. Not even the typical rodent infestation that one might imagine of such a dank, dark place seemed to be present. Groggle had an explanation for this as well, which admittedly had Xander a little on edge. He speculated that in particularly wet seasons, the deluge from the mountainous ranges of Kairos would easily fill the entire expanse of the tunnel… the result being the drowning and flushing of everything out onto the edge of the peninsula, where they had entered. The ragman had confirmed it only with a cryptic *Yes, yes, the way will close soon.*

Xander shook at one of the old mining lanterns, irritating the fungus spores within, trying to squeeze just a little more light from it. Groggle had produced a pair of them from one of his many pockets, obviously having spirited away the "parting gifts" that Remington Symmes' giant bodyguard had given them back in the Bizzarred mines, just after all this had begun. Xander wondered idly, like he had many times before, what else his young friend could possibly have tucked away in there. He imagined that more than half of the boy's girth was actually made up of things stuffed in his pockets.

Bringing up the rear, and still fiddling with the lantern in his hand, it took him a few moments to realize that he could no longer hear the ringing clop of Aldebarron's hooves. Just ahead of him, the rest of his party had stopped and were all looking upward, studying what looked like a wide, heavy round door in the ceiling of the tube. A ladder hung just above the reach of Xander's extended arms from the inset ledge that encircled the aperture.

"Ow, water hot! It burns Pipkin!" Pipkin scurried back from the slow drip of water that fell from the not-quite-solid seals of the door above, sucking at his fingers.

Pipkin had said very little since leaving the glade of the Wee Folk. He remained captivated with his own reflection, humming and whispering to himself about what the polished surface of the mirror gifted to him revealed. This was the first time Xander had heard him speak since then.

"Wow, jeez, he's right, it *is* hot!" Groggle sucked at his own fingers after his exclamation; but then his eyes got that excited look about them, like they always did when he was thinking about how something worked. "You know what this is? It's got to be the outlet for the city's steam boilers. For, like, the elevated cable cars' drive cable, and, well, a bunch of other stuff! Bet they have to empty it every now and then; probably a lever up above they pull to release it. We must be really close to Kairos now."

Xander hadn't bothered with anything else that Groggle had said, but a nod from an irritated Raggabrash confirmed Groggle's guess. Xander's spirits lifted slightly, and he was about to wrangle Groggle and get going when he heard the steady clomp of metal upon metal echoing about the tube and getting louder. At first, he thought it was Aldebarron, but the stallion stood motionless, his attention drawn back to where they had come from; and Pipkin had scooted back behind Groggle and was mumbling to himself in a frightened tone. The warhorse stepped forward to Xander's side, shaking his leather mane and snorting a challenge at the two figures that halted at the edge of the dismal light cast by the mine lanterns. The Forgotten Ones stared at Aldebarron, apparently apprehensive about coming any closer.

Xander recognized the pair of beautiful dancers from their initial encounter in the Tunnels. He knew he would never forget these two in particular — the painful memory of his first sight of the faces of the Forgotten Ones still haunted him. So they had followed Pipkin and him down the spillway, and had probably been hunting for them ever since, despite the merry chase that Xander supposed Pipkin had sent them on.

The Fool's words from the Ward echoed back to Xander: *Pipkin forgetting the Forgotten Ones, and Pipkin goes finds more friends to help!*

"Here, bug-eyed one must take Pipkin's mirror. Pipkin trusts his pockets." Xander took his eyes off of the seething faces of the metal women behind them to see Pipkin trying to get Groggle to take his mirror.

Xander pointed out, "Pipkin, you won't be able to hold them off us; it's probably still too far to the end of the tube. Maybe Aldebarron can outrun them." He looked around desperately for some escape, but his eyes only met the smooth, curved surface of metal and the black maw forward. Xander thought that maybe Aldebarron could buy them some more time. The Forgotten Ones seemed to be fearful of the horse; but he knew that it was only a matter of time before one would get by the horse and run the rest of them down.

"Please, Groggle, take Pipkin's mirror. Pipkin trusts him."

Groggle nervously looked to Xander for what to do, and Xander nodded to him to go ahead and take it. Groggle carefully took the mirror from Pipkin and stuck it in one of his inner pockets. The Fool looked relieved and thankful… and then abruptly stood erect. In a fluid movement, he raced to the side of the tube and then launched himself to the ladder above them. Hanging from a rung by a single arm, he turned; his eyes no longer fearful but full of mischief, he said to Xander, "*Your Highness must ride fast.*" Smiling broadly and looking up at the boiler tank hatch above him, he added, "*You know, like a toilet. Woosh!*"

It took Xander a moment to understand Pipkin's intent, and then he was grabbing for both Aldebarron's reins and Groggle. As he pushed Groggle up into the saddle and motioned for the ragman to come, Xander turned back to Pipkin. "Thank you, Pipkin. Raggabrash, jump on!"

Pipkin smiled and pulled himself hand-over-hand up the ladder. Xander had just taken his place upon Aldebarron when Pipkin yanked free the lever holding the circular door in place. The Forgotten Ones, finally understanding the Fool's intent as well, raced forward; but the deluge of water swept to the sides, and then raced down the slight decline that led back to the far peninsula of Kairos. The metal women held in place for a few seconds, but very quickly even their weight was not enough and they slipped, receding backwards along the smooth surface of the storm sewer. Xander saw Pipkin hold on for just a moment longer than the dancers, but then he too disappeared from sight.

Aldebarron shot forward, the wave of heated water cascading around him, quickly filling not just the space behind, but the space forward as well. Raggabrash, who hung onto the very back of the saddle, screamed in pain at the scalding he received, and Xander flinched as little droplets dotted the skin on the back of his neck and arms. The stallion's surefooted and heavy footfalls soon outdistanced the wall of water, though; and the water, finding the easier path backward, receded about the stallion's hooves.

Aldebarron slowed his gait as they exited into the midday sunlight shining over Mererid Bay. The intake of the massive drainage tube was nestled discreetly in the hills just above the wharf. Xander started to urge Aldebarron forward, but a groan from the back of the saddle caused him to pause and turn around. Raggabrash was slumped against the back of Groggle, pushing him forward; he was conscious, but was in obvious pain, having taken the brunt of the scalding during their escape.

He met Xander's eyes and said, "I am all right, little brothers; you must continue. The Wee Folk will look after me."

Xander wanted to help the ragman further, but thoughts of Kristane's peril ached at him. He simply nodded and extended his arm to help Raggabrash down from the saddle. The ragman slumped slightly, but kept his feet under himself. Giving Xander an encouraging smile, he waved them on.

All along King's Way there was a mass of gathering people, dressed in their finest. A variety of laborers were in the process of cording off the thoroughfare with elaborate stanchions and brightly colored ribbons. The stallion and its riders mostly went unnoticed, Aldebarron being mistaken for just another beast of burden, its riders too ragtag for the denizens of Kairos — preoccupied with whatever was happening — to give a second glance. Xander wondered at this, and was about to ask Groggle if he knew what was going on when a Brigger called out for them to halt.

By this point, the street had been cleared, and the Brigger who was directing the crowd to the sides and had called out to them began to approach. Xander could see that the way ahead was all but clear; the

Praetorians of the Bridge would be the last to stand in their way, and he could see them from here. Xander whispered to Groggle to hold tight; and as he kicked at Aldebarron's flanks, there was a long, resounding bellow from Kaer Kairos that carried clear across the bays. The Brigger who had tried to detain them turned to fearfully stare back at the old ruins, and panicked screams and murmurs replaced what had just been a festive atmosphere. Aldebarron did not lessen his stride; instead, he surged forward, passing the Brigger and running past the inattentive guards at the land bridge, whose thoughts were occupied with an instinctual desire to flee, unlike the fools riding towards the danger.

I TOLERATE THE FOOLISH

Kristane, on the edge of wakefulness, heard voices and cracked open her eyes. She recognized one of the brothers from the Abbey standing a short distance away, addressing several others; but what struck her as odd was the elegance of his robes. He was speaking, but the words were just not registering with her. She felt a shoulder against hers and turned to see Rellion, his arms no longer crooked and broken, but bound behind him. He seemed to be pointedly ignoring her. She couldn't figure out why, and wanted to ask him, but couldn't find her voice. Giving up with a strangled little mumble, she cast her gaze, with a great deal of effort, to her left, where she saw a kneeling Beezy trussed similarly to Rellion.

Beezy; is that his name? How can he manage to look both grumpy and concerned at the same time? She felt like tweaking his nose for the oddest of reasons. She suspected then that her mind was wandering. *Please, Xander, where are you?*

A crackling noise buzzed above her like an annoying insect, and she motioned to wave away the bugs, only to find that her arms were tied behind her as well. Concentrating on what the regally adorned priest was saying, she saw a beautiful golden statue standing next to him, and thought it odd that it had moved. She heard the priest say, "Let us now—" before he was interrupted by an intense bellowing. With a jerk of her head, her mind cleared. *The incessant crackling above her head — not bugs but the fiery leaves of the tree that didn't burn, and oh God, golden clockwork murderers. Please, Xander, where are you?*

Kristane's eyes whipped back and forth with nervous fear, instinctively looking up and around for the source that generations of tales had warned her of. A large shadow circled about the cupping edges of the dale, disappearing and reappearing, its image obscured intermittently by the shading of the high-hanging clouds that darkened with each passing minute as the sun retired into evening.

With a final deafening roar and a suddenness that terrified her, the enlarging shadow coalesced into a nightmare of shimmering black. The dragon perched itself menacingly on an enormous cropping of rock, eyeing the gathered throng with a single gold-speckled orb with a black pupil, the other eye a pale white sphere. Kristane watched as the gathered crowd started pushing backwards and elbowing each other out of the way, some tripping over those who had fallen to their knees, their haste creating a bottleneck of desperation to leave the dale.

"Hold!" Remarkably, the Holy Shepherds held their ground out of some sense of faith in their High Priest, or perhaps the feeling that escape was impossible anyway; it was hard to determine which. "Be gone, wyrm, servant of darkness! I am High Priest Cristobal Zekel! I bring your conqueror and master, the Saint of Kairos!" Kristane watched, dumbfounded, as the man first pointed to the Saint's casket, and then made shooing motions with his hands.

As Cristobal's statement echoed into the eerie stillness, the dragon slowly turned his attention to him, his reptilian lips curving into a contemptuous sneer before he started laughing; and then he spoke. "You confuse one tale for another, priest. The one interred there holds no sway over me, or any determination as to whether you live or die this day."

Kristane felt like her heart was going to beat itself out of her chest, and she found herself gasping for air. That fanged mouth had spoken; she couldn't have imagined it.

Rellion paid attention to her then. Turning to her, she could see the concern in his eyes. He nodded encouragingly at her, miming slow breaths through his gagged mouth.

Gathering herself, she watched Cristobal as he went white with fear and astonishment, his robes swaying with the wobbling of his legs. It was obvious he, too, had not expected the dragon to actually respond. "I tolerate the foolish, but rarely suffer them," rumbled the dragon. "I will suffer you just a little while longer for my own amusement, though… for what passes this day, must." Chuckling again in a menacing way, to everyone's discomfort, the dragon Thran continued. "I see you believed your sermons to be nothing more than dramatic enhancement for the masses. Foolish men!" The last roared out of the black serpent's mouth, and Kristane shivered with something other than cold. "What other forgotten marvels of this world will be your end, I wonder?… But I grow bored. Proceed with your ceremony, priest."

Kristane swore that the dragon had met her eye at the mention of a ceremony, and it was still staring straight at her. She was beginning to get the impression that this was going to turn out much worse than she could have possibly imagined. *Really? I'm already going to die. What could possibly be worse? I'm going to die!* Delirious with fear, she almost laughed out loud at her own thoughts. Attempting to hold it in, she ended up hacking and coughing through her cracked and bleeding lips. Beezy attempted to scoot closer to support her, but was forcibly pushed by his shoulders to a bowing position by one of the Forgotten Ones hovering above them.

Recovering from her fit, Kristane glanced through her knotted hair at the automaton standing closest to Cristobal. She motioned the other dancers to bring the Saint's coffin to where they stood. They marched the graying wood box up the wide steps that encircled a round and cracked rostrum tucked within the roots of the tree, like a stack of flat dishes of decreasing size.

After they set the simple coffin down, one of the clockwork dancers smashed at it with both fists. The old, dry wood splintered and nearly turned to dust with her hammering. A second yanked at the broken sides, inelegantly tossing the pieces off the platform with little care for who or what they might strike. Kristane prepared herself to see the skeletal frame of some man, or maybe a woman. She found herself disappointed that there was just another box within the box, like getting a pair of socks for

King's Day when you wanted a bracelet. She shook her head; she knew her thoughts were wandering again.

The second funerary box was much more opulent than the graying, decrepit skin of the first. It was hard to tell if it was constructed of hardened wood or burnished metal, but Kristane had the distinct impression that this sarcophagus was built not to be opened. She wasn't sure of whether it was the look or just the uneasy feel she sensed from it, but she knew she wasn't the only one. Those curious spectators who had gathered closer backed away as if they had inadvertently stepped too close to a nest of a vipers.

Cristobal ran his hands along the length of the box reverently, his eyes alight with a hungry glint.

"You wonder how I will open it, don't you, Rellion?" Cristobal smiled down at them with a sickly triumphant smirk. "I must admit, I had become disheartened by your futile attempt at keeping it from me. Turns out that my concern was unnecessary. For where there is one, there is another. I am beginning to believe that there may be several." Cristobal stuck his hand deep into a pocket that blended easily with the outer folds of his robes, and pulled out a silvery circular band pinched between his thumb and forefinger.

"Where…?" Rellion mumbled through his gag, then silenced himself, as it must have dawned upon him; he just nodded.

"Yes, that's right. Seems the long-term *guest* of the Manor Hall left a few personal effects behind." Kristane had no idea what the two men were talking about, but watched as Rellion's shoulders slumped just a fraction lower at the monk's declaration; and though she didn't see it, from higher up in the dale, hidden from sight, a red-haired beauty smacked the back of the head of one of her companions.

"Be on with it, priest! I tire of your gloating!" The dragon's guttural rumble made Cristobal shake, and he hurriedly ran his fingers across a series of indentations atop the second coffin. Staring at the embossed emblem upon the ring and matching it to one near where the entombed person's chest must be, he inserted it. Once the ring snapped in place with a slight *click*, he turned the shank, like the bow of a key, all the way around. For a long moment, nothing happened; and then, accompanied by a whirring of small gears, the surface of the sarcophagus began to fold and slide in upon itself like a puzzle box, becoming ever smaller until only a single plank of it remained.

Kristane thought that she knew what to expect, but what she saw was nothing she could have imagined. Atop the plank, draped in dust like a death shroud, was the body of the Saint of Kairos; but instead of a moldering ancient corpse in dull robes, he was a young man, as still and silent as the air about him. The faces of Cristobal, the Stewards, and the rest of the gathered throng who were close enough to see him were masks of consternation. Only the Forgotten Ones and Rellion seemed unsurprised. The young man wore, from what she could tell — the layers of dust hiding their true colors — a deep blue half-coat and tails with golden lace about the cuffs and trim. His billowy trousers, which were strapped with stirrups around high-lacing black leather shoes, were a creamy color; but that too could have just been age. The oddest thing was the body itself. The Saint looked as though he had just this moment laid down to take a short rest. His skin didn't display the pink hue of a health, but it wasn't flaking off in pieces either.

Kristane observed the confused face of Cristobal as he was shoved to one side by the Forgotten One beside him. With a flourish of her hands, she motioned to the automaton standing above Kristane. Grabbing hold of the back of her grimy cloak — as well as a good portion of her hair — the automaton dragged her toward the base of the rostrum, never allowing her to gain her feet. Behind her, she could hear the quickly silenced protests of both Beezy and Rellion. As she was spun around, her hands and backside bounced hard against each of the ascending levels of the stone stage. Kristane could tell that her knuckles, already scraped raw, were bleeding freely; and as her tailbone cracked against the edge of each of the risers, it sent a shock up her spine.

She saw that Beezy laid sprawled upon his face, blood blossoming along his scalp and puddling upon the flagstone beneath him. Rellion too had been further subdued, one side of his face pressed forward against the stone surface of the dale. The Forgotten Ones to either side of him seemed determined to imprint his features into the flat rock. One of them brandished his cane, as if she were going to bludgeon him. Kristane didn't realize how afraid she was until that very moment. The man who always had the answers and knew what to do, if not always forthcoming as to why, met her eyes, and she saw the shadow of dread that lurked there. Not for himself, she knew, but for her.

Frantically, Kristane searched the faces around her. She was met only by fearful and uncaring expressions — the Stewards in particular, their countenances bordering on a callous disregard for her fate. She knew then that she was truly alone. *Please, Xander, where are you?* She continued looking for a friendly face in the crowd, but as she was jerked around, all she found was the Forgotten One and the pinched and perturbed visage of the priest, obviously put out that the proceedings seemed to be no longer in his control.

Slowly, the metal woman unwrapped a pair of necklace chains from her wrist, and dangled the familiar heart-shaped pendants in front of Kristane until she had her attention. The Forgotten One gave a vicious and victorious smile, the curl of her metal lips enough to freeze Kristane's blood.

With her eyes, the automaton guided Kristane's gaze to the body of the Saint. The young man's face was pale in death, but handsome — well, half of it, anyway. It looked like the Saint was wearing half of a death mask, but it wasn't a vertical line that divided his face in two; it slashed across his face from right to left. And it wasn't really a death mask at all, Kristane realized. The edges of the mask melded too neatly with his nearly alabaster skin; it was more a part of his face, as opposed to something he actually wore. The mask was made of a combination of silvery metals, its portion of the eye, mouth, nose, and chin all in exaggerated size, like those worn by theater troupes for the performance of *Comedie Tragica* — but in a character Kristane didn't know.

There was a slight tugging of the bonds behind Kristane's back, and then a searing pain. She had received enough rope burns, jumping from building top to building top across banners and laundry lines in her life, to know the feeling. The Forgotten One behind her had freed her arms without cutting or loosening the rope. Kristane imagined that if she could have seen it, most of the skin on her wrists and the backs of her hands was scraped and hanging against the woolen braiding.

With an unrelenting grip, Kristane's left arm and hand were forced upwards into a praising salute by the metal automaton before her. Blood seeped through the creases between the metal fingers of the Forgotten One and ran down Kristane's arm, mixing with the dirt and grime already there. Pulling her forward, the Forgotten One stepped aside, revealing a section of the enormous root draped across the rostrum with a broadsword embedded in it. Tapering roots growing from the lateral base clung to the hilt and cross-guard, like the tree itself had plunged the blade into its own skin and was holding it there. The sword seemed otherwise insignificant, in that it was dwarfed by the enormity of the tree; but it shone and pulsed as the tree did, giving it its own elegance.

Forcing her outstretched palm to the blade's edge, the metal dancer ran Kristane's hand down its length. Kristane blinked back tears of pain as a burning sensation enveloped her hand with the opening up of the skin. Placing the pieces of the clockwork heart upon the chest of the Saint, the automaton slapped her bleeding palm upon the pendants. Crimson ran down over them and stained the breast of the Saint's jacket and the green paisley vest underneath. Attempting to pull away, she was held fast by the Forgotten One.

Kristane felt and saw, through her splayed fingers, the two halves of the Broken Heart slowly knitting together, the wooden parts becoming one. And then it began to faintly pulse, the light beginning to throb in a rhythmic manner as if a heart that had stopped had started to beat again. With each pulse of light, the space in between beats became shorter, and there was a slight movement of the young man's chest as it began to heave with the intake of air. The plated metal and gears that made up one half of the Saint's face curved into a smile, while the rest of his face remained immobile. Kristane watched with a fascinated horror as she considered the young man before her, and the mask, which seemed to almost have a personality of its own.

With a quick motion, the Saint's right hand reached up and clasped both Kristane's and the Forgotten One's. Kristane's gaze switched fearfully back and forth between the pale hand and the ever-so-slowly opening eyes of the Saint. Peeking through shuttered lids with faded blonde lashes, the Saint's eyes were a striking blue against his white skin, like the light blue of a spring day peeping through a bank of cottony clouds. Kristane felt his awareness, and her skin began to itch under the scrutiny of those beautiful and horrible eyes. She knew that his hardened gaze was weighing her life against that of a common bug and his desire to crush her beneath his heel.

Moving their hands away from his chest, he fondled the clockwork heart with his fingers. Lifting it up so that he might clearly see, he peered at it with a longing contempt. As her blood painted his long and tapered fingers, the Saint clasped the pendant in his fist, as if wishing to crush it; and the pulsing light within it ebbed.

Wetting his lips with a tongue that was just as stark white as the rest of him, he said in cracked and whispered voice, as if his mouth were full of the same dust that covered the rest of him: "But to live once more, I have become death…"

BEGONE FOUL BEAST

Standing, the Saint brushed away the dust from his long sleep, ignoring Kristane and only giving a cursory glance to the High Priest and the Forgotten Ones. He seemed oblivious to anything and anyone else around him, completely discounting the men, monks, Stewards, and even the dragon as just parts of the landscaping.

Idly tossing the clockwork heart up and down in his hand like it was just some bauble or plaything, he sauntered from the rostrum to where Rellion was still being pressed down into the stone pavers. "Ah! Rellion, it is delightful that you are attending my reawakening!" Kristane had the distinct impression, by the way he drawled Rellion's name, that he was *anything* but delighted. The Saint's actions were playful, but the tone of his voice bordered on incensed, as if each breath Rellion took was a personal affront to him.

The Saint waved lazily, and the Forgotten One yanked free the gag about Rellion's mouth. After spitting out blood and composing himself, Rellion replied, "I assure you, Fooney, that it is an event I had hoped to never have to attend, much less hear of." Even with his lips nearly kissing rock, Rellion carried off a distinguished air, as though his and the Saint's positions were reversed, and it was the Saint that was actually getting to know the flagstone in such an intimate fashion.

"Always the pompous fool, aren't you, Rellion?" The young man's tone was calm and subdued, but the masked side of his face contorted into a maniacal rage, while the other half merely smirked. "How quaint of you to use that long-forgotten and inappropriate moniker. It is the adolescent nonsense of a foolish little girl who is just as *dead* as that nickname."

"That little girl cared a great deal for you, Foon —"

Despite Rellion's haughty attitude, Kristane wondered if she was the only one who picked out the troubled strain hidden in his voice as he was cut off mid-sentence.

"She cared *nothing* for me! It is because of her I wear this mask! It is because of her I have laid here *asleep* so very long! It is because of her that…" Foon trailed off on his rant, the mask finally calming its features long moments after his true face had settled. It was then that Kristane, despite her fear, became curious as to which side of Foon's face was the true one.

Regathering himself, and donning a mischievous smile, Foon turned his attention to Kristane. "But who is this moppet?"

The Saint didn't wait for a response, and it appeared that Rellion didn't have one forthcoming. Foon sauntered over to where she was being restrained by the Forgotten One, carelessly swinging the pendant around his finger by its chain. He smirked at her with his metal lips, and those beautiful blue eyes stared hard at her. Kristane tried to look away, but she was yanked back by her hair so that she had no choice but to meet his gaze. Slowly, the Saint placed the chain over her head. The moment the clockwork heart touched her chest, it glowed brightly; not pulsing in danger, but with a constant, even light. Kristane felt guilty that, for the first time in her life, she wasn't gaining any sense of comfort from wearing her necklace now that it had been joined to the tarnished half.

"My, now, isn't that pretty. Wherever did you find her, Rellion? By the look of her, under some rock or garbage heap." Kristane felt anger rising in her chest at the sheer contempt with which Foon spoke and looked at her. Yet it was even more than that; this young man regarded her as nothing, and that infuriated her, the thought of it burning away any fear that she had held before. *I am someone; I am something.* "No doubt, the spurious offspring of some tavern maid, or possibly the illegitimate wretch of some stable boy." Bending over, Foon flicked his finger at her chin. "Oh, how far the royal blood thins once spilt, yes, Rellion?"

Kristane decided that if her mouth wasn't so dry, she would have spit in Foon's face; and then, in a rush of awareness, she played back in her mind what Foon had just said and what she had learned recently. She replayed the playful voice of Pipkin in a wet and musty cavern. *The pretty, pretty princess was lonely and wanted a friend, so the clockmaker made her a handsome and princely friend... The pretty, pretty princess's friend was hurt, so the clockmaker made him a new face...The beautiful, beautiful Queen broke the heart of her friend, and maybe just a little bit of her own.* Clasping the necklace, Kristane stared in wide-eyed shock at the handsome young man, the pretty, pretty princess's friend. Foon, as if reading her mind, gave her a wink with his masked eye, and turned expectantly back to Rellion.

"As you say, Foon, she is no one."

"So quick to discount her? How very unlike you, Rellion." Standing upright, he studied the older man. "Well, we will see." Not getting the response he wished, his mask cast a shadow of anger across the other-wise placid and uncaring side of his face as Foon continued. "I suppose I should be thankful, though, that a trickle of the blood still poisons Kairos. By the looks of it, my long slumber might have gone on even longer had none been found." Foon turned on his heels, taking in the ruins. "Much, much longer." His gaze lingered on the burning tree, and then the still-silent gathering of assorted monks, soldiers, and Stewards. Lastly, he gazed upon the High Priest and said, "You have the look of authority. Tell me, priest, your name, and the year of our Lord."

Cristobal, whom had been staring at Kristane, gave a start when he realized he was being addressed, but then stood up straight, dabbing at his nose with a kerchief. "O Saint of Kairos, I am High Priest Cristobal Zekel." Kristane had thought Rellion full of himself until she watched the lowly monk she knew from the Abbey declare himself. "This year and this King's Day marks the five-hundredth anniversary since you walked and fell upon your path of righteousness."

"Saint?" Foon tasted the word in his mouth like a piece of candy, savoring its sweetness. Kristane could see the delight in his metal features and a twinkling in his eyes. He looked at Rellion and said, "Clever, hidden in plain sight. Saint, Saint, Saint. I think I quite like the sound of that; it just rolls off the tongue like an eloquent appellation. Tell me more, *High Priest* Zekel." Foon said the High Priest's title as if he himself had just bestowed its use.

Zekel was nearly beside himself that the Saint of Kairos had emphasized his honorific in front of everyone. With a sweeping arm, the High Priest projected his voice to the still-tensed gathering of people. "All know the story of your path from the royal throne to the Abbey, at the bequest of the Queen, to secure the treasures of her heart; whereupon you were besieged by many a foe and fell wielding the King's own blade, but not before banishing the talking black demon from our midst and saving all!"

"Did I really?" Foon did not sound surprised; in fact, he looked as though he was weighing memories within his head. His mask twitched with a sly smile. "It does sound much like something I would do, of course. But which black demon are we speaking of?"

"Why, the one discussed in the Gospel of the Dragon, the Saint, and the Broken Sword, your Holy Being. That one." Cristobal pointed.

Foon looked over his shoulder to Thran, who had been watching over the proceedings in silence, then said. "Let's not be too formal, High Priest. You may call me Saint, or Your Saintliness." His masked mouth quirked upwards in amusement.

Kristane, listening to the conversation, directed her attention to the dragon. Unnervingly, she found his one good eye focusing solely on her, a liquid dot of black floating in a pool of white, which shimmered with pinpricks of the faintest of lights in concentric circles. She did not sense the hate or the anger that she had expected to from the deathly menace, but rather a sense of curiosity. It was fleeting, and while she still feared the dragon, she was confused by his look. She found herself unable to look away. Was her mind still playing tricks, mistaking hunger for curiosity, while the beast was merely deciding how many bites it would take to make a meal of her instead?

"Black demon, is he? Silly old crow of Kairos, says I." Thran turned from Kristane to regard Foon and his mocking tone. She could see the hate in the beast's narrowing eye return, but he did not rise to the baiting playfulness of the Saint. Foon was slight of frame in a sinister way, and lithe in a frolicsome way. He was equally boyish and ageless, and both were on display currently. With his metal mask displaying a calculating and shrewd grin, he said, "Begone, foul beast, and bother not the peoples of Kairos! Shoo, be off with you, or feel yet again the wrath of the Saint!" The young man gave a somewhat limp-wristed and backhanded dismissal, and while turning to the throng of people, his masked eye gave a conspiratorial wink.

Thran stared intently at the Saint for several long moments; and then, finally nodding his assent, spread his wings. With a couple of wide sweeps of the scaled membranes, which caused several small but forceful whirlwinds to displace the stone wall below him and Kristane's clothing and hair to push back like she was caught in a gale, Thran launched himself skyward. The talons of his back claws caused those in his path, below the canopy of the burning tree, to duck low; and then he was lost in the darkness that was quickly enveloping what remained of King's Day. There was a collective sigh of relief, which Kristane had to admit she felt herself, and the collection of Cristobal's minions looked on in awe at their savior, their Saint... but then it was disrupted by a long and final bellow from above that sobered the crowd.

Foon chuckled at everyone's discomfort, and Kristane noticed that the young man no longer looked as pale as he had. "Well, now that that is done, shall we continue? Remind me, High Priest, how was it that I fell?"

"Why, your heart was cleaved and broken." Foon's masked mouth grimaced as if he had tasted something spoiled, and he quickly glanced at Kristane and then away just as hastily as Cristobal continued on with reverence, "Yet such was your righteousness and innocence, the blade also broke against you."

"Did it? Yes, it is coming back to me now," Foon said thoughtfully. "Righteousness and innocence; that truly does speak of me." Foon took a moment to look the High Priest up and down, and then, in a calculating manner, examined the Stewards that flanked him for the first time. Both sides of his face smiled as one with delight, like a little boy who has been caught doing wrong but doesn't care. "High Priest, you remind me much of another priest I use to know… leadership will be needed in the coming times. Name the rewards you seek in this life."

Cristobal nearly quivered with anticipation. He had long awaited this moment, and as the High Priest stole a quick look at the tree, he did his best to respond humbly. "My only desire is that I should be granted the *time* that I should be able to serve."

Foon's masked lip smiled broadly, his other half again placid. Casting his twinkling and knowing eyes upward into the canopy of the tree, he said with a happy little chuckle. "Yes, that desire bears much *fruit*. I think you and I will get along famously, *High Priest* Zekel."

Foon then dropped the smile that he had granted Zekel, replacing it with a haughty grin for Rellion. "To the business at hand. Don't you think, Rellion?" Raising his hand imperiously, the Forgotten One complied with the silent order and raised Rellion back to a kneeling position, bits of dried weeds and pebbles falling away from his cheek and chin from where they had been compressed into his skin. "So many things to catch up on, so many things to do. *Where* does one start?" Pressing his finger to his chin in a pose of thoughtfulness, the eye of his mask giving Rellion a little wink, Foon continued. "Of course! I should start by removing the greatest threat."

"I would be saddened to see you gone, Fooney," Rellion said dryly. "It would take me some time to get through the loss."

Foon's mask twitched with irritation and rage, but the young man composed himself before replying, "Always the pithy retort. I wish I could say that I have missed your *endless* banter, but I would just as soon be without it."

"Do what you will with me, Fooney."

"I will, and *I don't need your permission!*" Foon lost all control of himself for a moment, both sides of his face contorted with rage, his outcry startling everyone watching. It was with a visible effort, his fists pulsing at his sides and his fingernails digging into his palms, that he composed his features and continued in a calmer but no less incensed tone. "Such self-flattery. It must be exhausting, thinking the whole of Kairos and its kingdoms rests on your shoulders. Oh, you *are* a grand manipulator, but you and your ilk of Amaranthine are but dust… or, at least, once the Tree is healed of this poison that afflicts it, you will be." Foon smiled broadly with the flesh-covered half of his face, encompassing the canopy of the tree with a sweep of his arm, but this time the metal half stayed stoic; and Kristane wondered at its meaning. Was the Saint lying?

"Yet I digress; there will be time enough for you." Foon, turning away from Rellion, stared at Kristane contemplatively, like a painter examining the model of a portrait, affixing her image in his mind. "You know, she even looks a bit like the pretty, pretty Princess. And the beautiful, beautiful Queen she became. Does she not?" Foon, speaking more to himself then the captivated assemblage, even went as far as to lift his thumb at arm's length, eyeing her, turning the extended digit from side to side. "Of course, she *would* be beautiful, wouldn't she?" Only the cold malevolence hidden deep within his brilliant eyes told Kristane that he wished to rearrange her face into some grotesque mockery of itself.

In an unsure and fearful voice, Rellion nearly pleaded. "You cannot harm her, Foon." As it dawned on Kristane, she thought, *Of course I would be the greater threat, as keeper and bearer of his heart.*

"You care for her?" Again the vicious smile marked both sides of his face. "This will make this so much more delightful, then. It's true that I cannot harm her directly, but…" Foon nodded to the automaton. "There is so much more one can do, and will do, with a broken heart, Rellion."

With the quick sweep of her arm and a slashing motion, Kristane did not even feel the cut that the automaton made — at first. She watched, both dazed and horrified, as her arm was opened up from her wrist to halfway up into the softer meaty flesh of her forearm. She was reminded of the slow ticking of a second hand on a clock face as the deep red seeped from the long line in slow motion. Then she was tossed to the side like a repugnant piece of rubbish, her back slamming into the root of the tree upon the rostrum. As she slumped there, she watched with a strange fascination as the blood pulsed from her wound, and the ebbing light of her necklace slowed. Through a fog of sound that Kristane suspected was much louder than her ears were registering, she heard a number of voices yell out; but above them all was Xander with an anguished "No!"

I knew you would come, but it's too late. Kristane realized she was dying.

Doing Her Best not to Throw Up

The pitch-black galleon lay berthed amongst the remnants of an ancient harbor and lighthouse. The hush that hung over the harbor felt as if it had weight; only the lapping of waves about the dark hull of the Lady's Grace proved that there was still sound in the world. Sailors' shoulders hung just a little lower, and furtive glances to the left and right at imagined whisperings only added to the gloom and sense of foreboding that permeated everything. Instead of simple stone or wooden pylons, massive, short towers of sculpted granite with black and green graining acted as support for the crumbling mass of a stone pier. Statuesque heroes of old with stone faces, some of them smoothed on one side as centuries of weather and crashing waves had finally made the sculptor's artistry succumb, stood just as silent as the living people who now passed beneath their outstretched arms and armaments.

Prya found herself about mid-column of those braving the legends, imagined or real, of Kaer Kairos, with Lathan at her side. A small group of the Dame's crew remained aboard as sentries. Silhouetted ahead, as the elevation of the island reached to the dusking sun, its rays casting a long shadow back upon Prya and the others, she saw the Dame dwarfed by the height of her Quartermaster, along with Ix and the Warder Blackmore.

Both the Dame and Ix claimed to know where they were going, but neither could convince the other that their path was the best. Though she couldn't hear them from where she was, Prya knew that they were still arguing. They were headed for something called the Dale of the Baennaith Tree; or maybe it was the Sanguis Glaive. Whatever it was, they were arguing about that, too. Prya imagined that the two would most likely argue as to what shade of blue the sky was, if nothing else.

Fatterpacker spoke animatedly behind her; he had demanded to come along, claiming that Their Highnesses would be expecting him. The adults had balked at Pyra's equally fervent demand to come as well, with attestations of danger, but had finally relented with a terse warning from the Dame. *Listen hard, my little cutie, you and your lot live or die upon your own merits. I'll not have this rescue go arse-up because of some childish heroics.* Prya didn't care; she was going after her friends.

Just as they were about to crest a hill, there came something that caused Prya to stop in her tracks, the rantings of the adults and the supposed danger all but forgotten. It started deep in her chest, and flushed throughout the rest of her body with a suddenness that nearly made her ill. It seemed to come from nowhere and then everywhere at once. Prya looked around and knew by the pained and fearful looks upon the faces of all of those around her that they had felt and heard the same: the growling roar of a predator that shook them to their bones and made their limbs ache to flee. Each of them instinctively knew that whatever it was, it never, never *ever*, was prey itself… and then there was silence.

"That was a little scary," Prya said quietly, trying to lighten her own mood and giving a half-hearted giggle to those around her.

A few of the braver sailors and Warders gave her nervous smiles back, but then the sound erupted again and everyone, including Prya, fell flat to the ground and squirmed for cover.

Prya was beside herself with anxiety and fear as she sneaked occasional glances over the rock outcroppings that lined the lip of the bowled dale below, which they had all hidden behind. She could see a collection of men, monks, Forgotten Ones, and most importantly, Kristane and Rellion, below. Blackmore kept referring to one of the monks as the High Priest, but Prya just thought of him as the mousy and bossy one from the Abbey, the one with the perpetually runny nose. And of course, there was the source of that terrifying roar that had sent them all scurrying and hiding in the first place: the black death with wings. All seemed unsurmountable obstacles to helping her friend. *God, really, a* dragon*?*

Her heart ached with each short glimpse of Kristane. She wished to run to her friend and hold her in her arms, to let her know that she wasn't alone; but she was paralyzed by fear and the sense of uselessness that was borne of her damaged arm. She swore that the dragon knew exactly where they were, his predatory gaze occasionally swinging from the happenings below to stare intently at the exact place where they lay hidden.

The adults were again bickering in hushed voices, and Captain Polly had smacked the fellow named Ix several times so far. *Ix; that's such a stupid name,* Prya thought, though the Dame was the only one who dared call him Richard. The voices below were a mumble, the acoustics of the amphitheater-like dale carrying only the distinct voice of the dragon to their ears. *God, seriously, not just a* dragon *but a* talking one*!* Prya shivered at the thought.

She could probably hear what was going on better if she went up over the lip of the bowl… but that dragon looked hungry. Working up her courage, Prya stole another quick glance over the edge at the place where her friend knelt, bruised and battered. For some odd reason, she imagined a courtly bard or musician sitting in that same place, upon the cracked and round rostrum tucked within the roots of the tree, entertaining ladies in beautiful dresses and gentlemen adorned in fine jackets… not this.

"What kind of distraction do you think is going to work, exactly?" Blackmore asked in a hushed and doubtful voice.

"I have an idea."

"Dammit, Richard, that is *stupid*, and it has *never* worked!" the pirate queen chastised Ix for what seemed the hundredth time since they'd all hidden themselves. "And don't look at me like I just kicked a puppy, I know exactly what you were thinking!" *Funny how the Dame can still seem to be shouting at him while still talking in a whisper,* Prya mused to herself.

"I believe Their Highnesses would best be served by…"

"Hush now, sweet man, the adults are talking again," Pollyanna interrupted Fatterpacker, patting him on the knee consolingly. "And you might as well shut it, Richard! I know what you're going to suggest next, and that's stupid too!"

The only thing that kept Ix from yet another prolonged tirade of protest with the Dame was another predatory roar from the dragon. Prya found herself trying to press herself farther into the rocks that she leaned against, her right shoulder tight against Lathan's, her hand trying to squeeze the fear she felt out of both their hands.

As before, the rumble of the beast thumped hard in her chest, and it was all she could do to keep herself from standing and running back to the ship, screaming like her hair was on fire. *Which is probably the most likely of scenarios, with a fire-breathing dragon on your tail.* Prya suppressed a bitter chuckle at the image that came to mind of Cayson and the moron brothers aflame.

Concentrating on her own feet sprawled out before her, Prya was doing her best to keep herself from throwing up on Lathan when a shadow passed over them. Prya knew it wasn't just a low-flying cloud blocking the sun's setting rays, and her heart pounded even harder. "He's gone." Ix almost made the statement a question, and in answer, the Dame just shrugged at her equally confused thoughts as to why the dragon had disappeared. Prya, on the other hand, didn't care why, and felt like dancing a jig; but it was several arguments later before she found the courage to let go of Lathan's hand and peer with the others back down into the dale.

For Kristane, things seemed to have taken a decided turn for the worse, and Prya once again had the desire to reach out to her friend and let her know that she was there and that it was going to be all right. Even Lathan was becoming more agitated by their inaction, and looked like he was considering soon going down there.

It may have been the horrifying sight of her friend being cut and tossed away like an old ragdoll, or it may have been the dismayed and heart-wrenching cry of "*No!*" from a brother whose heart had been shattered in the space of a heartbeat, but suddenly all the arguments about strategy and distractions were over. Prya found herself following the Dame, the

Warder lieutenant, and the others who were scrabbling over the edge of the bowl, trailing a bellowing Ix.

The Hope of a
Single Word

Xander crested the bowl of the Dale of the Blessed Tree astride Aldebarron, doing his best to take in the gathering below him. His gaze focused on the bedraggled form of his sister as she was cut and flung to the side by the metal wraith that had haunted their footsteps since Hallow's End.

"*No!* Kristane!" He had failed, he wasn't enough, and he couldn't do enough. The trivial hope of a single word: *no*. The desire of some little boy who wants desperately to have something returned, but whose protests have fallen on deaf ears. Xander's agonized scream even sounded hollow in his own head, but it was anything but. At the sound of Xander's cry, Aldebarron reared upward, his front hooves cartwheeling and his massive metal shoulders rotating beside his expansive chest plate. The metal warhorse sprang forward, as if the exclamation were a command to traverse the very depths of hell with demons on his tail. He was a veritable blaze of copper, brass, and gold, his flanks and chest shimmering from the assortment of lighted torches and the fiery tree.

Xander barely managed to cling to the saddle horn as Groggle rolled off the back of the horse, falling to the ground, and a startled Purdy took wing, squawking his indignation. Xander gave a cursory thought to

Groggle's well-being, but his anguish had quickly been replaced by anger and fear for his sister. He had get to Kristane, and if he wasn't enough, then maybe Aldebarron could be.

Barreling straight ahead, Aldebarron's heavy footfalls sparked against the stone stairs, taking several of them at a time, each trouncing hoof cracking the treads and risers and chipping away the crumbling edges. The great horse gave no mind to those too slow to get out of his way, and Xander heard more than one leg or arm snap at the horse's passing.

To his left Xander, could see from the corner of his eye a rush of individuals hastening down the terraced dale, dodging rock outcroppings and yelling incoherently. He gave them no mind; he and Aldebarron had but a single goal now.

With a leap from the final terrace to the rostrum, the warhorse vaulted the line of armed men and robed monks who had formed a circle around where Kristane lay dying. Their shocked exclamations as the horse passed over their heads were drowned out by the fierce bellow that Aldebarron issued in challenge. Whipping his leather mane from side to side, the great horse took the converging wraiths head on, spinning at the last moment to bring his back hooves up in a bucking motion. The crash of metal sent two of the Forgotten Ones sprawling into the armed men, and the others gave way to the raging stallion. Xander watched as a half-masked young man sidestepped one of Aldebarron's onslaughts, the features of the mask forming an amused grin as the bulk of the horse's body passed him. Xander wondered for the briefest of moments who he was.

Aldebarron fought his way through the metal automatons, but their moves became more and more sinuous as the battle raged, as if they were learning the steps to a new dance that Aldebarron was performing. His hooves and plated sides made contact with them less and less often. Xander could see his sister, and urged the horse in that direction. Jumping from the saddle, Xander ran to Kristane and cradled her head in his arms as Aldebarron continued to buck and swing his haunches at anyone who came close to them. "Kris-Kristane." Pushing back her matted hair, Xander choked over her name, emotion nearly silencing him. There was so much blood.

Her eyes flitted half-open and she said with a weak smile, "I knew you would come."

"Always, Kris." Xander tore a ragged piece of cloth from his cloak, securing it across his sister's wound. He knew that it might give her a few moments, but more needed to be done. Helplessly, he looked around, hoping for a way to mount the metal stallion and spirit Kristane away; but Aldebarron had troubles of his own.

"There, hook its leg there!" High Priest Cristobal was running about the periphery of the battle, shouting instruction to his Shepherds. A half-dozen men were swinging ropes with grapples at the great warhorse. A few of the barbed heads had already found purchase, entwined about Aldebarron's legs and across his back. Despite Purdy desperately diving and raking his talons across exposed knuckles and faces, dozens of others manned the loose ends of the ropes, doing their best to pull in opposite directions in an attempt to bring the metal stallion down. Even with the restraints, Aldebarron continued to yank the men from one end of the deep bowl of the dale to the other, but it was only a matter of time before he would be overwhelmed. Finding the metal stallion otherwise occupied, the Forgotten Ones began to converge on Xander and his sister. Leading them was the same half-masked young man that Xander had seen earlier. He didn't know who this man was, but Xander cared little for the cold look in his eyes.

Stopping short of the siblings, Foon's mask twisted in vicious delight. "My, my, my, who would have thought that there would be one, not to mention two? Still only one, really; very soon, anyway." Foon gave a heavy sigh and hung his head, pretending concern for Kristane's condition, but then peeked up and smiled again at Xander. "Might as well make it none, don't you think?" He motioned forward the Forgotten Ones who remained poised behind him.

Kristane mumbled something incoherent, which went unheard over the commotion of the stallion and those still trying to entrap him. She squeezed Xander's arm, but then fell listless again. Xander had no idea what the odd young man was talking about, but if the metal wraiths were listening to him, then it couldn't be a good thing. Carefully, he laid his sister back against the large root of the burning tree, and removed a stick about the size of his palm from his pocket. He shook it once, twice, then thrice.

Foon and his minions were caught unawares, utterly surprised by the force that emanated from the staff given to Xander by King Frobly. Foon's mask transformed from the malicious delight of a few moments before to pure fury. The Saint's eyes became transfixed upon Xander's staff, as if his stare alone could snap the weapon in half.

While Xander was no expert with a staff, the force that accompanied each swing made even his mistakes powerful enough that the Forgotten Ones gave ground. The first two who had reached him were just now regaining their footing after being launched into the lower terraces of the Blessed Tree's amphitheater. Xander looked to Aldebarron, who was now trussed about his head and legs, with several more ropes strung across his broad back; but still the great stallion stood. The ropes, taut with the effort of many men from all sides, attempted to force him to the ground; but the idea of falling to his knees in defeat was foreign to the mechanical horse. Xander instinctively knew the horse would never concede. If he could just free the stallion, they could still get Kristane away to safety.

The metal wraiths circled Xander, not bothering any further with Kristane, their deadly work already done upon her. Xander barely dodged a quick swipe of one of the metal dancers' hands and felt it brush against his cheek, followed by the biting sting of a fine cut, even as he heard several throaty battle cries sound out.

Ix launched himself from the final terrace, his feet landing on the large roots of the tree and increasing his momentum. Sliding upon his knees, his sword grasped in one hand and a dagger in the other, Ix split the space between Aldebarron's legs, simultaneously slicing at his bonds. Freed, the stallion screamed a boisterous challenge and was once again a blur of metal, bucking and spinning. The men not wise enough to release their holds upon the few remaining restraints shouted in pain as the heavy cords tore at the flesh of their palms and fingers.

As the Warders laid into the High Priest's Shepherds, Ix ran to Xander's side, taking a blow from a metal wraith meant for the boy's undefended back upon his notched sword. Ix didn't say anything, just eyed Xander and gave him a solicitous grunt. Xander had never thought that he would be glad to see the gruff and always-angry man, but his sudden appearance gave him the hope he needed for Kristane. With a renewed faith in how this might end, he took the legs out from under another Forgotten One with his staff.

The Dame of the *Lady's Grace* pranced and twirled her way to the two figures that remained hogtied at the stone base of the dale. "Why, Polly, how lovely to see you — and accompanying Richard, no less!" the man said conversationally.

"Shut it, Rellion!" Deftly, Polly sliced away his bonds. "I'm not here with him; *he* is here with *me*, and I won't have you playing village matchmaker today!" The Dame motioned for Taff to release the dwarf as she handed over Rellion's staff, which she'd found lying not far from where he laid, pulling him to his feet at the same time.

"No, quite right, Polly; more important things to be about at the moment." The end of Rellion's shillelagh glowed at his touch as he graciously bowed the pirate captain back into the fray. "After you, Polly. We must see to the young heirs."

You Were Never Mine to Protect

Kristane found herself falling in and out of consciousness. Her necklace, the broken heart, began to ebb slower, no longer a constant light; and a chill came over her body as the blood continued to flow from her arm, albeit slower since Xander's bandaging. Kristane knew the light was ebbing because she was fading, not because of any lessening danger. She could see Xander fighting with several of the Forgotten Ones all at once with a long, thin staff, alongside a man adorned in a piecemeal uniform. Kristane absently thought it odd that the Forgotten Ones were being thrown aside so easily by the force of Xander's blows. Foon was nowhere in sight. She tried to call out to her brother, but was too weak. Looking up into the canopy of the tree, she felt like she could almost touch the low branches from where she was slumped. In fact, it looked as though the branches were reaching down to her. At the very tip of a particular stem, Kristane saw something that looked like a fiery blossom: just a single perfect flower that opened up and smiled at her as if she were the sun. It was so pretty that Kristane had the sudden desire to touch it. She figured it was really all just her imagination, but it was so beautiful... and she had the strangest feeling that it was just for her.

Dipping lower, the branch of the Blessed Tree dropped to within a hair's breadth of the tip of her longing and outstretched finger. Slightly frustrated but filled with an overwhelming desire, she urged herself to fill the space that separated her from the flower. With the slightest of touches, more like a soft kiss, she brushed a single petal, and her arm fell away. The petals of the flower shivered as from a soft wind, and instantly a small, pure white silique pod formed at the center of the flower. It was like the world had gone away. The sounds of battle fell silent, and the throbbing of her arm quieted. With fascination, Kristane watched as the pod grew rapidly, expanding its shape into a perfectly formed heart-shaped fruit only a little bigger than a plum, the skin of the stone fruit burning and reforming like the leaves and bark of the tree that had birthed it. Kristane just stared at its beauty, entranced by the gift she was being shown by the tree in her final moments. With a faint smile, she laid down and succumbed to the darkness.

"Impossible! It cannot be!" Something of the tone or inflection of Ix's voice cut through the battle, drawing every eye to where he looked. "Quickly, boy, feed her the fruit! Force it down her throat if you have to!" Ix bodily pushed Xander towards Kristane; Xander didn't understand, but he obeyed, stumbling the last few steps to kneel by his sister's side.

Confused, Xander plucked the fruit from the extended branch. It burned in his hand, and he nearly dropped it. Apparently he wasn't moving fast enough for Ix's satisfaction, and the man yelled again. "Dammit, boy, I said feed her the fruit! There's not much time!" Ix turned away, taking a blow upon his sword from a Forgotten One. The metal wraiths seemed more wary of his blade now; Xander had noticed that Ix's sword alone seemed to nick at their metal skin. "Whiskeys, to me! Hold to your oaths — none shall harm the heirs of Alesdair!"

Blackmore was the first to Ix's side, with blood, a little of it her own, staining her ragged uniform tunic. Banes followed close on her heels, as did the other, also blood-soaked Whiskeys. Some hobbled and others clutched at wounds, but to a man and woman, those still standing came and formed a perimeter about Xander and Kristane.

"No! It is mine; it should be mine!" A high-pitched careening and selfish cry of dismay emanated from behind the ranks of the Shepherds.

The High Priest looked as though he had gone a little mad, his robes twisted about his legs and sweat pouring heavily from his brow. He had not even bothered to wipe at his nose; mucus had formed on his upper lip like some grotesque mustache. Cristobal smacked at the backs of those Shepherds and monks in front of him, screaming for all he was worth. "Stop them! Retrieve the fruit!"

There was a renewed clash of steel with the incoming wave of Cristobal's zealot followers. Unarmed monks fearful of their High Priest's displeasure fell upon the swords of the Whiskeys with a fervor, and the Forgotten Ones, urged on by the just-as-hysterical commands of Foon, clashed in a deafening scream of the dying.

The line of Whiskeys was buckling when Aldebarron plowed across the line of battle, doing his best to engage the metal dancers, who were taking the largest toll on both the Whiskeys and the Dame's crew. Rellion had been able to toss a few bursts from his cane, but had fallen to a single knee, his exhaustion and mistreatment at the hands of the Forgotten Ones evident. He, after all, was only one of The Undying, not invincible. Rellion and the members of his Rogue and the others now acted as a secondary line of defense for the twins, behind the Warders.

For Xander, the battle was something that didn't exist in the space he occupied with his sister. He couldn't tell whether she was still alive, and getting her to eat the fruit that burned in his hand seemed all but impossible. He still didn't know why he should, though Ix seemed so sure... She looked so peaceful, with almost a little smile upon her face. He had the oddest feeling that he should just let her rest, but then he would surely be without her. He was still grasping the fruit with both hands as it continued to burn his skin, and his eyes welled with tears from the pain and his frustration for his dying sister. The feeling that he hadn't been enough just about broke him.

The skin of the fruit, though resilient, covered a ripe flesh beneath, and Xander squeezed it as hard as he could over Kristane's slightly parted lips. Slowly, drop after drop, its juice pressed between his fingers, scalding and scaring them as each bit of moisture fell to her mouth. Ever so slightly, Kristane stirred, and her tongue licked across her chapped and cracked lips. Encouraged by this glimmer of hope, Xander put everything he had into crushing the fruit.

Kristane's eyelids fluttered, and the unnatural white pall of her skin flared a deep, fiery red along her veins, as if the juice had gone straight into her bloodstream. Those parts of her skin visible to Xander on her face and arms burned and glittered like the canopy of leaves above; but still his sister's chest did not heave with life. Xander began to sob; he was too late.

Then Kristane's eyes shot open, accompanied by a rattling gasp that arched her back, posing her on her heels and shoulder blades. Falling back to the ground, she screamed in a voice of anguished pain that silenced the ongoing battle. Xander was nearly afraid to touch her, fearing that he might cause her further harm; but he reached for the ragged strip that bound her arm. Before him, the long laceration made by the Forgotten One began to close upon itself, the skin still burning and reforming brightly as if it were on fire, but did not burn.

"Kris." As the burning faded from her skin, Xander tentatively met his sister's eyes. She was looking at him but not seeing, her gaze somewhere far away, staring through him.

Abruptly, Xander was spun around by a strong pull on his shoulder. Such was the force that he fell onto his backside, only catching himself from sprawling by planting his hands on the flagstones, the remnants of the skin and stone of the fruit rolling away and nestling under a root of the tree. The shock of his burnt hands striking the stone buckled his arms at his elbows, and Xander winced at the pain. Opening his eyes, he found himself staring up at the half-masked young man, his cold blue eyes looking through him like Kristane's had, his mask contorted with rage. Glancing from Xander to Kristane, the masked man said, "So, the spawn of Alesdair still draws breath? What a funny little look on her face, though — like she is not really there. How upset you must be, hmm?" He regarded Xander with a smirk as he reached out to stroke Kristane's cheek.

Xander moved to grab for the man's arm, but with surprising speed, the stranger struck Xander across the face with a thin stiletto he had clasped in his other hand. As Xander grasped at his jaw, he felt the warm and wet trickle of blood from where the blade had broken skin. The young man seemed to be not just surprised, but astonished at his own action. "Seems that there are advantages to having a broken heart. The curse of Alesdair is lifted from me. Had I known, I might have broken it myself... but then again, you were never mine to protect anyway. Were you?" With his finger poised at his chin in contemplation, Foon studied Xander for a long moment, and finally the mask gave him a wink. "No matter; I'll figure it out later. Seems that this day's events will not be a complete waste, don't you think, rider?"

Xander, not for the first time today and many of those preceding, understood little if anything of what was happening; but the masked man's grip on the thin blade, and the wanting look in his eyes, was enough for Xander to deduce his intent. Xander looked past his assailant for the help he hoped might come, but there would be no last-minute rescue for him. Ix was thick with blades and wraiths about him, with the raven-haired Blackmore and a red-haired woman to his back. Rellion and his friends were pushed far to the opposite side of the dale, and Aldebarron was nowhere to be seen.

The masked man's face was alight with pleasure, and he smiled broadly with both sides of his face at Xander's helplessness. "You are forsaken, heir of Alesdair; no help will come." The young man moved nonchalantly towards Xander, savoring his position over him, studying him from head to toe as if mentally deciding where he might cut first.

Kristane felt trapped in a dream, with Xander standing on the edge of it. She could hear his voice, but could not make herself reach out to him. She also heard another voice and recognized it as the pretty, pretty princess's friend, the deceiver Foon. He was saying something upsetting, she knew, but she couldn't quite get herself to understand. *Brother, I knew you would come*, she thought. But then Kristane heard the deceiver say something else, clearly: *no help will come*. And with a rush of awareness, the dream was broken.

Xander pushed himself backwards on his burnt fingers and palms, just trying to get a little more distance between himself and the dagger that

Foon flipped and played with, passing it from hand to hand and balancing the tip of it upon his finger.

The movement was so quick that Xander didn't see his sister rise and bring her hand up to the young man's chest to halt him. Her frail arm quivered from what little strength it took to even hold it aloft, but upon her touch to his chest, the skin of her hand and arm began to burn once again. The pair of them, Kristane and Foon, screamed in unison, like they were both on fire. Where Kristane's hand touched the rich fabric of Foon's jacket, vest, and shirt, it burned away. It was as if the two were now locked together, Kristane unable to drop her hand and Foon unable to back away. The fleshy side of Foon's face grimaced in pain, and his mask distorted into fear; but the mask seemed confused, as if it didn't know how to project the emotion, the plates of the mask rotating from a smile to a grimace. Kristane was still screaming, but her eyes had gone back to the dreamlike state from before, as if she were no longer there.

The screams continued as Rellion appeared and pulled Xander to his feet. "You must stop her, Xander, she'll burn herself away as well as him! You must reach out for her before it's too late —you are the only one who can!"

Xander didn't hesitate, his thoughts of inadequacy lost to the immediate danger his sister was in. The burning had crept up Kristane's arm to her neck and face; she sparkled from it, but Xander reached for her cheeks regardless. The pain he felt was instantaneous despite his already burnt and numb fingers; the heat flowed through him, and it was all he could do to keep himself from joining the two in their chorus of pain. Somehow he resisted; his sister needed him now.

Meeting the eyes that didn't see him, Xander pleaded through gritted teeth with his sister: "Kris, please just let go. Please, Kris, I love you; don't leave me. You have to let go."

Kristane didn't feel the pain, but did. Again, she was just on the edge of that dream of not knowing who she was. She could feel her body leaving her, burning away; but for some reason she was angry, and she wanted someone or something to know it, and if she burned away in the process, she didn't care. Yet there was Xander again, and he was reaching for her.

I knew you would come. This time she heard Xander say something: *I love you, don't leave me,* and with a rush of emotion, Kristane knew who she was, and she let go of the burning.

Xander barely had time to grab for the small of his sister's back as she crumpled in his arms. Her eyes were closed and she no longer burned, but it wasn't until her chest moved with the intake of air that he felt relieved. Quickly remembering that the strange young man was still there, Xander spun about, still clasping his sister's limp form.

Foon had stumbled back a few paces, his hands clutched to his chest, the stiletto lying on the stone where Kristane and he had been connected. He stood there panting, staring at Kristane with a hate that looked like it might envelop him entirely. Slowly, he pulled away his clawed hands, his fingers rigid and tense like a man who had clutched at life as his heart betrayed him. He didn't speak, but looked at the hand-shaped burn on his skin, and if possible grew even more incensed. He turned and ran, shouting for his beautiful metal dancers.

The High Priest, seeing his Saint and his angels retreating, joined them in a mad dash that was far below the station in which he perceived himself. Oscar Piggleback, amazingly, trailed him with a speed that belied his great girth, and the rest of Cristobal's devotees quickly lost heart without the whip of condemnation striping their backs. Rellion's Rogue, the Warders, and the pirate crew found themselves alone under the burning light of the Blessed Tree, its beauty marred by the stain of blood, the injured, and dead strewn out below it and amongst its roots.

Kristane twitched in Xander's arms, and opened her eyes with a gasp. His sister was still covered in grime and drying blood, but her eyes were bright, and her skin no longer had pale cast of death. "I knew you would come," she whispered.

Xander pulled her tight into a hug and sobbed into her dirty and matted hair. "Always, Kris."

Blackmore swatted off Banes as he attempted to tie off a gash on her arm, and motioned for him to attend to the Warders who were in greater need than herself. She had, miraculously, lost only two of her Whiskeys, and she had ordered their bodies placed near the base of the Blessed Tree.

The other injured were already being attended to by those less injured, and the Dame of the *Lady's Grace*, standing nearby, was supervising a group of her men to secure the entry to the dale from which the High Priest and his entourage had made their escape, in case any of them had the stomach for more battle.

Blackmore warily eyed the man who had visited her and had turned her and her men's lives upside down as he approached her and the Dame. She contemplated whether she was angry or grateful for the man's visit. Watching the brother and sister, the supposed heirs, together with their friends, Blackmore decided that purpose and hope had once again filled her... and maybe even for the first time in her life. She found that she was both angry and grateful.

Rellion, with Ix in tow, nodded to her as he donned his most winning smile and, bowing low, addressed the Dame. "My dearest Polly, am I to assume that you have transportation nearby?"

"Yes, but that doesn't mean I'm giving you a ride, Rellion. Oh, don't look so hurt, sweetie, you deserve worse for getting us caught up in this again! You too, Richard!" The Dame turned without another word to both men and, hoisting Blackmore up and taking her in arm, began marching up the terraces, trailed by her ever-present giant Quartermaster.

"You can*not* believe how glad I am you're here. Dammit, but these men will get us all killed. Well, some of us, anyway, you know, girl-to-girl. And Taff, we will need tea set for two." The Dame stopped for the briefest of moments, blowing a kiss at Fatterpacker, who was standing next to a disheveled Noodle. "Come along, sweet man, *you* can come with me."

Fatterpacker seemed unsure for a moment, but when he saw Kristane, with a purring Purdy nestled in the crook of her neck and Prya supporting her, and Xander, with bandaged hands leading Aldebarron, all turning to follow, the medicine man scampered after the pirate captain.

"She's not wrong." Rellion just smiled knowingly at Ix's comment, and slapping his reluctant friend on the shoulder, the pair walked silently together back to the *Lady's Grace*.

ANYONE WHO DOESN'T LIKE IT WILL BE THROWN OVERBOARD... BUT THAT'S ANOTHER STORY

Kristane found herself staring at the horizon, where the ruins of Kaer Kairos were no longer visible. She supposed that they had been sailing for nearly a week now. Her clean and unmatted hair tickled at her cheeks from the ocean spray, and for the first time in a while she was enjoying a moment of solitude. She was nearly alone; the deckhands still went about their work behind her, and she could hear the light singing voice of a young boy up in the rigging. Pipkin sat there in the flapping cloth and swaying ropes, happy, occasionally letting out an awed cry and clapping his hands when one of the many porpoises riding the leading wake of the *Lady's Grace* breached the water especially high.

No one was surprised to discover, when they had first reached the galleon after leaving the Blessed Tree, that the Fool was sitting nearly in the same place as he did now, smiling and looking like a drowned rat. After learning of everyone's exploits, she had tried to thank him for all that he had done for her, Xander, and the others, but he had gotten embarrassed and ran off before she could finish.

"Kris, they're waiting for us."

Giving a heavy sigh and taking one last look at the horizon, she turned to look at her brother. Xander was calling her for yet another discussion with the adults, "discussion" being a vague term for the actual clash of personalities and yelling that took place. Thankfully, they never seemed to last very long, ending when one or more would turn and stomp off. In fact, the only clear thing that had been decided was that they were headed back to Kairos. Kristane assumed that was only because the Dame had declared it her ship, and that she had "cargo" to pick up there — and anyone who didn't like it would be thrown overboard.

Kristane gave another heavy sigh; she should have known the relative quiet wouldn't last long. It wasn't that she hadn't wanted all of her friends as close as possible after what had happened to her, but the attention, the experiences of all, and the so-many new faces was a lot to handle all at once.

Xander's hands were still bandaged, and he had a thin cut along his cheek, but he smiled broadly at her. She felt guilty that she hadn't had a scratch on her after the Blessed Tree had gifted her a fruit, and she wondered at what had happened to her. Was she now like Rellion? Rellion didn't seem to think so; nor did the others, for that matter. They all seemed more than a little worried by it. Rellion had told her that what Foon had said was true: that the tree had been poisoned, but not by the poison that Foon had meant. *One man's poison is another's man's wine, but that's another story for another time, my Princess.* Just like Rellion to try and confuse the situation.

Kristane returned her brother's smile. Wrapping her arm around him and placing his on her shoulders, she walked with him back to the foredeck.

THE END

ᶜACKNOWLEDGMENTS

Eight years ago we embarked on an adventure through the land of Kairos, although we did not take this road alone. There were many along the way that helped to shape this journey.

We would sincerely like to thank our early readers, Cari Shein, Megan Duncan, Becca Meyer, Layna Bender, Natalie Madej, Chloe Zepkin, Margo Plieseis, Barbara Melhouse, Becca Schmidt, and Phelicity Wiese for their feedback, perspective, and encouragement. Your thoughts were truly helpful.

Thank you to Kellie Patton, James Kamb, Ryan Fountain, and everyone at Barnes & Noble in Chandler, AZ for letting us live in the YA Fantasy section scouring the shelves for the best books, new and old. Your support, input, and expertise is very much appreciated.

A thank you to our wonderful editor, Floyd Largent, who truly understands the world of fantasy, and to Mark Sean Wilson who helped bring the story to life with whimsical illustrations. Our brilliant cover design courtesy of Despina Panoutsou of Athens, Greece. Thank you for a cover that truly represents the story inside.

We would like to thank Debbie Felt, Cary Johnson, Shawn Stacy, Marty Flanagan, and everyone at APG for bringing us new opportunities, and getting our books into the hands of readers.

To our friends and family we are eternally grateful for your love, support, and patience in putting up with all our shenanigans. Thank you for your encouragement throughout the years. Thank you Reba Rose (RIP), Cari Shein, Jackson Neff, Susan Stoltz, Margo Plieseis, Barbara and Ole Melhouse and Conner Plieseis.

And to our readers, thank you for picking up, *A Tale of the Broken Heart*! We truly hope you enjoyed it!